Home Fires

Also in the Hope Springs series by Lois Greiman

Finding Home

Published by Kensington Publishing Corp.

HOME
FIRES

LOIS GREIMAN

KENSINGTON BOOKS

KENSINGTON BOOKS are published by

Kensington Publishing Corp.
119 West 40th Street
New York, NY 10018

ISBN-13: 978-1-62490-485-1

Printed in the United States of America

To Tara, who, despite the fact that I've made her ride horses with me since she was five days old . . . will still spend time on the trail with me. Thanks for being my best friend. I love you more than cookie dough.

HOME
FIRES

CHAPTER 1

"That was hotshot Brooks Hedley, riding Smokin' Jet Stream." Skip Jansen's singsong voice could barely be heard above the reverberating discharge of Brooks's single-action revolvers. But even before the blue smoke dissipated into the dusky evening air, the applause of the crowd echoed the .45s' explosive reports.

Onlookers were spread across the rolling hills of the Lazy Windmill ranch like frolicking puppies, perusing the vendors' varied wares, sharing local gossip, or admiring Hedley's marksmanship. Skip paused to let the crowd applaud, then boomed on in his best auctioneer voice. "As you all know, Brooks is South Dakota's very own mounted shooting champion. Double-barrel shotguns or single-action forty-fives, don't make no difference, he's top dog in both. So if you wanna know more about America's fastest-growing equestrian sport or just to grab an autograph, this is the chance of a lifetime, cuz Brooks and Smokin' Jet'll be right over there between the windmill and the—"

"If you ask me, that cowboy's the one that's smokin'," Emily said.

Casie Carmichael turned toward the girl. Regardless of her mocha complexion and wild dreadlocks, it was easy to see that Emily's face was flushed. But it was anyone's guess whether that blush was caused by the unseasonable September heat or by her own fired up endocrine system. Emily Kane was eighteen years old and eight-and-a-half months pregnant. Hormones ruled the day.

"Don't get yourself all excited," Casie warned.

"Too late." Emily didn't bother to shift her attention from the cowboy's midsection as he rode his prancing roan from the arena. Maybe it was because his belt buckle was as big as a hubcap, or maybe there were other distractions.

"I mean it," Casie said. "If you deliver that baby in the alfalfa field, I'm taking it out of your wages."

"You don't pay me any wages," Emily reminded her, and shifting her gaze a little higher, smiled at the approaching horseman. Perhaps her protruding belly was hidden behind the glass cooler that dispensed her homemade cider. Perhaps not.

"Drop that child on the Lazy and that unpaid status isn't going to change any time soon," Casie said, but Emily just gave her a jaundiced glance.

"Despite the fact that I plan to transcend the pains of labor by focused meditation and mental imaging, I fully intend to take advantage of St. Luke's übermodern birthing center while doing so."

Casie glowered at her a second longer, then sighed in relief. "Thank God. I was afraid you were going to go full-bore hippie on me," she murmured and slipped her attention back to the vendors. While many of the wares were agrarian in nature, there were products of every imaginable sort. Emily herself had planned to sell hot chocolate and scones, but the unexpected heat had convinced her to go with raspberry cider, assorted jams, and picture frames she'd crafted from weathered barn wood. Emily was enviably creative and constantly considering new career opportunities.

"Besides, I'd have to be a cretin to pass up the chance to enthrall an illustrious doctor at said birthing center," she added.

"Really?" Casie kept her tone dry and didn't comment on the girl's terminology. Apparently, Emily had read somewhere that using advanced vocabulary while pregnant could increase her unborn's IQ. She'd rarely uttered a monosyllabic word since.

"Indubitably," Emily said and offered the approaching cowboy her best come-hither smile.

"Don't you think you're going to be kind of busy while in labor?" Casie asked.

The girl shrugged and pressed her knuckles to the small of her back. "I'm sure I'll have copious hours to seduce a senior citizen during baby massage classes or Kindermusik or something."

"Kindermusik?"

"Sure. I'll bet there are scores of doctors with flagging libidos and receding hairlines who'd give their false teeth for a spunky trophy wife with a ready-made family."

Casie lifted one brow. "Spunky?"

Emily grinned. "Some consider that a euphemism for ... challenging."

Casie tried a daunting scowl, but in the half year since Emily's arrival at the Lazy, she had not once managed to quell the girl's indomitable spirit. It hardly seemed worth her effort now. "There's something wrong with you," she said instead, and tried, at least, to quash her own grin.

"I concur," Emily said. Hedley had stopped his mount to speak to a bleached blonde. The tramp stamp on the small of her back was almost entirely visible thanks to the shirt that barely reached her belly button. "Like hormonal overload and swollen ankles. This has been a pretty great gig though, huh?" she asked, and slipping an absent hand over her belly, she glanced around the bustling property.

In the past few months, the Lazy had undergone a host of changes. Fences had been added, buildings had been re-roofed, and the chicken coop that had once been a bunkhouse had, with the help of kindly neighbors, been restored enough to house guests who wanted a chance to experience ranch life.

Casie had no idea how things had gotten so out of hand. After her father's unexpected death, she had fully intended to sell the ranch and hightail it back to her life in the city. But a few unforeseen circumstances and the surprising arrival of a trio of teenagers had convinced her to stay a while . . . maybe take in a few paying guests, perhaps give a couple of horseback-riding lessons. But then one of those above-mentioned guests had suggested a symposium on cattle sorting. Emily had come up with the grand notion of inviting equestrians from other disciplines, and suddenly they had a dozen little-known sports represented and scores of vendors.

"I don't even know how all these people heard about us," Casie admitted. She also wasn't sure how she felt about having so many people on her private property, but the extra income was more than welcome. As was all the help that had been so freely given over the past few months. There was rarely a day that some generous neighbor didn't amble past her after planting a new post or mending an antiquated implement.

"It's called the Internet," Emily said. "If you'd come in from the barn every once in a while, you maybe would have heard of . . . Hey," she said, employing an exaggerated drawl as she smiled up at the man on the blue roan, "that was some mighty fancy shootin'. If those balloons were desperados, the townsfolk would have pinned a star on your chest by now."

"Thanks." Brooks Hedley glanced down at them from his stout gelding. Not past his twenty-fifth birthday, he had unruly blond hair curling out from beneath a stiff felt hat. To Casie, his round face and pointy goatee always made him look a little more like a billy goat than the Old West sheriff he hoped to emulate, but he seemed extremely popular with the female faction. "It's hotter than the Fourth of July out here, huh?"

"Climate change," Emily said.

He shifted his head, camel-colored hat tilting a little. "What's that?"

"Climate . . . Never mind," Em said, making Casie think she really must be attracted to Brooks if she wasn't going to venture into her environmental spiel. "Want some cider? It's made from the Lazy's own raspberries."

"Sounds great," he said and swung his leg over the gelding's hindquarters. His fringed chaps flared for a moment before settling around lean thighs as he took the glass she offered. He drank it in one gulp, not seeming to notice that the cup was made of one-hundred-percent-compostable material. Emily was hell on wheels when it came to details. "That's not half bad," he said, eyeing the empty receptacle. "What do I owe you?"

"Not a thing," Em said. "We just appreciate you coming to the Lazy."

"That's awful nice of you," he said and shuffled his well-polished boots, setting his jingle bob spurs to jangling. "Well, I guess I should be getting over there." He jerked his goatee toward the wooden water tank that sat at the base of the windmill. "Folks will want to pet Smoke, here," he said, and nodding a farewell, sauntered away. The blue roan followed.

"Some folks might want to be petting *you*," Emily murmured to his back.

"Emily!" Casie scolded softly.

"What?" she asked, and tilting her head a little, watched him walk away. "He's got hindquarters like well-watered garlic cloves."

"Will you quit staring at him?" Casie glanced around nervously, though the crowds seemed to be ignoring them entirely. "They'll think we're all a bunch of perverts here at the Lazy."

"Don't be ludicrous," Em said and tilted her head in the opposite direction. "People will think you're a perv if you *don't* appreciate that. I mean, seriously, that's some prime grade A, all-American—"

"Em!"

Emily raised her brows a little and managed to draw her attention from the retreating sharpshooter. "Admit it."

"What's wrong with you?"

"Admit he's got a great ass or I'm going to march up to Skip's bird's nest there and tell everyone that Cassandra May Carmichael can no longer identify prime beefcake when she sees it."

Casie glanced after the reigning mounted shooter, hoping the last hundred gunshots had rendered him mostly deaf. "Will you lower your voice?"

"Say it," Emily ordered.

"I'm trying to build a decent reputation for us."

"Say it," Emily repeated.

"Fine," Casie said through gritted teeth. "The man's got a decent . . . hind end."

"What's that?" Emily turned her head as if to catch a faint murmur. "I can't seem to hear you."

Casie rolled her eyes, but couldn't quite resist being drawn in by the girl's ridiculousness. "All right," she said. "If his ass was any prettier, I'd—" she began, but suddenly Emily shifted her gaze slightly to the right and opened her eyes wide.

"Hey, Mr. Dickenson," she said, voice suddenly dulcet, face the picture of innocence.

Casie felt her mouth go dry. Felt her heart thump in her chest as she froze, mortified into immobility, but in a moment she realized her foolishness. Emily had a penchant for practical jokes, but she had tricked her one too many times. "Very funny," she said and shook off her fear. "Extremely amusing." Richard Colton Dickenson hadn't been spotted anywhere near the Lazy since he'd galloped back to the rodeo circuit more than four months ago. Not that it mattered. He wasn't her type anyway. But Emily had always had a soft spot for him.

The girl grinned and shrugged in a win-some, lose-some gesture. "Dickenson has a better ass than that old wannabe sheriff anyway," she said.

"Dickenson *is* an ass. In fact—" Casie began, but something in Emily's expression stopped her cold. She shifted her eyes sideways.

"Hey, Case." Colt's voice was little more than a dark rumble from behind her.

Emily grinned sheepishly and Casie turned, not quite ready to relinquish the hope that she was imagining the deep timbre of his voice. But she wasn't. He stood not four feet from her, rust-colored shirt open at the collar, sleeves rolled away from broad, dark-skinned wrists.

"Dickey," she said. The easy tone she had shared with Emily was immediately absent. Her more usual stiffer-than-hell, stick-up-her-butt persona had returned. But Dickenson just smiled.

"It's nice to know you're thinking about me," he said.

She cleared her throat. "I thought you were in—"

"Hell?" he asked.

She felt her face flush. They had shared a similar conversation some six months before. "What are you doing here?"

He shrugged, an economical lift of capable shoulders. In some ways he had changed little since their shared childhood . . . Native American complexion, black hair, sharp humor shining in his earthy eyes. But a new scar nicked through the corner of his right brow, unsettling her stomach. "I was in the neighborhood."

"Are you saying the Lazy is close to hell?" she asked, but if she was looking for a fight, he ignored the gauntlet.

Grinning, he glanced to her left. "How you feeling, Em?"

"Gigantic," the girl said and placed both hands on her ponderous belly. "Heard you've been teaching those Wyoming broncs a thing or two. Won All-Around at Big Sky, huh? Not too shabby."

His eyes smiled at her. It had been abundantly clear that he'd liked Emily since the first day they'd met. He treated her like a sweet kid sister while he mostly reacted to Casie as if she were a case of hoof-and-mouth. Not that she cared. "Listen to you, with your cowboy lingo," he said.

Emily had been pure city before landing at the Lazy. And though she had become a dynamite cook and a first-rate organic farmer, her dreadlocks and ghetto chic wardrobe still spoke of a different world. "Casie said you were pretty good on bulls, too," she added.

He raised a brow and glanced sideways. Casie clenched her teeth, holding in the curse words that threatened to boil out.

"Head Case said that?" he asked.

"I may have said you were *full* of bull." She gave him a level stare. "Well, if you'll excuse me, I should talk to—" But he interrupted her. No big surprise there. If she had a nickel for every time he had done so in their lifetime, she could invest in another hundred acres.

"Quite a shindig you put on here."

She nodded, proud despite herself, of what they had managed to put together. "The kids did most of the work."

"So Ty's sorting cattle these days?" Dickenson's eyes were as mesmerizing as she remembered, alternating between quiet playfulness and outright impishness.

"Yes."

"He's getting to be a hell of a rider. And that spavined old gray you brought home . . ." He grinned as if remembering their fractious meeting at a sales auction some months before. "It's hard to believe she's still on her feet, much less winning competitions."

But he *would* have known if he had stuck around. He would have seen the gray blossom like South Dakota sunflowers. Would have watched her bloom right along with Ty, Casie thought. She forced a casual shrug. "She seems to like the work."

"I gotta admit, she moves pretty good."

"So you saw Ty's demonstration?"

Maybe there was something in her tone that alerted him, because his brows lowered a little. "Just the tail end of it."

Which meant he had been there for more than three hours and hadn't deigned to speak to her until this moment.

"Well . . ." It didn't matter. Heck, she didn't care if he visited every cowpuncher in the Dakotas before coming to see her. It wasn't as if she had any ties on him. She didn't even like him. But maybe for a while last spring she had thought . . . She gave herself a mental shake. "Well, I'd better say my good-byes before people start packing up and—"

"It was nice of Mr. Dickenson to stop by, though, wasn't it?" Emily said.

Casie felt her brows lower. Even after six months she knew little enough about the girl's former life, but it had been abundantly clear from the get-go that she wanted Casie and Colt together in the worst possible way. "Yes," Casie said, unlocking her jaw with a Herculean effort and turning her gaze on Dickenson. "I'm so glad you could take a minute out of your busy schedule to come see us—" She stopped herself before the word *peons* slipped out. What was wrong with her? It wasn't as if he owed her anything. Or as if she wanted anything from him.

"I *have* been busy," he said. His voice was low and maybe a little defensive.

She forced a smile. She used to be top-notch at faking smiles . . . and other things . . . back when she was engaged to be married. "That's what I said."

His body stiffened. "It's not as if you asked me to stay." His voice was low.

And suddenly, he was all she could see, all she could think about. "It's not as if you *wanted* to stay."

"You told me flat out you didn't need my help."

They stared at each other. Tension gathered like storm clouds, but she felt the change in the weather and forced a shrug, pulling her shoulders back, glancing around. "And I guess I was right."

"Far be it from Cassandra Carmichael to ever need—"

"Oh, for pity's sake!" Emily snapped.

They jerked toward her in unison.

"Will you two just . . . just get a room!" she said.

They stared at her in tandem bewilderment. She waved wildly between them. "If there was any more sexual angst between the two of you, I could set a match to it."

Colt scowled.

Casie cleared her throat, embarrassed and fidgety.

"I'm going to go take some pictures," Emily said, and snatching her camera from the table, turned toward the bustling hills. "Try not to kill each other while I'm gone."

CHAPTER 2

By the time Skip Jansen had stowed away his auctioneer equipment, most of the vendors had packed up and left. Only a few stragglers remained. Casie had made a noble effort to speak to each of them individually, though it went against every reclusive instinct she possessed.

"I'm glad you're still here," she said as Brooks Hedley straightened over a photograph he was signing. "I wanted to say thanks again."

"Hey." He grinned, then winked at the girl to whom he handed the signed portrait. It was no big secret why he was a heartthrob. "I should be thanking *you.*"

"So it went all right?"

"Yeah. Went pretty darn well," he said. "Sold a few products." He lifted a tooled gun belt that had been handcrafted on the Running W, his family's ranch not thirty miles to the east. There was a bunch of Hedleys. Two girls and five boys, several of whom worked in construction to help pay the bills. Brooks himself had lent a hand in restoring the Lazy's wooden water tank, though it was not yet fully functional. "Got orders for a few more."

"Well . . ." She kept herself from fidgeting like a toddler caught in the cookie jar, though it was a close thing. Men had always made her nervous. "You do good work."

"You think so?" he asked, and raising the belt a little, squinted past it toward her. "Hey, this one would look mighty good on you."

She laughed, nerves twittering. "Thanks. But I don't . . ." She shook her head. "I don't compete."

"Well, you should," he said and rounded the corner of his cowhide-covered table with a swagger. "I bet you're a deadeye."

"I don't think so."

"Your friend said you're hell on horseback."

"My—"

"The pregnant girl."

"Oh, Emily. Well, she exaggerates."

"She said you'd say that, too. Here. Try this on," he said and approached slowly, as if she might skitter away if he moved too quickly.

"I'd like to, but I need to talk to the other—"

"You don't wanna hurt my feelings, do you?"

She scowled at him. "I didn't know cowboys were so sensitive."

He laughed. "Fragile as kittens. Listen, I made this belt special for a gal down by Kansas City, but she never paid."

"I'm sorry to hear that."

He shrugged. "It just needs a good home."

"Like I said, I don't—"

"It's an orphan," he said. "Very sad. It was destined for a new mommy and now . . ." He shook his head. "It's out in the cold world all alone."

"I'm sure you'll find it a good mother somewhere."

"That's just the thing, most of the women are *too* . . . motherly."

She gave him a look. He grinned roguishly.

"I don't meet a whole lot of girls built like you."

She blinked. True, in the last several months, something indescribable had changed. For years she had seemed all but invisible to men. Not that she had minded. In fact, she often preferred that kind of safe anonymity, but lately something was different, as if a light had clicked on inside of her. Maybe it was the risks she was taking. Maybe it was the lack of eligible women in these parts. Or maybe it was the low-cut jeans and chest-hugging shirts Emily insisted she wear. She cleared her throat. "I . . ." She was at a loss.

"I meant that as a compliment," he said and grinned again. "You right-handed?"

"What? Oh. Yes."

"What a coincidence, so was she. It's like kismet or something."

"Almost ninety percent of people are—"

"Here," he said, and stepping forward, eased the tooled leather around her. His hands brushed her hips. A narrow strip of brindle cowhide embellished each holster. She raised her arms to accommodate his reach. He wrapped the leather around her, then buckled it in place before stepping back to admire his handiwork. "That looks damn good on you."

"Well . . ." She stared down at the belt, too self-conscious to look up. "It's very pretty."

"Yeah, it is," he said. There was something in his tone that forced her chin up.

His crooked grin quirked up higher. "Let's try it with some firepower."

"Oh no. I don't—" she began, but he was already pulling his own pistols from the holsters near his hip. In a moment he had settled their considerable weight into the allotted slots.

"How does it feel to be packin' heat?"

"I'm not a shooter," she said, but the truth was it felt pretty good. There was something powerful about the weight of the pistols lying side by side against her hip.

"You ever shot before?"

"Not really, no," she said, which was kind of a lie. Long ago, perhaps shortly after her father had completely despaired of ever having a son, he had taught her to shoot tin cans with an old Winchester.

"Not even as a kid? What the hell was your old man thinking?"

"Maybe he didn't know it was a mandatory part of raising a daughter."

"Was he from the city or somethin'?"

"No," she said and laughed at his ridiculous expression. "He was raised right here on this ranch."

He shook his head. "Well, that's just messed up. Here . . . let me show you how this works," he said and eased around behind her. "See how the belt is pretty high up?"

She nodded.

"Not like in them old spaghetti Westerns where they was practically hangin' down by their knees. You want 'em snug up on your waist so you can—Shit," he said, grinning over her shoulder, breath warm against her ear. "You don't hardly have no waist at all. Don't you ever eat?"

"Of course I . . ." He was very close. Uncomfortably close, his hip snug against her seat. "I eat."

"Yeah? Maybe I could take you out to supper then."

"I just . . . now?" she asked and turned slightly. Her shoulder brushed his chest. Their faces were inches apart.

He grinned down at her. "It won't hardly take me a New York minute to finish packing up."

"I can't tonight. I still have to do chores and help—"

"I think you're lying to me."

She felt her eyes widen, felt her heart rate bump up a notch. His chest brushed her shoulder. "I'm not. I really need to—"

"I bet you don't eat no more than once a week."

"Oh." She laughed, faced forward, and abruptly spied Colt Dickenson. He stood not eight feet away. She felt his presence in the pit of her stomach.

His expression was atypically serious. "I thought I should say good-bye," he said.

"Oh." She took a step forward, leaving the heat of Hedley's chest behind her. "Are you . . ." She resisted the impulse to glance back over her shoulder, *tried* to resist the impulse to blush. She didn't owe Colt any explanations. Neither did she owe him her loyalty. Hardly that. "Are you taking off?"

"Yeah. Thought I would," he said and raised his gaze to Brooks for an instant. "Hey, Hedley."

"Dickenson."

She cleared her throat and turned sideways so as to keep them both in her sights, like a gunfighter with two assailants. "You two know each other?"

"Oh, we go way back," Colt said.

Their gazes met and clashed, brown on green. "I used to do some rodeo," Hedley admitted.

"Oh?" She didn't mean to wear out the word, but urbane conversation wasn't exactly her forte.

"I tell you what . . ." Hedley grinned a little as he shifted his gaze back to hers. "There ain't nothing like bull riding to beat the hell out of the boys."

"The boys?" She scowled.

He winked. "I figured if I wanted to keep the ladies happy, I better find a sport that was easier on my . . . tender parts."

Casie blushed, but neither of the men seemed to notice. Hell, neither of them was looking at her at all. Instead, they seemed to be engaged in their own silent showdown.

"Was that it?" Colt asked. "I thought you quit because you couldn't keep the bull between you and the ground for more than two seconds at a time."

Anger or something like it flashed in Hedley's eyes. "I decided to leave the rough stock to those of you who got faces ain't going to look no worse after getting smashed in a few more times," he said and eyed Colt's latest scar.

It sliced through the outer edge of his right eyebrow. Casie scowled. Sometimes it was almost impossible to remember she didn't care.

"I suppose toy guns *are* a whole lot safer," Colt said.

A muscle jumped in Hedley's jaw. "Broncs are like merry-go-round ponies compared to them brahmas I rode."

"Yeah, you're a hell of a man."

Hedley forced a smile. "That's what they say."

"Those weren't Jess's exact words."

"Listen, you—" he began, but a gasp from Casie's left interrupted the conversation.

Emily stood not two yards away, bent double, face scrunched in pain.

"What's wrong?" Casie took one truncated step toward her, hands already reaching out. "What's going on?"

"I don't know." Emily was panting. Terror was stamped on her face by the time she straightened a half inch. "It hurts."

"I'll get the truck!" Casie's voice was no more than a rasp of terror to her own ears.

"Puke?" Emily winced at the mention of the Lazy's rattletrap pickup. "It'll pop the baby out like a cork in a wine bottle. Couldn't—"

"I've got it," Colt said, and taking the three strides that separated them, smoothed his hand down Emily's right arm. "Hey, you're going to be okay, Em. You hear me?"

She lifted adoring, desperate eyes to him, and tried a jerky nod.

"Thatta girl. Just breathe. Everything's going to be all right. Stay with her, Case." His eyes were dead steady. "Keep her calm. I'll be back in thirty seconds."

"That long?" Casie hated the weakness in her voice, hated the unsteadiness of her hands, but she couldn't seem to stop the words any more than she could stop the panic. Her knowledge of human births was confined to what she'd seen on television, and mostly that involved a lot of screaming . . . and someone boiling water.

"Hang in there," Colt breathed and then he was gone.

CHAPTER 3

"I thought she wasn't due for another couple of weeks." Colt's voice sounded strained as they fishtailed from the gravel onto the tar toward St. Luke's cushy birthing center.

Emily sat between him and Casie. She was panting and concentrating hard on her performance. Holy crap, what was wrong with these two? Didn't they know they were perfect together? Of course, Colt *was* a Neanderthal for returning to the rodeo circuit, and Case could be as stubborn as a jug-headed mule, but . . .

"She's not," Casie said. Emily couldn't help but notice that she looked awfully pale. Perhaps that was a testament to Emily's own acting ability. And maybe she should be proud of her acting prowess, but just now she didn't feel all that great about lying. "You okay, Em?"

"Sure. I'm—" She paused to close her eyes and groan pitifully. "I'm okay."

"Did her water break?" Colt's eyes cut to Emily. His knuckles looked white on the steering wheel. But she kept panting, avoiding specific questions and staring glassy-eyed at her knees. Holy shorts, they were the size of summer cantaloupes. Labor was a bitch even when you were just faking it.

"I don't know." Casie's voice practically crackled with worry.

"How far apart are the contractions?" he asked.

Casie squeezed her hand. Emily just shook her head, as if too focused on her internal agony to answer.

"Can't you drive any faster?" Casie asked.

"If I want to get us all killed."

"I'm sorry I interrupted your day," Emily said. She was still panting. She was pitifully good at it. "I know you have a lot going on."

"Are you kidding?" Casie's voice was raspy.

"Shoot, Em—" Colt glanced at her. The fear in his eyes made Emily's guilt intensify to the point where she would almost *welcome* labor pains. But if they hadn't been acting like such douche bags, she wouldn't have had to go to such drastic measures. "Don't worry about *us*. When was your last exam?"

She shrugged, shook her head, and exhaled rapidly. If she was any better at acting, she was going to push herself into labor for real. "Two weeks ago, maybe."

"Had you started dilating yet?"

"Just a little."

"You did?" Casie's voice was shocked. "Why didn't you tell me?"

"Didn't want to worry you." Obviously, she had no such inhibitions about lying to Casie, however. At least, that used to be true. What had happened to that blissful lack of conscience?

"Had you begun effacing?" Colt asked.

Em glanced at him, temporarily caught off guard. But not as much as Casie was.

"*What?*" Colt asked, catching her eye.

"Been through this a number of times, have you, Dickenson?" Casie asked.

"Geez, Head Case, not everyone's as naïve as—"

"Aaah!" Emily moaned and, tilting her head back, squeezed Casie's hand with all the strength she could muster. Which was considerable. Organic gardening was no job for sissies. Then again, birthing might not be for the pansy patrol, either.

"Hang on," Colt said.

"It's going to be all right," Casie added.

Emily panted and considered telling them that when the real deal began in earnest, they might want to beef up their platitudes. "Are we almost there?"

"Just another few minutes," Colt promised and he was right. They were pulling up to St. Luke's automatic doors before she had a firm game plan in mind, but it was too late to back out now. And she'd learned to punt before she'd learned to walk. Absentee parents and a flawed foster care system were aces at teaching a girl to think on her feet.

"I'll help her in," Colt said, gaze hard on Casie. "You alert the staff."

"Alert the—"

"Start the paperwork. Tell them we have an emergency."

Oh crap, Emily thought, but Casie was already gone, rushing through the doors and into the abyss beyond. Too late to call her back. And now Colt was trotting around the bumper like a border collie on a mission. She slid sideways along the bench seat and prepared to step down, hands bracing her belly, but he reached for her before she could dismount.

"I can—" she began, but he stopped her.

"Let me help you, honey," he said, and there was something in his voice that stopped her world. Something she'd never heard in the entirety of her life. Not from the myriad foster parents who had temporarily crossed her path, not from the unimpressive legal system, and certainly not from the father of her unborn child. Tears stung her eyes. Which was just plain weird. She wasn't the weepy type. In fact, there was little enough evidence that she still *had* tear ducts. She bumped a nod. He slid his arms gently around her and drew her to his chest, maybe like a father would. Maybe like he cared about her. Guilt solidified like a chunk of lead in her belly.

She found his face with her eyes "I . . ." She winced, cleared her throat, and cut her eyes away. It wasn't really surprising that she'd never found a guy like this to love her, she supposed. Men like this, good men, real men, probably didn't care to be lied to. To be made fools of. "I'm sorry, Mr. Dickenson. I'm not really—"

"Don't. You don't have to apologize for anything," he said, and pivoting toward the solid block building behind him, hustled her inside. A wheelchair stood beside the door, a nurse at the ready. A plastic name tag proclaiming the woman to be

Chelsea was pinned on her plum-colored scrubs. "I can carry her," he said.

Chelsea gave him a brittle smile that would have challenged a sumo wrestler. "We'd prefer to have her in a wheelchair."

He straightened a little, chest hard against Emily's swollen right boob. Mr. Nice Guy was gone, taking a quiet backseat to the rodeo cowboy who carried her. "Yeah, well—" he began but Emily stopped him.

"It's okay," she said. Her heart twinged again. Who knew that having a champion would be so painful? "The chair will be fine."

"You sure?" he asked, and there was such concern, such gentleness in his voice that the tears almost fell loose.

"I'm sure," she said and shifted her eyes away lest the sight of him send the truth spilling from her lips like poison.

Chelsea took her place at the wheelchair. Casie stood not ten feet away, speaking earnestly to a woman behind the reception desk.

Colt settled her carefully onto the vinyl seat. Chelsea smiled with all the sincerity of a hungry coyote.

"I can take her in from here," she said.

"Do you want me to go with you, honey?" Colt asked. His hand felt warm and solid when he slipped it around her fingers.

His deep voice, so typical of Native American men, threatened her tear ducts again. "No. I'm okay."

He stared at her a second as if trying to ascertain her level of pain, then nodded toward the front desk. "What about Case? You want her to go along?"

"I'd like to come," Casie said, turning toward them, eyes earnest. "If you don't—" she began, but Nurse Chelsea jerked suddenly, setting the wheelchair slightly atremble.

"You'll have to leave," she said.

The three of them shifted their eyes to her in surprise. The smile, cool as it was, had left her face and was now replaced by brittle condemnation.

"Leave?" Colt said.

"What are you talking about?" Casie asked.

"Our rules are very clear," she said and dropped her gaze to Casie's hips. Hedley's hand-tooled gun belt remained firmly fastened around her waist. "There are absolutely no firearms allowed in this facility."

The noise that left Casie's lips might have been amusing under different circumstances. "I didn't . . . I don't . . ." she began and dropped her hand to the butt of a pistol.

"Security!" snapped the nurse.

"No!" Casie said, lifting one hand in a futile attempt to wipe away any misunderstanding. "I just—"

"Maybe you'd better wait outside," Colt suggested. "I'll take care of Em."

"She's not your responsibility," Casie said, then snapped her gaze back to the hospital's temporarily immobilized staff. "Besides, the guns aren't even loaded." She smiled at the nurse and slipped the gun belt from her hips. "Probably." It was then that one of the pistols clattered to the tiles. The noise was loud enough to wake the dead . . . or at least the nearby patients. An octogenarian jumped, eyes wide above her oxygen mask. An elderly gentleman gasped, almost teetering off his walker. Nearby, a little boy grinned from ear to ear as he tried to tug free of his mother's grasp.

Colt swore under his breath.

"Where's security?" snapped the nurse, but just then a pot-bellied man in an overtaxed uniform rushed around the corner toward them.

Casie scooped the gun off the floor, shot Emily a look heavy with apology and angst, and slunk toward the front door.

"Well, I think we can assume we made an impression," Colt said. Casie could just hear his voice as he and Emily approached the pickup truck where she waited.

"Maybe I should be a doc," Emily said.

"Well, you'd be cute as hell at it. Let me hear you say, 'Take two aspirin and quit riding broncs, you moron.' "

Emily laughed. Casie watched them in the side-view mirror, two beautiful people sharing an easy camaraderie. The wheelchair had been left behind. Emily was, quite obviously, ambulatory. Colt was, of course, charming. She had never resented him more.

"Hey, Deadeye," he said, glancing through the open passenger window at her. "You okay?"

"Sure." She didn't look at him, but kept her gaze on Emily. "How about you? Are you all right?"

"Yeah. Sorry," she said and didn't make eye contact as Casie stepped out of the truck to give the girl the middle seat. "False alarm, I guess."

"So the contractions stopped?"

Some unknown expression crossed Emily's gamine features. It almost looked like guilt. Which was unexpected since, four months earlier, Casie would have sworn the girl didn't know the meaning of the word. "Yeah, stopped almost as soon as I got in there. Weird, huh?"

"The doctor says that happens sometimes," Colt said and handed Emily a plastic bag filled with who knows what. "The mom gets stressed out and then the labor stops." Casie stared at Emily from the paved parking lot as Colt rounded the bumper to approach the driver's side.

"Do you think that's what happened?" Casie said the words softly, for Emily's ears alone.

The girl didn't so much as glance at her as she hoisted herself laboriously onto the seat. "Must have."

"So you really *were* having contractions?"

"What?" Colt asked the question even before he had fully opened the driver's door. Stupid cowboy had ears like a basset hound. He shifted his gaze to Casie. "It was a false labor. Happens all the time. Get in, Head Case. Em needs to get home to rest."

Emily shifted her gaze to the windshield as Casie climbed into the cab. Colt fired up the truck. The diesel engine rumbled like thunder, but little else was heard on the twenty-minute drive to the Lazy.

Once home, Ty Roberts appeared beside the passenger door before Casie had even touched the handle. Outside, it was almost fully dark. Just a few magenta layers lighted the western sky. The vendors were gone, leaving little more than flattened grass and a few scraps of detritus across the scalloped hills.

"What's going on?" The boy spoke as soon as Casie pushed open the passenger door. Beside him, Jack, border collie and resident security, turned circles in excited anticipation.

"False alarm," Colt said and stepped out of the cab. "Holy Moses, boy, you must have grown a foot since I last seen you." In fact, his height now exceeded Colt's by half a hand. Casie had no idea why that truth made her feel better. "Doesn't look like you're going to make a bronc rider after all."

"Bronc rider!" Casie scoffed, then wished she hadn't opened her mouth.

Ty shifted his worried gaze to her, then on to Emily. "Everything okay?"

Colt rounded the bumper. "Casie's just mad that hospitals have that silly rule about not allowing target practice in their facilities."

Ty's brow wrinkled.

"You could have warned me," Casie said and stepped out of the truck.

Colt laughed. "And spoil the fun?"

"What are they talking about?" Ty asked, directing his attention to Emily, who slid carefully off the seat and shook her head as if trying to disavow the entire episode. Casie wondered with vague mortification if she had embarrassed the girl. Generally, Em had the toughened attitude of a veteran warhorse, but she was bound to feel vulnerable in her current condition. Wasn't she? Uncertainty stole through Casie like a cat on the prowl. After all, it wasn't as if *she* had ever experienced the pangs of pregnancy, emotional or physical. And in all honesty that was probably for the best; she was barely up to nurturing newborn calves. God help her if she ever had a child, she thought, and let her misty gaze settle for just a moment on Em's rounded belly.

"Was there any trouble with the vendors?" Emily, true to her entrepreneurial nature, was glancing with concern around the all-but-empty property.

"Not that I know of," Ty said and shuffled back a half pace, making room for her bulk. "Everybody seemed pretty happy. But hey, some guy from Lead was interested in your rhub-apple jam. Said he thought it could go mainstream. Whatever that means."

"Yeah?"

"Said it was rhubalicious."

"Seriously?" Emily made a face that suggested both delight and the burning need to mock. "He said that?"

Ty grinned, just the slightest twitch of his lips. He did that more these days, though he would probably never match Colt's irritating jocularity. "He left his card."

"Where is it?" Em's voice was breathy with excitement. She was ever determined to find a way to increase the ranch's profitability.

"I put it on the table . . . or on the counter or . . ." He paused. "Maybe I better come in and find it," he said. "Things got a little hectic at the end."

"Here . . ." Emily handed him the plastic bag. "Carry this, will you?" she asked and shifted the sack into his possession before they headed toward the house together. Watching them walk away was almost painfully poignant. They looked ridiculously pretty, hopelessly vulnerable.

"Cute, huh?" Colt said.

Casie swallowed the tears building up in her throat, pursed her lips into a solid line, and changed the subject with careful single-mindedness. "What did the doctor say?"

Colt shrugged, still watching the pair disappear into the darkness. "She's doing fine. He's a little concerned about her blood glucose, but gestational diabetes is a common occurrence, I guess."

She nodded, as if she had known that little factoid since infancy, and glanced back toward the shadows just ascending the porch steps.

"You might want to cut back on her duties a little, though." His words were soft, as if his mind was elsewhere.

Casie snapped her attention back toward him. "What?"

He shrugged. "She looks kind of tired."

She felt her back go up, and though she knew better, opened her mouth immediately. "You think I'm standing over her with a whip or something?"

"Whip? Naw." He grinned, pulled open the passenger door, and yanked the gun belt out from under the seat where she had stowed it. "I'm thinking these would be more effective."

A half-dozen razor-sharp rejoinders came to mind, but she kept them at bay and grabbed the tooled leather.

He pulled it closer to his chest, effectively tilting her off balance. They were inches apart. His grin disappeared. She blinked. He cleared his throat. Seconds ticked into the gathering darkness. "He's not for you, Case," he said.

She forced herself to breathe and felt her brows rise toward her hairline. "What?"

"Hedley," he said. "I know he's got a dreamy smile and the cutest little butt ever." He said the words in a breathy falsetto, then inhaled as if he was trying to control his temper, which was simply weird because, as far as Casie knew, he didn't even *have* a temper. Still, his dark eyes snapped. "You don't want to get involved with him."

"Well, that's great because I'm *not* involved with him."

"Really?" He tilted his head at her. "Cuz if you two get any cuddlier, you're going to be in the same fix as Emily."

She felt her jaw drop, heard herself snort. "And this from the man who knows more about women in labor than an obstetrician."

He narrowed his eyes a little. Flexed his jaw. "I'm just trying to help," he said.

"Help?" She stepped back a pace. "Is that what you call it when you disappear for months at a time? When you—" She stopped short, since it was apparent that she was losing her mind. After all, she had *told* him to leave . . . had insisted, in fact, that he return to the rodeo circuit. She could manage things on her own. She didn't need a man in her life. After her ex-fiance's departure, she was thrilled to be on her own, she'd said. But it was clear now that she hadn't really expected him to believe her, and the truth of her own disjointed illogic made her temper rise like a springtime flood. "How do you know so much about childbirth anyway?"

He tilted his head at her as if she'd lost her last marble. "Geez, Head Case, is that what's bothering you?"

"Where did you even hear the word *effacing?*"

"Everyone knows that stuff," he said.

"I don't." Her voice sounded a little pissier than she'd intended and seemed to raise his ire.

"Well, you keep seeing Hedley and you'd better be a quick study."

She shook her head. "What is it with you and Brooks?"

"Brooks . . ." He said the name with an odd accent, then drew a deep breath, slowed down. ". . . is a jackass."

"Well, then you two have a lot in—"

"Hey," Sophie said. Casie jumped, nearly dropping a pistol as she found the girl in the darkness. "What's up?" Sophie Jaegar had arrived at the Lazy six months ago as a guest. It was hard to say exactly what her role was now.

"Casie is going to become a sharpshooter." Colt's voice sounded atypically bad tempered.

"What?" Even in the near darkness of the front yard, Sophie Jaegar was beautiful. Despite a hectic day of giving tours and riding demonstrations, every hair was in place, every fingernail immaculate. Casie had no idea how she did it. Perhaps it had something to do with breeding, or money. Both of which the girl had in spades. Functional family—that's what she lacked. Hence her original arrival at the Lazy. Her subsequent stay there was a little more complicated.

Colt shrugged. Casie could feel him trying to unwind. Odd. She'd never even known he could *wind*. She felt an evil little tug of satisfaction at the advent of that knowledge. Served him right to get all cranked up after the years he had tormented her in high school.

"How you doing, Soph?" he asked.

The girl glanced at him. While Emily had adored Colt from the day they first met, Sophie was more reserved, about everything. Casie had never appreciated that fact more than she did right now. "You're skinnier," she said.

He grinned, seeming amused by his lack of ability to charm her. "Shortage of home cooking on the road. How's that colt coming along?"

She shrugged, but even in the uncertain light, her enthusiasm was obvious. Damn him and his honest interest in other people. "I'm ground driving him now."

"Yeah?"

"I bet he's grown a full hand since you saw him last."

"You must have him and Ty on the same diet then."

Sophie pursed her lips at the mention of the boy she had crossed swords with since day one. "I thought he cared about that old mare of his."

"What?"

"Angel," she said, referring to the emaciated gray Casie had bought at auction less than a year before. As it turned out, Ty had arrived along with her as an unforeseen bonus. "I thought she was going to keel over right in the cattle pens. He rides her too hard."

"She loves to work cattle," Casie said, reluctant to jump into the conversation but no longer able to resist. "She probably just got keyed up."

"Roberts was the one getting excited," Sophie said.

They stared at her in tandem. She glanced from one to the other, scowling heavily. "He'd do anything to be the center of attention."

Colt raised his brows.

Casie tilted her head in dubious uncertainty. If Ty Roberts said fifteen words a day, he was ten words over his limit. Maybe that was because of the abuse he had suffered at the hands of his parents, or maybe he was being ultracareful not to cause any problems that might run him afoul of the law. In the past, he had been in some trouble at school. But since Casie had met him, he'd walked the line as carefully as a tightrope artist. "Ty?" she said.

"I mean . . ." Sophie's scowl darkened even further. "I know he's not too bright, but I thought he knew better than to over-work a horse that has splints."

Casie stared at her. The splints on Angel's forelegs had calci-fied years ago and were unlikely to bother her. Sophie knew that if anyone did. But Casie didn't bother to mention it. "Is she okay?" she asked instead.

"It would serve him right if she wasn't." Sophie's shoulders drooped a little.

"Take it easy on him," Casie said. She kept her tone low. She and Sophie had argued over Ty on more than one occasion, but she didn't really need Colt to know of their battles. "He's found something he excels at, something the mare loves. I think it's good for both of them."

"You *would* take his side." Despite Sophie's frequent acts of maturity, she still had painful teenage outbursts.

"I'm not taking sides," Casie said. "I'm just saying—"

"And I'm just going to bed," Sophie said, but she felt the need to add more . . . maybe as a sort of surly apology for being six-teen. "I fed the yearlings. The stalls are cleaned and bedded. Lark has a little thrush in her left front frog. I painted it with io-dine."

"Thank you."

She nodded, tight lipped, and turned toward the house.

Casie exhaled evenly. The night went quiet as the girl's foot-steps faded into the darkness.

"Kinda cute how you have the fun of raising teenagers when you don't know anything about giving birth," Colt said.

Casie's temper exploded like a time bomb. She pivoted to-ward him, fists clenched, teeth bared. "Emily was lying."

"What?" His quizzical expression might have been comical if it wasn't for the guilt that detonated in Casie's gut immediately after she dropped the bomb.

"Nothing." She inhaled, steadied herself, and backed away a step. "It's nothing. Well . . . maybe I'll see you around some-time," she said and turned away, but he caught her arm.

"What do you mean, *nothing?*" He searched her eyes. His were as dark as midnight. "You don't think Em lied about being in labor, do you?"

She pursed her lips. She appreciated the fact that Colt thought so highly of the little mother-to-be. Really, she did. The girl needed a man in her life who wouldn't ignore her or seduce her, and Colt had managed that much. So far at least, she thought cattily.

"I'm going to go check on the horses," she said and tugged at her arm, but he held on.

"You think maybe she's faking the pregnancy, too, Case? Cuz I've gotta tell you, it looks pretty real to me."

"Well . . ." She gave him her best fake smile. "You're the expert."

He scowled at her, shook his head once. "You don't need to be jealous," he said.

"Jealous!" She sputtered something inarticulate. "Are you nuts?"

"Could be." He tilted his head. That old mischievous light shone in his eyes again. "Are you *jealous?*"

"No!"

"Really?" His grin peeked out. She wanted to slap it off his face. Or something. "Cuz it kinda looks like you might be."

She huffed a laugh. "Listen, if you want to fawn all over a girl who's half your age, I think that's great. God knows she's been neglected most of her life, but—" She stopped, realized his brows had shot toward his Stetson like stray bullets, and wished she could disappear into the earth beneath her feet.

The night went silent. Somewhere far off a cow bellowed. Beyond that a coyote yipped and was answered.

"I meant, you shouldn't be jealous that she's pregnant," he said.

"I . . ." She swallowed, mind spinning. "I know what you meant."

"She's not really half our age," he said. Silence settled in again. "You're not too old to have kids."

She felt herself stiffen. "I'm so relieved that you think so."

"Are you?" he asked and moved a fraction of a step closer.

"No!" she said and yanked her arm out of his grip. "I'm just curious how you know so much about the whole thing."

He shrugged, a single lift of one lean-muscled shoulder. "I've known where babies come from for quite a while, Case."

"Oh, you're funny."

He laughed. "Always have been."

"Night, Casie," a voice rumbled from the darkness. A man passed by on her left, little more than a shadow carrying a toolbox.

"Oh . . ." She cleared her throat. "Good night. And thank you."

He raised a hand and vanished into the darkness.

Dickenson blinked after him. "What's Will Sommers doing here?"

She shook her head, rarely sure what any of the myriad men were doing who roamed through the Lazy. She only knew that the bunkhouse had been restored, the arena fence was solid as a rock, and the new porch was a sight to behold. Of course, *all* of her neighbors' efforts weren't charity. She'd offered Sommers and a dozen others free booths at her symposium. Emily gave away her wares like cider was river water, and the daughters of half the people in town had gotten a free riding lesson or two.

"Listen . . ." she said, getting back on track with some difficulty. "I'm going to take a look at the horses. Then I'm going to bed."

"Is he here a lot?"

"What? Who?"

"Will. Geez, how many other men are floating around here in the dark?"

She stared at him a second, then said, "Don't be an ass."

He gritted his teeth. "Well, not everyone can be the upstanding citizen Hedley is."

She shook her head at him, honestly confused. "What have

you got against Brooks? You two fight over the same buckle bunny or something?"

"Why? You want us to fight over you?"

"I couldn't care less if you—" she began, but in that second he kissed her.

CHAPTER 4

His lips touched hers, firm and warm. She knew beyond a shadow of a doubt that she should do something drastic. She should slap him or curse him or duck and cover, but she was too shocked to move, and then he was slipping his hand beneath her hair, pulling her closer, and suddenly the air was sucked out of her lungs, and every flickering brain cell went limp. For a moment she teetered on the edge of uncertainty, and then her body made an executive decision. Dropping the gun belt, she curled her fingers into his shirt and shoved him up against the pickup truck like a bag of crimped oats.

His left hand was on her butt. She scrabbled with the buttons on his shirt. But they were so damned small. One popped into the air and pinged off the cab like an errant bullet, but she was light-years beyond caring.

He had a chest mounded with muscles that ran down toward abs that bumped a toboggan's course to the silver buckle cinching his jeans. She flicked his belt open with one simple motion.

"Geez, woman!" The words were little more than a breath of air against her face. "You—"

"Shut up!" she growled and kissed him harder.

He fumbled with the door handle behind her. She stood in the opening, not quite lucid enough to climb inside as she clawed at the zipper on his jeans.

"I'm taking off," said a voice from the abyss. It took her muzzy mind a full second to recognize the voice as Ty's.

She gasped and jerked her hands from Colt as if stung. He hissed a curse. Ty strode toward them through the darkness.

"You might want to check on Tangles," the boy added, just coming into view. "He was acting a little funny."

"Funny?" Casie's voice sounded like she was possessed by a demon, and maybe she was. Good God, had she just torn open Colt's shirt? She slammed the thoughts away and ran a shaky hand over her hair. Colt remained facing his truck, making her wonder if she'd ruined his zipper, too. "Funny, um . . ." She shot her gaze toward Colt. He was buttoning his shirt with lightning-quick fingers. She refrained from closing her eyes. Refrained from groaning. Refrained from hiding under his truck. Holy crap, she was mature. "Funny how?" And what the hell had they just been talking about?

"I don't know. Maybe it was nothing," Ty said. "He was just lying down."

"The dun?" Colt asked.

Casie shot him a glance, hoping like hell that they couldn't see her blood-infused face.

"Yeah." Ty shuffled his feet and glanced at Colt as he faced them. "We turned them all out to graze after the shindig was over. Thought he'd be hungry, but he didn't eat more than an hour or so before he laid down."

"Did he seem restless or anything?" Casie's voice sounded a little more normal, though she could feel her heart beating against her ribs like an overzealous blacksmith.

"Not really. Just thought I'd let you know."

"Oh, okay." She cleared her throat again and wished she'd quit doing that. "Thanks. I'll check on him right away."

"Sure," Ty said and shoved his hands into the front pockets of his jeans. The movement was reminiscent of Colt, or maybe he'd picked up the idiosyncrasy from Colt's father. The boy had been living on the Dickensons' neighboring ranch ever since Casie had had a run-in with his mother some months before. The fallout from that debacle was still falling out, something Casie was careful not to let Ty know about. Despite his carefully maintained veneer, the boy had wounds too raw to be ignored. "Well, good night."

"Yeah," Casie said. "Thanks for your help today."

"Sure," he said and backed away.

"I'll, um . . . I'll see you tomorrow."

He nodded once and then he was gone, swallowed into the darkness. Since the Dickensons' Red Horse Ranch was less than a half mile down the road, he often insisted on walking.

Casie stared at the spot where he'd disappeared until her eyes watered.

"You okay?" Colt's voice sounded a little funny.

"Yes. Sure. Of course. Well . . ." She backed away, knees wobbly. "I'm just going to . . ." She jerked a thumb over her shoulder. ". . . check on . . ." Holy Hannah. She couldn't remember the horse's name. "On . . ."

He tilted his head at her. "Tangles."

"Yes!"

"I'll go with you."

"No!" The word exploded from her lips. She tried a smile. It didn't feel any steadier than her knees. "It's been a long day. I'm sure you want to get home."

"I don't," he said and made an odd noise.

She stared at him. Was that laughter? Was he laughing? Because this situation was *not* funny. This situation was light-years from being funny.

But when she studied him with narrowed eyes, she realized she could just make out the slant of his devilish grin.

He cleared his throat, fought down the grin before she had a chance to slap it off his face, and shifted his attention toward his scruffy boots. "You sure you're okay?" he asked, glancing up past the brim of his hat. "Cuz you seem kind of . . ." He shrugged. "Embarrassed."

She inhaled through her nostrils. "I'm fine," she said again and turned away. For one exhilarating second she almost thought she'd escaped, but then she heard his footsteps on the gravel behind her. She closed her eyes and walked faster, but the

horses weren't far away. Just past the windmill she could see
their dark shapes. She ducked between the twisted wires and approached them, hoping, at least, that the fence would slow her
stalker down, but it didn't. She pulled a peppermint candy out
of her pocket and offered it to the nearest animal. Reaching out,
Tangles took the treat between his teeth and munched, nodding
happily as the others gathered around.

"They all here?" Colt asked.

She scanned the two herds, separated by gender to prevent
problems, four males on one side of the fence, five females on
the other. Nine horses in all. "Looks like it."

"Everybody seems okay."

"Yeah."

"Maybe the dun was just tired."

"Maybe."

"Sophie rode him kind of hard."

"Yeah."

"I never saw a western dressage performance before."

"It's a pretty new discipline."

"She's a heck of a rider."

She closed her eyes, remembered to breathe, and pulled out
another piece of candy. The night was quiet. Somewhere not far
away an owl called for its mate.

"You're *not* embarrassed, are you?" There was laughter in
his voice. She gritted her teeth and tried to make herself turn toward him. No go.

"Casie?"

"No," she said and offered Blue the peppermint. The gray
colt snatched it from her hands and trotted away, knees lifting
in a jaunty manner that belied the sorry condition in which he
had arrived at the ranch. "Of course not."

The other horses were beginning to crowd in hopefully.

"Cuz you shouldn't be. I mean, it was just a kiss, right?"

She tried to speak. Failed again.

"Case?"

"Right," she said. "Of course. Just a . . ." She couldn't force
out the last word.

"Kiss." He finished for her. "And the . . . and the shirt thing. You didn't see where that button went, did you?"

Oh God.

"Well, never mind, maybe one of the kids will find it. I'll ask them tomorrow when—"

"Don't you dare!" She swung toward him like a missile.

He was grinning, which meant he was probably teasing her. She hated it when he teased her. She crunched her hands into fists.

"Now don't go getting all riled up," he said. "This is no big deal."

"Not to you!" She practically spat the words.

He tilted his head a little, Stetson cocked to the right. "But it was to—"

"I'm their . . ." She waved a hand. The motion may have seemed a little wild as she tried to think of appropriate words. "Their mentor. I can't be seen . . ." She sputtered a little.

He nodded, as if trying to help her spit out the applicable words. "Kissing," he said.

She closed her eyes and groaned. He laughed out loud. "Geez, Casie, ease up. It was just a kiss. Don't get all cranked out of shape. I'm sure the boy's seen people kiss before. It's just—"

"You think he *knows?!*"

"What?"

"You think he knows I . . . we . . . were . . ."

"Kissing?"

"Yes."

For a moment she thought he would laugh again, but the man wasn't, apparently, a complete idiot. Besides, they'd known each other for a score of years. He'd seen her at her craziest and probably didn't care to witness such a thing again. He shook his head. "No. Naw. Probably not."

"Really?" She was grasping at straws, desperately searching his face for sincerity. But in that instant she realized that his collar was off-kilter. Skimming her gaze down his chest she saw now that his entire shirt was kittywampus. She quit breathing.

"What?" he asked and glanced down.

"Your shirt's buttoned wrong."

"What?"

"Your *shirt* is buttoned wrong." Her voice had risen a couple of octaves and a number of decibels.

"Now just settle down," he crooned. "You're scaring the horses."

"The horses are fine! *Emily's* fine!" She leaned toward him, anger erupting. "You're the problem!" She stabbed at his chest, which she remembered as dark and broad and hard as granite. How the devil was she supposed to think coherently when his chest was . . . his chest?

"Me?" He sounded genuinely confused. Maybe she had been wrong. Maybe he *was* a complete idiot. "How do you figure?"

"How do I—" She threw up her hands. Had she really torn open his shirt? "You disappear for months on end, then show up like some knight in—" She stopped herself with an effort.

He was staring at her. She pursed her lips. He narrowed his eyes.

"You said you didn't want me here, Case."

"I didn't."

"You didn't say that or you didn't want me here?"

"I said I didn't *need* you here."

"But you do *want* me?" His voice was breathy. He took a step forward.

She stepped back. Was he out of his mind? She'd torn a button off his shirt in her haste to . . . "No. I . . . ." She shook her head, trying to joggle out the unwanted thoughts. "You're twisting my words."

He took another step forward, eyes narrowed. "Then say what you mean, Case. Now's the time."

She swallowed, found his eyes in the darkness. "I don't . . . Men . . ." She paused, trying to think, trying to breathe. "Bradley . . . My fiancé," she explained, as if he might have forgotten the name of the man whose nose he had broken not six months earlier. "I thought I'd be with him forever. But he's . . . he's gone."

"Brad's a moron." His words were absolutely level, earnest, matter-of-fact. And very likely correct.

"You left, too."

He narrowed his eyes. "Seemed to me like maybe you had a few things to figure out."

"Don't put this on me," she said.

He watched her.

She gestured wildly, then managed a wheezy laugh. "Geez, Dickenson, you're a rodeo cowboy. There couldn't be anyone less likely to settle down."

"That *your* opinion or your ex-fiancé's?"

She exhaled sharply in disbelief. "Are you saying this doesn't scare you?"

"This?" he asked.

She swung her hand sideways. "Money troubles, pregnant teenagers, pending lawsuits, rank horses . . ." She laughed. It sounded maniacal. "Choose your poison."

He watched her in silence for a moment. "Lawsuits?" he asked.

"Good choice," she said, and feeling inordinately tired suddenly, glanced toward the soothing hills that had framed her world for most of her life.

"What lawsuits?" he asked.

She shook her head. "Probably nothing will come of it. I mean . . . it's been months already. It'll probably never go to court."

"What lawsuits?" he repeated.

She scowled into the distance. "She's claiming I'm unstable."

He remained silent.

"Said I gave her a concussion. Says she's in constant pain, that she has to medicate to relieve the agony." She laughed. "Holy Hannah, she was three sheets to the wind at seven o'clock in the morning."

"Ty's mom," he guessed.

She didn't respond. Hadn't she learned not to depend on a man for help? Wasn't she better than that? She inhaled carefully. He stepped toward her, curled his hands around her arms.

"The boy's parents are suing you?"

She winced despite her resolve to be strong. "Guess his mom is kind of carrying a grudge."

She could feel his gaze on her, and when she shifted her eyes to his, she scowled. Was he grinning?

"Is something funny?" she asked.

"You *did* beat the living crap out of her," he said.

"This is not amusing!"

"No. It's . . . *amazing!*" he said.

For a second she was mesmerized by the light in his eyes, by the warmth in his voice. Did she see admiration there? she wondered, but she shook the thought away. "What's wrong with you?" she snarled and jerked out of his grip. "I attacked another woman. A mother! I must have been nuts. Bradley was right. This place is making me crazy."

"She beat Ty," he said. "Left bruises. Left *scars!*" There was danger in his voice suddenly, anger in his face. "Does it really seem crazy that you'd try to protect him?"

"I . . ." Why did he make it all sound so logical? She wasn't a violent person. Usually. "He's so young."

"I know." He nodded. "But he's doing okay. He's a hard worker, dependable, good with the livestock."

"He deserves better."

"Dad's doing the best he can."

"I didn't mean . . ." She shook her head, feeling manic. "Your parents are fantastic. I can't thank them enough for taking him in. I mean . . . I'd keep Ty at the Lazy if I could, but with the girls here . . ."

"Things are working out okay."

"Are you kidding me? Holy crap, Dickenson, I *assaulted* her! What was I thinking? I should have never gone to their farm. I should have never—"

"I think you should have."

She snapped her gaze back to his. He shrugged. His lips curled up a little at the corner. "Kicking her in the ribs that last time may have been a little over the top, though."

"Oh man . . ." She groaned. "I *should* be locked up."

"Is that what they're saying?" The humor had disappeared from his voice.

"They don't want me seeing Ty." Her voice sounded broken to her own ears.

"They're the ones that should be locked up, Case. Anyone who would do that to a kid should be put away forever."

"Maybe they'll settle out of court."

"Does Ty know about this?"

She shook her head, thinking about the last phone call she'd received from the Robertses. So far there had been only threats of legal action, but that could change at any time. "I hope not. He thinks everything's his fault as it is."

Colt scowled. "I know a good lawyer in Sioux Falls. I'll give him a call. I think he'll be able to—"

"No," she said. "This isn't your problem."

"Hell, Case!" He ground out the words, shook his head, glared into the distance. "If this goes to court, you might never be able to take in another guest."

Worse, she could lose the right to see Ty. And Emily. And Sophie. Her throat closed up. Her heart squeezed tight in her chest. "You think I don't know that?"

"You could lose the ranch."

She stifled a wince, glanced at the ancient windmill. "I'll be all right."

"Let me help you."

She shook her head. "Thank you." She cleared her throat, shoved her hands into the back pockets of her jeans. "I appreciate the offer, but I . . ." She allowed herself to glance at his chest for one moment before returning her attention to his face. "I don't seem to be real . . . sane when you drop by."

"Maybe if I quit dropping by . . ." He was staring at her. "Maybe if I were around on a more permanent basis."

She laughed, astounded. "What are you thinking, Dickenson? Are you saying you're going to give up rodeo? You saying you're going to stay forever to babysit teenagers and . . ." She flipped a hand toward the decrepit house. "Fix the plumbing?"

He watched her, body still, voice low. "Is that what you want?"

She watched him, unblinking. A thousand frenetic emotions swooshed through her. A thousand pictures of tranquil domesticity eased into her soul, but she forced a laugh. "You're a rodeo cowboy. A bronc rider. Songs are written about how you love 'em and leave 'em. About how you—"

"I could be something else."

She blinked, held her breath, forced herself to speak again. "For how long?" His eyes made her chest hurt. A hundred uncertainties squeezed in. "If you were here and then changed your mind, it would break my . . ." She stopped herself. "It would break Emily's heart."

He stared at her.

She glanced away. "She's been disappointed too much already."

"Maybe I won't disappoint her."

She shook her head, feeling frantic. "She's fragile. I know she . . . she doesn't seem like it, but she's been through a lot, and now . . . What if something goes wrong? I've tried to make sure she eats right and doesn't work too hard. But I don't know anything about prenatal care and—"

"It'll be okay."

"You don't—"

"Everything will be all right."

She drew a deep breath and remained silent for a while, trying to yank herself from his gaze, but it was almost impossible. "How do you know?"

He scowled at her.

It wasn't like her to question, to hound. But maybe she was growing up. "How do you know so much about pregnancy?"

The night was absolutely quiet for a moment before he spoke. "I'm an uncle, remember?"

She raised one brow at him.

"Sissy has a couple of kids."

"And what were you?" she scoffed. "Her designated birth coach?"

He shrugged. "Carson was in Iraq. Second tour. She was alone on a couple thousand acres when little Tuff was due. I thought it wouldn't kill me to pitch in for a while."

"Oh." She felt sheepish and small and petty. "I guess I forgot."

"That she has kids?"

She drew a deep breath and decided to go with honesty. "That you're not always an ass anymore."

He laughed. "Geez, Case, that's so flattering. You're not trying to seduce me or something, are you?" he asked and stepped forward.

For a moment she forgot to step back. Forgot to deny everything.

"Cuz if you want, we could start back up where we left off."

She opened her mouth, but in that moment he slipped his fingers behind her neck. Her lips remained parted. He kissed her.

She felt the blood rush to her extremities. Felt herself weaken.

"I mean . . ." He breathed the words against her lips. "My shirt's buttoned wrong anyway. And you look . . ." His nostrils flared as he stared at her. The expression in his eyes made her swallow, try to back away, and fail completely. Men didn't look at her like that. Men mostly ignored her. But her hair had come loose during the debacle by his truck and curled around her face like the morning glories on the front porch. Her lips felt bruised, and her shirt seemed to be shrink-wrapped to her breasts. "Good God, Case, you look good enough to eat."

She blinked. Tried to think of something to say, came up empty.

He raised his brows a little. "I think all the kids that are going to interrupt us have already passed by. And your last guest already left, right?"

She managed a nod. If she lived to be a hundred she would never know how.

"Which means the bunkhouse is empty?"

Another nod. This one was a little less steady. He skimmed his thumb over her lips. She shivered and swiped them with her tongue.

"No one would know if we put it to use."

She couldn't seem to do anything but stare at him.

"Case?"

She blinked. "Yeah?"

He watched her for an eternity, finally chuckled, then leaned in and kissed her again. Her lips melted first, then her neck, then her spine, then her knees, until she was sure she would flow out from under his hands like a sun-warmed Popsicle, but in a moment he pulled away. They stared at each other for an eternity. A thousand emotions shone in his eyes.

"Good night, Casie," he said, and turning, disappeared into the darkness.

CHAPTER 5

"I left it in the bathroom." Sophie's voice was loud, clear, and as pissy as hell from the kitchen below.

Emily's was calm and level, steady with the kind of exaggerated patience that made you want to grind your teeth. "Then chances are good that it's still in the bathroom."

"I already told you, it's not there."

"Then maybe you should look somewhere else."

Public radio played quietly in the background; a contingent of world-renowned scientists agreed that the earth was losing over five thousand species a year to extinction. The straight-talking district court judge, known by some as Judge Heartless, had recently resigned due to health problems. Emily was a self-confessed news junkie, but Sophie's harangue could not be ignored.

"Where'd you put it?"

Casie rubbed her knuckles into her left eyeball and stumbled out of her bedroom. Teenagers . . . she thought . . . probably not God's best invention. The fourth stair from the top groaned beneath her feet. She wasn't positive, but she was pretty sure she hadn't gotten more than two seconds of sleep during the entire night.

"Seriously?" Emily's voice had become increasingly patient. As it turns out, there aren't a lot of people who can fully appreciate the patient voice of a pregnant eighteen-year-old. "You think I stole it."

"Yes. I do."

"Have you seen my hair?" Emily Kane's dreadlocks were her trademark . . . nearly as well known (but not as dreaded) as her stellar sarcasm . . . or her patient tone.

"Listen, you may have Roberts fooled into thinking you're some kind of blessed saint, but I know you're nothing but a—"

"Good morning!" Casie sped down the final steps and lurched into the kitchen before open warfare was declared.

The girls turned to her in a second, both talking at once.

"She took my curling iron."

"Why would I take her stupid . . ." Emily paused, brows rising as her attention settled on Casie. "What happened to you?"

Casie raised her fingers to her face and darted her gaze from one girl to the other. Sophie was scowling. Emily was grinning. It wasn't until that moment that Casie realized her lips felt bruised, her face flushed. "Nothing. Nothing happened to me. Why?" She tried to calm her tone and her expression and wondered if they knew she'd spent the night restless and conflicted. Wondered if they knew she'd never found the strength to turn Dickenson down. That it had been Colt himself who had called a stop to . . . whatever it was they had started.

Emily's grin hitched up a notch. "What time did Mr. Dickenson leave?"

"Mr. . . ."

"He looked good, huh? A little skinny maybe, but cowboy yummy."

"I . . ." Casie's mind went momentarily numb, then snapped into action. "I'm sorry, Sophie." She turned with robotic precision toward the younger girl. "I was the one who used your curling iron."

"You?"

"Yeah, I . . ." She laughed, hoping rather manically they wouldn't think she had gussied up for Dickey Dickenson, the bane of her existence. "I just wanted to look decent for the festival. You know. Not that my hair is the curling type. Either one of them." She chuckled rustily at her own joke and dismissively flipped her hair behind her shoulder. It was thin, fine, and the unexciting color of caramel, but she had to admit that it almost looked decent when curled and shellacked into submission.

"It looks sexy," Em said. "What did Mr. Dickenson say?"

"I . . ." She remembered him saying she looked good enough to eat. Remembered the heat in his eyes, the strength in his hands as he slid them up her—

"Where?" Sophie said.

"What?" She yanked her attention back to the conversation at hand, feeling oddly immature in this house of teenage estrogen.

Sophie looked disgruntled and maybe a little disgusted. "Where'd you put my curling iron?"

"Oh. I left it in the bathroom."

"I *looked* in the bathroom."

"I'm pretty sure it's still—" she began, but Emily had never been above interrupting her at any given moment.

"I suppose it's too much to hope that you have him sated and ecstatic in your bedroom upstairs, huh?"

Casie zipped a reprimanding scowl at the older girl. "Emily!"

"What?" She looked honestly affronted. "Geez, Case, you don't have to live like a nun just because we're here. We know about sex. Least I do." She made a wry face and caressed her belly, which seemed to have expanded overnight. "You've heard of sex, too, haven't you, Soph?"

Sophie rolled her eyes. "I don't think it's too much to ask that I have a few possessions of my own in this house. A couple pair of jeans . . . a curling iron. Maybe a—"

"Holy cats!" Emily said. She and Casie had had long, grueling discussions regarding acceptable expletives. Holy cats had become her favorite, with holy shorts coming in a close second. Casie refused to consider what her unacceptable favorites were. "Will you just go look in the bathroom already?"

"The bathroom's the size of a turtle's egg. You think I wouldn't have seen it if it was—"

"In the drawer," Casie said, remembering suddenly. "I'm sorry. I put it in the top drawer. I thought that's where you kept it."

"I . . ." Sophie began, but Emily stopped her.

"That *is* where she keeps it."

"Stay out of this," Sophie warned.

"I don't know why you're getting so hot-wired," Emily said. "It's not like it's the Holy Grail or something. It's just a frickin' curling iron."

"It's *my* curling iron."

"Yeah, well, it's not as if you even need it. I mean, good God, *golly*," she corrected, glancing at Casie. "It's six thirty in the morning and you look like you just stepped off a high fashion runway." She scowled. When Emily was honest, which was a sporadic thing at best, she was spooky honest. "Makes me want to eat my weight in salami."

"That's . . ." Sophie, though pampered like a princess before her arrival at the Lazy, never quite seemed to know how to handle compliments. "It's not as if it makes any difference. He doesn't even . . ." She paused, shifted her gaze from one to the other, cheeks coloring a little.

"What?" Casie said.

"He *who?*" Emily said.

"Nothing," Sophie said, and turning, rummaged noisily through the silverware drawer.

"He *what?*" Emily asked, sparing a grin for Casie. "Hey, you don't have a thing for that shoot-'em-up cowboy, do you? Cuz he's mine. Soon as I pop out this baby, I'm gonna throw him over my saddle and bring him on home to the Lazy."

Casie watched Sophie's jerky movements. It wasn't like her to get embarrassed, but Casie herself was all too familiar with the pangs of self-consciousness and drew the conversation in a different direction.

"I thought you were looking for an elderly doctor, Em," she said.

"A sugar daddy. Sure," Emily conceded happily. "Brooks Hedley's just for sport."

Casie shook her head. "You're a terrible influence."

"Yeah, well, Sophie's not as innocent as she seems."

"I meant for me," Casie said.

Emily laughed with her usual effusiveness. "I'm surprised you can even blush anymore after stashing Mr. Dickenson away in your bedroom last night."

"She's down!" Ty burst into the kitchen like a tornado. There was terror in his eyes, a quiver in his voice.

"What?" Casie was in full panic before another word was spoken.

"It's Angel!" He spit out the words. "I think she's collicking."

"What happened?" she asked, but she was already rushing toward the foyer, searching for her boots with eyes too recently open.

"She was flat out when I went to feed her. I thought she was just resting cuz she got up as soon as she saw me, but when I dumped the oats in her bucket she wouldn't eat."

Casie swore in silence as she smashed a Marlboro cap onto her head. Horses didn't turn away from oats unless they were sick. Prior to this, she'd been pretty sure Angel would have to be dead to refuse breakfast.

"Did you take the grain back out?"

"Didn't have time. Came straight here. What are we going to do?"

"Do you think she's been rolling?" They were already rushing out the door together.

"I don't know."

"What's wrong with rolling?" Despite her bulk, Emily was only a half pace behind them.

Sophie was closer still. "Horses have an esophageal sphincter that won't allow them to throw up. They thrash around to try to alleviate the pain. Sometimes the agitation will cause a gut to twist. After that . . ." She fell blessedly silent.

Thank you, Miss Happiness, Casie thought, and lengthened her strides. It was no secret that the Lazy could barely afford equine feed much less equine surgery.

Inside the barn, Al, the follicly challenged goat, greeted them with an early-morning bleat, but Angel's head remained unseen above her stall's Dutch door. In a moment Casie was looking inside. The mare was down again, and there was no question that she was in pain. Her head was stretched out on the ground, her eyes half closed. Little moans of agony escaped at irregular intervals.

"Get a halter on her," Casie said.

Ty was quick to do so. In a second he had crouched down to slip the nylon behind the mare's long ears, but she was already rolling miserably onto her side.

"Get her up!" Sophie ordered.

"I'm trying." Ty's voice was raspy as he jerked on the lead line. But the old mare didn't notice. Groaning, she rolled onto her back, legs flailing.

"Quit trying and *do it!*" Sophie yelled.

Casie stepped inside the stall, adding her strength to the lead. But suddenly, there was a crack of noise. Angel jolted to her feet, nearly trampling them in her haste to rise.

Sophie stood behind her, whip in hand.

"What the hell are you doing?" Ty rasped.

"Saving her life!"

"Well, you don't have to hit her."

"You want her to die? Is that what you want? Cuz if you don't, you shouldn't work her so hard."

"I didn't work—"

"Showing off for the buckle bunnies was what you were doing. It would serve you right if—"

"Sophie!" Casie barked the girl's name.

The barn went quiet. Angel pawed frantically.

"That's enough," Casie added and caught Sophie's gaze in a hard stare. The girl turned back to the horse. All eyes shifted in that direction.

There was hay scattered in the old mare's scraggly mane, white rimmed her terrified eyes, and her coat was dark with sweat behind her ears and along her neck and flanks. She ground her teeth in hopeless agony.

"What now?" Ty's voice was little more than a whisper. In the past, he had proven to be a quick thinker in an emergency, but his wits seemed dim now, his reactions jerky.

"Better get her walking," Casie said.

"Not if she twisted something," Sophie said.

Ty turned toward her. "What do we do then?" Perhaps it was a testament to his worry that he voiced the question to the girl he despised.

"Surgery's the only option."

Casie felt her stomach knot. She knew it was true. A twisted intestine was rarely, if ever, corrected without extremely invasive surgery. Extremely *expensive* surgery. She could feel Ty's attention shift to her.

She shook her head, only vaguely aware that she was doing so. "I can't, Ty. I just . . . The Lazy . . ." The truth was, the Lazy was barely clearing expenses, and if she was going to fight a lawsuit . . . going to fight for the privilege of continuing to see the battered boy who had captured her heart, she would need every penny. But if she let him down now, would he even *want* to see her?

"You don't got the money?" His voice was low.

Her own was barely audible. "I don't."

"How about paying on credit?" Emily spoke for the first time. Her face was pale, her mocha eyes wide in the barn's dim interior. She and Ty had shared a bond since before she'd ever set foot on the Lazy. "Or a loan."

"Dad didn't . . . The Lazy doesn't have a very good rapport with Dakota Equine."

Emily shifted her gaze to Ty's face and winced. "There must be other places we could take her."

"Not that can handle this kind of surgery," Casie said. "Not within a hundred miles."

"Then I guess we'd better get her to that one," Sophie said.

The three of them stared at her in uncertain silence.

"Unless you just want to shoot her between the eyes," Sophie snapped.

No one breathed. Casie shifted her gaze to Ty. He stood absolutely still, watching her with dread and painful hopefulness.

"I'll hook up the trailer," she said.

CHAPTER 6

The trailer door moaned like a ghost as Casie pulled it open. Her expression was taut with worry, pale with uncertainty. Ty couldn't bear to look at her. She didn't have the funds necessary to pay for major surgery. He knew that just like he knew he didn't have a pot to pee in. But Angel . . . She shifted her dark eyes toward him. They were wide with the kind of fear he understood all too well. He put a hand on her neck and urged her forward. Pain, he knew, was driving daggers through her belly, but she did as she was asked and took a staggering step toward the trailer.

"Call the hospital," Sophie said.

Ty glanced at her, barely understanding her words.

"Emily!" the girl snapped. Em jerked toward her. "Call Dakota Equine. Tell them we're bringing in an emergency."

"I don't . . ." Em shook her head, looking dazed and worried. Maybe she was thinking of her unborn baby. Maybe she was wondering how she was going to pay *her own* hospital bills. God knew Casie would help her if she could, but how was she going to do that when she was sinking money into vet bills? Em glanced at him, eyes as worried as Angel's. "I don't know the phone number. Maybe I should—" she began, but Sophie stopped her.

"Well, find it. Tell them we have a colicky horse. Older. Early twenties, maybe. Mixed breed. Nine hundred pounds. Generally good health. We'll be there in forty-five minutes."

"How are you going to get all the way to Rapid City in forty-five—"

"Just call them," she barked and turned her attention to the mare. "All right." She calmed her voice, pursed her lips. Casie came around the back of the trailer, expression strained.

"We ready?"

Ty clenched his fists. He was trying like hell to be strong, but he *wasn't* strong. Never had been. "What if she goes down in the trailer?"

"She's not going to," Sophie said.

"What if she *does?*" He was sick to death of Sophie Jaegar with her glowing skin and stinking superiority.

"She's not going down," she repeated, "because we're going to hold her up."

"What? No, you're not," Casie said, but Sophie had her back up.

"Angel's not going to . . ." She paused and took a deep breath. "She's not going to die."

"You can't ride in the trailer!" Casie said. "It's not safe. It's not even sane."

"Well, this whole thing is crazy, isn't it? Ty said himself the horse isn't worth the cost of a bullet." Her tone was harsh, her eyes bright with emotion. She was probably mad about the waste of money, too. Blue, the colt she adored, needed supplements. Hell, every animal on the property needed something. "We're wasting time. Let's get on the road."

"All right," Casie said, "but you're not riding back there."

"Then she's as good as dead." The girl's tone was steady and absolute.

Ty felt the words in his gut. He knew it was stupid. The old mare should probably just be put down. In the long run it might be kinder, but . . . He shifted his eyes to Angel's. They were wide with fear, dark with a hundred memories of time they had shared together, of times he had wept when no one else could see. Of times he had whispered his deepest fears, his most closely guarded secrets. He felt his throat close up, felt his hands shake.

For a moment he could feel Casie's gaze on him, hot as a heat lamp.

"Load her up," Casie said, but he couldn't bear to look at her. To thank her. Neither could he argue, though he was sure he should. His mother would be screaming mad if she knew they were throwing away good money on this worthless nag.

He tugged the mare toward the vehicle.

Angel stumbled as she heaved herself into the trailer, groaned as she hoisted up her hindquarters. But she didn't refuse. She never refused. Casie had once said the old girl would walk through fire for him. He swallowed, trapped in Angel's eyes, as Sophie stepped up beside the mare, hand braced on her neck.

"Shut the door," she ordered. Her tone was abrasive, her expression taut. But she didn't sound angry. Maybe she was scared, too. Maybe this was what she was like when she was afraid . . . more irritating than ever. God help them all.

"Listen—" Casie said, but Sophie spoke first.

"We'll be all right." Her voice had dropped a few decibels. "We will."

Casie scowled at her, then shifted her gaze to Ty. "You okay?"

"Yeah." He nodded. It was hard as hell to speak past the lump in his throat. His mother was right. He was weak. Weak and sentimental. He swallowed the lump.

"Drive fast," Sophie ordered.

"If you have trouble, stick your hand between the slats on the left side," Casie said. Her voice was tight with worry. "I'll pull over as soon as I can."

"It's like living in the dark ages," Sophie said. "If you had a cell phone I could—"

"Complain about my Neanderthal ways later," Casie said. "You ready?"

They both nodded. She closed the door. It swung on rusty hinges, groaning as if in pain. Inside, it seemed unreasonably dark. Puke rattled loudly when Casie turned the key. The first few crunching feet of gravel were as bumpy as a roller coaster. It was a little smoother on the road. Angel flipped her tail and cranked up her left hind leg. He put a hand on her neck. It was wet and cold with sweat. Forty-five minutes was an eternity, and he had no idea how they could make it that fast.

Sophie moved around Angel's tail and stepped up next to him.

"I know you think I'm a bitch," she said.

Her words, pitched high to be heard over the sound of the wheels, surprised him. For a moment he tried to come up with a disclaimer, but seriously, she *was* a bitch. And although he didn't exactly consider himself a social genius, he didn't think now was exactly the right time to voice that opinion. He remained cautiously mute.

"But I don't care what you think. We're going to have to work together on this."

He managed a nod. It was stupid hard to think when she was standing right next to him. He scowled, trying nevertheless.

"I don't like it any better than you do, you know."

He nodded again, not sure if it was called for.

"Whatever," she said then. "Let's push her up against the side of the trailer. Then we can both support her on this side. Okay?"

He blinked, tried to marshal his senses despite her proximity and managed to shake his head. "No."

"What?" She sounded dismissive and already angry. "Listen, if she goes down, we'll never be able to—"

"She's my horse."

She snorted. "Like I'd even *want* her."

He felt his molars grind. "So I'll be the one taking care of her."

"Well, that would be just awesome if you could, wouldn't it? But since you can't, I'm going to help out."

"That's fine by me. Just so long as you do the helping out from over there," he said and jerked his chin toward the back of the rumbling trailer.

"Oh sure," she said and hissed a laugh. "Because you're the *man?*"

Her words seemed to stop his heart for a moment. Was it possible that she thought of him like that? he wondered, but he found his footing in a moment. "Because if something happens to you, your father'll kill me dead."

"Are you kidding?" She snorted again. "My dad couldn't care less if I—" She stopped herself.

He scowled at her, wondering. What the hell was she thinking? Her father had probably never even raised his *voice* to her. Then again, maybe there were different forms of hate. Forms he didn't understand. The idea made his gut cramp up.

"Listen," she said, breaking his line of thought. "Hercules wouldn't be able to hold this horse up alone. So we'll both stay on this side. If she starts to go down we'll keep her tight between us and the wall."

"Sounds like an okay plan," he said and shifted his eyes to her for a second. She glowed in the dark. Swear to God she did. "If we want to get dead fast."

She scowled at him. "You have a better idea?"

Angel lifted a sharp forefoot and pawed with rapid-fire panic, nearly striking Sophie's leg.

Ty drew her lead up tight, lifting her head, doing his best to keep her from collapsing. "Yeah," he said, heart in his throat. "If she goes down, we'll just keep her down. Make sure she doesn't roll. Make sure she doesn't hurt herself."

"That's asinine."

"It'll be easier than trying to keep her *up.*"

"Then how are we going to get her out of the trailer once we—" she began, but in that second, Angel's knees buckled.

"Hold her head up!" Sophie rasped.

Angel stumbled, trying to right herself. Her left forefoot swung erratically sideways, striking Sophie's leg. The girl staggered to her knees an instant before Angel collapsed atop her.

Panic roared through Ty. He yanked at the lead, trying to pull Angel up. "Sophie! Sophie!" he yelled, but the girl was already dragging her legs out from under the mare, already crawling forward and stretching out on top of the gray's outstretched head. It took him a while to realize she was actually taking his advice. Shoving that weird knowledge aside, he dove down beside her, covering Angel's neck with his body.

"You all right?" His voice shook, not to mention his hands.

"Yeah."

Beneath him, Angel struggled to rise. Ty threw himself forward, adding his weight to the girl's atop the mare's head. She lay back down with a grunt. "Thatta girl," he rasped. "Just stay put, now. It's going to be okay," he crooned, but he knew he was lying.

Inside the cab, Casie wheeled around the final turn and came to a jolting halt in front of Dakota Equine Veterinary Hospital. The driver's door resisted for a moment, but she shoved it open and held her breath as she raced toward the back of the trailer.

"Is this the colic?" A voice from the concrete building stopped her in her tracks. She turned to see a young woman in jeans and a sweatshirt standing in the doorway.

"What?"

"Is this—"

"Oh yes. This is Angel."

"You can bring her right in," she said and disappeared back inside.

Casie yanked herself from her stupor and rushed toward the trailer door. It creaked open. She stared inside, then jerked her gaze lower; both kids were stretched across the mare's head.

"Holy—"

"We there?" Sophie asked.

"Are you all right?"

"Can we let her up or not?" Sophie snapped. Apparently, the ride hadn't softened her disposition.

"Yes. Be careful, though. If—" she began, but Tyler was already rising to his feet. Sophie was a little slower. Reaching out, he grabbed her by the shoulder of her shirt and dragged her with him.

Casie was sure the old mare was dead, but in a moment she raised her head.

"Come on," Ty crooned. Angel blinked, shoved herself onto her belly, then heaved herself to her feet. Sophie shifted out of the way, limping a little.

Casie snapped her gaze to the girl. "What happened?"

"Hurry up," Sophie said. "Let's get her inside."

"What—" Casie began again, but Ty interrupted her.

"Angel fell," Ty said. "Sophie was underneath."

Casie felt herself blanch. She'd be lucky to survive a violence lawsuit. Add neglect to that and she might never again see the light of day, much less keep the ranch.

"You okay?" Her voice sounded a little rusty.

Sophie didn't even glance in her direction. "They ready for her in there or what?"

Casie skimmed the girl's legs. There were no protruding bones or spewing blood. Was it a bad sign that that was the best she could hope for? "They said to take her straight in."

"Then what are we waiting for?"

"I just want to make sure—"

"Let's get going," Sophie said, but she winced as she stepped down from the trailer.

Casie exchanged a glance with Ty. His expression was solemn, his brows low under his frayed, ever-present cap.

"So this is Angel?" The girl in the sweatshirt was back, holding open an oversized door and watching the procession as they eased toward her.

"Emily must have gotten ahold of you," Casie said.

The girl nodded and stepped back, directing them across the bare concrete floor to an exam room where a metal frame of heavy steel tubing was anchored into the floor. "How's she doing?" she asked.

"She's hurting," Ty said.

"I bet you are," she said, addressing the mare. "But hang in there, old girl. Lead her into the stocks, will you?"

Ty tugged Angel into the metal frame as the girl continued to croon.

"But you're a tough old bird, aren't you, sweetheart." She approached slowly and placed her hand on the mare's muzzle. Lifting the gray's upper lip, she glanced at her gums. Even to Casie's uncertain eye, they looked pale. The girl pinched the skin on the mare's leathery neck, testing for dehydration. "You Ty?" she asked, glancing at the boy.

"Yes, ma'am."

"Are you the one who takes care of her?" It didn't take a genius to recognize the worry in Ty's eyes, the tender caring in his hands.

"I try to," he said.

She gave him a solemn glance. "Do you know how long it's been since she drank?"

"I gave her a five-gallon bucket last night," he said. "It was half gone this morning."

The girl nodded. Her blond hair was pulled back in a tight ponytail. Her face was unlined. She glanced into Angel's eyes again. "Such a nice girl, aren't you, sweetheart. Just a peach. So polite, even with a tummyache.

"Any recent change in her diet?" she asked, not glancing toward the humans.

"No, ma'am. Lots of pasture, a little hay and crimped oats at night. But . . ." He winced. "I worked her pretty hard yesterday."

"Worked her how?"

"Cattle." He slipped a hand onto the mare's broad cheek as if he couldn't help himself. "She's real good with cows."

"I bet she is." Easing the stethoscope from around her neck, she plugged the bifurcated ends into her ears and placed the flat end on the mare's belly. Her hand looked gentle but firm against the mare's spine when she steadied herself to lean down. "I bet you show those cows who's boss, don't you, sweetheart?" She listened for a second, moved the stethoscope toward the mare's flank, and listened again. In a matter of seconds, she let the stethoscope drop to the end of its cord, lifted the old mare's tail, and carefully inserted a thermometer. "Any history of colic in the past?"

Ty shook his head. "She's been real healthy ever since we first got her. Except she was lame for a while. But that was just a gravel."

She glanced up from where she was palpating Angel's belly. "Did she work that out on her own?"

"Yes, ma'am."

"How long have you had her?"

He scowled. "Year. Year and a half, maybe."

Angel lifted a hind leg, cranking it painfully up against her belly.

"Well," the girl said, "she's lucky to have found a man who takes such good care of her. There are lots of people who wouldn't have even noticed—"

"The animal's in pain," Sophie snapped. "Are you going to get a vet in here or what?"

The blond girl straightened slowly. "I guess I didn't introduce myself," she said. "I'm Dr. Sarah."

Sophie's brows dipped even lower.

"Are you Ty's sister?"

"No!"

"Girlfriend?"

Sophie actually paled. If Casie hadn't been worried out of her mind she would have laughed out loud.

"Not—"

"Sophie and Ty help out on the ranch," Casie said. "I'm Cassandra Carmichael." Once the words were out she wished she could call them back. The name Carmichael had gained something of a reputation with her father's declining health. It wasn't a good one. "What can you tell us?"

"Well . . ." The young doctor shook her head and glanced toward Sophie, who was atypically silent. Dr. Sarah exhaled, scowled. "There are virtually no gut sounds."

"Is that bad?" Ty barely seemed able to force out the words.

"It means she's twisted an intestine." Sophie's voice was low, lacking inflection. Casie glanced at her. "Right?" she said, turning her attention back to the vet.

"It's possible," she said. "I'm going to give her something for the pain. Then I'll examine her more thoroughly, but I'd be willing to bet that she's going to need surgery."

Ty winced. "How much would that cost?"

"It's not cheap, I'm afraid."

The boy's hand tightened on the frayed lead rope. His fingernails were chipped, his knuckles white. "How much?"

The vet shook her head. "The techs usually handle that sort of thing, and they're not in yet." She scowled, watching Ty's expression. "But the costs will be in the thousands for sure. It all depends on the severity of the situation, how fast she recovers, how long we keep her here. . . ." She shrugged.

Ty's face looked as pale as his knuckles now. "When is that money due?" he asked.

The doctor glanced from him to Casie, expression apologetic. "We usually ask for payment at the time services are rendered."

The room went silent. Angel moaned low and desperate.

"I'm sorry we can't defer payment." Dr. Sarah flicked her gaze from face to face. "But with the economy like it is, we've had a lot of clients fail to pay."

"I'll get the money," Ty said.

All eyes turned toward him.

"I'm a hard worker," he said.

Something changed in the veterinarian's expression. She met his eyes with a quiet blend of regret and admiration. "I'm sure you are, Ty, but—"

"And my word's good. I just can't . . ." He paused, tightened his fingers in Angel's mane for a moment. His cheeks had turned red. "I just can't pay it all right up front."

No one spoke. From a distant part of the building a horse nickered hopefully.

Dr. Sarah flicked her gaze to Casie's. Maybe she read something there; maybe she made some sort of decision on her own. Casie would never know, but she spoke again in a moment.

"Listen," Dr. Sarah said. "I have a call in to the techs, but they probably won't be here for another half hour yet. If you can help out, I should be able to take a little off your costs, but the bill could still be upwards of eight thousand dollars."

Casie felt like she had been gut punched, but one glance at Ty's wounded eyes was all she could bear. "All right," she said. "Let's get at it."

CHAPTER 7

Three hours later they were gathered outside a roomy stall. It was bedded in fresh-smelling wood shavings and padded with rubber on the walls and floor.

"What are her chances?" Ty asked. His face was solemn as he curled his fingers around the steel bars that separated him from the mare standing alone on the far side of the door. Her head drooped near her knees and her eyes were half closed, but she was back on her feet.

Sophie stood a couple yards from the stall. Her face was no longer green, but it had been clear early on that despite her usual commanding presence, she would not be much help during these particular proceedings. Although her interest was obvious, she'd barely been able to assist in shaving the surgical site and catheterizing the jugular before leaving the room on wobbly knees. While Ty and Casie watched the doctors incise and empty the mare's intestines into huge, wheeled garbage cans, Sophie had rushed outside to empty her own stomach.

"Her chances are decent." Turned out little Dr. Sarah didn't pull any punches. She stood beside them, the top of her head barely reaching Casie's nose. A spray of blood still festooned her left cheek. "As you know, there was a torsion, a twist, in the posterior portion of her ileum. It had already become somewhat necrotic. But when we removed that portion of the intestine and sutured her back up, things pinkened up nicely. Still . . ." She scowled as she glanced at the mare, who looked small and forlorn in the oversized stall. "Her age is against her. But you got her here really quickly." Lifting her gaze, she stared at the IV that hung from the center of the ceiling and dripped steadily into the mare's jugular. "We'll know more in a few hours. Do you want to wait around?"

Casie shook her head. They'd talked about it at some length between Sophie's rushed trips to the restroom. "We can't. I've got chores to do, and if we hurry, the kids can still get in a couple hours of school."

"Sure," Dr. Sarah said and smiled. "Well . . ." She reached out to shake Ty's hand first. "We'll take good care of her. That's a promise."

He nodded. "When can I see . . ." He cleared his throat. Boys in general tended to be uncomfortable with emotions. Cowboys viewed them as lethal. "When do you think we'll be able to take her home?"

"I'm not sure yet, but we've got your contact information, right?" she asked and glanced at the clipboard hanging on the stall door. "Let's see, we've got Sophie's cell, Casie's landline, Emily's e-mail address, and the Dickensons' home phone. Looks like we should be able to reach you without sending up smoke signals." She smiled.

"And you'll . . ." Ty paused, unsmiling in the face of her upbeat humor. "You'll call me either way? I mean, if things get worse . . . I'd like to . . ." His lips twitched. "You won't put her down or nothing without my permission, right?"

"No." She sobered, then reaching out, put a hand on his arm. "If things go poorly, I'll do my best to make sure you have a chance to say good-bye."

For a moment Casie was sure he would argue, would assure them all that that wasn't what he had meant at all, but in the end he just mumbled a thanks and turned away.

The walk to Puke was silent. The day was overcast. A stiff wind blew from the northwest, rustling the needles of the fir trees that grew alongside the parking lot and wafting the pungent scent of sap and autumn over them.

"You okay?" Casie asked, but at that moment Ty turned un-expectedly toward his nemesis.

"You got money," he said. His voice was low, nearly inaudi-ble. It took a moment for Casie to understand his meaning.

Sophie was even slower on the uptake. Apparently, the sight of seventy feet of intestines being unraveled from Angel's in-verted body was still having some negative effects on her equi-librium. "*What?*"

Ty pursed his lips, body stiff, eyes narrow. "I'd pay you back. You got my word on that."

She scowled. "What are you talking about?"

Casie dug Puke's keys out of the pocket of her canvas jacket and tried not to interrupt. She'd never been comfortable with controversy, but there was no way of avoiding this. God knew she'd pay Angel's medical bills on the spot if she could. Then again, if she could fly, she'd get them all home quicker. Chances were about equal for both.

"Your dad'll give you the money if you ask him," Ty said.

Sophie shook her head, glossy hair rippling as she finally caught his drift. "Surgery costs . . ." She scowled as if still trying to get her bearings. "The bill's already in the thousands. If she needs additional—"

"I'll pay him back."

For a moment there was absolute quiet and then she breathed a snort. "How?" The sound was caustic, ushering in her return to normal. "Everyone knows your family doesn't have a pot—"

"Sophie." Casie kept her voice low. In the time she'd known Ty, he'd never asked for so much as a dime. But his face was flushed with dark emotion now, his body stiff, as if it took every fiber in his being to beg.

"I'll pay him back," he repeated. "With interest. You got my word."

For a second Casie was sure the girl would laugh again, cer-tain she would come up with some sharp-edged rejoinder, but she just glanced back at the building behind them. Maybe there was something about the cold concrete blocks that convinced her to pull a cell phone from the pocket of her riding breeches. She jabbed a single number and skimmed her eyes away as it rang.

"Hi, Daddy." She kept her gaze carefully averted.

"Soph?" His voice was clear from halfway across the state.

"Yeah. Hey, I'm sorry I didn't call you back." She sprinted her gaze to Ty for a second, then shot it away. "We've been . . . I've just been really busy."

"The agreement was that you'd contact me daily," he said. "But I didn't mean you had to call me during school hours."

"Oh, well . . . I'm not in class right now." She glanced at Casie and, lowering her voice, turned away. "Listen, something's come up," she said, and pacing toward a row of horse trailers that lined the hospital's drive, let her voice dwindle away.

Casie sent Ty a fleeting glance. His lips were clamped tight, his body tense, but it was the silent worry in his dark eyes that made her heart hurt, that made her ache to reassure him, to make him smile. But she had nothing to give. No heartfelt wisdom, no salty humor, not even a father with deep pockets.

She was still searching for platitudes or punch lines when Sophie reappeared a few seconds later. The girl's brows had dipped low over her angry eyes. Her lips were pursed in her trademark expression of irritation. "He wants to talk to you," she said, and stretching out her arm, handed Ty the phone.

He took it with obvious misgivings, but his voice was low and steady when he spoke. "Hello?"

They could hear a similar greeting on the far end of the line. "I hear you need a loan."

"Yes, sir."

"I'm Googling equine colic surgery right now. Says here it could cost as much as ten thousand dollars."

For a moment Ty looked as if he was going to be sick. He failed to speak.

"That's an awful lot of money, Tyler."

"Yes, sir." He nodded, face pale, and tightened one hard-working hand into a fist. "I know, sir."

"How much of that can you pay yourself?"

Ty shifted his gaze to Casie. She felt herself wince despite her best efforts at stoicism.

"I can't pay more than a couple hundred right out of the chute," Ty said. His face was ruddy now, but whether that was caused by embarrassment or worry, Casie couldn't tell. In the end, however, it didn't matter, because she spoke without thinking, without censor.

"I can come up with a thousand." Her voice was extremely low. Maybe because it was an out-and-out lie. She had no means of garnering that kind of money, but the painful gratitude on the boy's face made it worth the fabrication.

"Twelve hundred, maybe, altogether," Ty said. His voice was quiet but determined. His course was set. "But I'd pay you back, sir. Every penny. That's a promise."

Jaegar sighed. "Listen, I've made quite a few investments lately. I don't have a lot of available cash. Maybe your parents could help you out."

Ty clenched his teeth. His eyes gleamed with unspoken emotion. "My folks don't have that kind of cash, neither."

Another sigh. "Listen, Tyler, I know Miss Carmichael thinks highly of you, but the economy isn't picking up as well as we had hoped and—"

"You can have the horse," Ty said.

The world went silent. Casie held her breath, trying not to think of the boy's chafed hands caressing the old mare's gleaming hide. Trying not to remember the grueling hours of work he had done in an effort to pay *her* back.

"What's that?" Jaegar asked.

"If you cover the bill you can have her. I'll still pay you back. She ain't much. I mean . . ." Ty's voice cracked. "She's old and she ain't got no papers or nothing, but she's cowy and she's quick. Your girl, Sophie . . ." His lips jerked as he shifted his gaze to her. He looked like little more than a cornered animal now, the hope all but gone from his eyes. "She could give riding lessons on her or something."

"That's very generous of you, I'm sure, Tyler. And I'd like to help you out, son. Really, I would, but—"

"Give me the phone." Sophie's face was tight as she stretched out her hand for the second time.

Ty scowled.

"Give it to me," she demanded, and with obvious uncertainty, he handed it over.

She turned away with military precision, silky hair swinging. In a moment she had disappeared from sight. Even her voice was gone. Ty shuffled his feet on the graveled parking lot. Casie cleared her throat. The tension was tight enough to strangle them both, but in a matter of moments Sophie had returned and was shoving the phone back into her pocket.

The silence stretched away like a tightrope.

Ty's face was absolutely devoid of color. Casie felt like shaking the girl until her teeth rattled. "Well?" she rasped finally.

"He's calling the hospital with his credit card number," Sophie said.

They were the last words spoken until they turned onto the Lazy's bumpy drive.

"You okay, Em?" Casie asked and rose from the table, taking her plate with her. In the background, Josh Turner crooned softly about dancing up the stairs.

Emily glanced sideways, still up to her elbows in soapy dishwater. Fresh-smelling herbs lined the windowsill in one long terra-cotta pot. The tiny leaves of thyme nestled cozily against the broad herbage of purple basil. "Sure. Why do you ask?"

"You only ate a gallon or so of chili."

"Baby Osgood was ravenous this afternoon. We had half a loaf of barley bread before you got home. I was thinking, maybe I should be a vocalist."

"You can't sing."

"Yeah, that could be a drawback," Emily said, ruminating silently for a second. "Do you think Ty's okay?"

Casie scowled as she returned for the remainder of the dishes on the table. Sophie had wandered upstairs to catch up on homework nearly an hour earlier. "I don't know. Sometimes he seems so strong, but sometimes . . ." She sighed, heart aching. "He's not as tough as he seems."

Emily snorted. "Ya think?"

"Guess you knew that already, huh?"

"Je . . . eez," she said, remembering just in time to avoid using God's name in vain. "Sophie probably even knows *that*." She glanced toward the stairs. "How bad was she anyway?"

"Who? Soph?"

"No, the Wicked Witch of the West." She cocked her head to add a dose of attitude to the sarcasm. "Yeah, *Soph*."

Casie stifled a grin. She had no idea why the girl's sass amused her. "She wasn't so bad."

Emily raised her brows. "I guess the fact that you allowed her to live tells me something."

Casie remained silent for a moment, considering that statement. If Emily thought she favored Ty, she didn't seem to take offense. Sophie, however, was a horse of a different color.

"It was nice of her to ask her dad for the money," Casie said.

"Nice?"

"Yes."

"You know she's going to make us all pay, right?"

"What do you mean?"

"Oh, Cassandra May." Emily sighed, long-suffering, as she shook her dreadlocks. "So innocent."

"How's she going to make us pay?"

"Far be it from me to divine what devious means she'll devise, but I tell you this . . ." She lifted a soapy forefinger to shake it at Casie. "If she hurts Ty I'm going to kick her skinny ass from here to Sunday."

"Well, it better happen soon then," Casie said, skimming her gaze over the girl's ever-burgeoning figure. "While you can still lift your feet off the floor."

"Don't underestimate the power of mom hormones. I can still—" she began, but the doorbell rang.

"Who's that?" Casie's stomach cramped with nerves.

"You know what?" Emily asked. "Even mom hormones don't necessarily make one psychic."

Casie gave her a glance. "You're not expecting anyone?"

She glanced meaningfully at her belly. "No one capable of using a doorbell."

Casie rolled her eyes. They stood faced off. "Don't you want to get that?"

"Do I look like I want to get that?"

Casie scowled and headed toward the front door like a convict to the scaffolds. To say she was an introvert was an understatement, but she forced herself to open the door. Colt Dickenson stood gazing off over the cattle pastures. She cursed in silence as he turned toward her. The tendons in his dark neck shifted. A grin tilted up the left corner of his lips. Something contracted warily in her gut. What the hell was that about?

"Hey," he said. He had one hand braced against the door frame. The other was stuck in the back pocket of his jeans. His arms were half bare, the skin dark and smooth where his worn cambric sleeves were rolled just past the elbow. The muscles there were lean and well defined, traced with veins that did nothing but add interest to a too-intriguing physique. "How's it going?"

"All right," she said and waited for him to say something meaningful, or maybe she was waiting for her stomach to cease threatening treason.

"Nice night."

She had no idea how he could get her flustered without half trying. "Yes. A little windy this morning, but . . ." she began and fought the hopeless impulse to chatter on like a manic chipmunk. "Did you need something?"

"Yeah. A good roping horse."

She canted her head and raised a brow. "What?"

"I need a good roping horse," he said and shuffled his scuffed boots on the newly painted porch as if his knees were sore. "Bronc riding is hell on the joints."

She gave him a WTF look, hoping it was half as potent as Emily's.

"I'm thinking of quitting the rough stock."

She let that soak in for a minute. Odd as it might seem, she had always thought of Colt Dickenson as a rodeo cowboy, even before he was one. There was something about the way he moved or looked or smelled or . . . something. "You're quitting bronc riding." It wasn't a question exactly. More like a skeptical exclamation of disbelief.

"Thinking about it."

"Are you serious?"

"As hip replacement."

It took her a second to work that out. Then she shook her head as she remembered that this man had been messing with her emotions for as long as she had emotions to mess with. "Why are you here, Dickenson?"

"I like the look of your bay."

"My bay?" She glanced toward the horse pastures. "Are you serious?"

"As a broken—" he began, but she interrupted him. Encouraging his sense of humor had been a mistake since he'd begun telling her knock-knock jokes in second grade.

"He's not even gelded yet."

"I know. Testosterone." He shifted his hand on the door-jamb, making his biceps flex like pythons. "Puts some nice muscle on them, doesn't it?" he asked and raised his brows a little. She refrained, with some difficulty, from glancing at his arms. She also refrained, with more difficulty, from smacking him upside the head.

"He's also incredibly irritating," she added dryly.

"Yeah?" He grinned, perhaps understanding the connection she was making between him and the horse.

"Causes more trouble than he'll ever be worth," she added.

"Well . . ." He shrugged. "Us Indian cowboys know some tricks."

Holy Hannah. "Do you?" She made certain her tone was rife with boredom.

"Yes, ma'am," he said and cracked a grin. "Want to see?"

"Not at all."

"Hey, Case, thanks for the chili," someone called from the darkness.

"Emily made it," she said, entirely unsure to whom she was speaking. "But you're welcome."

"I pulled the heating element out of your old water tank. Be back tomorrow with a new one."

"Oh, okay, thank you."

"You bet," he said and disappeared into the darkness.

"Who the . . . ?" Colt began, then softened his tone and tried again. "Who was that?"

She shrugged, peering past his shoulder for a second before bringing her attention back to the present. "Why are you really here?"

He straightened, exasperation beginning to show on his face. "You don't think I came to see *you,* do you?"

"Of course not! I mean . . . No!" she said and hoped to hell he couldn't tell she was blushing. "Why the bay?"

"He looks like he'd be a nice ride."

"What's wrong with the way Madeline rides?"

He made a face at her. "My old piebald?"

"Is there another Madeline?"

"There was a Maddy in Albuquerque a few months back. Cute gal. Didn't get a chance to ride—"

"Yes, the piebald!" she snapped, then took a deep breath and calmed herself. "What's wrong with your pinto?"

He grinned. "She's got a shoulder like a giraffe. It don't make for the smoothest ride in the world. Like I said, rodeo will jolt the crap out of a rider . . . even a great rider like me." That grin again, cheeky but somehow self-effacing at the same time. It was one of the things she hated most about him. And one of the things that had kept her sleepless on more than one long night. "I'm looking for something with a nice, easy stride."

"Oh." She could almost believe that. The bay, though often fractious and frequently naughty, had a dreamy lope. Watching him canter across the pasture made her smile every time. "He *is* a pretty mover."

"What do you want for him?"

"Oh, I don't know." She refrained from rolling her eyes. "Ten thousand should do it."

He nodded, shrugged, glanced toward the pasture again. "Okay."

"What!" she said and laughed out loud.

Another shrug, just a slow lift of shoulders wide enough to make a lesser woman sigh. "I need a horse."

"Are you nuts? Six months ago you were hauling that bay up to the killer pens."

"Yeah, but you fattened him up. He looks real good now. Kinda catty. I think I can make something of him."

"You're crazy."

He shook his head. "Buddy of mine is the number-two-ranked heeler on the circuit. His header took a header off his mare just coming out of the box." He grinned at his own play on words. There was no one who found Colt Dickenson funnier than Colt Dickenson. "I figure if I step in, I can make a quick buck."

Casie scowled at him.

Colt shuffled his feet uncomfortably. "A heeler's the guy who ropes the steer's hind legs," he said. "The header ropes its—"

"I know what team ropers do!" she snapped. "The point is, the bay isn't trained. He's basically worthless."

"Listen, Head Case . . ." He sharpened his glower. "I'm not sure you know how this horse-trading thing works. But see, I offer a price, you say you need more. I raise my price, you say you'll—"

"You just want to give me money." The truth hit her like a hammer.

"What?" he said. He sounded honestly aghast at the idea, which just made her madder.

"Listen . . ." She shook her head. It was entirely possible that the anger spurring through her was unwarranted, but it was there nonetheless. "I don't know what you're thinking, but I don't need your charity."

"What the hell are you—"

"Or a patron."

"A—"

"Contrary to your macho way of thinking, I neither need nor want a man to finance my lifestyle. In fact . . ." She stopped short and narrowed her eyes as a new thought struck her. "Emily called you, didn't she?"

"I don't know what you're getting so riled up about. Holy cow, every damn male between here and Montana is . . ." He stopped himself abruptly, though there did, in fact, seem to be someone pounding on something near the windmill. "I'm in the market for a roping horse. That's all. You've got a perfectly good animal just frittering away in your—"

"We don't need your help."

"Yeah?" He leaned toward her a little, fully aggravated. "Well, maybe Ty does."

The world went silent. She drew a deep breath, steadied herself, found her center. Whatever the hell that meant.

"Then I suggest you talk to Ty," she said.

Knocking the heel of his hand against the doorjamb, he glanced to the right, showing his profile. "Damned if you're not just as stubborn as he is."

She blinked. Something softened in her gut at the quiet frustration in his voice, but she held herself back. "You already asked him."

A muscle bunched in his jaw. Maybe it was his way of stopping any unwarranted information from spilling out. "I just want a damn roping horse."

"Go home," she said and closed the door, but he caught it with his right hand.

"Listen . . . I don't like you owing . . ." He drew a deep breath as if to calm himself. "These big business guys . . ." He glanced toward the pastures again. Fire flared in his eyes. He gritted his teeth. "You don't know what they'll demand for their loans."

She raised her brows at him. "Did Emily tell you what I had for lunch, too?"

"Everyone knows that realtor fellow comes around here a hell of a lot."

She made a face. "It just so happens that his daughter lives here."

"Right!" he said and chuckled without mirth. "How much do you know about him?"

Anger. She felt it flare in her soul. It was as common as buttonweed when he was around. "Well, I know he looks dreamy in a three-piece suit and Italian loafers."

For a moment she thought he would comment, but he stopped himself. "Sell me the bay, Case."

"For ten thousand dollars."

"Do you need more?" His voice was low as if he tried to stop the words.

She stood there, flabbergasted. Holy Hannah, how much did he make on the rodeo circuit? "Are you drunk?"

He shook his head. "Talking to you makes it look like a pretty good idea, though. You going to sell him to me or not?"

"Not."

"Fine," he said, and raising both hands in the air, backed away.

"Fine," she said.

"Fine," he repeated and stomped across the porch and into the darkness. In a moment, she heard his truck fire up. The headlights made a clean sweep across the bunkhouse and front yard before cleaving a path into the distance.

She stood there listening to the silence settling back in.

"You turned him down, didn't you?"

She squawked at the sound of Emily's voice all but crackling in her ear.

"Didn't you?" she asked again, appearing only inches away.

"Holy Hannah . . ." Casie put her hand to her chest. "You scared me half to—"

"You're ridiculous," Emily said, and turning on her heel, waddled up the stairs to her bedroom.

Sighing, Casie prepared to follow her, but a voice spoke from the darkness.

"Hey, Case, you got a minute?" In a second, Brooks Hedley appeared in the porch's diffused light.

"Oh, yes, hi," Casie said and hoped to hell this entire day was nothing more than a bad dream. "You probably want your guns back."

He shook his head once as he mounted the steps. "Looks like maybe you need them more than I do."

"What?" she asked, and stepping onto the porch, closed the door behind her.

"Dickenson giving you trouble?" he asked.

"Who? Colt? Oh . . ." She cleared her throat. "No. We just . . ."

"Because I'll talk to him if you want me to."

About what? she wondered but didn't ask. "No, it's just a . . . little disagreement."

"About whether you should sleep with him or not?"

"No!"

He chuckled at the way she said it, then took the few steps that remained between them and sobered. "I just don't want you to get hurt."

"What?"

He shrugged, looking uncomfortable in the dim light. "Dickenson's an okay guy, I guess. I mean . . . I don't wanna spread any rumors or anything, I just want to make sure you're okay."

"Okay how? What do you mean?"

He glanced away. "It's just that sometimes Dickenson ain't real . . ." He shook his head. "Loyal."

"What are you talking about?"

"I mean, I understand why he done it. He was ranked pretty high on broncs and didn't want to give up rodeo, but that don't mean he couldn't have married her. Or at least offered to take care of the kid."

She felt her stomach pitch. "What are you talking about?"

"Jess," he said, finding her gaze with his and holding it

steady. "She's a real nice girl. Not real . . ." He tilted his head a little. "Not real standoffish maybe, but sweet. You know?"

"Colt got her pregnant?" Her voice sounded funny and her throat hurt.

"Yeah."

"Then left her?"

"Guess he wasn't ready for no family."

She nodded once, then stepped into the house and closed the door behind her without another word.

CHAPTER 8

Emily stirred diced apples into the cinnamon muffin batter and stared out the kitchen window. The sky was gun-metal gray. The wind blew rough and sporadic from the northwest, and the temperature had dropped overnight. She had tried to stay in bed, but it was becoming impossible to find a comfortable position on her lumpy mattress. Not that she was complaining about the accommodations. They were a hundred times better than the foster homes where she had stayed. Infinitely better than the flophouse where Stevie had introduced her to Ecstasy.

Guilt and worry brewed to a toxic blend in her bloodstream. She felt Baby Pascal kick against the mixing bowl, a tiny contraction. He didn't move as much as he used to, and though the doctors said that was normal, they didn't know everything. Not about medicine, not about life, and certainly not about her. Try as she might, she couldn't remember the last time she had gotten high, but what if it had been after conception? What if her own ugliness had messed with the baby's development? What if—

"You okay?"

She turned at the sound of Casie's voice.

"What's wrong?" Casie's tone was instantly worried.

Emily shook her head.

"What is it?" Casie asked, and crossing the floor, took the bowl from Emily's hands.

"What if I ruined it?" She tried to keep the words to herself, but they spilled out, sounding silly in the early-morning gloom.

"What?" Casie asked and set the bowl on the cracked Formica.

"The baby. It just. . . . He deserves better."

"What are you talking about, Em? What happened?" Casie stared into Emily's face, trying to catch her gaze. Her hands felt warm against Emily's. "Here. Come on. Sit down. Are you all right?"

"No." She shook her head. "I . . ." She laughed. It sounded crazy to her own ears. "I'm going to . . ." She took a deep breath, braced herself, and spoke slowly. "I've decided to give him up."

"*What?*"

Emily shook her head. The movement felt wild, out of control, like the rest of her life. "Come on," she said and barked a laugh. "You know I can't take care of a kid. I can barely take care of myself. I used to do drugs. Did you know that? I used to—"

"Emily, slow down. Relax."

But she couldn't. She shook her head. "My mother was practically twice my age when she had me. Twice! And even *she* couldn't cope with the . . . with the . . ." she began and had to swallow so she could continue to breathe.

"Emily. Hey," Casie said and pulled her into her arms. She was warm and gentle, exuding all sorts of things Emily didn't deserve. Had never deserved. Nevertheless, she melted into the embrace, letting her tears soak Casie's sweatshirt. "You're not your mother."

Emily gasped a laugh. "Isn't that the truth? I don't even know where she is."

Casie was quiet a moment, then said, "Maybe that's best, Em. I mean, if you'd stayed with her, you wouldn't have come here. We would never have met and I . . ." She paused. "You've been so good to me . . . and to Ty."

She snorted a laugh. "Don't you ever get tired of being Pollyanna? Of picking up the pieces? My pieces. Sophie's. Ty's." She shrugged. The movement felt jerky. She drew a shuddering breath.

There was a moment of silence. "I'm not a complete idiot, Em."

Emily scowled and pulled away a little, swiping her knuckles beneath her nose. "I never said you were. I would never—"

"I know I'm lucky to have you here."

Emily laughed again, but Casie pushed her out to arm's length.

"I am, you know."

"Yeah. Yeah." Emily's throat felt tight. She wiped her eyes with the back of her hand. Her hand shook visibly. "Cuz who doesn't want a pregnant teenager with anger management problems and no insurance to look after?"

"You won't be pregnant much longer," Casie said, and that's when Emily began crying in earnest. The sobs racked her, making it all but impossible to breathe.

"Emily, come on . . ." Casie's voice sounded tortured. "Don't do this to yourself. You're going to be a good mom. A *great* mom."

She laughed. The sound cracked like a witch's cackle in the cozy little kitchen. "Sure," she said. "I mean, take a look at how fantastic *my* mom was. She was a meth addict. Did you know that?"

Casie shook her head.

"Yeah. The story I told you 'bout my dad burning down the house . . ." She swallowed, feeling sick to her stomach. "He wasn't really my dad. Just a guy. Some guy. He was just flopping with us. He called himself Ray Edgar, but that wasn't really his name." She laughed again. "Second thought, maybe he *was* my old man. Maybe that's where I got my aptitude for lying. Maybe that's where I got my stellar ability to make decisions. To—"

"Quit it," Casie said.

"I hated her, you know."

She felt Casie's scowl like a sunbeam on her face.

"Hated her. Even then. Even before I turned six. She . . ." Emily shook her head, remembering back. "She was always . . ." She winced. "She was pretty. Even after all the drugs . . . after all the . . ." She exhaled. "There were men. Always men, in our house . . . in our . . ." She swallowed. "She'd be passed out on the couch and I'd be alone . . . or worse."

Silence permeated the morning, soaking into her skin. Emily closed her eyes, knowing she had said too much, had gone too far. Honesty had never been her friend. She stared at her fists squeezed tight in her lap and forced a laugh. "I'm just kidding," she said. "Things weren't that bad. It's not like I was working in the coal mines or—"

"It's her loss." Casie's voice was very low, very quiet, very sure.

Emily lifted her gaze slowly. "What?"

"Your mother . . ." Her expression was absolutely sober, her gaze ultrasteady. "She's the one who's missing out."

"Yeah." She laughed. "Poor thing. I'm sure if she knew the situation, she'd come running."

"She would if she understood."

Emily scowled, searching her eyes.

"Every morning I get up and laugh at your jokes and . . ." Casie nodded toward the abandoned mixing bowl. "Eat your muffins and . . ." She swallowed. Her eyes were extremely bright as she shrugged and lowered her gaze to Em's belly. "Watch you become a mother."

Emily felt herself blanch. "I can't do it," she said. "I can't go through what I put her through."

Casie watched her, gaze steady.

The faith in her eyes made Emily's stomach turn to jelly, but she forced a laugh. "Guess I didn't tell you that I was the reason she ended up in jail in the first place, huh?" Or maybe she hadn't mentioned that her mother had done hard time at all. It was becoming increasingly difficult to keep her lies straight. "Yeah, one fine morning I trundled off to school with her stash of coke in my backpack. Didn't try to hide it. Didn't even . . ." She cleared her throat. "You know what will really get a second-grade teacher excited? Bringing five grams of blow to show-and-tell." She shook her head. "I'm a super liar. The best. You know that. But I didn't even try. I just said it was Mom's. Served her right, I thought. Served her right for not being there for me." She felt a tic jerk her jaw. "But at least she wasn't eighteen and pregnant and unemployed and—"

"Don't do this to yourself, Em. It won't help anything."

"At least she kept a roof over my head. Kept an apartment."

"Everything's going to be fine."

"When I was little . . ." She swallowed again, trying to ease the pain in her throat. "She used to read to me . . . when she wasn't . . ." She shook her head. "She used to read to me. Dr. Seuss was my favorite. *Oh, the Places You'll Go!*" She remembered the rhythm of it. "She had a really pretty voice. Not all gnarly like mine, but—"

"Damn her!" The words exploded in the room. Casie's hands were like talons on her arms.

Emily blinked.

"She was your mother! Your *mother!*" She took a deep breath, closed her eyes for a second, then loosened her grip. "She was supposed to take care of you."

"It wasn't—"

"Don't say it wasn't her fault, Em. Don't say it. Sometimes people just have to step up to the plate. Just gotta . . ." She shook her head. "They just have to ride the horse they saddled."

They stared at each other, emotion sharp as a blade in the room before Emily finally managed to open her mouth.

"You sound like Ty," she said, but Casie remained absolutely somber.

"Do you have any idea what half the women in this country would do to have a daughter like you?"

Emily forced a grin, but Casie tightened her grip. "They'd give their lives, Em. She was supposed to be willing to give her life."

Seconds ticked away. Her throat felt tight, her stomach quaky. "What if I'm not?" The words were nothing more than a whisper. "What if I'm not willing to do that?"

"You will be."

"You don't know that."

"I do. And so would your mother, if she'd stuck around. If she'd been half as brave as you are."

She wasn't going to cry. Hell, she didn't even know how to cry. But her cheeks felt wet. She swiped at them with her knuckles.

The front door opened behind her. Sophie, probably, coming in for breakfast, and Emily couldn't bear to be seen bawling like a baby.

"Your guest is here," Sophie said from behind.

Casie lifted her gaze slowly from Emily to Sophie. "Guest?" There was a pause. "What's going on?"

Emily was having a meltdown. That's what was going on.

"What guest?" Casie asked.

"Said her name was Linette. Or something. What's with Emily?"

"Lin . . . Oh . . . shoot! Linny Hartman? I thought she wasn't coming till tomorrow."

Sophie's shrug was almost audible. It wasn't until that moment that Emily remembered the phone call she'd taken two days before. The phone call asking if Lin Hartman could come a day early. She closed her eyes.

"I'm sorry," she murmured.

Casie lowered her gaze to Em's for a second before lifting it back toward Sophie.

"Can you take care of Linette, Soph?" she said.

"I'm already—"

"Sophie." Her tone wasn't sharp, wasn't demanding, just serious, just strong. "I need your help."

"Okay," she said, and that was the end of it.

Casie would make a hell of a mother, Emily thought, and burst into tears.

CHAPTER 9

Casie took a deep breath before knocking on the bunkhouse door. Emily had branded the word *welcome* into the rough timber before framing it with a wreath made of dried weeds she'd found down by the creek. The effect was earthy and surprisingly charming, but Casie barely noticed. Her few minutes with Brooks Hedley on the previous night had been painfully revealing, her morning not much better. She'd received two phone calls before noon: one from Cap Emerson, who supplied her hay, one from Dakota Equine. Neither had exemplary news. Although Angel was on the mend and able to return home, the bill was going to be somewhat higher than expected. That little factoid had been delivered just moments before Cap's message bemoaning the lack of rain and subsequent increase in *his* fee. And *that* news had come shortly before Emily's atypical breakdown. Which meant, once again, that there would be no time for Casie to have the meltdown she'd been waiting so long to enjoy. In which case she'd better get her head in the game, she thought. Planting a smile on her face, she knocked again on the rough-cut timber.

"Hi." The woman who opened the door was small and thin. *Frail* might have been a word used to describe her if she didn't stand quite so straight. She held a wineglass loosely in one hand.

"Linette?" Casie asked.

"Lin. Yes. Hi. You must be Cassandra Carmichael."

"Casie," she said.

The other woman nodded. Her hair was silvery gray and cropped close to her head in a stylish cap that would have been better suited for Wall Street than the Lazy Windmill. "Or Linny, if you like. You have a beautiful place here."

"Oh." Casie glanced to the right. The heifer fence needed fixing and the alfalfa was past its prime. Basically, the entire ranch was held together with duct tape and baling wire. But the pastures were still green and the oak trees were pretty spectacular, a burnt sienna color that stood out in rustic glory against the lady's slipper yellow of the aspen behind them. Still, the arena was short one gate and . . . She stopped herself, remembering to make her guest feel welcome. "Thank you. It's a pretty time of year."

"Yes." Lin laughed. The sound was low and husky. "I bet it's as ugly as sin most times."

Casie grinned, took a deep breath. "Maybe I take it for granted sometimes."

"Really?" The woman glanced around, probably not even seeing the dozens of tasks that needed doing. "What a heinous crime that would be."

"I guess you're right," Casie said and felt herself relax a little. Emily believed that Casie was uncomfortable around guests because she was uncomfortable with *herself*. But Emily thought too much. The reason Casie wasn't comfortable was because there were always a hundred thousand things that needed doing. Having guests added another hundred thousand, but she liked the feel of this woman. There was an honesty to her, a solid earnestness. "Have you settled in okay?"

"Absolutely. Everything I need. Sophie was very kind. Lugged all my luggage in for me. Answered all my inane questions. Gave me a bottle of wine." She lifted the glass. "She seems like a nice girl."

Sophie? Casie thought, but even though the morning had been less than sublime, she was still coherent enough to catch herself before her skepticism slipped out. "Yes, she's been a huge help to us here on the Lazy."

"Will she be the one giving me riding lessons?"

Lessons. Casie felt herself tense up again, but managed to refrain from clearing her throat. "About that, I know you said you wanted to get some horseback time in, but you were mainly concerned with relaxing and getting a little fresh air, right?"

"Well, yes. I like to hike, and I thought I might even do a little bird-watching. But once I saw the horses . . ." She gazed past Casie toward the pastures and something lit up her eyes. It wasn't an uncommon thing. There was some inexplicable bond between women and horses. Something indescribable and magical. It grabbed them in adolescence and often didn't let go until the grave. "Is that little one a grullo?"

Casie raised her gaze to the east where the geldings grazed, heavy manes splashed over glossy necks. "Blue? Yes, he is. You know your horses."

Linette laughed. It was a pleasant sound, low and earthy. "Just through research, I'm afraid. Horses have been an interest of mine for as long as I can remember, but I never had a chance to get to know them. Lately, I've had more time to read, though."

"I remember reading," Casie said, displaying more dreaminess that she had intended. The woman laughed again.

"The ranch keeps you pretty busy, I take it."

"I don't play a lot of checkers," Casie admitted.

Linette tilted her head. "Truth is, I've had a little too much time on my hands since I retired. Too much time to think, so I decided to do some things for myself."

Too much time . . . It sounded wonderful, Casie thought, but didn't say as much. "What are you retiring from?"

"Drudgery. Backbiting." She shrugged. "Stress."

Casie laughed. "Sounds like my old job."

"Let me guess," Linette said, eyeing her up. "I bet you were a top-notch administrative assistant, too."

"I'm afraid I wasn't a top-notch anything," Casie said and let the memories remind her how lucky she was to be here, a hundred thousand chores notwithstanding. The rain-washed air felt soft against her skin. Somewhere just within hearing a meadowlark sang to the sky. "And I think the word is *secretary*."

"Well . . ." Linette raised her glass. "Here's to undervalued laborers everywhere. Say, do you have time to join me for a drink?"

"I'd love to," Casie said, "but Emily has dinner ready, and believe me, we don't want to get in front of that train."

"Dinner?" She twisted a speckled wrist to check the time. The watch face was framed in understated gold vines and looked as if it might be worth more than the Lazy's mortgage. Linette Hartman must have been a more valued employee than Casie had been, despite the backbiting to which she'd referred. "It's not even one o'clock."

Casie smiled. "Out here in the sticks, we call lunch dinner and dinner supper."

"Oh, okay, I'm all about change these days."

"Great. Well, come on up whenever you're ready. The door's open anytime."

"Thank you," Linette said. "I'll be right there."

Despite Emily's recent meltdown, dinner was awesome, though Sophie would have rather stuck a fork in her eye than admit as much. She reached for another fresh-baked roll. It was misshapen, freckled with tiny seeds she couldn't identify, and phenomenally delicious.

"So, Sophie, are you in college?" Linette Hartman was several inches shorter than Sophie and even skinnier than Sophie's mother, but she seemed to enjoy the meal with carnivorous enthusiasm. The fact that she could remain so tiny and eat like a lumberjack would have driven her mother to distraction. Monica Day-Bellaire ate about a teaspoon of imported yogurt a day and not much else.

"I'm a senior in high school," Sophie said, realizing she'd been silent longer than etiquette demanded. Thoughts of her mother often made her reticent. The rest of the time they made her crazy.

"Oh. And are you . . . I'm sorry. I've never been known for my tact so I'll just ask straight up." She glanced about the table. "How are the three of you related?"

"We're not," Sophie said, then lowered her eyes at the harshness of her tone. "I'm just . . ." What was she? Unnecessary? Unwanted?

"Sophie's the equine manager here at the Lazy," Emily said.

Sophie glanced at her. Despite the fact that she enjoyed resenting Emily almost as much as she liked hating Ty, she felt an unwanted flush of gratitude wash over her. There were few things she detested more than feeling grateful.

"Really?" Linette glanced from Sophie to Emily and back. "How do you manage the horses and still find time for school?"

"I take some of my classes online," Sophie said and slathered butter onto her roll. Monica Day-Bellaire eschewed shortening of any sort, but Emily had been fiddling with homemade honey-butter recipes. Only an idiot would eschew homemade honey butter, and Sophie liked to think she wasn't an idiot. A bitch maybe, but not an idiot. "It gives me more time to spend training horses."

"You do the training?"

"Casie and I," she said.

"Mostly Soph," Casie said. "She's got a gift."

Gratitude turned to something warmer. Good God, if she wasn't careful she was going to become as mushy as Emily, without the hormonal glut to blame it on.

"Well, that's great," Linette said, "because I'm afraid it's going to take all the gifts you can muster to teach me to ride. I'm not quite as spry as I was a hundred years ago."

Sophie reached for another roll.

"I think it's great that you're so independent," Emily said as she took her seat beside Casie.

"How do you mean?"

Em shrugged and took a sip of what she liked to call razza-dazzle tea. It was anyone's guess what was in it. "You know, most of our guests come with a support system . . . a friend, mother, daughter. *Someone.*"

"It might have been nice bringing Elizabeth."

"You have a daughter?" Emily asked. Her tone was a little dreamy. How weird would it be to have another person growing inside you and not even know what gender it was?

"Well, yes," Linette said, and glancing down, took a sip of her coffee. "As a matter of fact, I do."

"You're lucky," Emily said. "Are you and Elizabeth close?"

"Quite close." She fiddled with her fork. The tines were bent. Emily hadn't gotten around to replacing the cutlery yet, but she probably would soon. She could find a bargain in a hay field. "We've spent a great deal of time together."

"That's so great. There's nothing more important than family," Emily said.

Casie watched her intently, as if ascertaining her mood before turning her attention back to their guest. "Maybe you can bring her next time."

"She's pretty busy with her own family."

"You have grandchildren?" Emily asked.

Linette drew a heavy breath as if not entirely comfortable with the conversation. "Well, grand*child,* actually."

"Then we're just flattered you could tear yourself away long enough to visit—"

"Wait a minute," Sophie said, and, zipping her attention from her second fresh-baked roll, speared Linette with a sharp gaze. "You don't know how to ride?"

"Never been on a horse in my life."

"But . . ." True, Sophie had given lessons to newbies before, but they were young, less . . . breakable, and those lessons had always been given on Angel because she was . . . well . . . she was an angel. And Sophie would rather *die* than admit that to Ty, who acted as if the mare walked on water.

"But what?" Linette asked, one silver brow raised slightly.

From her vantage point, Sophie could see Casie clench her fist beneath the table. Sophie pursed her lips and forced herself to remain silent.

"One of our beginner horses is just now recovering from surgery."

One of them? Sophie thought and nearly laughed out loud. Angel was their *only* beginner horse. The rest were barely even *horses.*

"I'm sorry to hear that. Nothing too serious, I hope."

Sophie felt her gut knot up. The image of Angel, drugged and disoriented, had been bad enough. But the sight of Ty's haunted eyes as he watched her through the cold steel bars of the equine hospital was a memory she couldn't seem to shake. The ensuing conversation with her father came in an ugly second.

"I think she's going to be all right," Casie said. Her tone was light, her expression upbeat. Casie Carmichael could make a full amputation sound like a hangnail. "They think she'll be able to come home today."

"They do?" Sophie asked and felt her heart pick up its pace. "Does Ty know? I mean . . ." She pursed her lips. All eyes were turned toward her. She felt her cheeks flush, but refused to shift her gaze away. "It's his horse. He should be the one taking care of her."

"I'm sure he will once we bring her home," Casie said.

"Um, speaking of which," Emily said. "Is that a diesel engine I hear?"

Casie turned toward her. "What?"

"Ty called." Emily smiled, bright as a sunflower. "Said Colt offered to pick Angel up."

"Oh." For just a second Casie looked like she had bitten into a lemon. Interaction with Colt Dickenson tended to affect her that way. Sophie wasn't sure why, but hey, sometimes you just had to hate people, no matter how hot they looked in their ratty caps and old blue jeans. "Well, that was very nice of him."

"Yeah, in fact, that might be them pulling up right now."

"What?" Casie said again. Her upbeat tone had slipped a little.

"I told him I was sure you'd appreciate the favor," Emily said.

"Appreciate the—" Casie began, then cleared her throat and set her fork carefully on the edge of her plate. "Of course. Thanks, Emily. If you'll excuse me, Linny, I'd better see to the mare."

"Sure," she said. "I think I'll get some air, too. I ate enough to feed an army. The meal, by the way, was exquisite, Emily. Five stars," she said, "but I'm afraid I'm not accustomed to such rich food anymore. Maybe I'd better walk it off before it settles in for good."

"Oh," Casie said, finding her usual conviviality. "Of course. Feel free to roam anywhere on the ranch," she said, and though she rose smoothly from her chair, her journey toward the door could only be called stalking. Sophie followed. Casie's disjointed relationship with Colt made her feel almost normal by comparison.

It took them all a second to pull on their footwear. Linette was quicker, simply shoving her feet into a pair of low-heeled sandals, and then they were out the door.

By the time they reached the barn, Ty was already swinging open the back door of the Dickensons' long aluminum trailer. His stupid-ass cap, frayed almost beyond recognition, was pulled low over his eyes, but Sophie could see the stubborn slant of his jaw and, below that, the sharp jut of his shoulders. He had practically no hips and his legs went on forever, but it was his hands that put her stomach in freefall. His damned hands. They were always dirty, his nails ragged, his knuckles scuffed, but as he led Angel from the trailer, he caressed her neck. And it was that touch, as gentle as a lullaby, that got her. It was so tender, so ultimately caring, as if he could protect her from the world with that one careful hand.

"Soph?" Casie said. Sophie jumped, realizing she'd missed something.

"What?" She tried not to look guilty. Geez, she had nothing to feel guilty about.

"I was wondering if you'd mind cleaning Angel's stall."

"Oh." Her cheeks felt warm again. Maybe she was getting sick. She didn't have time to get sick. "I already did that."

"You did?"

"Just because *he's* slacking off, doesn't mean we all can."

Casie raised a brow at her.

Sophie lowered her eyes. "I'll get her some fresh water," she said and scurried away.

* * *

Casie watched her go. Holy Hannah, she thought, if this place got any more flooded with female pissiness she was going to change the name of the farm to Estrogen Hills or something. As for herself, she took a deep breath and lifted her lips into a smile as Ty turned toward her.

"How's she doing?" she asked.

The boy's face was as solemn as a dirge, but there was a guarded meld of hope and worry in his eyes.

"Okay, I think. She seems pretty stiff."

Casie nodded, doing her best to ignore Dickenson as he rounded the trailer carrying a lead rope. "She's been through a lot. We'll have to be really careful with her."

"The doc left a catheter in her neck and sent along the IV bag just in case. Said we should give her more fluids if she don't drink enough. And she's gotta be confined for eight weeks."

"In the stall?"

"I guess," Ty said and steadied the mare as a half dozen horses ran up to the fence to see her. Blue reared, mane flying. Tangles stretched his neck over the wire and snorted a greeting. Angel shuffled sideways, excited by their attention. "Easy now," he said, then to Casie, "She ain't going to like to be holed up like that."

"No," Casie agreed.

"They said to hand walk her five to six times a day," Colt said, striding up beside them. She'd been ignoring him until this moment. That couldn't go on forever, but what was she supposed to do? Pretend she didn't know his secret? Pretend it was perfectly fine to abandon his own child, to leave the baby's mother to her own defenses? She felt her stomach twist.

"I didn't know she was ready to come home," Casie said, "or I would have picked her up myself."

He shrugged. "I was in the area."

"In the area of Rapid City . . . with your dad's stock trailer?"

He grinned as Ty let Angel wander away a little, nosing the grass. "Now don't go getting all riled up, Case."

"I'm not riled up."

"I'm not trying to buy the boy's affections or anything."

"Buy the boy's—"

He leaned closer, lowered his voice, and shoved his hands into the front pockets of his jeans. "Couldn't do it anyway. Kid thinks you're Beyoncé and Taylor Swift all rolled into one. Sexiest thing to ever rock a pair of cowboy boots."

She felt her jaw drop, felt her blood pressure rise, and remembered how much she hated being teased. She had never been a sexy kind of girl, but he didn't have to remind her.

She opened her mouth to blast him, but Ty spoke. "I guess I'll get her settled in."

"Just grass hay," Colt reminded him, his tone even.

Casie ground her teeth. "We can take care of her," she said, but Dickenson was already stepping past her, arm outstretched as Ty led Angel slowly toward the barn.

"Hey," he said, nodding. It took Casie a moment to realize her guest was standing only a few feet behind her. "You must be Linny Hartman."

Her mind was reeling. How did he always know more about what was happening on her ranch than she did? She slammed her gaze into Emily, who gave her an ethereal smile edged with a noncommittal shrug.

"Yes." Linette's voice sounded very precise beside Dickenson's cowboy drawl. "And you are?"

"Colt Dickenson," he said and grinned in that slow way that made women act like idiots and idiots act like giggling chimpanzees. "How long you going to be staying at the Lazy?"

"Well . . ." She had to cock her head a little to gaze into his face, a feat she seemed more than willing to do. "I don't have a *lot* of time, but I hope to be here for a couple weeks at least."

"It's a nice place to unwind."

She raised her brows a little. "I've already unwound," she said. "I'm starting to think it might be time to challenge myself some."

"Yeah?" He shifted an almost grin toward Emily. "You going to try Em's razzapple kuchen then?"

It took Linette only a moment to catch up, then she laughed.

Emily raised a brow. Casie was just happy she didn't raise more than that . . . like a middle finger perhaps.

"I'm hoping to master horseback riding."

"Good for you." Colt sounded honestly encouraging as he shifted his attention back to the older woman. "How much experience do you have?"

She laughed. "Just a little less than none. How about you?"

He shrugged. "I can keep 'em between me and the ground if they ain't too rowdy," he said.

"Mr. Dickenson was ranked thirteenth All-Around cowboy in the PRCA," Emily said. "Before he got too old and crotchety to get out of bed unassisted."

He grinned, shifted his gaze back to the older woman. "Em's a heck of a cook, can't ride worth a hoot, though. Head Case, on the other hand . . ." He winked at her. "Rides like Annie Oakley, and you should see her throw a punch."

Linette raised her brows. "Are you a pugilist, too, Casie?"

"No," she said. "Mr. Dickenson's just trying to be funny."

He laughed. "In two weeks, Case'll have you galloping around the Lazy like Shoemaker at the Derby," he said, then raised his brows a little as if thinking. "Who you planning to put her on, Case?"

She refrained from spitting at him. He knew good and well that Angel was the only horse suitable for beginners. "I'll have to give that some thought."

"Sophie said you have Tangles coming along pretty well."

"Yes," she said, but inwardly cringed. Last time she'd ridden the dun gelding, he'd taken a surprising dislike to a loosed tumbleweed and had just about lost her while pivoting away in a panic. Those quick spins looked pretty spiffy during a reining competition, but they were rarely appreciated by neophytes whose knees were shaking in time with their hands.

"What about the Dickensons' piebald?" Emily asked. "Madeline, isn't it?"

Casie turned to her like an automaton. How the hell did she know about Colt's old pinto?

Em glanced at her and shrugged, steady under fire. In fact, she was practically catatonic under fire. "Colt said she's a sweet-heart," she added.

"Yes, well . . ." To be honest, the bond between Dickenson and Emily had always irritated her, but never more so than now. Who was he to act like the girl's guardian angel when some-where he had a child of his own? A child he had never even bothered to mention to her. Something in her midsection twisted at the thought. Last night's chili, she thought, come back to haunt her. "I'm sure Mr. Dickenson has plans for Mad—"

"I don't," he said.

Casie gave Linette a fleeting smile, silently promised retribu-tion to everyone concerned, and turned smoothly back toward Colt. "I can't ask you to donate your mare for—"

"You didn't."

Her smile turned gritty. "That's very kind of you, Mr. Dick-enson, but I'm sure we'll figure something out."

"Piebald," Linette said. "That's a black-and-white pinto, right?"

"Good job." Colt sounded honestly impressed. "It's kind of an old-timey term. Not everyone knows it."

"Like I told Casie, I've been reading," she said. "And I've al-ways had a predilection for pintos."

"Predilection," Em said, quietly trying out the word for later use.

"Yeah?"

"I was a Scout fan."

They stared at her and she laughed. "*The Lone Ranger.* Tonto's horse . . . Scout." She waved a hand at them. "Before your time. Listen, I don't mean to make this difficult for you, but I surely don't want to cut short Angel's convalescence, either." She stared up at Colt, silvery brows raised a little. "The last few months have been somewhat . . ." She shrugged. "A little rocky. Truth is, I wouldn't mind returning home with a few bragging rights."

"Bragging rights?" Casie stared at her. "I'm afraid I don't

know what you—" she began, but Colt was already sweeping the Stetson from his dark head.

"I'd be proud to provide them for you if I can."

Casie scowled at him. "Provide what?"

"Bragging rights," he said and grinned. "Turns out I'm going to be giving Ms. Hartman riding lessons on old Maddy," he said.

CHAPTER 10

Linette Susan Hartman paced the horse pasture fence, cell phone to her ear as the recorded message played out for the umpteenth time. "Please leave a message and I'll get back to you as soon as possible."

It was an out-and-out lie. She'd learned years ago to smell a falsehood from miles away, was known for that ability, in fact, but she left the message anyway.

"Yes, it's me again," she said. She tried to make her tone upbeat and confident, tried to find that hard-line demeanor she'd always been known for, but instead, her voice sounded pale and sadly forlorn in the soft darkness. It had been a long time since she'd sounded this desperate. Decades, in fact. But she'd just been a child then, and certain her world would shatter without her daddy's presence. She had been wrong, of course. She had survived just fine. Had grown stronger because of his departure. Had learned to survive entirely on her own. Had learned to succeed, to excel. But everything was different now. Everything had changed. "I just thought I'd try you once more. I'll be out of town for a while, but if you have time to get together, just give me a call and I'll . . . Well, just give me a call," she said, and clicking the phone off, she closed her eyes.

She was tired, exhausted really, but the night sounds soothed her. Yards away, the horses grazed together, tails flipping at unseen pests. A cow bellowed. A calf answered. From some indiscernible direction, an owl called. Every sound was quiet and melodious, as old as the earth itself. She filled her lungs with the crisp fall air and let her mind wander. Light-years ago, when she was a little girl, before she had become too scared or too busy to dream, she had thought she would have a ranch of her own some day. Somewhere in Utah, maybe. Or Idaho. She'd marry a cowboy with narrow hips and irresistible dimples who would adore her for the rest of her days. But her life hadn't turned out quite that way.

A noise distracted her. She turned toward it. A dark pickup truck pulling an aluminum trailer was being driven down the gravel road. Slowing down, it turned onto the Lazy's bumpy lane and rumbled into the yard before stopping beside the barn.

Colt Dickenson got out. She knew him even in the dark. He had that sexy, narrow-hipped look she had once dreamed about.

Sauntering past the tailgate, he flipped the lights on inside the trailer, then opened the back door. The horse inside was tall and broad, bi-colored and sleepy looking. It blinked at the lights as if just awakening from slumber. Loose in the entirety of the enclosure, the pinto made no move to avoid the cowboy but stepped forward when Colt spoke to her. In a moment she had ambled outside to glance around with unhurried curiosity.

It was a dreamy picture. A cowboy and his horse, backlit with little more than the trailer lights, framed by a thousand acres of rolling cattle country.

"Here we are, old girl." Colt's voice was soft, his hands slow as he shifted the mare's parti-colored mane to the off side of her lengthy neck. "Gonna get you settled in before Casie decides to evict—"

But his words were interrupted by the slamming of a door.

Colt's sigh was almost louder than his words had been. "That'll be her," he said. "She's probably already madder than a hosed skunk, so you gotta be on your best behavior."

The mare glanced at the shadowy figure that paced toward them, then lowered her head to crop grass, unfazed by any human drama about to unfold.

"Hey, Case," Colt said. "Nice night, huh?"

"What are you doing here?" Casie's voice was low, but

Linette had been a student of human nature too long to miss the sizzling emotion that punctuated it.

Colt, however, showed no sign that he had recognized that emotion. Instead, he glanced at the mare with all due casualness. "We're just catching a little moonlight. Isn't that right, Maddy?"

There was a moment of silence. "Something wrong with the moonlight at your house?"

"It doesn't have the same scenery." He grinned. Linette could see his teeth flash in the darkness. The dimples she had to leave up to her imagination. But she'd been playing them around in her head for so many years it hardly mattered.

"I got your message," she said.

"Yeah? Well, I didn't want to get you all riled by showing up unannounced. Just thought I should get the old girl here tonight."

"It could have waited until morning."

"Old Mad's been around," he said, stroking the mare's neck absently. "But horses need some time to settle in. Woulda thought you'd know that, Case."

Even from where she stood, Linette could feel Casie stiffen. "I know what horses need," she said, then paused and drew a hard breath. "But it's late."

"Yeah," he agreed equivocally. "That happens a lot about this time of day. I didn't wake you, did I?"

"No."

"Doing some bookkeeping?"

"No."

"You're not having trouble sleeping, are you?" Reaching up, he laid a casual arm across the mare's withers. She didn't bother to stop grazing.

"No. I'm not."

"You sure?" The pinto shifted her weight a little, bending her left foreleg and bearing Colt a half step closer to Casie.

"It's almost midnight," she said. "I could sleep right there on the gravel if people would quit coming down my drive."

"Was someone else here?"

There was a slight pause. "Phil Jaegar," she said finally.

"Who?"

"Phil Jaegar." Her tone was becoming increasingly taut. There was obviously a history between these two, Linette thought, and couldn't help wondering what it was.

"Oh, yeah. Sophie's dad, right?"

She didn't respond.

"The hot-shot realtor. You're not thinking of selling out again, are you?"

She remained silent.

"Hey, listen, I know it's hard," he said. "But your folks worked their tails off for this place. "

Still nothing.

"They loved this land. And each other. I mean, maybe it seemed like they were at each other's throats sometimes, but that doesn't mean anything. Hell, some folks even get mad at *me*. Not you, of course. You adore me. But people who haven't recognized my innate charm and irresistible—"

"I know you know."

"What's that?"

She drew a breath. "You probably know more about what's going on at the Lazy than I do."

He shrugged. "Wouldn't think so. Why would you—"

"I need you to stop it."

He canted his head a little, his movements slow, his voice the same. "Stop what, Case?"

"It's not fair to Emily."

He shifted his stance, slipping his arm from the mare's back, stiffening a little. "What's Emmy got to do with this?"

"She's pregnant, Dickenson. Pregnant. You know what that means?"

"I think I got a pretty good idea."

"I bet you do."

"What does that mean?"

There was a stiff silence, then, "I want you to leave her alone."

"What are you talking about?"

"Quit confiding in her. Quit making her confide in you."

"I like confiding in her. We're friends," he said.

"*Friends!*" she scoffed. "She's a teenage girl. You're . . ." She waved a hand up and down at him. "A wolf in sheep's clothing."

"A . . ." He snorted a chuckle. "First of all, sheep don't have clothing. I would think you'd know that, Head Case. Second, if I have to be in clothes, which I'm not all that crazy about—"

"Just . . . Just quit leading her on."

"Leading her . . ." He laughed out loud. "You have flipped your—" He paused. "Is that what *you're* doing?"

"What? No! I have *never* led you on."

There was a pause filled with a thousand tangled emotions. Linette knew she should leave, knew she should slip quietly into the night and let them have some time alone. She also knew she would do no such thing. Perhaps she missed the drama after all.

"Not me," he said and barked a laugh. "You're definitely not leading *me* on. I'm talking about Jaegar."

"I'm not . . . I've never . . ." she began, then drew a noisy breath and tried a new tack. "So you *did* know he stopped by."

He paused, making it clear, once again, that even a wolf can be caught in a carefully laid trap.

"Emily might have mentioned it," he said finally.

"Might have mentioned . . ." Casie chuckled. "That's the only reason you're here."

"What?"

"Admit it," she said. "You're not interested in me. You never have been. You just like the chase."

"What are you talking about?"

The night went quiet for a moment. "I know about Jess."

Silence seeped in again, and when he next spoke, his tone was atypically somber. "You've been talking to Hedley."

"He said she was pregnant with your baby."

He glanced away for a second. "There's more to it than you think."

"So it's true," she said. There was a world of agony in those few words.

"Case—"

"But you didn't marry her."

"I didn't love her, Case. It wouldn't have been fair to—"

"Not fair!"

"Casie . . ." he began, but she was already turning away.

"Go home," she said and disappeared into the darkness.

He stared after her and swore quietly.

"We don't owe you nothing," someone rumbled.

Linette jerked her gaze to the left. A new shadow had worn a hole in the darkness.

Colt turned toward the boy with a sigh. "That's not why I offered the loan, Ty."

The boy shuffled his feet a little. "It ain't like I don't appreciate the offer. It was good of you to want to help Angel out."

"But you'd rather owe Phil Jaegar than me. Is that it?"

The boy shrugged, his face barely discernible in the dim light. "If I owed you, she'd feel like *she* did, too." He jerked his head toward the ranch house into which Casie had disappeared. "That's how she's put together."

"So now she owes the Jaegars." He paused. "And so do you."

"Couldn't be helped."

"Yes, it—" Colt stopped himself with an obvious effort. "What the hell have I done to make you distrust me? Why are you always so pissed?"

"You left her." Ty's voice was little more than a growl in the darkness. "You left her when she was down."

"She told me to go!" Colt said. "Practically pushed me out with both hands."

"Leaving's the quickest way to nowhere."

Colt jerked his gaze toward the barn, shook his head. Frustration rolled off him in waves. "She was on the rebound. I didn't want to confuse her. She needed time to think."

"Seems like you're the one should do some thinking."

Colt watched him in silence for a moment, then exhaled softly. "I've been thinking since we were kids."

"Then you should have pretty much figured things out by now, I'd say."

"It's not as simple as it seems to you."

"Maybe it ain't as complicated as it seems to *you*."

They were faced off like bad-tempered bulls.

"She's special," Colt said, nodding tightly. "I get that."

"Then how come you run off?"

"I didn't run off!" he rasped, then drew a deep breath and chuckled. "I would rather have faced her old man than you."

"Well, he ain't here," Ty said. "He up and left her, too, didn't he? But I tell you what, you hurt her . . ." He spread his legs, shifted his slight weight in an aggressive stance as old as the earth upon which they stood. "You'll answer to me."

For a moment Linette thought someone would throw a fist. Thought there would be blood and accusations and acrimony.

But Colt finally shook his head and handed over the mare's lead line. "You win," he said and turned silently away.

CHAPTER 11

"You look good up there," Colt said and meant it. Linette Hartman might have been as slight as a june bug, but she had fire in her eye and steel in her spine. That much was clear even to him. "Just ease up on the reins some." Stepping up beside his mare, he took the woman's hands in his own and flexed her fingers a little. "That's it. How do you feel?"

"Okay," she said. It was early evening and they were in the Lazy's newly built arena. It still smelled of fresh pine. Only the gate was missing. But there were probably a half dozen local men feverishly working on it at that very moment. Maybe Hedley was at the helm of that project, he realized, and did his best to contain the anger that thought incurred. "Still scared stiff, though."

"That's because you're no idiot," he said, focusing on his student again and wondering what the hell he was doing there. Casie didn't want him on her property. That much was certain.

"There are a fair number of people who would disagree with that assessment," she said.

"Yeah?" He squinted up at her. The sun was bright and warm on his face.

"It's a documented fact."

He chuckled, marginally more relaxed as the image of Hedley faded a little from his mind. "Go ahead and squeeze her into a walk."

She did so, grinning as the pinto settled into a cadenced four-beat gait.

"Well, maybe they're the idiots," he said, studying her form. "Believe me, anyone who doesn't have a little honest fear of a thousand pounds of opinionated equine doesn't have all his ducks in a row."

She didn't respond. Her fingers looked stiff against the leather reins and her legs were clasped around the mare's broad barrel like metal tongs.

"Breathe," he suggested.

"I *am* breathing."

"I meant more than once every ten minutes."

She laughed a little, and with that he could see her shoulders loosen up some. Laughter did that. When Casie laughed, the world lit up like a Roman candle. And why the devil couldn't he get her out of his mind? The kiss they'd shared had fired up a sparkler of hope in him, but that was before she'd spoken to Hedley.

"So, it's not unusual to be afraid up here?" Linette asked. He watched her try to force herself to relax. It was a little like trying to make yourself fall in love. Impossible. He had found that out the hard way, and still mourned the truth of it.

"Maddy here outweighs you by ten times or more. You'd have to be dumber than a cob of corn not to be a little scared."

"How long before the fear subsides?"

"That depends."

"On what factors?" she asked, still circling him at a snail's pace.

"Lots of things, I suppose. Mostly how many times you make unscheduled departures from your mount."

She immediately clamped on again. "I'm hoping to avoid that," she said, and he chuckled.

"Nobody *wants* to do it, Lin. But we all take a fall one time or another," he said and thought riding a horse could maybe be a metaphor for life. He'd fallen hard. "Unless we chicken out first," he added and glanced toward the house, where a few periwinkle blossoms still graced the front porch.

Linette gritted her teeth, drawing his attention back to her. He stifled a grin, impressed by her stubborn determination.

"Like I said, the most important thing is just to keep the horse between you and the ground."

"I remember."

"Well, remember it when you pick up a trot, too," he said.

"A trot!" Her eyes widened in fear.

He stared at her for a second, then stepped forward and lifted a hand to Maddy's reins, stopping the mare before motioning to his student with his free hand. "Come on down here."

"What? Why?" She scowled, expression determined. "I'll trot if you insist."

He smiled at her fire. "Just come on down for a second."

She did so, hauling her right leg carefully over the cantle before stepping stiffly to the ground.

Leaving the reins crossed over the mare's crest, Colt touched a hand to the woman's narrow back and steered her a few feet from Madeline.

Turning, he removed his Stetson, sat down on the ground, and lay back.

Horse and woman stared at him. "Lie down," he said.

"Aren't you supposed to be giving me lessons?"

"I am."

"I already know how to lie down. I've had a fair amount of practice at it, lately, in fact."

"Yeah?" he asked. "You been hospitalized or something?"

She stared at him, long and hard. "Retired," she said.

It might have been a lie, he realized, but he let it go. Sometimes pride was all a person had to hold on to. "Well, then you should have learned how to relax by now. Come here."

Scowling a little, she finally settled down beside him.

"Pretty sky, huh?" he asked.

She turned toward him, brows raised beneath the helmet Casie's insurance company insisted she wear.

He chuckled. "I just wanted you to get used to the view from down here."

She remained silent for a second, then, "Because this is where I'm going to land?"

He nodded. "Sooner or later."

She exhaled slowly. He could feel her unwind. Sensed her turning toward him.

"How much is it going to hurt?"

"Like the devil."

She turned back toward the sky. "I'm beginning to wonder if you're the wrong person for this job."

"I could sugarcoat it for you if you want me to."

"I think that ship may have already sailed."

He grinned, liking her. "Sometimes things hurt, but if you want them you still go after them, right?" he asked and refrained from glancing toward the house.

"I don't have a lot of time."

"I thought you were retired," he said and watched her closely.

Their gazes met. "I have to be getting home eventually."

"I suppose your family misses you."

Emotion flitted across her eyes, but it was gone before he could identify it. "Elizabeth worries," she said and winced a little as she turned back toward the sky.

"Well, let's make this time count, then," Colt said. "Get back up there."

"All right." She rose to her feet, determination replacing her uncertainty of moments before. "But if I'm incapacitated with fear from your pep talk, you're culpable."

"When I figure out what that means, I will consider myself duly warned," he said.

"You know what that means," she said and managed to mount the mare under her own considerable steam.

By the time they'd progressed to a shuffling trot, her face was alight with a mix of excitement and terror.

"Hands low and steady," he said. "Heels down, seat firm."

"I'm as old as the hills," she said, attention strictly focused between Maddy's ears. "My seat hasn't been firm for decades."

He couldn't help but laugh.

Traversing the path between the cattle pasture and the kitchen garden, Ty gave him a disapproving glance as he passed by. A few seconds later, Casie headed in the same direction. Her cream and caramel hair was loose and swung against her shoulders in time to hips just wide enough to make a perfect target for his gaze. Her jeans were low cut. Her T-shirt barely met her belt.

"Colt!"

"Yeah." He jerked toward his student's voice with some chagrin.

Linette was staring down at him as if she'd been doing so for some time. "She's being a little stubborn."

"Yeah, well . . ." He snorted in frustration. "You should have known her in junior high."

Her silvery brows jerked toward her hairline, but her tone was deadpan. "And here I thought horses rarely made it past fifth grade."

There was nothing he could do but grin at his own obsessive behavior. "Well, old Maddy here was a star student. I used to copy her geometry papers."

"Really?"

"She could conjugate a rhombus like nobody's business."

"Conjugate a rhombus, you say."

He grinned again. "It's been a while since I've been in school, too," he said, to which she shook her head.

"You're in deep, aren't you?"

He lowered his brows and decided now was neither the time nor the place to discuss the depth of the hole he had dug for himself. Instead, he would give the riding lessons he'd promised, then get the hell out of Dodge.

"Push your hands forward," he suggested. "Don't shake the reins. Don't lean back. Just give her head some room and squeeze with your legs."

She did so. Nothing happened.

"Give her a little boot," he said.

Her legs moved the slightest degree. He grinned, placed his hand on her calf, and glanced up at her.

"Here's the thing, Lin," he said. "This here horse is sensitive enough to feel a mosquito land on her back and shake it off by moving nothing more than her skin." In his peripheral vision, he saw Casie bend to pull a weed from the potato patch. He was pretty sure it wasn't as fascinating as it seemed and forced himself to concentrate on his student. "But on the flip side, she's out in the elements twenty-four seven. She's tougher than nails and can be meaner than a rattlesnake. So if she wants to ignore a thing, she ignores it. Right now, she's pretty serious about ignoring you."

Linette scowled down at him. "You're saying I'm going to have to be more forceful."

"Can you do that?"

She tightened her jaw. "I'm not called heartless for nothing."

"Heartless?" His memory niggled him a little, but the approach of a black Camaro drew his attention like a circling wasp. Turning into the driveway, it pulled up to the house and crunched to a stop on the sparse gravel where it regurgitated a man in carefully distressed blue jeans and a suit coat with pushed-up sleeves. He looked young and lean, unbent by bucking horses, disappointment, or a hundred myriad worries. Colt felt his molars grind as Casie shaded her eyes against the sun and headed toward him.

He couldn't hear their voices as they spoke. But he could hear her laughter. His teeth were beginning to hurt.

"Everything going all right there?" Linette's voice was soft but maybe held a hint of humor.

Colt didn't feel quite so jocular. "Not if she gets into that car," he rumbled. There didn't seem to be much point in lying.

"Ever consider just telling her how you feel?"

"Doesn't seem like a very good game plan," he said and failed, yet again, to drag his gaze from the pair by the Camaro.

"Maybe it shouldn't be a game."

He drew a heavy breath and managed to turn toward his student. "There's been a little water under the bridge between us."

"Let me guess." She narrowed her eyes at him. "You liked the cheerleader type."

He glanced at the pair by the car again. "I mighta had a little trouble seeing past their pom-poms."

"Then later on you left her for the rodeo."

He raised his brows in surprise.

"I know your type. And . . ." She shrugged. "Maybe I heard your conversation a couple nights ago."

He couldn't have been more surprised. "Linny Hartman, you're an eavesdropper."

"I'm an insomniac."

The man by the car, little more than a boy really, laughed. The sound was deeper than it should have been. Colt felt the hairs at the back of his neck stand up. He turned toward them, fists forming without his permission.

"South Dakota still carries the death penalty for manslaughter," Linny said.

"You sure?"

"Trust me on this."

He drew a deep breath, fought his most basic instincts, lost, and shifted toward the Camaro, but in that instant Sophie Jaegar stepped out of the house. She wore a silky yellow sundress, strappy sandals, and a trio of bracelets on her right arm.

The breath stopped in Colt's throat.

"Curiouser and curiouser," Linny said.

Sophie spoke. The boy answered. Casie stepped away. The young couple slipped seamlessly into the Camaro and rolled out of sight.

Colt swore again, and Linny grinned.

"You make love look awfully tiring, cowboy," she said.

For a second he considered denying her words, but it hardly seemed worth the effort. "You wanna go for a ride?" he asked instead.

"I thought that's what I was doing."

"Give me a second," he said. "I'll throw a saddle on one of those broncs in the pasture."

"Are you sure Casie won't mind?"

"Yeah, well, if she gets pissed she'll have to talk to me, won't she?" he asked.

"I think I see a chink in that logic. I'm just not sure where it lies."

"You'll find it soon enough, I suspect. It's probably fair sized," he said and went to tack up one of Casie's favorite horses.

CHAPTER 12

"Casie!" Ty's voice sounded loud and squeaky-scared in the stillness of the kitchen.

She appeared in the doorway in an instant, eyes already frantic with worry. "What is it?"

"Something's wrong with Angel." His stomach, already knotted, knotted again.

"What do you mean? What—"

"She's standing funny."

They stared at each other, a dozen possible scenarios zinging through them in horrific tandem.

"They said she was okay when they released her," she said. "It couldn't be. . . . You don't think she's foundered, do you?"

"I don't know. Can you come look?" he asked, but it was a foolish question. She was already shoving her arms into the sleeves of her father's old Carhartt jacket.

The yard was dark as they stormed across it. Hell, it had been dark for hours already, and Sophie still wasn't home. Not that he cared that she was with that city boy, but sometimes she was kind of handy in an emergency.

Inside the barn, Al bleated. The chickens roosted precariously on the goat's nearly hairless back, bobbled, then flapped wildly as he pushed himself to his little split hooves.

But Angel remained exactly as she was as they approached her stall.

"Hey," Casie said, opening the door and stepping inside. "What's up, big girl?"

Behind her, Ty remained silent. Before them, Angel stood stretched out in a frightening impression of a sawhorse.

"When did she start this?" Casie asked. Her voice was soft, serious, scary.

"I don't know." Ty shuffled his feet, feeling sick. "She seemed okay when I come out earlier tonight, but maybe I just didn't notice."

She turned toward him, scowling a little. "What do you mean?"

He shrugged, trying to look casual, trying to look as though he wasn't sure this was his fault. "There was a lot going on. Colt was givin' that lady lessons, the lambs needed feeding, and Em wanted some help with the taters."

"So you fed her like usual?" she asked and turned back toward Angel.

"Didn't have no reason not to."

"And you gave her her meds?"

"Yeah."

"The Bute, too."

" 'Course I did." His voice had gone sharp.

She glanced at him in surprise. He caught her gaze for an instant, then shifted his eyes miserably toward the floor.

"I just . . . I should have checked her earlier," he said. "Soon as I got here."

"You're doing everything you can," she said, but she was like that . . . always saying things to make a guy feel better.

"You think it's founder, don't you?" he asked.

She tried to look tough, but he could see the worry in her eyes. "Her feet seem tender."

Founder, he knew, affected the sensitive lamina of the interior of the horse's hooves, causing tremendous pressure, enough pressure, sometimes, to make them lose their hooves entirely.

He swallowed his bile. "Should we give her more stuff for the pain?"

She shook her head once, uncertainty stamped on her face. "Anti-inflammatories can be hard on the stomach. The last thing we need is for her to colic again."

"I've been giving her that ulcer prevention stuff pretty regular."

"All right." Her voice was uncertain, but she made a decision. "Then let's give her more painkiller."

"She don't like it much. It's awful bitter."

She raised her brows at him, momentarily distracted. "You tried it?"

He shuffled his feet again, feeling foolish. "Ain't right to ask a man to ride no horse you ain't willing to break yourself."

She stared at him a second, then shook her head. "Let's bed her down deeper. Give her a little more cushion. I'll call Dr. Sarah, then mix some Bute into Em's applesauce and load it into a big syringe."

He nodded, then broke open a new bale and scattered additional oat straw around the old mare's feet. They were neatly rasped, carefully shod, and somehow the sight of them brought tears to his eyes. They'd been so ragged in the past, long and untrimmed and broken, but at least *then* her very survival hadn't been threatened. At least . . . He wiped his nose with the back of his hand.

She was just a horse. He knew that. Old and lug-headed. But . . .

Angel turned toward him. Expressive wrinkles folded above her dark eyes as she shifted her attention to him. His throat constricted, tight with emotions he shouldn't be feeling. Just a worthless horse, he reminded himself, but when he slipped a hand onto her face, he could feel her pain like a knife between his own ribs.

"Don't you give up," he whispered. "Don't you never give up."

"How's she doing?"

Ty jumped. Caught red-handed with his heart on his sleeve, he cleared his throat and glanced behind him. Colt Dickenson was leading the palomino called Evie toward him. As far as Ty knew, the mare hadn't been ridden more than a half dozen times, but everything seemed to be okay. The lady guest followed them, looking particularly small so near the beefy pinto she led.

Ty drew his hand away from Angel's face and swallowed his fear. "Not so good."

Dickenson swore and paced across the barn to look over the stall door. His brows lowered. His eyes narrowed. Evie dropped her head to sniff the floor. "You think it's founder?"

"Don't know."

Colt remained still for a moment, then turned and handed his reins to the guest, who took them with obvious misgivings. One horse was probably more than she'd handled in her lifetime. Two was going to give her fits. "Go find some low buckets," he ordered, watching Angel again.

"What?" Ty's voice cracked with strain.

"Hurry up now," Colt ordered. "Find some buckets or pans or something. Anything that's waterproof and big enough to fit her feet in."

Ty shook his head, half obstinate, half hopeful. "Casie said to give her more bedding."

"Let's not worry about that just yet."

"Linette," he said, addressing the lady behind him, "tie our mounts to the hitching rail out back, will you?"

"I'm not sure how to—" she began, but she stopped herself. "Okay," she said and turned away, carefully jockeying the pair of horses between farm equipment and a dozen other obstacles.

"What's going on?" Casie glanced toward Linette's retreating form. Her hands were full of bottles and syringes.

"We're gonna hose down her feet," Colt said.

"You think it's founder." There was terror in her voice.

"Even if it's not it won't hurt her."

She zipped her gaze to Ty's. Tears stung his eyes, but he wouldn't let them fall.

"You okay?" she asked.

"Sure," he said and heaped a little more guilt on the already teetering pile; it wasn't right to lie to Casie.

"I told him to fetch something to put her feet in."

She nodded. "Look in the sheep barn," she said. "We've got a bunch of buckets in there."

"You got a hose in here?" Colt asked.

Casie shook her head. "Closest one is by Em's garden."

"Get that, too, will you?" Colt said.

Ty hurried away. By the time he had returned, Linette was there, too.

"How serious is it?" she was asking. Her tone was smooth and unruffled. But then Angel hadn't listened to her fears in the deepest part of the night.

Ty shifted his gaze to Casie and felt her worry like a knife in the heart. "It can be pretty bad," she said.

The woman nodded. "How can I help?"

Casie shook her head and managed a smile. If he lived to be a hundred he would remember that smile every day of his life. How it could shine through in the darkest times. How it lit up his life. How it made the world better. "Don't worry about it, Linette. You're on vacation. We can take care of this."

"I want to do something."

"Really, there's no need. You should go to bed. We'll just—" Casie began, but Colt interrupted without looking up from where he was attaching a hose to the hydrant a few feet from Angel's stall.

"You get them horses taken care of, Lin?"

"Yes." She nodded, face solemn, wrinkles highlighted by the uncertain light. "I put the saddles in the tack-up room."

Tack room, Ty thought, but no one corrected her.

"Explain this scenario to me," she said and nodded toward Angel.

"Laminitis causes the sensitive structures of the foot to become inflamed," Casie said.

"And then?"

"If it gets bad enough the swelling can cause the coffin bone to rotate inside the hoof."

"What causes it?"

"There are a bunch of possibilities, but it could be a result of the colic."

"We're going to try to get her to stand in cold water to reduce the swelling," Colt said.

Linette nodded. "I imagine an animal as opinionated as a horse could resist that."

"Most do. Getting them to remain still long enough to do any good can be a real pain in the—" Colt began, but Casie interrupted him.

"She'll do it," she said and glanced up. "She'll do it if Ty asks her to."

And despite everything, his ignorance, his terror, the knowledge that he was not, and would never be, the person Casie thought he was, Ty felt his heart swell a little.

"Then you better ask her nice, son. Get her right foreleg in here," Colt said. And the struggle began.

By midnight Ty was exhausted and wet and cold, but Angel was finally standing perfectly still, all four feet fetlock deep in icy water. She heaved a sigh, looking more relaxed. Cocking her right hind, she shifted her weight a little. Linette, stationed beside that leg, hurried to steady the bucket she was standing in.

"She seems to be feeling a little better," Colt said.

Casie nodded. "Yeah." She glanced toward the cowboy, but didn't quite meet his eyes. "Thanks."

"No problem," Colt said. "Linny was tired of riding anyway."

She smiled from her position on the floor. "*I* wasn't tired," she said. "But my derriere *was* beginning to voice a few complaints."

"You're going to have to get some calluses on that thing," Colt said.

"I can't thank you enough," Casie said to the little woman

seated in the straw by Angel's hind legs. "This probably isn't what you had in mind for your vacation."

Linette shrugged, a leisurely lift of narrow shoulders. "Your Web site *did* say all inclusive."

Dickenson grinned. "Consider this a crash course in equine management."

"Well, the lesson's over for tonight," Casie said. "Sleep in as long as you want. We'll make breakfast whenever you get up."

"*We?*" Colt asked, raising a brow toward Casie.

"I can cook if I have to," she said.

Ty shifted his gaze toward Colt, whose lips hitched up some at the corners.

"If you don't wanna get even skinnier than you are, you're gonna have to get on Em's good side," he said and winked slyly at Linette.

"Listen," Linette said, "you don't have to worry about me. I can look after myself."

"Well, you should look after yourself in bed," Casie said. "You've done more than enough here."

"What about Tyler?" she asked. "Doesn't he have school to-morrow?"

"She's right. You have to get home," Casie said, worry edging her tone, but Ty shook his head.

"I can sleep here. In the stall. One day won't matter. I'll just—" he began, but Casie was adamant.

"If your grades slip they might not let you—" She shifted her gaze toward the door, throat constricting. "We'll take care of her. You don't have to worry."

And yet he did. About Angel, about himself, about *her*. But she was right. He could lose the right to come here, to see her, to breathe. He watched her for a second, then nodded and stepped toward the stall door.

"How about *I* stay?" Linette said. "I can take the first watch, keep changing the water so it's good and cold. If there's a prob-lem I'll wake you immediately. Otherwise, I'll let you sleep for a couple hours."

"No," Casie said. "Absolutely—"

"I think it's a good idea," Colt said.

From his position outside the stall, Ty saw Casie shoot Dickenson a withering glance, but the cowboy didn't wither easy. Instead, he shrugged. "I'd stay if I could, but I gotta get home. We're sorting calves tomorrow, and Dad'll bust my hump if I ain't bright eyed and bushy tailed come dawn. Hey, hold up, Ty," he said. "I'll give you a ride."

Ty considered refusing, but one glance at Angel's contented expression changed his mind. She was good for now, but she would need him later. "I got some stuff to get from the house first," he said and headed out.

Their voices murmured behind him, arguing softly, but when he stepped out of the barn, another noise distracted him.

A car turned into the driveway. Sleek and dark, it pulled into the turnaround spot fifty feet from the house and went silent. The yard light was distant and far overhead, but it glowed off Sophie's hair as she turned toward the driver.

Her date was good looking. Even in the poor light, Ty could see that much. His hair was blond and carefully unkempt. He was broad shouldered with well-proportioned features. His lips turned up, showing expensively aligned teeth as he laughed at something she said. One wrist was draped over the steering wheel in a casual sign of passive possessiveness.

Something twisted like a blade in Ty's gut, but he continued toward the house. He didn't care what Sophie Jaegar did. Didn't care if she dated every money-soaked hipster west of the Mississippi. It had nothing to do with him.

He picked up his pace, striding resolutely up the hill. A light remained on in the kitchen. It only took him a moment to gather up the corn muffins Emily had left for him on the kitchen table. Stepping out the door, he refused to glance at the sleek Camaro. Neither would he wait around for Colt. It wasn't far to walk to the Dickensons' farm. He'd done so a hundred times and he could sure as—

But a noise interrupted his thoughts, a raised voice coming from the Camaro. He snapped his gaze in that direction, breath held. Even from that distance, he could see arms flailing.

And that was all he knew. One moment he was standing outside the house, the next he was jerking the car door open and dragging the driver out by his suit coat.

$\mathscr{C}$HAPTER 13

"**H**ey!" The hipster stumbled, trying to get his footing, but Ty slammed him up against the back door of the car, knocking the wind from his lungs.

"Leave her alone!" His voice sounded guttural, barely recognizable to his own ears. Rage flared through him like a torch, burning his gut as he glared up at Sophie's date.

"What the hell, man!" Hipster began, but Ty knocked his fist up against his chest, rapping his spine back against his slick muscle car.

"Ty!" Sophie's voice was shrill as she bounded out the passenger door and around the bumper. "What are you doing?"

"What's *he* doing?" he snarled, but he didn't allow himself to glance toward her, didn't let his gaze stray in that direction because he knew what he would see. Beauty and class and brains, none of which were meant for him. He tightened his grip on the other kid's coat.

"Ty, for God's sake!" Sophie hissed. "Let him go."

"Did he hurt you?" Rage had burned down to glowing embers now, allowing a little more normalcy to his tone, enough lucidity to permit himself to glance her way. She was exactly as he saw her in his dreams, strong and stunning and dismissive.

"What?" Her voice was pitched high and frenetic.

The hipster laughed, spine bent back against his car, body almost relaxed, smirk firmly in place. "Dude, who the hell are you? Her lapdog?"

Rage flared again, causing Ty's fist to tighten without intent in his shirt, but Sophie spoke before the rage turned to something more deadly.

"Shut up, David!" she snapped but didn't turn toward him before speaking to Ty. "Let him go," she ordered, but he couldn't.

Instead, he clenched his jaw and twisted his fist in David's coat. "Did you?" he asked.

"Did I what, dude?" His voice was rife with disdain.

Ty's fist trembled with his emotion, but he held himself in check. It was not a simple task. "Did you touch her?" he snarled, but in that second, David snorted and brought his arms sharply up, knocking free of Ty's grip. There was a loose-limbed strength to him, an almost unconscious bravado that had been familiar to Ty since the day he was born.

Ty backed carefully away, narrowing his eyes against the rage, steeling his body against the violence that was sure to come. "Have you been drinking?" His voice was little more than a feral whisper, now.

"What? Who the hell is this guy?" David asked, but he didn't turn toward Sophie as he voiced the question.

"Ty," she said, addressing him instead. There was something in her voice that drew his gaze, his attention, the weakness in his soul. "Just let it go."

But he couldn't. "There's alcohol on his breath," he said.

"What the hell is it to you?" His words were scoffed.

A dozen emotions stormed through Ty, but he corralled them all, cordoned them off, reminded himself that some people were social drinkers. Some people could do that without anyone getting hurt. "You okay?" he asked instead.

"Yes," she said, but her tone was taut. "I'm fine. He just . . ." She sent David a caustic glare. "Forget it. It's nothing."

He swallowed, suddenly shaky, marginally sane. "He didn't touch you?"

"Touch her! Good God, get a grip, man," the hipster said. "What do you think she is, the Virgin Mary?"

Ty felt something roil in his stomach. Felt his eyes narrow. He knew he should back off. Knew he should back away.

"What'd you say?" he asked.

"Geez, man . . ." He snorted and lowered his voice to a conspiratorial whisper. "That's a prime little piece just waiting to be stroked. But maybe you already tapped that, huh? Maybe you already—"

That's when Ty hit him. He had no choice, no will of his own, and no compunction to stop. He just raised his right fist and slammed it into the other man's face. David spun like a top against his shiny car, but in a moment he had steadied himself. In the next he had turned and was barreling into Ty, bent double. They went down in a tangle of legs and arms. The breath rasped from Ty's lungs in a hard whoosh of pain. He brought his knee up with all the force he could muster, driving his opponent away from him, but David came back at him, swinging with both fists. Pain snapped against his cheekbone. He rolled in a fury, pinning the other man beneath him, scrabbling to hold him down.

But suddenly he was dragged away, punches landing in thin air, kicks falling on nothing.

"I said stop it!" The voice rumbled through the yard like a freight train. It did nothing, however, to slow David. He leaped to his feet and plowed toward Ty, but suddenly he was stopped, too, pulled to a halt and bound in place. It took Ty a moment to realize Colt Dickenson had his arms wrapped around the bastard's torso.

Ty struggled for a second, then forced himself to go perfectly still, forced himself to think. His breath was still coming hard, but his mind was settling into some kind of sanity. Colt's dad, Monty, held him from behind, arms like iron bands around his chest.

"What's going on here?" His voice was like Colt's, only more so, deeper, older, craggy as the bluffs overlooking the Chickasaw. Ty didn't answer.

"He attacked me," David said. "Came out of nowhere. Pulled me out of my car and started beating on me."

The night was silent but for the sound of their breathing. Sophie stood flush against the Camaro, watching Ty as if he were a wild animal. Casie watched him, too. He didn't know when she had arrived, but he could feel her gaze on his face, could feel her disappointment like a knife in his gut.

"Ty . . ." Her voice was soft, low, heavy with concern. "What's going on?"

He wanted to speak, to ease the worry in her eyes, but the guilt was too thick to allow his tongue to move. He looked away, but she didn't give up. Why didn't she ever give up?

"Ty, talk to me," she said and moved a step closer. "What's going on?"

It was almost impossible to open his mouth, to defend himself, but he would do it for her. "I thought they was fighting. Thought he was . . ." Words failed him. Rage boiled up, curling his fingers into fists again, making his chest ache as if it were about to explode.

"Simmer down," Monty said. "Just take it easy."

"Sophie?" Casie said.

He could feel her turn her attention toward the girl, could feel Sophie's glare sharpen even though he wasn't looking at her.

"I'm fine," she said.

David snorted again. "Of course she's fine," he said.

Ty ground his teeth, and perhaps he leaned into Monty's containing grip again, but the older man tightened his arms.

"She's okay," he rumbled. "She ain't hurt. You hear that, son?"

Ty forced a nod. Monty loosened his grip a little. "You gonna be good now?"

Good! Like a kid who can't be trusted with the cookie jar. He nodded again, face flaming.

"How about you?" Colt asked.

David straightened. "Yes, sir," he said. "I'm sorry, sir."

Colt turned him loose. David shook out his arms.

"He took me by surprise. That's all. One minute we were sitting in the car talking and the next he was coldcocking me."

The night went silent again.

"Is that what happened?" Monty Dickenson asked. Even in the darkness, his eyes looked hard as steel as they turned toward

Sophie. For one crazy second, Ty was tempted to step between them, tempted to shield her from his glare.

But *her* glare was just as potent when she turned it on the old man. "I said I was fine," she repeated.

Mr. Dickenson's brows rose. Ty had learned fairly early on that most folks didn't question Monty Dickenson's authority. "That's not what I asked," he rumbled, but Sophie had already turned her attention back to Ty.

"You stay out of my business!" she snarled.

"I'll do that," he said, "so long as you don't go acting like some—"

"Hey!" Colt spoke up as if shot. "That's enough now."

Silence echoed in the yard. Ty pursed his lips and gazed off toward the creek.

"We're all tired," Colt said. "You, what's your name?"

"David Pritchard, sir." He sounded like an ingratiating pup. The words scraped against Ty's ears like steel against steel. "I'm Jim's son."

"Jim and Stephanie Pritchard, the attorneys?" Monty asked.

"Yes, sir."

Colt exchanged a glance with his father. "Well, I'd suggest you get home," Colt said. "We've had enough trouble here for one night."

"Yes, sir. You're right. I'm sorry for any misunderstanding." He turned toward Sophie. "Good night, Miss Jaegar."

She didn't respond. In a minute he was gone, driving sedately out of the yard and turning carefully onto the gravel.

The night went quiet.

"What do you mean you've had enough trouble?" Sophie's voice sounded strident and tight in the soft darkness.

No one answered.

"What happened?" she asked.

"We're having a little trouble with Angel," Casie said finally.

"What? What do you mean?" She turned toward Ty, eyes gleaming. "You were supposed to be watching her."

"Sophie . . ." Casie warned.

"What?" She swung toward their mentor. "Dad made me go

out with that stupid . . ." She swung disdainfully toward the departing car, but stifled her next words. Ty scowled, mind churning. She drew a deep breath and narrowed her eyes. "Dad paid a ton of money to keep Angel alive, and you let her colic again?"

"It's not colic," Casie said.

"Then what is it?"

"We think it might be laminitis."

"Lamini—" She paused, swallowed, jerked her gaze to Ty's. Her eyes shone bright and tragic. "Did you get the vet out?"

"She's on another call."

"So what'd you do?"

"Force-fed her Bute, cold water on her hooves."

"How long ago did you quit hosing?" Her voice was like a jackhammer, demanding, facing off everyone. Like a lioness on the prowl.

"Just simmer down," Colt said. "She's standing in buckets right now."

"Alone?" she asked and turned with a snap toward the barn, but Casie caught her arm.

"Slow down, Soph. Linette's with her."

"Linette? Your *guest*? What does she know about horses?"

"Enough to call me if things take a turn for the worse."

She glared for a second in silence, then turned back toward Ty. "You pulled her shoes at least, right?"

"What?" The single word sounded dumb even to Ty, but her direct attention always deadened his tongue, dulled his mind.

"Her shoes," she said, enunciating clearly. "Didn't anyone think to pull her shoes?"

"She was in a considerable amount of pain," Colt said, his voice smooth and quiet where Ty's had sounded thick as concrete. "We thought it best to get that under control before we worried about farrier work."

"But you called somebody in," she said. Her tone was haughty as hell, pure evil . . . or pure Sophie, whichever you chose.

"I'll pull them in the morning," Colt said, "if it's not too hard for her to stand on three feet for an extended period—"

"You can't just yank them off," she said. "She'll need therapeutic shoeing. Pads, probably bar shoes to keep pressure on her . . ." She sighed heavily as if they were all too dense to tolerate. "Tell me you called a specialist."

"It's one o'clock in the morning," Casie said. "I didn't really think anyone would appreciate getting a call at this hour of the—"

But Sophie had already dragged her cell from the ridiculously small handbag draped over her left arm. She snapped it to her ear, listened for five seconds, and spoke. "Yes, Darren, this is Sophie Jaegar."

A murmur sounded from the other end of the line.

"Sophie Jaegar," she repeated, her voice slower now as if she was speaking to the mentally impaired. "We have a possible founder."

Another dismal murmur.

"No, it can't wait," she said, and suddenly her voice was thick with an emotion Ty couldn't quite identify. She turned away, and though her tone sounded oddly unsteady, she could still be heard. "The horse is in pain."

She paused as he spoke.

"What I expect is for you to remember that it was *my* recommendation that got you the Rosemount account." She paced away and lowered her voice, but her words could still be heard. "Then I expect you to get your ass out here within the hour." There was a pause. "Good. I'm at the Lazy Windmill." Another pause. "The Lazy Windmill," she repeated, then rattled off the address and shoved the phone back into her purse. She was back in view in a second and skimmed her gaze from one to the other. "I'm going to take over for Linette," she said and turned crisply toward the barn.

"You've got to get some sleep, Soph," Casie said.

The girl raised one haughty brow. "And you don't?"

"I'm going to rest until Linette wakes me up."

"I'll be the one waking you up."

For a second Ty thought Casie would argue, but she just sighed and let her shoulders sag a little. "Okay. Just . . ." She paused and lowered her voice, picking her way carefully, like a collie through a herd of fractious mustangs. "Just remember that Linette's a guest."

Sophie lowered her perfect brows. "I realize that."

"A *paying* guest. You know what I'm saying?"

Sophie pursed her lips. "I'm not going to offend her, if that's what you're worried about."

"No," Casie said, and it almost looked as if she was tempted to smile. "Of course not. I don't know what I was thinking. Well . . . wake me up when you're tired."

"I'll wait till after Darren comes," Sophie said.

"Okay," Casie said and watched as Sophie strode toward the barn. "Well." She exhaled heavily. "Good night, everyone. And Ty . . ." She turned toward him. He made himself face her, though he honestly didn't know if he could bear to hear her reprimand. Didn't know if he could stand her disappointment, but her expression was soft, her eyes bright with unbearable forgiveness. "Try not to worry, okay?"

He gripped his hands into fists and managed a nod, though his throat felt tight, his face stiff.

Reaching out, she placed a hand on his arm. Her touch was gentle, but somewhere in his soul it burned like hell. "I'll call you if anything changes."

He nodded again, though he didn't really know why. She smiled and turned toward the house. They all watched her go.

"Holy cats," Monty said. His voice was little more than a sigh in the darkness. "You got your hands full here, son."

"I know," Ty admitted.

"You've no idea," Colt said.

The two of them glanced at each other in surprise. Monty chuckled, wide face amused. "See you at home, Colton. Come on, boy," he said, and raising an arm, settled it over Ty's shoulder.

The weight felt awkward but not unbearable, unnatural but not unwanted. They walked in absolute silence to Monty's old truck.

"I'm sorry." Ty's words came of their own accord, uncalled

for, unexpected. He had learned long ago that apologies rarely improved circumstances. But neither did excuses. Or anything else.

"Listen, son . . ." Monty lightly squeezed the strained muscle above Ty's right arm. "Where women are concerned, sometimes there ain't nothing you can do but cinch up tight and pray to God," he said, and Ty felt his heart break just a little more.

CHAPTER 14

"Yes, I'm very sorry about that," Casie said. She had the phone receiver pressed firmly to her ear, her fist pressed just as tightly to her chest. "But it was just a misunderstanding. Tyler thought your son was taking advantage of—"

"A misunderstanding." Mrs. Pritchard's voice was low and steady, perfectly modulated, as if she had trained for years for just this type of warfare. "He was abrasive and confrontational, verbally and physically abusive even though David was simply doing a favor."

"A favor?"

"Philip Jaegar said the girl was lonely. David agreed to show her a good time out of the goodness of his heart."

So that was the payment Jaegar had extracted from his daughter for the use of his funds. Sophie seemed a little young to be the bargaining tool between two wealthy families, Casie thought darkly, then prodded her mind back to the conversation at hand.

"Like I said, Mrs. Pritchard, I'm extremely sorry about the entire incident, but believe me, Tyler is *not* aggressive. Not unless he believes someone to be in trouble. He was just trying to protect Sophie."

"Protect her from what?"

"From . . ." This was tricky territory. "Mistreatment."

"Are you saying my son is a sexual predator?"

"No! I just—"

"Defamation of character is a serious issue in the state of South Dakota, and it's a documented fact that Tyler Roberts was previously accused of assaulting a classmate. In light of that fact, Mr. Pritchard and I will be consulting with the criminal attorneys in our firm to determine how best to proceed from here. We'll know more after David has had a thorough examination."

Casie closed her eyes, but a noise from the porch forced her to jerk her attention in that direction. The last thing she needed was for Ty to hear this conversation. Stepping around the corner into the narrow hallway, she lowered her voice.

"He's okay though, right?" she asked. "Your son, he seemed fine when he left here. I know—"

"Miss Carmichael, I, for one, do not think it's *okay* for someone to physically attack another without provocation."

"I just meant, he's not seriously injured, is he?"

There was a taut silence. "We'll know more after X-rays and a CAT scan."

"CAT—"

"We will also have an estimate of damages done to David's automobile some time this week."

"His car? Nothing happened to—" Casie began, but just then footsteps rapped across the kitchen's curling linoleum, making her heart beat faster.

"Okay." She tried to sound upbeat or at least as if the sky weren't about to come crashing down around their heads. Even though she was pretty damned sure it was. "I'll wait for your call." Hanging up the phone, Casie closed her eyes and tried to remember to feel grateful. After all, Angel was doing better. Although, come to think of it, she hadn't seen the mare since morning. Anything could have happened since then. Suddenly seized by panic, she jerked her head out of her hands and stormed into the kitchen. "What's wrong?"

Linette and Sophie glanced at her with identical expressions of surprise. Despite Sophie's casual ensemble of jeans and jersey, she looked cool and chic. Beside her, Linette looked small and serviceable in khaki pants, zip-up sweatshirt, and SmartWool socks.

"What's going on?" Sophie asked, pouring a cup of coffee into a chipped mug.

"Angel," Casie said, trying without much success to tamp down the galloping worry. "What's going on with Angel?"

"Not much," Sophie said. Her lips jerked with irritation as she glared at the coffee cup she handed off to Linette. The older woman sighed, murmured her thanks, and settled stiffly into a nearby chair. Her daily hikes along the Chickasaw had been getting longer. "Darren hasn't come back yet to reset her shoes." Darren, the farrier Sophie had bullied into showing up long before dawn, had pulled Angel's shoes some hours before. "I think he was just too lazy to do it while he was here."

"I rather doubt that," Linette said, and taking her first sip of Emily's famous coffee, visibly relaxed.

They both studied her. She settled back against the wooden slats of the chair and raised her brows at them.

"Honestly," she said, clearly surprised by their scrutiny. "People called *me* heartless, but you're a force of nature, Sophie. I just hope he made it home without wetting himself."

"What are you talking about?" Sophie asked, but Casie was pretty sure she understood the reference.

"What did you do to him?" she asked, but before she got an answer, Emily burst into the kitchen like a freight train.

"Hey, Case, come see what I got."

Casie shifted her gaze to the girl near the door. "Can it wait just a minute?"

Emily eyed the trio already inside the room. "What's going on?"

Linette took another sip of coffee, palms still wrapped reverently around the mug. "Sophie's telling us how she charmed the nice young blacksmith who made an emergency house call last night."

Sophie narrowed her eyes. "If he was so nice he would have been here half an hour earlier and done his job correctly."

"Sophie." Casie tried to soften the warning in her tone, but worry was making her tired. Or maybe it was the fact that she was running on four hours of sleep and a near-constant supply of adrenaline. "We can't afford to terrorize a farrier. There aren't many around."

"I didn't terrorize him." Sophie sounded honestly offended, but her cheeks were a little pink. "I simply suggested he should get the stick out of his . . ." She lowered her brows. "I thought maybe he should do the job he was hired to do."

Linette chuckled almost inaudibly and sipped again.

"Sophie . . ." Casie said again, but the girl had had enough.

"I didn't do anything wrong."

"Nothing?"

"He knew he was doing a slipshod job," she snapped.

"I don't think so," Linette argued.

They turned toward her as a unit and she shrugged. "Admittedly, this isn't exactly my area of expertise, but I do know people, and I can tell you this—if that young guy could have justified slapping a set of shoes back on that horse, he would have done so with alacrity."

"Alacrity," Emily murmured.

"It would have been a far cry easier than putting up with the harangue from Sergeant Sophie here."

"I didn't harangue any—" Sophie began, but Emily laughed.

"Oh, please . . . that's like saying that Father *doesn't* know best," she said. It took Casie a second to understand the reference. Emily loved retro TV. "Who is this poor guy? I'll send him a jar of rhubapple jam as an apology."

"I don't harangue—" Sophie began again, but Linette held out a hand.

"I didn't say being tough was a bad thing," she said and gazed solemnly at Sophie. The two women remained silent for a moment, a quiet meeting of steely minds. "But sometimes it can be hard on the people we care about most. On the other hand, it's perfectly obvious that if that horse doesn't make a full recovery, it won't be because you didn't do everything you could."

Casie watched Sophie blink, watched her brows rise, watched her straighten a little.

Linette observed her, too. "Ty's going to be extremely grateful," she said. Her voice was low, her gaze steady.

Sophie's cheeks brightened. "Like I care," she said.

Emily snorted and shook her head. "Come on," she said.

Casie turned like a robot, more than ready to escape from the house, but when she stepped through the doorway, she stopped short even before she reached the porch steps.

"What's that?" she asked, staring numbly past the newly erected support beams to the yard beyond.

Emily was grinning like a happy cherub. "They're goats."

Casie nodded numbly. "See, here's the thing," she said. "I realize they're goats." In fact, there were three of them, a doe and two kids, all tricolored, all potbellied, all trouble on the hoof. She knew that from experience. "But funny thing, Em, we already have a goat. Our quota is full."

"What? Are you talking about Al?" Emily asked. "He can't give milk."

"Well, no," Casie agreed evenly, "but—oh no," she said, realizing where this was going. "Please tell me you're not planning to milk that doe."

"Good news," Emily said, beaming up at her from the bottom step of the porch, where the morning glories bloomed bright and cheery despite every ongoing catastrophe. "I'm planning to milk her."

"Emily . . ." Casie resisted the urge to press the heels of her hands into her eye sockets and scream like a banshee.

"Listen, Case," Emily said, pattering up the steps to grab her arm and drag her into the yard. "I know you think we have enough to do already, but—"

"*Think?*" Casie said, mind spinning with the number of things that had to be done yesterday.

Emily grinned like an urchin. "But Bodacious will actually *save* us time."

"Her name's Bodacious?" Sophie asked. She was staring at the potbellied trio with a certain degree of disbelief.

"Good gracious," Linette murmured, still nursing her coffee cup, as the kids butted heads, then twirled away to leap off in opposite directions. "That's the cutest thing I've ever seen."

"I know, right?" Emily said.

Casie shifted her gaze back to the girl, who sobered immediately.

"I mean, not that that had any bearing on my decision to buy them."

"You paid money for them?" Sophie asked.

Casie would have liked to echo that sentiment, but in actuality, Al hadn't exactly been free, either. Insanity, apparently, was contagious.

"They were a steal," Emily said, tone reeking with enthusiasm, but when Casie turned back toward her with rising brows, she scowled. "Not literally. Geez, Case, who do you think I am?"

And that was the thing. Despite the fact that they had spent six months working and talking and laughing together, she really had no idea who Emily Kane was. In fact, it was fairly unlikely that that was her real name. "Listen, Em, they're really adorable."

"Aren't they!"

"But we can't keep them. I mean, Al's enough trouble. We can't—"

"They're not going to be any trouble. They're going to be helpful. They're going to supply milk. We won't have to go to the store so often. Or pay three something a gallon. And do you know what goat milk sells for? Two bucks a pint. That's like liquid gold. And that's *if* you can find it."

"That's great, but—"

"And their milk is naturally homogenized. So it's easier on our digestive systems. It's higher in amino acids, protein, vitamin A, and niacin."

Bodacious glanced up, marbled eyes blinking, tiny mouth chewing rapidly.

"They're sustainable on less acreage, making them more environmentally friendly, and their milk is higher in virtually all the essential minerals such as—"

"Emily, think about this. You're not going to have time to milk her. You're going to have a baby. I mean, I don't know much about raising children, but I'm told it can be rather time-consuming and—"

"That's why this idea is so exemplary," Emily said. "Instead of running to town every other day for milk, we'll have our own . . . maybe a little extra to sell to the neighbors, and hey . . . you know I've been wanting to make the Lazy's own brand of earth-friendly soap."

Casie felt the heinous weakness take hold, but she bolstered herself with the memory of fatigue and good sense. "Dairy animals have to be milked twice a day, Emily. Twice a day, every day. How are we going to manage that?"

"See, that's the beauty of it."

Casie raised her brows, waiting for a glimpse of that elusive beauty.

"I talked to Bess at some length about this."

"Bess?"

"Bodie's owner. *Former* owner," she corrected and grinned.

"Oh, sure." The kids were rearing again, pawing at each other with cloven hooves, ears flapping wildly, distracting as hell, cute as bunnies.

"She said we don't have to treat this like a traditional dairy operation."

Casie raised her brows and refrained from glancing about. She thought it fairly obvious that they were not in danger of being considered traditional. Or a dairy. Or possibly sane.

"She said if we don't have time to milk her for a few days or a week or whatever, we can just turn the kids back in with the doe. Then when we want to begin milking her again we just remove the babies and—"

"Wait," Sophie said, "we have to take her kids away from her?"

"Of course," Emily said, but her own expression was somber suddenly. "How do you think the big operations do it?"

"I thought you just said we weren't a traditional dairy."

"Well, we're not," Emily said. "But the confinement farms take the babies away immediately, put the calves in solitary confinement, and start milking the moms with machines. Bess said these little ones have had plenty of time with Bo. They've gotten all the colostrum and stuff they need." She was still scowling, despite her upbeat tone. "Plus they have each other so they won't get too lonely. Besides that, they'll still be able to be with Bodacious sometimes. Like when I go into labor. That way you guys won't have to worry about anything."

"Anything?" Sophie asked, tone dubious. "I heard that if a fence doesn't hold water it won't hold a goat, either."

"It's great that you checked into all this," Casie said, trying to stop her head from spinning. "And your ideas seem . . ." Crazy. "Sound. I just don't think now's the time to introduce another—"

"Listen," Emily said, expression absolutely sober again. "I know I'm a burden."

"What? No. Emily—" Casie began and took a step forward, but the younger woman held up her hand.

"Just let me say this, okay?" Her lips were pursed into a puckered mound, her dark eyes wide with sincerity. "There's no way I can ever repay you. I know that. I'm not delusional. I just want to . . ." She swallowed. Her mouth twitched. "I just want to earn my keep, you know. I just want to feel like I'm doing *something* to help pay for me and Baby Roxbury."

"Something?" Casie felt her heart crack. "Are you kidding me? Em, you do everything." The girl shook her head. One fat tear bulged at the corner of her eye, threatening to fall and break her world apart. "I mean it. All the cooking, all the gardening, all the cleaning."

"I don't know anything about horses."

"Horses!" Casie swung her gaze toward the pasture where her little herds grazed, then laughed out loud. "Holy Hannah,

Em. We have horses covered. People *pay* to work with the horses. People travel . . ." She waved vaguely toward Linette. "Hundreds of miles to work with horses. But I'll tell you this for sure, no one's going to pay to make our meals. No one's going to pay to clean the basement and bottle-feed the lambs, and . . . and . . ." She glanced toward the little mother-to-be again, hoping against hope that that one fat tear wouldn't fall. "And take care of every godforsaken emergency that pops up in the middle of the night."

"It's not enough," Emily said. Her eyes were dead steady, her expression absolutely impassive.

"What?"

"You're giving my baby a home, Case," she said. Her lips were pursed again, her eyes round and solemn. "You're giving us a place to live. Keeping us off the streets." She swallowed. Her neck was dark and smooth. "I know I can't repay that. Not ever. Not in a thousand years." She cleared her throat. "But I want to try. I *have* to try. I mean . . . I know it won't be much, but maybe I can make a little profit on homemade soaps. Maybe I can repay you in some small way. Maybe I can—" she began, and that's when that fat, traitorous tear fell.

"Oh, Em," Casie said, and because she couldn't resist, she pulled the girl into her arms. "There's nothing to repay. I'm glad to have you here. I'm *thrilled* to have you here. And if it's that important to you, you can keep the goats."

"No." Her shoulders bumped up on a sharp sniffle. "No. It's all right. I'm just being silly. Endocrine overload." She swiped her knuckles across her cheek. "I saw Bodacious in the field and I knew Bess couldn't keep her and she had those babies and I thought about what it would be like to have kids and no home and I . . ." She paused, struggling for breath. "But you're right. They're going to be a lot of trouble, so—"

"No. I was wrong." Casie shook her head with vigor, wishing she could call it all back, make it all right. "What's one more goat?"

"Three more—"

Casie laughed, feeling a dozen odd emotions swirl inside her all at once. "Three more goats," she said and pushed Emily to arm's length. "We'll work it out."

"You sure?" Emily asked and raised her watery gaze to Casie's before swiping her hand across her cheek again.

"I'm sure," Casie said. "You okay?"

Em nodded.

Casie smiled.

Emily cleared her throat. "I thought I'd put them in the corncrib."

"The corncrib?" Casie said, dubious.

Emily blinked. "It's empty and secure. They won't be able to get through the wire."

"But—"

Emily's lips twitched.

"Yeah," Casie said. "That's a good idea. Go ahead."

"Are you sure?" Emily's voice was very small.

"Positive," Casie said.

"Okay. Thanks," Emily said and almost managed a smile before wandering off toward her new wards.

"Maybe you could help her, Soph," Casie said.

Sophie gazed at her a second, then shook her head with almost sad restraint and meandered down the steps after the older girl.

The five of them made a strange picture trailing across the yard toward the empty corncrib.

"Wow," Linette said, coming up beside Casie, coffee cup in hand. "I've never seen anything quite like that."

Casie sighed. The thing about living with teenagers was that you could never be sure whether you had won or lost. "Yeah. They're cute, aren't they?"

"Oh yes, they're adorable," Linette said. "They're all cuter than hell. But that wasn't exactly what I was referring to."

Casie glanced down at her.

"I just haven't seen anyone be played quite so beautifully before, and I've got to tell you . . ." She shook her head. "I've been around."

"I wasn't . . ." Casie scowled, opened her mouth, glanced at the girls herding the goats toward their new enclosure. Sophie said something. Emily smiled. "Holy Hannah," she said. "I've been played."

"Like a fine violin," Linette said.

"Again," she said, and despite everything . . . the impending lawsuits, the turbulent teenagers, the hundred thousand things that needed doing, they laughed out loud.

CHAPTER 15

"Then don't bother coming at all," Sophie said and snapped her phone shut.

Ty tightened his fingers in Angel's mane, breath held as he swept his gaze toward Casie. It was five o'clock in the afternoon. Fewer than twenty hours had passed since they'd realized Angel's new troubles. It felt like two hundred. School, which used to be a respite from the weighty tension of home life, had dragged on forever. Even Charles Dickens couldn't hold his attention.

Finally home, it had been a relief to see Angel standing square and quiet on all four feet, but she was heavily medicated and needed therapeutic shoeing as soon as possible. Thus the recent phone call.

"Sophie . . ." Casie's tone was a warning, but judging by the girl's petulant glare, she was in no mood for advice of any sort.

Sophie's gaze caught on his for a second. He felt the heat of it like an acetylene torch long before she turned her attention to Casie.

"What?" Her tone was abrasive. It would be crazy of him to like her. Probably crazy to like any girl . . . especially a bossy girl like her. He might be young, but he wasn't entirely stupid. "We can't wait around forever just because Darren is too lazy to get his butt off his recliner."

"He probably had appointments with other clients," Casie said.

"And what about Angel? Isn't she important enough for him to waste his time on? Maybe we should just put her down, then, if we can't get someone to take care of her feet."

Ty was familiar with Sophie's dramatics, was fully aware that Casie had no intention of giving up on the mare that had captured their hearts, and yet he felt his stomach knot up tight, felt his hands tremble.

Casie glanced at him before shifting her attention back to Sophie. "Let's avoid the histrionics," she said.

"Histrionics?" Sophie said. "What do you think is going to happen if we don't get her feet taken care of?"

"We *are* taking care of them. We've got the pain under control. And I'm sure Darren will be here in a couple hours."

"A couple of hours! She could be dead in a couple of hours. She could be—"

"Another relaxing day at the Lazy?" Colt asked and silently stepped into the doorway of Angel's box stall.

Ty felt something strike his gut, a feeling oddly balanced between relief and turmoil, jealousy and gratitude.

The women glanced at the new arrival. Had they turned their collective attention on Ty like that, he would have been tempted to duck and cover, but Colt Dickenson seemed comfortable in the eye of the storm.

"How's she doing?" he asked. Blithely ignoring Sophie's dark glare and Casie's uncertain body language, he lifted the door latch and stepped into the stall.

Ty shrugged, Sophie fumed. Only Casie spoke.

"About the same as this morning, I think. She doesn't seem terribly uncomfortable, but she's probably higher than a kite, so it's hard to tell." There was something in her tone that hadn't been there earlier . . . worry, maybe. Why? Was she increasingly concerned, or was there something about Dickenson's presence that allowed her to let down her guard? His stomach knotted up tighter. "I'm not sure what else to do," she said.

"The farrier isn't in a rush to come back, huh?" Dickenson asked and grinned a little as he glanced at Sophie.

"It's not my fault," she said tersely. That was one thing about

Sophie. She was as caustic as battery acid, but at least she wasn't bowled over by Dickenson's rough charm. Then again, if the rodeo cowboy couldn't win her over, what chance did lesser men have?

Dickenson, however, seemed completely untroubled by his inability to enchant and grinned crookedly as he crouched to place his palm flat against Angel's left forefoot. In a moment he switched to her lateral hoof.

They all remained silent. It was impossible to see his expression beneath his Stetson, but finally he stood.

"What do you think?" Casie asked. Oh, he didn't *like* Colt. There was no getting around that, but the man was Monty's son, and Monty wouldn't raise no fool.

"I'm no expert," he said.

Casie lowered her brows. "They're still hot, aren't they?"

He sighed. "Feels that way to me."

Casie nodded. She was trying to look casual, relaxed, but Ty knew her better than that, knew she smiled when she was worried, knew she was the gentlest soul on earth but would fight like a mad dog to save those she cared about. The image of her face after her return from his parents' farm still haunted his dreams. His eyes stung, but he blinked. Being a baby wouldn't do anybody no good. "Maybe Doc Miller can help us out."

"Doc Miller?" Sophie's tone was skeptical at best, but he didn't glance at her. Seeing her gleaming hair and too-perfect features wouldn't help anything, either. "The pig doctor?"

"He works on other livestock, too," Casie reminded her.

"Yes," Sophie said, "if the other livestock has a rumen. Horses, if you recall . . . do not."

Casie lifted one brow at her. And Sophie, to Ty's surprise, merely glanced away diffidently. When she spoke again her tone had lost its biting edge. "I don't think Doc Miller will be much help."

It was a strange interaction. Sophie backing down, Sophie not being a bitch.

"Have you got a better suggestion?" Casie asked.

Sophie scowled, then after a second's hesitation pulled the cell phone out of her pocket again. It was then that Ty could no longer remain silent.

"I ain't taking no more money from your dad," he said. All eyes turned to him. He was as surprised as any of them that he had spoken.

"Listen," Sophie said, brows pulled low over storm-cloud eyes. "Now's not the time," she began, but he shook his head, interrupting her before she could dig her heels in further. Memories of the hipster in the Camaro streamed through his head like poison arrows.

"I ain't," he said.

"Fine. Let's just let her die then," Sophie said. Her left fist was clenched by her thigh. Her lips were pursed in her signature expression of anger, and though her eyes were narrowed dangerously, they seemed unusually bright. "It doesn't matter to me if—"

"Soph," Casie warned, but Ty barely heard her. He was drowning in the liquid brilliance of Sophie's eyes. It wasn't until that second that he recognized the worry in them. The worry masked as anger.

"What?" Sophie snapped, and when she turned toward Casie, the moment had passed. "Dad paid good money to fix her and now . . ."

"Sam'll know what to do."

Colt's voice was quiet, but somehow it pierced the echoing emotions, the turbulent angst. Ty had no idea how he managed that.

"What?" Sophie asked.

"Who's Sam?" Casie said, but Colt was already pulling a phone from his own pocket.

"Hang on a second," he said and pressed a single button. In a moment he was speaking into the tiny receiver. "Yeah, hey, it's me." There was the slightest pause. He laughed, rocking back a little on his worn heels. "Not recently. Say, I've got a problem. Was wondering if you could help me out." Another pause. "Close.

We got a mare might have a case of laminitis." He lifted his eyes toward Casie, caught her gaze, and nodded. "Yeah. Recovering from colic surgery."

Al bleated as he wandered in, followed by two frolicking kids. Colt raised a questioning hand, but in a moment he was distracted again.

"Cold-water baths, Bute, Banamine, deep bedding. The usual stuff." He glanced outside, listening for a second, then, "She's barefoot now." He nodded again, rhythmically. "Okay. Yeah. "Where do I find that?" He grinned at the answer. "Well, that's great, but it's not in the back of *my* truck."

He shifted his gaze to Casie again. "I don't want to put you out." A murmur. "You sure? Okay. We'll keep her comfortable till then. Thanks, Sam. I owe you one." He narrowed his eyes and laughed again. "All right. I owe you three," he said and hung up.

Al bleated again, breaking the ensuing silence.

"How long do we have to wait?" Sophie asked.

Colt shrugged and glanced at Casie. "It takes a while to get here from Pine Ridge."

"He's coming all that way?" Casie asked. "That's going to cost a fortune in gas alone."

"Don't worry about it," Colt said.

"I *am* worried about it," Casie said.

Dickenson shrugged. "I've helped Sam out a time or two."

"It sounded like you're already in his debt."

Colt cleared his throat. "Well, we trade favors."

"I don't want you to owe him more than you can afford to—" Casie began, but just then Bodacious galloped into the barn, head high, frayed rope dragging behind her. Emily appeared a half second later, out of breath as she gave chase. The three of them stared over the stall door at her. She stared back, then dropped her hands to her knees, breathing deeply.

"Holy shorts. Maybe someone who's not pregnant could chase after that thing," she panted.

*   *   *

A half hour later they were *all* out of breath, but the hole in the corncrib had been repaired and Bodacious was once again confined. An hour after that, chores had been completed, Dickenson had given Linette another riding lesson, and Ty had once again soaked Angel's feet. The worry in his gut had receded marginally.

"Milk or water?" Casie asked. She was pouring beverages from ceramic pitchers that boasted raised pictures of roosters. They matched the glasses to perfection and beat the crap out of the chewed-up plastic ones they used to use. Emily was exceptional at consignment shopping. Even better at taking a run-down house and making it into the kind of home that insisted you kick off your shoes and settle in with a bowl of warm apple crisp and a sigh. But that was only one of the reasons Ty liked her so well. She was also loyal and smart and funny . . . a friend when he'd desperately needed a friend.

But Sophie . . . He shifted his gaze to where she sat beside Dickenson. Guilt crept up. *Emily* was the one who needed attention. Emily, who was always there for him. Emily, who had never had nobody. Sophie turned her glowing gaze toward him and he jerked his nervously away.

"Is that goat milk?" Linette asked.

"You bet your extraordinary brainpower," Emily said. Bending, she retrieved a hotdish from the oven. It steamed into the relatively cool kitchen air. "It'll make you brilliant, stalwart, and more bodacious."

Linette raised her glass toward the milk pitcher. "I'd give my spleen to be more bodacious."

"Amen," Emily said and began dishing up the casserole. The kitchen smelled of melted cheese and contentment.

"You know that it hasn't been pasteurized, right?" Sophie asked.

Casie was already handing over the full glass. The milk looked thick enough to walk on. Linette stared at it a second, then shrugged. "Here's to living dangerously," she said and raised her beverage in an impromptu toast.

Dickenson clicked it with his own ceramic rooster.

"Speaking of dangerous," Emily said, sucking gooey cheddar off her thumb. She seemed in good spirits today, though her latest environmentally conscious T-shirt looked stretched to its limits over her belly. "How was your riding lesson?"

"Well . . ." Linette tasted the milk, made a "not bad" face, and continued on. "I rode over four cavaletti at a trot and still made it onto the porch under my own steam."

Casie settled into a chair and raised her own glass to the older woman's. "Going over ground poles already. Congratulations." Her voice was soft, exuding comfort.

"I've never been more proud," Linette said.

"Or more lucky," Emily said.

Linette glanced at her.

"Horses," the little mother-to-be explained, shoving her spatula under another helping of the still-steaming entrée. "You might as well strap a jar of nitro to your a . . ." She paused. They all stared. Emily had been outspoken since the day she'd first come to Ty's rescue in a temporary foster home in Buffalo Gap. Her looming pregnancy wasn't lessening that characteristic. "Ankle," she finished and delivered another plate to the table.

"Nice save," Dickenson murmured and took the plate.

Linette laughed. Sophie stared down at the pan. "What's the mystery meal of the day?" she asked, but she didn't waste any time lifting her plate for a helping.

Emily canted her head. "I call it Hotdish Bodacious."

Sophie scowled at it as she settled a piece onto her plate. "It looks like . . ."

Casie cleared her throat.

". . . good," Sophie finished, and Dickenson grinned.

"It tastes like . . . good, too," he said, having just tasted his first bite. Mrs. Dickenson was a pretty good cook. Which made the number of meals her son ate at the Lazy seem kinda suspicious. But then, Ty supposed the same could be said of him.

"Wow," Linette said, sampling a bite. "That's better than good. Where'd you get the recipe, Em?"

Emily shrugged and settled her belly beneath the table. "I just try stuff."

Linette tasted another bite, closed her eyes for a second, and smiled around her fork. "What's in it?"

"Bodacious milk, three kinds of cheese, a bushel basket of fresh herbs, and Magenta eggs."

"Don't ask," Sophie warned. Ty glanced at her for a second, then skimmed his gaze away, stomach already unsettled.

Linette glanced at her, but asked anyway. "Magenta eggs?"

"I have a theory," Emily said.

"God save us," Sophie said, but Emily continued unperturbed.

"Magenta is our little purple chicken."

"You have a purple chicken?"

"No," Sophie said. "We don't."

"Well, she looks purple in the proper light," Emily said. "Anyway, she's the littlest chicken we have. We lock them all up in the coop in the evening, you know, to keep them safe from . . ." She waved her fork, indicating the world at large. ". . . everything. But one night I couldn't find her."

"Here we go," Sophie said, taking her first bite of a biscuit.

"The next morning she was limping and missing half her tail feathers."

Linette waited in expectant silence.

"There were coyote tracks around the coop."

"Or they could have been Jack's," Sophie said, mentioning the ranch dog.

"They were indubitably coyotes," Emily declared with finality and started in on the hotdish. Linette stared at her, waiting. But when Emily ate, not much else happened. Linette shifted her gaze to the others around the table, encouraging someone else to fill in the blanks.

"Emily believes that perhaps Magenta fought off the coyotes," Casie explained.

"Ahh," Linette said.

"They haven't been back since." Emily said the words around enough food to feed a family of pachyderms.

"Of course, Jack has been outside every night since then," Sophie said. "Can I get some vegetables?"

Casie passed the glazed carrots.

"This is the best egg thing I've ever tasted," Dickenson said, then glanced at Ty. "You tell Mom and you're responsible for my chores when she tans my hide."

"I'm still not sure what your theory is," Linette said.

Emily shrugged as she added a pair of baby dills to her plate. Maggie Janis, their closest neighbor to the west, was an award-winning pickle maker. It was no secret that Em planned to learn everything she could from the old woman, crotchety though she was. "Magenta is unusually courageous, so it naturally follows that her eggs will imbue us with that same bravado."

Linette remained silent for a moment, perhaps trying to figure out if Emily was serious. Ty could have told her unequivocally that she was.

"Eat up," Dickenson said, nudging Linette's elbow with her own. "We're going to lope tomorrow."

"I—" Linny began, eyes wide with fear. "I'm going to need a bigger plate."

Dickenson chuckled.

"He's just kidding," Casie said. "You don't ever have to lope if you don't want to."

"Well, I can't force you," Dickenson said. "But it's best to get it over with before you scare yourself out of it."

"I've already scared myself out of it."

"You can take as long as you want," Casie added.

"I wish that was true," Linette said. "But I don't have a lot of time left." Her voice was quiet, her gaze distant.

They all glanced at her.

She raised her brows at them, suddenly aware of their attention. "I mean, I'm not getting any younger."

A knock at the front door broke the ensuing silence.

"Who could that be?" Casie asked. Her tone was steady, but her eyes looked nervous. Why? Ty wondered. Had something else happened to make her skittish?

"I wouldn't be at all surprised to learn that strangers show up unexpectedly at dinnertime," Linette said.

"Emily would feed Jack the Ripper," Sophie said.

"She's probably hoping he could teach us some table manners," Colt said. "Hey, Ty, pass me the pickles, will ya?"

Ty did so without thinking, watching as Casie crossed the cracked linoleum.

"You didn't can those yourself, did you?" Linette asked.

"They're Maggie's," Emily said. "She's like a kitchen witch or something."

"Or just a witch," Sophie amended.

"Give Em half an acre, she'll feed you for the winter," Dickenson said.

Ty heard the door open and strained to hear the voices there, but the banter around the table was too loud.

"Give me an alpaca and I'll clothe Baby Quinton forever," Em said.

"You'll have to talk to Mom about *that*," Colt said.

"Alpaca?" Linette questioned.

"Warmest fiber in the universe."

"Where would you possibly find time to care for another animal?"

"Excellent question," Colt said, spreading rhubapple jam on a biscuit.

"I figure I'll just be sitting around for a couple months after Baby Ravel's born anyway, so I might as well have a hobby."

"Are you serious?" Linette asked.

"Well, you know, I won't be able to practice canning for a while."

"Or walk," Linette said. "After my daughter was born I could barely sit up."

"What's it like having a daughter?"

Voices murmured from the entryway.

"It's . . . nice," Linette said, but her tone was distracted.

"Nice like . . ." Emily shrugged. "Pickled beets? Or nice like your best friend in the world?" Her voice was a little tight, her eyes sharp. "I mean, there's nothing like family, right?"

"I'm starting to think that it's the most important thing in the world."

Emily nodded. "So when will we meet her?"

"Who?"

"Elizabeth. Your daughter. Hey, she should come pick you up. I mean, you don't have a car here. She could rent one in town, then stay until you have to leave. I bet Case would give her a couple nights free so you two could spend some time together. I'd take care of your granddaughter and..." She finished off her pickle, thinking hard. "What's her name again?"

Linette blinked. Her face seemed a little pale. Sometimes Ty wondered if she had been sick. If she had come here to recover. "Lila," she said.

"After her grandmother?" Dickenson asked.

Linette shook her head, then shifted her attention to Emily. "These biscuits are amazing, Em. You *must* have had a recipe for these. An old family secret maybe?"

"No, but my mother..." Emily began, then paused and glanced at Colt. He caught her gaze with a steady eye. "Probably didn't even know what homemade meant." She shrugged. Em was never real comfortable with the truth. "Like I said, I just experiment."

Dickenson smiled a little. There was something in his expression. Pride maybe. It made Ty's stomach feel odd. Dickenson gave Emily a nod before returning his attention to his meal. "We're like happy little guinea pigs," he said.

"Well, I'm going to be a potbellied pig if I stay here much longer," Linette said.

"I've gained ten pounds since last spring," Sophie said with a scowl.

Ty glanced at her. Maybe she *had* put on some weight since they'd first met, but it only made her more... He couldn't think of the word.

"If I pack on any more, my mother will disown me," she added.

Linette stared at her. "Sometimes mothers make mistakes."

Sophie shrugged. "I didn't say it would be a bad thing if she—"

"Hey," Casie said, returning to the kitchen. Another woman stepped up beside her. She was slightly shorter than Casie and somewhat heavier, but every ounce of that excess seemed to be packed into her chest, which was barely confined by a narrow-strapped, candy-apple-red tank top. Her hair was long, black, and shiny. It curled in a wavy mass around her shoulders. Her lips were plump, glossy, and just as red as her shirt. "This is Samantha Shepherd." She paused and smiled, but a tic jumped in her jaw. "Colt's farrier friend."

CHAPTER 16

"What a grand old mare," Sam said, and straightening, stroked the gray's speckled neck.

Casie refrained from gritting her teeth. She had no reason to dislike Samantha Shepherd. Especially since the woman had just spent the past hour and a half shaping therapeutic shoes over an acetylene torch. Sweat beaded her brow. It glimmered on her chest and arms. All of the above were extremely well defined. "Good thing you caught this early on, Ty, or her chances of a full recovery wouldn't have been nearly so good."

Ty shuffled his feet. "Casie's the one that took her in," he said.

The blacksmith turned toward Casie, who shrugged. This woman wasn't the enemy, she reminded herself. "I just supply the feed," she said. "Ty looks after her."

"Well . . ." Sam glanced at Colt. She had a crooked smile that could light up a cave. "Colt always could find himself people with soft hearts." She laughed, seeming to remember something the others weren't privy to. Casie felt her stomach tighten. "The world needs more of that kind. God knows them PMU horses could use some help. Right?" Sam said, and pulling her gaze from Colt's with an obvious effort, turned her smile on Casie.

Casie tried to smile back. "What horses?" she asked. Thunder rumbled off to the west. A storm was rolling in.

"The ones on that urine line."

"What?" Casie asked. Sophie scowled.

"You know," Sam said, and shifting Angel's left foreleg carefully onto the heavily bedded floor, straightened her back. The movement shifted her tank top a little higher, almost allowing it to hide half her boobs. "The mares that are kept for the urine that's used for hormonal imbalances and stuff. There's a farm around here somewhere, I guess. I mean, they didn't report any abuse on that particular property, but I've got a feeling the conditions might not be real cozy. They showed footage from other farms . . ." She shook her head and patted Angel's shoulder. "Well, I think we're done here."

"Thanks," Colt said. "I really appreciate your help."

"Yes," Casie added, trying to sound grateful. "Thanks so much for all your time. What do I owe you?"

"You?" She laughed. "Nothing at all. But Colt here owes me a roping lesson and a pair of red—"

"So you think she'll come along okay?" Colt asked.

Sam raised her brows at the change in course, but followed along easily enough. "Yeah," she said, and still smiling, turned toward Ty. "You keep taking care of her like you have been and she should come around just fine. I'll plan on stopping back in a few days to take a look at her. But you gotta promise to call me right away if she takes a turn for the worse, or if you have any questions. Call me . . . night or day."

Ty nodded.

Sam smiled. "You got my number?" she asked.

Ty shook his head and looked sheepish. Laughing a little, Sam slapped a hand to the pocket on the seat of her jeans. The fabric across her boobs stretched as tight as an overtaxed water balloon. She wiggled a little as she searched her pocket, but her hand came up empty.

"Sorry," she said finally. "I'm damn good with horses, but I'm not so hot with people. Looks like I forgot my business cards again." She made a face. "But Colt here's got my number if you need it." She smiled again, eye contact strong. "You'll call, right?"

"Yes, ma'am," Ty said, and she nodded before bending to pick up the half dozen metal tools that were strewn around Angel's stall.

Colt hunched down to assist, and when she tried to take them from him, he declined. "Least I can do is carry your stuff," he said.

"You're right," she said and laughed. "That is the least you can do."

Casie forced herself to look away as Colt walked Sam to her truck. It was a brand-new Chevy with all the fixings, as red as her tank top, as shiny as her hair. She cocked a hip against her open tailgate and faced the barn. When she laughed her boobs jiggled like just-set Jell-O.

"I'm going to take Angel out to graze," Sophie said.

"What?" Ty asked, pulling his attention from the pair by the truck.

Sophie scowled. Her cheeks looked a little pink, her eyes narrowed. "Angel . . ." she said. "Remember her?"

"Yeah." He scowled back, looking confused. " 'Course I remember her," he said and stroked the mare's neck.

"She needs grass."

"What are you talking about?" he asked and glanced toward the corner of the stall where they had piled her hay, two flakes of grass and one of alfalfa. The bedding was deep enough to swim in. "She's got plenty to eat."

Sophie pursed her lips. "It doesn't have the same nutritional value that fresh forage does. It's not as easy on her digestive system, and she doesn't like it as well. She wants to graze."

But he shook his head. "Sam said she needs stall rest for at least another week."

"Well, Sam is a . . ." She said the woman's name with a good deal of force and no small degree of distain. Casie raised her brows a little at the tone, making Sophie lower her voice and her shoulders. ". . . person who doesn't know everything."

Ty's scowl deepened a little. Casie watched the exchange with some confusion. But her thoughts about Samantha Shepherd were equally confusing. Who the hell was she to Colt? And what did she hope to be? And why would Casie possibly care? True, maybe for a while she'd been intrigued by Colt Dickenson. Maybe she had even thought he had changed. But her conversation with Hedley had proved otherwise.

"Such as how to wear a shirt, apparently." Sophie's voice had dropped an octave, effectively dragging Casie's attention back to her.

"Well . . ." Ty shifted his attention between the two women standing closest to him. His ears were a little red. "The weather *has* been mighty hot and . . ." He shrugged. The movement was stiff. It looked as if it was taking a good deal of discipline to keep his gaze off the object of their discussion. "Blacksmithing is hard work."

Sophie gritted her teeth. Casie swung into the conversation before it unraveled completely. "I think Ty's right, Soph," she said. "Doctor Sarah thought Angel should be kept as quiet as possible, too."

Sophie's scowl deepened at the sound of the veterinarian's name, making Casie wonder if Sophie disliked *her*, too. Holy Hannah, if she was going to hate every woman in the equine industry, she was going to be mighty lonely. Ninety percent of the equestrian world was female.

"Yes," Sophie agreed, her tone suspiciously saccharine. "But that advice came before Sam's brilliant scheme. Had the good doctor known our illustrious farrier was going to come up with something as earthshaking as egg bar shoes, she would probably be allowing us to run Angel in the Derby by now."

"I think them shoes looked pretty good," Ty said.

If Sophie's scowl got any deeper, it would swallow her whole face. "You sure that's what you thought looked good?" she asked.

From her left, the farrier laughed again. Casie didn't bother to glance at the pair framed in the doorway of the barn. She had seen enough jiggling boobs to last her a lifetime.

Ty shuffled his booted feet and also kept his gaze front and center. "I don't know much about horses' hooves," he said. "But them new shoes might just help Angel move around a little easier."

"Yes. She's practically a genius."

He shrugged again, red spreading from his ears to his neck. "Not a genius, maybe," he said. "But I wouldn't a never thought of them things."

"Well, you—" Sophie began, but stopped herself before Casie could jump back into the mix. "All right," she said. "I'll leave Angel where she is if that's what you want."

He nodded. They stared at each other. Casie tried to think of something to fill the awkward silence, but there was no one more awkward than she was, and her mind was half occupied by the couple near the truck anyway.

Sophie was the one to turn away first, but Ty stopped her.

"Soph." His voice was low, a testament to the fact that he was almost a man. His cheeks had turned pink . . . proof, perhaps, that he was still a boy. "Thanks."

The girl's back was very straight, her lips pursed, but her eyes seemed oddly haunted. Still, she forced a casual shrug. "She's your horse. You can do whatever you want with her."

He remained silent for an uncomfortable moment, then spoke again. "I meant . . . thanks for trying to get Darren to come back out."

For a second her face softened, but she caught herself. "Well . . . like Mother would say, a poor attempt is almost as good as nothing at all."

He lowered his brows, working out the logistics for a moment. "He come out in the middle of the night the first time. Who knows what would have happened if he hadn't pulled them shoes first thing out of the gate?"

Sophie glanced at the old mare. For an almost infinitesimal instant, tenderness shone in her eyes. "She would have probably been fine without any intervention," she said, but Ty shook his head.

"You done good," he said. "I know she ain't much compared

to . . ." He shrugged. "You're probably used to riding them Grand Prix jumpers or something, but it was a nice thing you done for her."

For a moment her expression was guileless. Her lips parted, her cheeks pinked. She backed away. "Well . . ." She said the word almost as if she was flustered, almost as if she was at a loss. "I'm just going to . . ." She waved vaguely somewhere between the corncrib and the creek. "I'm going to help Emily with the dishes," she said, and turning abruptly, practically stumbled over Jack before disappearing outside.

"She's *what?*" Colt asked, appearing in the doorway from the opposite direction.

Casie took a deep breath and refrained from looking him straight in the eye. "I believe she said she was going to help Emily."

"That's what I thought." Colt scowled, staring off toward the house. "Any other signs of the apocalypse?"

She could play this game, Casie thought, and forced a smile, happy to avoid the conversation she knew they should have. "I did see seven horsemen by the front porch this morning. And last night—"

"She ain't all bad," Tyler said.

They turned toward him in stunned unison. Was Tyler Roberts sticking up for Sophie Jaegar? Was this yet another sign of impending doom? Casie wondered. But he just shrugged.

"I'd best be gettin' back." They were still staring at him. "Promised Monty I'd oil up his ropin' saddle yet tonight."

They watched in tandem as he strode purposefully down the driveway toward the Red Horse Ranch.

Colt's eyebrows were lodged up against the weathered band of his Stetson. "What the hell was that about?"

Casie shook her head, trying to sort it out.

"I mean . . ." He exhaled. "Do you think it's true?"

"What?"

She could feel him turn toward her.

"Do you suppose Sophie *isn't* Satan?"

She glanced toward him. His expression was a ridiculous blend of awe and suspicion, but when she was just about to chuckle, she noticed the smudge of lipstick across the corner of his mouth.

She felt her fingers curl toward her palms. "Well . . ." she said. "I'd better get inside."

"I wouldn't risk it if I were you," Colt said.

She glanced at him on her way out of the stall. He shrugged. "If Sophie hasn't hexed Emily yet, it's probably just because they're in the middle of an epic battle of good and evil."

"Well . . ." She pursed her lips, reminding herself of Sophie's prissiest expression. "We can't all be saints."

"What's that?"

She heard him latch the stall gate behind them. But she didn't turn.

"We don't all have six hours to burn on a Tuesday night."

He was silent for a second before she felt him touch her arm. "Hey."

She kept walking.

He tightened his fingers around her elbow and tugged her toward him. "Sam's just a friend," he said.

"Really? Then cowboys must have changed a bit," she said and carefully extracted herself from his grip.

"What the hell are you talking about?"

"The lip gloss," she said. "I don't think it's your shade."

He stared at her for a second, then wiped his mouth with the back of his hand, glanced at the streak of red across his knuckles, and shook his head. But she was already turning away.

"Is that what you're mad about?" he asked, striding after her.

"I'm not mad." The words sounded a little like a growl. But the good news was that if she stormed along fast enough, *her* boobs could jiggle a little, too.

"Really?" Colt asked. "Then this is the jovial you?"

She swung toward him without intending to. "So what kind of favors do you trade with her exactly, Dickey?"

He stared at her, brows raised cautiously again. "What?"

She gritted her teeth. It wasn't that she cared what he did in his spare time. It wasn't as if she cared about him at all, but he didn't have to lie to her.

He was absolutely silent for a long moment, but finally he spoke. "It's not like you think, Case."

"Really! Because I think you slept with her." She practically spat the words at him.

He moved his lips, raised one hand, and failed to speak.

She gritted a smile. It felt kind of flinty on her face. "Turns out it kinda is what I thought, isn't it?" she asked, and turned away, but he was in front of her before she reached the doorway.

"Good God, Case, I'm a grown man. What did you think I would do? Wait in chaste hopefulness until you found it in your heart to return to the Lazy and my poor abandoned self?"

She stared at him a second, then snorted out loud and stormed around him.

"Okay!" He grabbed her arm as she torpedoed past. "Listen, I'm sorry. Sam's a nice gal. She'll give you the shirt off her back if—"

Something escaped her throat. It might have been some kind of animalistic snarl.

Colt stepped back a pace, then laughed nervously and continued on. "Could be that was a bad choice of words. But she really is a swell girl."

She felt her brows jump like trout at dawn. *"Swell?"*

"Nice. Sweet. Kind. Thoughtful. You name it," he said.

"How about fat chested?"

"Fat—" he began, then laughed. She swung around him, steeling herself in case he grabbed her again, but he just stepped back instead.

"Holy crap." He barely breathed the words. "Holy . . ." She heard his footfalls stop. "I never thought I'd see the day."

She told herself to keep walking, to march straight into the house and up the stairs. Maybe fetch Clayton's old shotgun . . . maybe . . .

But he spoke again. "You're jealous."

She stopped as if she'd been shot. Her cheeks felt hot, but she swung toward him anyway. "You're deluded," she said.

He stared at her a second longer, then laughed again. "It's true. Cassandra May Carmichael is jealous."

"What would I be jealous of?" she asked. In the back of her mind she thought that if he said, "Her boobs," she just hoped she had enough shotgun shells left to do the job right.

"I don't know," he said instead. "She's a great gal."

"Yeah? As great as Jess?"

He winced, froze, then exhaled slowly. "I've been meaning to talk to you about that."

"About the mother of your child?"

"She—"

"The child you abandoned?"

"I didn't abandon her."

So it was a girl, she thought, and had no idea why that made things worse. Made her want to cry. "So maybe you married Jess and just forgot to tell me that, too."

He glanced out the door, eyes haunted. "I wouldn't have made her happy."

She drew a deep breath. "So you talked about it. You considered it."

"Yeah."

"And she wanted to marry you."

"She thought she did."

She laughed, despite herself. "But you knew better."

"I didn't love her," he said, and turned back to her. "There was someone else." His eyes were frightfully earnest, absolutely steady. "There has always been someone else."

She felt herself pulled in, pulled under, but she shook her head, trying to formulate the appropriate questions.

Suddenly, Emily's voice rang through the barn. "Sophie! Soph! Where are you?"

Casie gave Colt one last look and stepped into the doorway. "Emily . . ."

The girl turned toward her with a start. "Holy shorts!" she said, staggering away. "Scare the crap out of me, why don't you!"

"Sorry." She refused to glance at Colt as he appeared out of the shadows beside her.

"What's going on?" he asked.

Emily eyed him up, then shifted her curious gaze back to Casie. Her lips curved happily. "Excellent question." Her tone was suggestive.

"Why are you looking for Sophie?" Casie asked.

"Oh." Emily's happy expression diminished rapidly. "She's not with you, huh?"

Premonition cranked Casie's stomach up tight. "She said she was planning to help you with dishes."

"Yeah," Emily said. "Weird, huh?"

"So she *did* go inside?"

"Ten minutes ago or so," she said and pulled a comical face. "Have you seen any other signs of end times?"

Casie could feel Colt's gaze shift to her face, but ignored the ongoing joke. "Where is she now?"

"I don't know. One minute she was in the kitchen. The next I heard an engine fire up. I didn't think anything of it for a while. Assumed it was you, but then I noticed the news clip."

There was a lull in the conversation. A lull that Emily failed to fill.

"What news clip?" Casie asked, already striding into the yard.

Emily followed. "The TV was on in the living room. I pretty much ignored it until I heard the words *abused horses*."

Casie felt the blood drain from her face. "What about them?"

Emily shrugged. "Apparently, there are some."

The three of them were standing in the yard now. But Puke was noticeably absent.

"Was the trailer still hooked up?" Colt asked.

"What?" Casie asked, mind numb as she turned toward him.

"The horse trailer," he said. "Was it still hooked up to Puke?"

"Holy Hannah!" She breathed the words like a curse. "She took the trailer? It doesn't even have lights."

"Where'd she go?" Colt asked.

"I don't know. I was in the bathroom. One minutes she was there, and the next she was gone. Kind of like a stomachache."

CHAPTER 17

Ty scowled into the distance as he strode toward Red Horse Ranch.

The moon, as bright and round as an October pumpkin, flirted with blue-black clouds. Thunder rumbled overhead. Fog rolled up like lacy blossoms, slowly enveloping the cattails that grew beside the Chickasaw. But Ty failed to notice the weather as he marched along. Colt sometimes gave him a ride home from the Lazy at the end of the day, but he didn't want to make a habit of it; he owed too many people too many favors as it was, and anyway, he needed this time alone, time to walk, to think.

Things had changed so dang much since he'd met Casie Carmichael that sometimes he still needed time to adjust, to make sense of things. He'd been beat down. Now he wasn't. Perhaps it was as simple as that. But the whys of the situation bedeviled him. Why did she waste time on a kid like him? A kid with too few skills and too many problems. She had enough troubles of her own. Sophie Jaegar, for instance. Sophie was like a hot-blooded thoroughbred on too short a lead. Trouble on the hoof. She made his pulse race and his hands sweat. But that was just because she was so temperamental, so impossible to understand. She ran hot and cold and scary as hell. But she was also so . . .

He shook his head and exhaled heavily. God knew there were far more important things to worry about than Sophie Jaegar's inexplicable moods. Emily, for instance, who always seemed tough and steady, but was scared spitless on the inside. Or Angel, with the dark, trusting eyes and the deep-throated nicker that made him feel needed, made him feel right. But Angel would have died days ago if it wasn't for Sophie. She'd saved the mare as surely as if she'd performed the operation herself. And why was that? Sophie Jaegar could buy and sell a thousand Angels with the kind of money her daddy had. So why had she decided to help *his* mare?

Against his will, he remembered the brightness of the girl's eyes when she talked about the old gray, but he was sure it wasn't tears. Sophie Jaegar was mean, he reminded himself. She was self-centered and vain and caustic. But sometimes, when he least expected it, he would shift his gaze just so and wonder if he saw someone else in her eyes, someone vulnerable and lost. Someone who needed a champion. Someone who could *be* a champion, who could fight to the death for a broken-down old plug that wasn't worth the price of a bullet. Someone who could fight for a guy who—

He shook his head, trying to dislodge the thoughts from his brain, but the lost little girl was stuck firm in the back of his mind.

Was that how his father had felt at one time? Had he looked at Ty's mother and longed to be braver or better or smarter or stronger? Had he wanted more than anything to be the kind of man that she needed? He shook the idiotic thoughts from his head. It wasn't as if *Ty* felt that way. But Gil Roberts must have had some kind of reason to marry a woman who would never be happy. Ty would be smarter, though. He wasn't going to get caught in that trap. It wasn't as if Sophie Jaegar meant anything to him. It didn't matter that her hair shone like a palomino's burnished coat or that her skin was the color of clover honey, or that now and then, when he least expected it, there was a breathtaking vulnerability to her that made him want to be something he could never be. Something better and—

A light struck him from behind. He jumped, feeling inexplicably guilty for his wandering thoughts. The pickup truck was coming up behind him. He shuffled diagonally off to the side of the road. It was darker than pine tar out here, but when he twisted toward the approaching vehicle, he recognized Puke's single headlight without half trying. Casie's ancient horse trailer rattled behind it, fishtailing on the gravel. Where were they off to at this hour of the—

Angel! Panic struck him like a blow. While he'd been festering over Sophie's mercurial moods, something had happened to Angel. Another bout of colic, probably. Or maybe the laminitis had taken a turn for the worse. They must be headed straight for the vet hospital.

Fear knotted his muscles, freezing him in place, but at the last moment he reached up and tried to flag them down with both hands. It wasn't right that they'd leave without him. She was *his* horse. He'd go with them no matter the outcome. Maybe they thought he was too weak to do what needed doing. Maybe that's why they'd waited until he'd left. He winced, realizing the horrible limitations of their options. Spending more money was out of the question. He knew that. He wasn't a complete idiot. Still, he wouldn't let Angel go through anything without him. He waved again, frantic now. But the truck didn't slow down. Instead, it swerved around him. For a second he caught sight of wide eyes and glossy hair and then dust swirled around him in a gritty vortex.

"Sophie?" he breathed, but she was already hidden from sight. Maybe it was the memory of those lost little girl eyes or maybe it was fear for Angel that made him act. He would never know for sure, but without thinking, without hesitation, he leaped toward the trailer. His fingers curled around the metal slats while his boots hit the rusty fender. His left foot slipped. For a second he was certain he would be thrown onto the gravel like a hapless grasshopper, but he scrambled for footing, tightened his grip, and managed to stay put.

Half choking on the dust and hyperventilating on the adrenaline rush, he gazed into the interior of the trailer. Nothing gazed back. He shoved his face closer to the slats and peered inside more intently, but the conveyance was empty. Even in the darkness, he could see that much. Uncertainty claimed him. Where the hell was Sophie going? And why? She didn't have no license. For a moment he considered jumping off, but she was already picking up speed and she was . . . *Sophie*. Closing his eyes against this new insanity, he flattened himself against the side of the trailer, and hung on for dear life.

Inside the rattletrap pickup truck, Sophie Jaegar curled her fists around the steering wheel and tightened her lips. Anger roared like a gale force wind inside her head. Footage of miserable horses tied in stalls so narrow they could barely shift their weight stormed through her brain. The pictures melded painfully with old memories, memories of Ty with broken lips and eyes cast in shadows. Cruelty, blatant and devastating. She swallowed her bile and stepped on the gas. Behind her, the trailer swiveled wildly. She eased up on the accelerator but didn't touch the brake. She wasn't a complete idiot. She didn't want to send the whole rig spinning into the ditch. That much she knew, but little else.

Rage had taken over. Standing in the living room watching the TV anchor talk about PMU horses with such bored disregard had shot her into action. Although the clip hadn't shown the interior of the particular barn she was headed for, she had recognized the farm featured on the news clip. It was an out-of-the-way place on a little-known gravel road, a road she'd often traversed between her father's condo and the Lazy Windmill.

Her hands shook as she turned off the highway. Puke's right front tire hit a pothole and she gasped. The anger had worn down a little, turning to bitter uncertainty. But she drove on. Another right turn brought her onto a rutted gravel road that wound around a murky slough.

The farm stood on a small hill a quarter of a mile or so to the north. It was fully dark now, but there was a light on in the yard. A shelterbelt, a narrow band of Russian olives and blue spruce, grew beside the road. She pulled past the edge of it, shifted into neutral, and shut off the truck. She would be all but hidden from view of the house now. Still, uncertainty kept her frozen in place. Who the hell did she think she was? Some superhero come to right the wrongs of the world? She was just a kid. If she had a brain in her head, she'd go home. Then she could rant and rave and insist that someone do something, knowing all the while that no one would expect that someone to be *her*. But the image of the horses loomed in her mind again. Reaching to her right, she curled her fingers around the camera she'd taken from Emily's room. Her left hand moved out of its own accord. The driver's door squeaked as she stepped out of the truck. Her knees felt less than steady as she eased the door shut, trying to be silent. Her nerve, so sharp and clear when she was standing in the Lazy's warm kitchen, seemed to have abandoned her completely. But the pictures on the television gnawed at her brain like nasty rodents.

She swallowed hard, straightened her spine, and took a step toward the farm.

"What are you—"

She jumped back with a shriek, raising her arms in a wild effort to protect herself from the monster that accosted her.

But the monster morphed quickly into human form. "Soph! Geez, Sophie!"

She stepped back, heart pounding, mind desperately trying to make sense of things.

"Ty?" The name sounded shaky and ridiculous to her ears, an unshapely meld of terror and hope. "Ty!" Anger came quickly on the heels of the relief she was sure she shouldn't be feeling. She hated surprises, and glanced around now, sure she'd been followed, sure her plans, unformed as they were, would be thwarted. She refused to admit that just seconds ago she had desperately hoped that would be the case. "What are you doing here?"

"What am *I* doing here?" He looked around. There was little enough to see, just a lone farm with a few run-down buildings and a yard light making a poor attempt to pierce the gloom. "Where *is* here?"

Her legs felt wooden, her hands sweaty. What the hell was going on? She paced past the trailer, looking for his vehicle. "How did you even get here?"

"How do you think?" He waved wildly at nothing in particular, anger or something like it making his tone tight. "You almost ran me over. You drive like a . . ." He shook his head and blew out a breath. "What the devil are you doing? You don't even have no license."

"Were you . . ." Things were unclear in her mind, skewed by fear, made jagged by the sharp rush of adrenaline. She shook her head, trying to see past the tail of the trailer. "Neither do you. How—" She stopped breathing, remembering she'd passed him on the road. "Did you grab on to the trailer? Were you hanging on to the side the whole time?"

"You gotta slow down when you're pulling a load, Soph. It can jackknife on you, you know. And if you're hauling a horse, you can't drive nearly so fast."

"I didn't have . . ." She shook her head. "You were hanging on the trailer?" She scowled at the rusty fender, the pockmarked slats. "Are you nuts?"

"No more than you, looks like. What are we doing here?"

"*We're* not doing anything here," she said, and gathering her nerve, skirted around him to head for the barn.

"Soph." She could hear him turn toward her, could hear him scramble after. "Sophie! What's going on?"

"Nothing! Go home."

"Sure. I'll do that." She heard him stop. "I'll just leave you here. But just so I got some idea what to tell Casie when they find your hacked-up body along the side of the road, where the hell *is* here?"

She felt herself blanch, hated herself for her weakness, and worked hard to dredge up a modicum of the rage she'd felt just a short time before. She straightened her back. "This is the place your hero was talking about."

"What?" Confusion echoed in his voice.

"The farrier," she said, lowering her voice. Off in the darkness somewhere, a dog barked. Her stomach knotted. "Sam told us about it."

He shook his head.

"The PMU mares are kept here!" she snapped.

"I don't know what you're talking about," he said, but his voice was low, too.

"Pregnant mare urine," she said, leaning close to rasp the words into his face. "I just saw it on the news. They collect the stuff here, then send it to the big pharmaceutical companies out east."

His brows were pulled low over his thousand-secrets eyes. "So?"

"So?" She hissed the word, glared at him, then, for lack of anything more constructive, ground her teeth and ducked between two strands of barbed wire fencing. Something rustled in the scraggly sour dock that grew to her left. She jerked spasmodically, then gritted her teeth at her own cowardice and crept silently forward, though she didn't have a reason for her stealth. She couldn't see two feet in front of her face. A bat wouldn't be able to find her in this darkness. Although a big dog might be able to. She winced at the thought and glanced to the side. Something slithered across the toe of her boot. She swallowed and resisted grabbing Ty's arm, though he had caught up to her.

"Why—" he began again, but she snarled at him.

"It's inhumane," she said.

"What's inhumane?"

"The way they treat these mares," she said and turned abruptly toward him. Reminding herself with every word that she had a mission, she dredged up her anger. "It's barbaric," she said and winced as she saw his face. In the darkness, it almost seemed that she could still see the discoloration around his battered eye. The discoloration that his own worthless mother had caused. But that wasn't *her* problem. Casie had come to his rescue. Sophie Jaegar wasn't anybody's hero. Not any human's anyway. But horses . . . maybe horses were another matter entirely. "It's cruel and stupid and—"

"I'm sorry."

His simple words stopped her cold. Because he *was* sorry. She could hear it in his voice. Could feel it in his presence. How could someone who had been hurt so much by his own mother still care? She was still angry because *her* mom hadn't given her a cell phone until her fourteenth birthday. "They're kept in tie stalls for months at a time," she said and carefully stifled the confusing emotions that stormed through her.

"Why?"

"Pregnant mares have something in their urine that's used in drugs for women's menopause problems. That urine has to be collected, and the easiest way to do it is to keep them immobilized."

His lips twitched. His brows lowered. "Well, that ain't right, Soph. But lots of animal ain't treated no better. Pigs are confined all the time. Dairy—"

"These aren't pigs!" The words left her lips in a rush, though she knew he had a valid point. "And they're not cattle. These are horses." Her eyes stung and her cheeks felt hot. "The species that's been serving mankind since people drew pictures in caves. Don't you think they deserve a little more from us than this?" She waved vaguely toward the farm.

Ty opened his mouth, but she hurried on, though she didn't know why. It wasn't as if she'd ever cared about his opinion.

"They don't need that urine anyway. There are synthetic ways to make the same type of drug."

"It sucks, Soph. I see that, but—"

"They constrict their water."

She watched his lips twitch, saw the pain in his face, but she didn't let that stop her.

"They're mostly draft horses, big mares that'll produce more pee, so being confined is going to be harder on their joints. And the tight spaces get even tighter as their fetuses grow and their bellies—"

"Soph!" He stopped her, sounding almost desperate. "There ain't nothing we can do."

"No," she agreed, and drawing a deep breath, straightened

her spine. "There's nothing. Go home," she said and turned away.

He caught her arm. She stopped in midstride and gazed down at his hand for a second. "Listen, Ty," she said. "You can't be here. I get that. Casie has enough legal trouble already."

He flinched and even as she reveled in her ability to strike a direct blow, she cursed herself. What the hell was wrong with her? It wasn't as if he didn't have enough guilt without her piling on more, but she blew out a breath and continued on.

"You shouldn't be here," she repeated and pulled her arm from his grasp, "but I should."

"What are you going to do?"

She turned resolutely away. "It's not going to do anyone any good if I tell you that," she said. Besides, her plan was sketchy at best.

"Soph!" He marched after her, strides long and noisy through the scraggly weeds of the pasture. "This is somebody else's property. You can't just go barging—"

"What about the foals?" she asked, and feeling herself buoyed by her belated revelation, faced him again.

"What?"

She pursed her lips. "There are tens of thousands of these mares," she said. "Maybe hundreds of thousands. Each one of them has to give birth every single year."

"Yeah?" He sounded tentative.

"What do you think happens to the babies?"

She could hear his teeth grind.

"The economy sucks." She kept her voice quiet, letting him think. "And it's not like these mares are anything special. They're just cash on the hoof. They're just bred . . ." She shrugged. "To be bred." Her eyes stung. She took a deep breath and marshaled her anger. "So if the mare's only value is in her urine, her foal has no worth at all."

"Animals are slaughtered all the time," he said, but his voice was oddly husky. "There ain't nothing better than Em's blue beef Stroganoff."

"So you think this is okay?" Her voice sounded self-righteous even to her own ears, but in the darkest part of her mind, she hoped he would say yes. It was fine. This was none of her concern. He would drag her back to the Lazy where she could seethe and carry on and blame him for being weak and uncaring and barbaric.

But somewhere far away a horse nickered. The sound was low and hopeful. Ty glanced up. His jaw was set. Silence set in. "What's our plan?" he asked. His voice was very quiet, barely heard above the night sounds.

Her stomach twisted. She tried to repeat that he wasn't included in her plan. But the look on his face did something to her. It weakened her, softened her, made her irresistibly grateful that he was there. "I'm going to take photographs," she said.

He stared at her.

"There were only pictures of the outside of the building. The news clip showed the interior of other barns. But nothing of this one. Maybe if I could get real footage of the horses' conditions to the local media, we could get this place shut down."

For a while she thought he would argue. For even longer she *hoped* he would, but finally he drew a deep breath and turned toward the farmstead in the distance. "Ain't never going to be no time like now, I suppose," he said and turned toward the light on the hill.

She swallowed, fear making her knees weak. "Maybe . . ."

He paused to glance over his shoulder at her. She could see little more than the outline of his face, the high jut of his cheekbones, the sharp cast of his jaw, but that was enough. There was something about his silhouette that looked absolutely resolute, not like her, not scared out of her wits even though she'd never suffered a real hardship in her entire life.

She nodded once and stepped up beside him. Their footsteps seemed ungodly loud in the stillness. The yard light vaguely illuminated five buildings.

"That must be the horse barn," he said. It was a long, low building sided with galvanized steel.

She nodded, unable to speak. Anger had worn off completely now, leaving her with nothing but the ashy taste of fear. Beyond the barn, the house stood tall and gray in the darkness. A light shone from one of the far windows. She swallowed, hating herself. "Maybe we should wait until they fall asleep."

He watched her in the darkness. It was not until that moment that she saw her own fear reflected in his eyes. But he spoke nevertheless. "We're already all saddled up, Soph."

"But we shouldn't have to wait long." She said the words too quickly, too eagerly. She slowed her pace, took a deep breath. "REM's the deepest shortly after people fall asleep and—"

"You think Case won't come looking for you?"

She had no idea why she hadn't considered that possibility. She blinked. "She doesn't know where I am."

"She ain't stupid, Soph. She'll talk to Em, know you seen that clip on TV, and put two and two together."

She felt herself wince. Felt herself nod.

"Okay," she said and ground her hands into fists. "Let's go."

They crept forward in tandem. The overhead light became brighter. It felt as hot and revealing as a spotlight against her face. She froze when they reached the next fence, unable to go on.

He looked at her, paused. Maybe there was something in her eyes, because he nodded once and said, "I ain't the best photographer in the world, but I can get the job done."

She couldn't speak. She wasn't sure why, but she hoped to hell it wasn't due to gratitude. Still, she remained silent, staring at him.

"Listen . . ." His voice was very low. He glanced at the farmstead again, just yards away now. "I think you should go back, get Puke outta here."

She blinked at him, barely able to do that much.

"I mean, what if someone sees it there? It ain't like it's inconspicuous. And I don't want to get Casie in no more trouble."

"Are you saying . . ." She swallowed. Even that was difficult. "You want me to leave you here alone?"

"Better I walk home unnoticed than I go in a squad car."

She felt herself pale. "We're not going to get arrested. We're just taking pictures," she said, but her voice was barely audible.

"We're trespassing, Soph." He leaned close when he said the words. "Some of these old farmers take that real personal. 'Specially if they got things to hide." He turned toward the barn. There was something about the place that felt wrong. Maybe it was her own fear that made her think so, but he narrowed his eyes, seeming to feel the same.

"We're not going to get arrested," she repeated, but her voice shook.

"Then you better get that rig outta here," he said.

He was right. He was so right. He would be better at sneaking around anyway. He'd probably spent half his life trying to be invisible. And if there were two of them it would make it twice as likely that they'd be seen. And . . .

And when had she become such a coward?

She stared at him, locked her knees, and straightened her spine. "You want the truck moved, *you* do it," she said.

They faced off in utter silence.

"Could be you're the stubbornest girl ever was born," he said finally, but his eyes spoke of something other than loathing. It might have been admiration. Dear God, it might have been *affection.* "Come on, then," he said, and curling his fingers around a smooth expanse of wire, pressed the other strand down with his foot before reaching for her with his free hand. Their fingers touched. Something sparked warm and hopeful between them. Their gazes brushed. Feelings rushed through her, but she reined them in and ducked through the fence, feet barely touching the ground.

She held her breath as they tiptoed through the darkness toward the barn. Every snap of a twig, every sigh of the breeze made her heart leap, but in a moment they were at the door. They shared one furtive glance before he twisted the latch. The door groaned as he pulled it open.

The odor was the first thing that assaulted her senses. Not the comforting scents of horse sweat and hay, but the rancid smell of rotting manure and despair.

Ty said something she had never heard pass his lips, something Casie would disapprove of. Maybe it was the sound of his suppressed anger that brought up her nerve, or maybe it was the smell of the place, the acrid odor of hopelessness, that strengthened her resolve.

His fingers tightened on hers, but not as if he was trying to tell her something. More like he couldn't help himself. As if the conditions reminded him of something too painful to be borne alone. She squeezed back and in that moment they were comrades. He was the first one to speak.

"That camera have flash?" he whispered and nodded toward the Canon that hung from her neck.

"It's Emily's."

She could feel his immediate disapproval. "You took Em's camera?"

She felt jealousy rise beneath the surface. What did Em have that she didn't? Sophie was richer, probably smarter, definitely bitchier. She contained her wince at the thought and felt her anger bubble down to a soft boil. "I'm just borrowing it," she said. Her tone was a little more caustic than she had intended, but he didn't drop her hand. The point of contact was as warm as sunlight on her skin.

"Well . . ." He was scowling. "I guess if anybody'll be for saving babies, it'll be Em," he said.

She felt her gut twist at the affection in his tone, but managed to keep her mouth shut.

"Anyway, her camera's got a flash. I'm sure of that, but I don't know if things'll show up good without there being a light on. And how we going to know what we're taking pictures of in the dark?"

Sophie swallowed, fear sloshing over her other emotions. "They'll see us for sure from the house if we turn on the lights."

"Maybe we can find something that's out of the way some. A room in back that'll be harder to notice. I'll go look," he whispered, but it was practically impossible to let go of his hand so she tagged along.

They stumbled over a threshold and into a larger area. The smell was stronger here. A horse nickered. There was the sound of heavy hooves shuffling.

Then something exploded.

Ty jumped. Sophie ducked. But nothing else happened. No shots were fired. No one screamed for them to leave. Neither did the noise cease. Instead, it became louder, more insistent.

"Pawing," Ty said, voice strained. "Just a horse pawing."

She nodded. They skimmed the wall to their left. A horse snorted and jumped, making them stop in their tracks, hearts racing.

"Easy. It's all right," Sophie soothed, but her hands were unsteady. They had no way of knowing how far they were from the horses. Nor did they know if these particular animals would kick. If she was as mistreated as these animals surely were, she might be a little mean. Hell, she was mean anyway.

Ty tightened his fingers and tugged her along.

He stumbled suddenly, making her gasp. But in a moment he straightened. "Watch your step," he said. "I think we've found what we're looking for."

She swallowed, not sure if that was good news or bad.

Feeling their way along a wall, they stepped into what felt like a smaller room. She shut the door behind them, then felt around in search of a light switch. She found one at last and pushed it up. Light blasted on above them, seeming hideously bright. Sophie blinked and shielded her eyes, but in a moment her pupils had adjusted. They stood in what had once been a milking parlor. Barely a hundred feet square, it had only one small window facing the road.

"You okay?" Ty's eyes were dark and earnest, his voice very soft.

"Yes." Her own was barely audible.

"You sure?"

"Of course." She cleared her throat and searched for strength. It was being pretty furtive. "Why?"

"No reason. I just . . . I think I might be losing circulation in my fingers."

She dropped his hand like a hot poker and waited for him to laugh at her, but his expression remained unchanged.

"It ain't too late to get that truck outta here," he said.

She stared at him, grateful to the core of her being, lost in his eyes, drowning in his kindness.

"Soph?" he said, and she jerked.

"*You* can leave if you're scared," she said and hated herself for the words.

He watched her for a moment in silence, then said, "I'm going to open the door a ways. You tell me when you think there's enough light to take your pictures."

She nodded. Unable to look at him, she turned toward the interior of the barn as he pushed the door open.

Dozens of horses stood in two long, ragged lines. Their shaggy heads were turned toward her. A harness was strapped to each mare. Even in the dim light, the chafing around the animals' flanks was apparent. A narrow rope was tied around each tail and rubber tubing ran from under their docks and away. The stalls were too narrow for them to lie down even if their harnesses would have allowed it. Their bellies were distended with unborn foals.

Sophie's vision was still blurred with tears when she began snapping pictures. The pawing continued, a hopeless, metallic sound that gnawed on her nerves and ate at her soul.

"Soph," Ty hissed.

"I'm almost done," she said, but suddenly the overhead lights snapped on. She gasped and jerked toward the doorway. A giant of a man was silhouetted there. Or maybe it was the rifle in his hands that made him look so huge.

CHAPTER 18

"What the hell's going on?" the giant growled at Sophie.

Ty had ducked inside a stall like a cowering rabbit. Beside him, a nervous mare stopped pawing to lean away from him in terror. "Easy," he whispered, then shifted his gaze to a narrow hole between the planks of the stall.

Near the west door, the giant shrank to human proportions. He was just a man, just a man, Ty told himself.

"What you doing here?" he asked and shifted his gaze from side to side, searching for others. Ty held perfectly still. Sophie, too, remained exactly as she was, poised between the two rows of horses. The camera was lifted halfway to her face. Her eyes were round and rimmed with white. She looked very small suddenly. Small and fragile and alone.

Ty knew he should save her, should grab her and run, but he was immobilized, frozen in the tight confines of a chestnut mare's stall. And that's where he remained, where his courage abandoned him completely.

"Christ, you must want it bad to be stumbling around in the dark like a damned ghoul." He scowled. His head was bare, his hair thinning, though he couldn't be more than forty years old. "Who sent you anyways?"

She stared at him, face pale in the glaring light. "No one sent me."

He cocked his head a little, thinking. "Then how did you hear about us?"

"I saw you on the news."

His brows shot up. "You're lying," he said and took a step forward. "I wasn't on TV."

She skittered back a step. "Not *you*," she said and jerked her head to the right as if indicating the place at large. "The farm."

"What you talking about?"

Sophie lifted her chin. "It's not right," she said.

He snorted. "It's not my fault if people shoot up, then—" He stopped himself. "What's not right?"

"The horses." She all but spat the words. "You can't keep them in these conditions."

"Horses," he said and laughed. "Christ, you're just a kid, ain't you?"

She didn't respond. Ty dipped a little lower and forced himself to glance to the side, to try to marshal his senses in an effort to plan a means of escape. There was another door at the far end of the barn, but there was no way to guess if it would even open. Lots of these old buildings had been boarded up tight.

A scrape of noise snapped Ty's attention back to the farmer, who propped his rifle against a nearby beam. He raised his hands as if to say he was harmless, smiled as if to assure her they were friends, and took a step toward her. "Listen, honey, let's start fresh. My name's Pete Whitesel. What's yours?"

She didn't answer.

He smiled. "Okay. How about this one? How'd you get here?"

Sophie shook her head, her gaze never leaving the man. They were only about forty feet apart. "What you're doing is wrong," she said.

He narrowed his eyes at her, tilted his head a little. "You a friend of Vick's?"

She scowled at him. "They deserve better," she said, but her usual bravado was missing, her voice barely audible.

"Guy's gotta make a buck," Whitesel said, "and it's not like we're shoving bamboo slivers under their little hooves or something. They're perfectly content. Except for that one," he said, nodding to the chestnut beside which Ty crouched. "She's one crazy bitch."

Sophie darted her gaze toward Ty's hiding place and away. "I'd be crazy, too, if you kept me caged up twenty-four hours a day."

"Maybe you *are* crazy," Whitesel said and grinned a little. He was short and stocky with a slanted grin and a round face. "How'd you get here, anyway? And who are you?"

Ty held his breath, willing her not to answer. But Sophie Jaegar was nobody's fool.

"I'm the voice of the horse," she said.

Whitesel paused, maybe taken aback by her melodramatic tone. "Really?" He chuckled. "I thought a horse's voice would be . . ." He shrugged. "Taller."

She pursed her lips. "I don't think this is funny."

"Well, maybe not," he said and settled a beefy shoulder comfortably against a nearby post. "But at least it's legal."

"What?"

"I'm not doing nothing illegal," he said, nodding toward the rows of confined mares. "I've got all the appropriate paperwork in the house if you'd like to see it. Listen, these animals is kept fed and dry. Hell, they're not even going to be eaten. That's more than can be said for half the animals in this state."

"That doesn't make it right."

He shook his head as if amused by her fervor. "Where did you come from, honey?" he asked. "I didn't hear you drive up." He cocked up one quizzical brow. "Are you even old enough to drive?"

"I'm old enough to know an injustice when I see it," she said.

He smiled. "A little girl with convictions." His eyes looked very bright. His mouth twisted up a little. He sighed. "Listen, why don't you come on up to the house? We can have some coke . . . a glass of Coke," he said, smiling as if he had made a joke.

"How can you live with yourself?"

He laughed. "You're a real Girl Scout, ain't you?" Something pinged on the metal roof. Ty jumped, but Whitesel just canted his head. "Sounds like it's starting to rain. Come on. I'll give you a ride home."

She hesitated. For a moment Ty thought she would glance toward him, would reveal his presence, but she was far braver than he. Brave enough to stand alone. "You're not going to get these pictures," she said.

He laughed again. "I don't want your pictures, cutie. Like I said . . . " He motioned to her to hurry. The rain was louder now, making it hard to hear. "This is all good and legal."

"So you're not going to try to stop me?"

"What do I look like? The big bad wolf?" His teeth looked yellow in the sharp overhead lights.

She didn't answer, and he laughed at her reticence. "Come on," he said again. "Before all hell breaks loose out there."

She remained where she was.

Ty swallowed, desperately trying to coax up a modicum of courage.

"Seriously," Whitesel said and stepped forward, "I'm not gonna hurt you. Why would I? You're just one girl voicing her opinion. Right?" He was only a few yards from her now. "Right?"

"I think I'll walk home," she said.

"What's going on?"

Ty jerked his gaze past the chestnut's hindquarters as someone stepped through an unknown door behind him.

"What took you so damn long?" Whitesel asked.

Maybe it was the dark timbre of his voice that made Ty act. Maybe it was some instinct older than time. But whatever the case, he suddenly snapped to his feet. Panicked, the chestnut reared back, and in that second Ty reached forward and jerked her tie loose. She reared, pivoting wildly. For an instant she was stuck in the stall's narrow confines, but then she jolted away, ripping her tail loose of its rope, tearing the catheter free. The falling apparatus only frightened her more. She leaped from her stall like a loosed torpedo. Racing around the corner, she charged for the door at the east end of the barn. Whitesel dove out of her path just as Ty jumped over the stall into the wide aisle.

With freedom in her sights, the mare careened past Sophie, then skittered onto the wet concrete outside. Ungainly and terrified, she crashed to the ground. The sound was sickening, deafening. But Ty was already beside her. He grabbed the flapping leather tie out of sheer instinct and steadied her as she lurched to her feet, but Whitesel was already coming, racing toward the door, rifle in hand, eyes wide with fury.

Terror spurred through Ty at the sight. "Let's go!" he yelled.

Sophie turned toward him in silent questioning, but he was already pivoting toward the mare. Grabbing her tangled mane, he swung aboard. She half reared, but he reached for Sophie's hand. "Come on!" he rasped.

There was a moment of hesitation and then their fingers met. Whitesel raised his rifle. A bullet exploded. The mare pivoted away in panic, nearly ripping Sophie from Ty's fingers, but somehow their grips held. The momentum snatched Sophie from the ground. Reaching for his waist with her left arm, she swung up behind him.

One moment they were standing still and the next they were galloping, racing across an open field, holding on for dear life, cursing and praying as they sped north, directly *away* from old Puke.

There were garbled shouts from behind them. "Get the car."

". . . busted my leg."

"Don't be—"

But the rest of the words were lost in the wind, in the rain.

"Turn her around!" Sophie ordered. Her lips all but brushed Ty's ear. Her breasts bumped his back. But he couldn't even think about *that*. Staying aboard was all consuming. "Hurry. Turn her."

It took all Ty's strength to get the animal turned around, all his teetering balance to stay astride. But the mare was game. She plowed off toward the south, leaping through the night like a wild mustang. Stumbling up the ditch, she nearly fell to her knees as she skittered onto the gravel road thirty yards from the horse trailer. She was huffing. Her heaving ribs felt like wooden lathes against Ty's calves. He pulled her in a tight circle. Headlights raced down the drive, then turned east before careening north.

Sophie slipped to the ground. Ty followed suit, his legs barely supporting him as he reached solid footing. "Let's go," he said, and setting the mare free, pivoted toward the truck, but Sophie had already grabbed the mare's lead and was tugging her toward the trailer.

"Help me."

He stopped in his tracks and flashed his gaze toward the speeding headlights. "No." He knew what she was thinking. Knew it beyond a shadow of a doubt. "They're going to find us in a second."

"Open the trailer!" she barked.

For a moment he considered arguing, but agreement was the quickest way to depart. He swung the door open. Sophie jumped into the vehicle, tugging as she went, but the mare resisted, hauling against the lead.

Ty swore quietly. The headlights were out of sight now, but it wouldn't be long until they circled the whole farm and found them in the middle of the road. "Let her go," he said. "Just let her go."

But Sophie didn't even seem to hear him. Instead, she stepped down from the trailer and raised a soothing hand toward the mare. "It's okay," she said. "It's all right."

Ty swore in silence this time, although it clearly was not all right; that man had a rifle!

"Sophie," he said, trying to keep his tone level, "we gotta go."

"I know it's dark," she said, her tone smooth as satin as she continued to ignore him. "I know you're hurt. But if you'll just trust me . . . just for a little while . . . I can help you."

The mare took a tentative step toward her.

Ty turned his attention to the north. The headlights appeared again, swinging wildly to the left, heading west.

"Sophie . . ." he warned.

"Get some grain," she said.

"Wh—"

"Oats!" she said. Though she didn't raise her voice or change the smooth cadence, the words were clearly a command. "I think there's some in the back of the truck."

Ty squeezed his eyes shut, gritted his teeth, and galloped off to do her bidding. Lightning cracked overhead, illuminating the contents of Puke's truck bed. Yanking the cover off a feed can, Ty scooped up some grain.

The mare jerked and snorted as he reappeared around the trailer door, but the headlights were getting closer and there was no time to lose. He shoved the pail under the mare's nose. She took a tentative taste. He pulled the bucket toward the trailer and she followed.

"Thatta girl," Sophie said. "Thatta girl." In a moment she had stepped back into the trailer. "Holy crap, I'd give a kidney for some lights," she said.

"Lights!" Ty's voice was as soft as hers, but breathy with un-bridled fear. "If you're going to be giving up internal organs at least trade them for something useful." He stepped up beside her. Rain struck the metal roof in a loud patter, soaking his right shoulder as he leaned into the onslaught, offering the grain again. The mare stretched her neck.

"Like what?" Sophie asked. "Come on, mare. You can do this."

"Like a hard-ass attorney," he suggested, and in that second the mare stepped into the trailer.

Sophie hurried backward and the mare hopped in. Nervous, but game, she thrust her head back into the bucket.

After that it was just a couple heart-thumping seconds before she was locked inside and they were racing toward the cab.

"You drive!" Sophie rasped and pressed the keys into his hand. Then, yanking the passenger door open, she dove inside.

There was nothing he could do but follow suit. His hands were still shaking as he shoved the key into the ignition. The engine rattled to life.

"They're coming!" Sophie said.

He slammed into first. Gears ground, but they jerked forward.

"Lights!" she said, but he was shaking his head.

"No lights."

"What?" She swung around to stare out the back window. "I can't see anything."

"It's not like we can outrun them," he said. Their tires spun on the gravel.

"Hurry up!"

He shifted into second, ground into third. The headlights had almost reached the crossroad behind, just about to turn toward them. They looked close enough to spit on. It was darker than hell. But there had to be a side road to turn onto soon. Maybe just past the stand of trees that grew beside—

"Turn right!" Sophie shouted.

"What?"

"Turn!"

He did so without thinking, without seeing. They careened off the road. Ty gasped, Sophie shrieked, the trailer bumped like a bucking bronco and then the engine died, spilling them into silence.

They held their breath. The car behind them fishtailed into the turn behind them. Headlights filled their mirrors. Their pursuers screamed up to them . . . and tore past.

Ty watched the taillights fade into the distance. He blinked, exhaled. "Holy—" he began, but in that second Sophie kissed him.

The air left his lungs. His hands steadied on the steering wheel. And his heart . . . his heart might have stopped entirely.

She smelled like courage and fear, like hope and despair and the kind of beauty that lasts forever. By the time she drew away, his head felt light.

"I'm . . ." He had no idea what he should say. Not an inkling what he should do. "I'm sorry," he said.

She blinked at him, then drew slowly back. Her hands, he noticed, weren't shaking. Her voice was perfectly level.

"We'd better get home," she said.

CHAPTER 19

"Where could she be?" Casie's face was taut with worry, her eyes wide and wild with it. Colt watched her pace the length of the kitchen. They'd made a quick circuit around the countryside. For a while they had hoped to catch Sophie. After all, Puke was hardly ready for NASCAR, but the cloud of dust they were following turned out to be made by Greg Ruff in his International Harvester. The soybean harvest was gearing up.

"I told you everything I know," Emily said. She'd given up washing dishes and was now focusing all of her considerable attention on Casie's frantic face.

"She was watching television, right?" Casie prompted.

"Yeah."

"The news."

"Case, I told you everything I—" she began, but in that instant Colt came up with an idea.

"What station?" he asked.

They turned toward him in unison, two women strong enough to scare the bejeezus out of him.

"What?"

"What station?" he asked again. "Maybe I can call them. Get more information."

Hope sprang into Casie's eyes, and for a moment, just a second in time, it took his breath away.

"The guy with the face caterpillar," Emily said.

Colt turned to her. He usually tracked her crazy thoughts pretty well, but this time . . . "Face . . ."

"The unibrow. You know," she said. "The weather guy with the Cro-Magnon—" She stopped herself. "Three. I think it was channel three."

Colt jerked a nod and pulled his cell phone from his pocket. Casie's eyes followed his hand as he jabbed in 411.

"What time was it exactly?" he asked as the phone rang.

"I don't know *exactly,*" Em said.

"Well, guess!" Casie said. "Just—"

"Hey," Colt said, jumping in. "Let's just calm down a little." In some distant portion of his mind, he wondered how many times he had said approximately the same thing in this very house.

"Calm down?" Casie turned on him like a cornered cougar, reminding him that saying those particular words had rarely done so much as a sliver of good. "Sophie's gone! She's gone! That could be even worse than concussed. I mean, at least when she was kicked in the head, we knew where she was. We knew—"

He held up a hand to stop her tirade when someone answered the phone.

"City and state, please."

He covered the mouthpiece and swore in silence. "What city is channel three out of?"

"I don't know," Em said.

"Sioux Falls?" Casie suggested.

Colt gritted his teeth. "Sioux Falls, South Dakota?"

"What listing can I find for you in Sioux Falls?" The operator's voice sounded ultimately reasonable.

"Channel three news."

"Checking Sioux Falls for channel three . . ." She paused. "I'm sorry, sir. I don't see any listing for channel three in—" she began, but suddenly there was a disturbance in the yard.

Casie spun toward the door. By the time Colt reached her side, Puke's lone headlight was sweeping across the yard.

Colt slipped the phone into his pocket just as Casie sprinted outside.

"Sophie!" Her voice was little more than a hiss as she galloped down the stairs and raced across the yard. The girl was out of the truck almost before it pulled to a halt. "Where have you been?"

Sophie stopped in her tracks and spun toward them as if surprised they were there.

"And what—" Casie's words sputtered to a halt as Ty stepped out from behind the steering wheel. "Ty?"

He nodded, his face shadowed in the yard light.

She stared at him, glanced at Sophie, turned to Colt. He shrugged. God knew he rarely had an inkling what was going on here.

"Where were you?" she asked. Her tone was breathless. "We were worried—"

It was then that something exploded inside the trailer. They jerked toward it in unison. It took a second to recognize the sound of anxious pawing.

Casie's face looked pale in the dim overhead light. "What's in the trailer?" Her voice sounded extremely reasonable.

Behind him, the screen door slammed again as Emily exited the house at a slower rate.

Ty cleared his throat. Sophie stiffened.

"Soph?" Casie said, tone absolutely steady now, low, soft, maybe a little eerie. "Talk to me."

The girl raised her chin in that cowboy up way of hers. "I had to do something," she said.

Casie turned her head toward the trailer a little. It was impossible to be sure, but it almost seemed as if she was holding her breath. "Something?"

"It's wrong!" Sophie said, emotion spewing up suddenly. "You know it's wrong. Those mares—"

Casie held up a hand. To Colt's never-ending surprise, the motion stopped Sophie dead in her verbal tracks. "What mares?"

No one spoke.

"Is this about the news clip Sam told us about?" Casie asked.

"This is about abuse!" Sophie raged. "This is about neglect and stupidity and—"

Casie held up her hand again. Again the verbal barrage stopped.

"Tell me what happened."

"It ain't her fault," Ty said.

They turned toward the boy in surprise. In the six months since he'd been hanging around the Lazy, Colt had never known him to interrupt the woman he idolized.

Ty winced, shuffled his feet, and looked like he would rather die than disappoint her.

"I mean . . . them horses *was* being mistreated."

Casie stared at him a second before turning toward Sophie with a grimace of apprehension. "Please tell me there's not a horse in that trailer," she said. When no one spoke, she turned like a marionette and goose-stepped past Puke. Curling her fingers through the open slats near the top, she pulled herself onto the fender and peered inside. The banging stopped for a moment. She stepped back down. "There's a horse in the trailer." She said the words numbly and turned to Colt like one in a trance.

He shrugged, cleared his throat, and tried a tentative grin. "Maybe they bought it."

It was a ludicrous suggestion. No one knew that better than he, but Casie was nothing if not hopeful and turned toward the kids with breathless optimism.

"Did you buy it?" she asked. No one spoke. "Please tell me you bought it."

Sophie pursed her lips. "They don't give them enough water," she said. The night fell silent for several beats before she spoke again. "Kidney failure is common among PMU horses even if—"

"Holy Hannah," Casie murmured.

It was then that Linette appeared. She looked like nothing so much as a small, wizened gnome in the darkness. "What's going on?"

"Oh!" Casie jumped as if shot. "Linette. I thought you were . . ." She skimmed her eyes to the kids. Emily took a step forward, braving the insanity with chipper ease. "Sophie just bought a new horse."

Linette's brows jumped up as she turned toward Casie. "Really?"

Casie blinked. Emily gave her a pointed stare. "Yes," she managed finally. "A . . ." Maybe she was in shock. Maybe she was just searching frantically for some kind of lie that wouldn't get them all arrested. "She just picked her up."

"Huh! I didn't even know she had her driver's license."

The yard went silent. Casie shot her gaze to Colt. It was frantic and hopeful and needy. And damned if he could think of anything to do but jump in, too.

"Friends," he said and took a step forward, though he hadn't a clue why he wanted to be closer to this fiasco. "Friends of mine. They've had this colt for sale for a while now."

"Mare," Sophie corrected.

"Mare," Colt mimicked and added a decisive nod.

Casie followed the conversation as if it were a tennis match.

"At eight o'clock at night?" Linette asked, and pacing toward the trailer, peered inside. "Wow, she looks kind of pot-bellied, doesn't she?"

Casie closed her eyes.

"She's pregnant," Sophie said.

Some sort of noise escaped Casie's lips. It might have been a moan. Might have been a hiss. Colt was just glad she stayed on her feet. In fact, he stepped up next to her as a kind of last-ditch support system should her knees fail. As for Linette, she snapped her gaze to the two of them. Casie forced a smile. It looked ghoulish in the darkness.

"You okay?" the older woman asked.

"Me? Sure," Casie said. "I just don't know . . ." She shrugged. "Pregnant mares can be difficult to . . . Well . . . I suppose we'd better get her out of there."

Sophie stared at her for a full four seconds, then nodded once and marched to the back of the trailer. The door groaned as she swung it open. The mare came out like a bullet, dragging the girl with her. She hit the ground hard with her front hooves then her knees before struggling up and circling wildly at the end of what looked like a leather lead.

Linette backed off. The woman was no idiot, Colt thought.

"Where should I put her?" Sophie asked. Despite the fact that the mare was still circling nervously, her tone was snooty and terse. For Sophie it was pretty subdued.

"She can use one of the new stalls."

"She doesn't really like to be . . ." The mare spooked, throwing her head up and springing off her feet, legs braced against the world. "Confined," she finished.

Casie looked as if she'd like to die . . . or kill.

Sophie tightened her grip on the lead and laid one hand against the mare's long, scrawny neck. "She's been locked up for so long."

"It's the best we've got for tonight."

Sophie almost argued. Even in the darkness, Colt could see the mutiny in her eyes, but finally she nodded and led the mare toward the barn. Ty hurried ahead and snapped on the switch beside the door. The others followed more slowly.

Inside the cluttered building, the mare danced on the end of the leather line, swinging her rear end this way and that to take in the sights.

That's when Angel thrust her head over her Dutch door and nickered at her. The mare jolted to a halt and trumpeted back, legs spread.

It took a few minutes for Sophie to coax the chestnut toward the newly finished stall, but finally she was inside. She circled the enclosure, stopping only to sniff Angel's nose through the open planking, squeal, and circle again.

"She looks kind of skittish," Linette said. Her tone was dubious. "Is that why they sold her?"

No one spoke for a moment. Ty jumped in, his usually slow voice atypically quick.

"They're moving," he said. "Had to get rid of the horses."

"So she was their only one?" Linette asked. Her tone was innocent, but her expression looked kind of foxy.

Ty and Sophie shared a quick glance. "No," she said. "They had . . ." She swung her gaze back to the mare, but not before

Colt saw the brightness of her eyes. "There are more." Her voice was very soft, barely recognizable. "Lots more."

"All pregnant?" Emily asked. One hand was holding her belly.

Sophie nodded.

Emily turned toward her, eyes gleaming in the uncertain lighting. "You're a royal pain in the ass, Soph. But if I wasn't such a godawful heterosexual I'd kiss you square on the lips," she said, and wiping her nose with the back of her hand, turned toward the house.

Everyone watched her go for a second.

"Well . . ." Linette said. Her eyes were just as bright as the girls', but it might have been curiosity that made them sparkle. "I guess I'll get to bed, too."

In a moment only two adults and two teenagers were left in the barn.

Casie shook her head. "How could you—"

"It was my idea!" Ty's voice was quick and anxious.

"Ty—" Sophie said, but he interrupted her.

"They had all them mares. And I couldn't help thinking what if Angel was in one of them tight little stalls. What if it was her? I had to get this one out of there. Sophie didn't think we should, but—"

"Ty—" Sophie said again. Her expression looked tortured. They stared at each other from inches apart.

"Don't lie to—" Casie began, but Colt touched her back with a careful hand. The kids weren't beating the crap out of each other; it hardly seemed the time to bring up a little thing like dishonesty.

"Not tonight." He said the words very softly, but she heard him.

Taking a deep breath, she nodded once. "Will you take Ty home?" she asked, not turning toward Colt, but keeping her gaze level on the boy's ruddy complexion.

"Safe and sound," he promised.

She nodded again. "You," she said, staring at Sophie. "You're okay?"

"Yeah." She nodded jerkily. "Of course."

"No one saw you?"

She pursed her lips.

"Sophie . . ."

"No," she said. "No one saw me."

Casie scowled and opened her mouth again, but Colt touched her back and spoke again. "Let it go, Case."

She exhaled carefully. "Just . . ." She shook her head, looking exhausted and relieved all at once. "Just get some sleep, will you?"

The three of them left the girl alone outside the stall. From the yard, they could hear the mare whinny again, loud and frantic.

Casie's shoulders slumped as they neared Colt's pickup truck.

"I'm sorry." Ty's voice was extremely quiet.

She turned back toward him, eyes soft in the darkness. "I didn't think you even liked her," she said.

"Soph?" His face looked pale. "I don't!" The words came out of his mouth fast enough to make Colt chuckle. Casie just raised her brows and headed dismally toward the house.

Colt tried to control his grin. "Don't worry about it, kid," he said, glancing over the hood of his pickup toward Casie's retreating form. "I used to give Case some trouble, too, and she *adores* me."

He wasn't sure, but he thought he heard her snort as she opened the door.

CHAPTER 20

Sophie was standing outside the arena behind the barn when Colt stepped out of his truck the next morning. Her back was to him, her corn-silk hair long and shiny in the slanting sunlight.

Inside the enclosure, the new mare was galloping wild circles about the pen. The hair was rubbed off the base of her tail, but she had it flung over her back as she ran. It curved over her spine as she broke into a high-stepping trot, neck arched, nostrils flaring.

"Hey," Colt said, settling his forearms against the top plank and shoving his right boot onto the lowest rung. "I see she's settled down."

Sophie refused to comment on his sarcasm. Instead, they watched the mare make another mad dash around the pen. Her withers were sharp and bumpy from lack of calories. A dozen oozing wounds and raw lacerations marred her scruffy coat. Throwing her head up, she trumpeted, then spooked at a random sound, bouncing from her feet, eyes rimmed with white as she darted in the opposite direction.

"Do you think she's crazy?" Sophie asked.

"I suspect we'd all be a little nuts if we'd been tied up for nine months at a time."

"Some of you are crazy anyway," she said.

He leaned away from her, brows raised. "Did you just make a joke?" he asked, but her jovial mood was already darkening.

"I don't even know when she's due," she said.

"Well, I think that's the least of your worries," he said.

She turned toward him. "What could be worse than . . ." she began, but just then the girl noticed Casie approaching from behind, strides purposeful, brows lowered.

Sophie winced. Colt couldn't help but chuckle to himself. When had sweet Casie Carmichael become the kind of woman who made a take-no-prisoners girl like Sophie Jaegar wince?

But when she arrived her eyes were only for the horse. Granted, the mare was the kind of animal that would always make people stop and stare. Oh, she looked rough, rubbed raw, worn thin, but she had what could only be called presence . . . that look-at-me something that made every head turn, made every eye misty. All three were silent as they watched the chestnut circle the arena at a snappy trot.

"She moves like a dancer." Casie's voice was very soft, almost reverent. The mare turned her head with haughty disdain, gliding along, potbelly distended, every rib showing. "Even with that scraggly mane and popped knee."

Colt shifted his gaze to the mare's left foreleg. Now that she mentioned it, the injured carpal joint was easy to identify.

"They're kept in narrow stalls twenty-four seven, so she pawed," Sophie said in explanation of the knee problem. Apparently, she had already noticed it. But then if Colt had spent the entire night in the mare's stall, maybe he would have, too. "Probably incessantly." They were all silent for another moment. "The others are mostly drafts, a lot calmer." She cleared her throat. Her eyes, Colt noticed even in profile, looked red and raw. It must have been a hell of a night for everyone. Even through his parents' well-insulated walls, he had heard Ty toss around like a thrashing crew until two in the morning. "Maybe they've given up . . . but Freedom . . ." Her voice broke.

Casie clenched her jaw, but refrained from turning toward the girl. "You named her?"

"Windflower's Freedom."

"Soph . . ." Casie's voice was soft with regret. She tilted her head toward the girl, expression worried. "We have to take her back."

"What?" Sophie asked, voice breathless.

"Think about it." Casie lowered her brows, expression beseeching. "She's stolen property. It's a felony."

"They abused her." Sophie's tone was low, steady, flat, and dangerous. "*That's* the felony. Or at least it *should* be."

"Well, it's not a felony that's going to get *them* put in jail."

The morning went silent.

"I'll do it," Casie said, exhaling carefully. "Just tell me where the farm is."

There was a moment of silence. "No."

"Soph—"

"You can't go there," she said. "It's not safe."

Colt's heart stopped. Casie raised her brows. "What?"

"They have rifles."

Casie's lips formed an O. Her face was very pale. "You said no one saw you."

"I lied."

"You . . ." She stopped herself. Colt held his breath.

"I talked to him. The owner." Sophie swallowed. Her expression was nothing if not fearful. It looked out of place on her kick-ass face. "I spoke to him."

"The owner with the . . ." Casie paused, winced, carried on. "The rifle?"

Sophie nodded. Colt stepped a little closer to Casie . . . just in case.

"What did he say?"

"He invited me into his house."

Casie reached out, grasping the arena's nearest two-by-six. "You didn't go."

"Of course I didn't go. Do you think I'm an idiot?"

No one spoke.

"What happened then?" Casie's voice was quiet.

"Then Ty set Freedom loose and she bolted out the door."

"Then?"

"Then we took off across the field."

"They didn't follow you?"

"They did, but we doubled back. They never found us."

"For real?" Em asked. Colt hadn't seen her coming. How the hell did she do that?

"Sophie . . ." Casie's voice had gone from quiet to breathless. "You're—."

"My hero," Emily said. "Sophie Jaegar . . . my hero." She scowled at the thought, seeming momentarily perplexed. ". . . And other signs of the apocalypse," she murmured, then shook her head. "How did you outrun them?"

For just a second a flash of something showed in Sophie's eyes. It would have been nice to believe it was regret. But it looked a little more like excitement. "Turns out . . ." She cleared her throat. "Turns out Freedom rides double."

Casie's knees actually buckled. "No." She shook her head. Colt propped her up with one hand on her elbow. "You didn't ride her knowing how wild—"

"Bareback double."

On the far side of the arena, the mare reared, dreadlocked mane dancing as she leaped into the air, spun to the left, and trumpeted again. The sound spoke of a hundred fears, a thousand wild hopes.

"Isn't she a pretty thing," Linette said.

Colt turned abruptly toward the newcomer. Holy cow, since when did women sneak around like furtive mice? And how long had she been there listening?

"Yes," Casie said, not looking surprised that the older woman was there. Maybe she was counting on Murphy's law taking precedence once again. "Even like this, she's poetry."

"How far along is she?" Linette asked.

Sophie shook her head, eyes mutinous. "The bastards didn't give a—"

Casie cleared her throat. Colt stared. Sophie wasn't usually the one to swear. The little mother-to-be, on the other hand, had a mouth like a storm trooper when left to her own devices.

Sophie pursed her lips at the censorship, but complied with the warning, finding that pitch-perfect snooty tone without any apparent trouble. "Her past owners just pasture bred their mares

. . . just turned them out with the stallions," she said. "They weren't sure when she conceived."

"Who's the sire?"

They all looked at her.

"That's uncertain as well." Sophie said the words through clenched teeth.

"Doesn't sound like your friends know much about horses," Linette said.

No one spoke. It took Colt a moment to realize she was talking to him, a moment longer to remember his lie regarding the mare's past ownership.

"Oh, yeah," he agreed. "I guess they aren't world-class equestrians, huh."

"They're world-class—" Sophie began, but Casie interrupted.

"Well, are you ready for that riding lesson, Linette?"

"Sure," she said, pulling her attention from Sophie with some difficulty. "If Colt is."

Colt glanced at Casie for a second, making sure she was okay. "Come on, then," he said and reminded himself that although Casie Carmichael's eyes could melt his heart, when the hammer hit the anvil, she was tough as nails. "You can show me what you remember about saddling up."

"Prepare to be astonished," Linette said.

He grinned as he turned away, but his student paused and glanced back.

"Best not to think about those people too much, Soph. Premeditation can prolong a sentence considerably," she said and turned away without another word.

Casie watched her guest walk away. "What did she mean by that?" she asked.

Sophie shrugged and changed the subject. "Well, I'm going to clean Free's stall while she's out here."

"We need to talk," Casie said.

Sophie scowled. "I thought that's what we were doing."

Casie narrowed her eyes. Ty was just turning onto the Lazy's pockmarked drive. It was Saturday morning, and he could have slept late, but she wasn't surprised to see him pacing toward the barn. "Bring Ty into the house," she said and turned away, gathering her wits as she went.

In a matter of moments, the three of them stood in a rough triangle in the living room. Twenty feet away, Emily sang off-key as she banged around in the kitchen.

"First of all . . ." Casie glanced at the pair. "I want to say that I understand why you did what you did. Horses shouldn't be kept in the kind of conditions you described. But that doesn't mean you can just *take* those horses. It's . . ." The word *crazy* came to mind. A couple other prime adjectives followed quickly on its heels. "Dangerous."

"We didn't take horses," Sophie said. "We took *horse*."

Casie turned on her, mind spinning, anger spurring up. "Don't you split hairs, Sophie Jaegar. What do you think your dad's going to say when he finds out about this?"

Sophie shrugged, looking bored.

Frustration made Casie want to gnaw off her own arm. "Is that what you want?" she asked. "Do you want your father to come around asking questions? Do you need his attention that badly?"

"This has nothing to do with him."

"This has everything to do with him," Casie snapped. "He's your legal guardian. He can make sure you never set foot on this property again."

"He wouldn't do that," Sophie said, but her face looked pale suddenly and her voice was breathy. "He doesn't care enough to do that."

Casie shook her head in disbelief as she turned toward Ty.

"And you," she said, but even to her own ears, she heard her tone change, felt her emotions soften. "You know better, Tyler. You can't afford to get into trouble."

"I know," he said and shifted his eyes toward the floor. "But Soph . . ." He paused, raised his gaze to Casie's, and caught himself. "It ain't right," he said. "The way they treat them horses. It just ain't right."

"I know it's not." Casie cleared her throat, searching for her already dissipating anger. When did she become the Wicked Witch of the West? It wasn't many months ago that she was the one bringing home the neglected and the abused. She'd never stolen them, though. And why was that? Just because she lacked the nerve? "But there's nothing we can do about it. As much as I feel for the mare . . . my main concern is you two." She hardened her jaw. "We have to take her back."

"Case—" Sophie began, but a noise from outside interrupted them.

Casie hurried into the kitchen to peer outside. A muddy pickup truck turned into the driveway. There was something about it, some premonition older than time that made the breath stop in her throat. "Get back," she said, seeing that Sophie had followed her.

"What?" the girl asked, but there must have been something in Casie's eyes because she backed away from the window.

"The guy with the rifle . . . Freedom's owner . . ." Casie continued to gaze through the window from an oblique angle, trying to see inside the pickup. "How did he look?"

"I'm not going to let you take—" Sophie began, but Casie stopped her with a glance.

The girl drew a sharp breath. Her eyes widened. "Do you think it's him? Is he here?"

"Stay put," Casie said, and gathering every ounce of nerve she could muster, paced toward the front door. Her mind was spinning, her body pressurized. Don't look tense, she told herself, but she was no actress. Still, spying the egg basket in the tiny entry, she grabbed it on her way out. Her knuckles hurt from her grip on the handle. Way to be casual, she thought, and loosened her fingers with a concerted effort.

The weather was still drizzly. She tugged the brim of her Marlboro cap lower over her eyes and tried not to pass out.

Jack turned a happy circle and loped back to her as the truck came to a halt not twenty feet from them. She tried to look surprised about this unexpected visitor. The man who stepped out from behind the steering wheel was somewhere in his early forties. He wore loose blue jeans and a brown plaid jacket.

A few salutations zipped through Casie's mind. *Greetings. Hey there. Top of the morning.* She stifled a groan. "Can I help you with something?" she asked and forced a gritty smile.

"Yeah." He shifted his gaze right and left, as if searching the premises. "I'm Pete Whitesel. Got a few acres west of here."

"Hi." She extended a hand. The kids had bought her a pair of buckskin gloves. The leather was soft and pliant, considerably superior to the duct-taped pair she'd been wearing just a few months earlier. His handshake was quick, his gaze unsteady. "Cassandra Carmichael," she said. "It's nice to meet you. I don't know any Whitesels. Are you new in the area?"

Her mind was spinning. She knew, absolutely knew, that he was Freedom's owner. Which meant that she should tell him the truth, admit the facts . . . or maybe . . . maybe she could say it was her idea. But either way . . . *any* way, she should return the horse to her rightful owner. *Had* to return the horse to her rightful owner. But in the back of her mind, she saw the mare's frantic expression, her wide, wild eyes.

"Fairly new. Say," he said. He stared at her a second too long, lips curling up a little. "I'm looking for a horse."

Why she laughed she would never be sure. But the sound was ridiculously convincing, at least to her own ears. She nodded toward the pasture where her own wild bunch grazed. "Well, you're in luck," she said. "We've got a good half dozen for sale. Most of them aren't broke yet, but if you're looking for a yearling or a 4-H project for your kids or something—"

"I ain't looking to buy," he said and grinned. The expression was kind of oily. Still, Pete Whitesel was a relatively attractive man . . . considering he was the scum of the earth.

"Oh." She made a confused face. It wasn't half hard. "Well, I—"

"One of mine was stolen."

"Stolen!" She was not meant for the stage, but anger had begun a slow boil in her soul. Why now, she wasn't sure. Maybe she had imagined the owner of a PMU farm differently. Maybe she thought he would have some horrible disfigurement that would make it impossible for him to make a living in a manner that didn't make her want to spit in his eye. "You're kidding! That's terrible. How did it happen?"

He shook his head, but watched her out of the corner of his eye while he did it. "Some damn kids come up and took her right out of my barn."

"No!" It took every bit of discipline she had to keep her gaze off the window from which those same damn kids were surely watching. Neither did she cut her eyes toward the arena behind the barn where Freedom was being kept.

"You sure they were kids?" Emily's voice broke into the conversation like a steak knife through suet.

Casie refrained from closing her eyes in misery. The last thing she needed was Emily's radical opinion at this point, but she turned, feigning nonchalance. The girl was dressed in a pair of oversized overalls. Her hair, the whole untamed mass of it, was shoved up under a cap that would have made Elmer Fudd proud. There was a red-checkered handkerchief hanging from one pocket, and her feet were bare.

Pete eyed her up and down, brows low, lips lifting into a lazy grin. She didn't even blink.

"I mean, kids these days . . ." she continued. "They're too busy with their 'pods and 'pads and whatnot to barely take a step outside. Why would they steal your horses?"

"They only got away with the one."

"Well, that's lucky anyway," Emily said. "How many do you have?"

He shrugged, still watching her, eyes alight as they rested on her protruding belly. "Forty head maybe."

She whistled, sounding impressed. "You must be an exceptional horse trainer."

"Trainer!" he scoffed. "I don't have no time for that sort of thing."

"Then . . ." she began but stopped suddenly. "Hey, you don't have one of those pee lines, do you?"

His eyes narrowed. "What's that?" he asked, brows lowered.

"Those pregnant mares," she said. "I heard their pee is worth its weight in gold. Listen, my aunt Carol just went through her change and I'll tell you what, it was a lifesaver."

He shook his head vaguely, but she was already expounding. You could always count on Emily to expound. At least if there was a lie involved.

"You know," she said. "Women's problems. I guess some people think the synthetic brands are just as effective, but I don't believe it. And why shouldn't we have access to the real deal? I mean, God put animals on this earth for us to use, right?" She shook her head. "Damn tree huggers."

He looked confused. It wasn't an uncommon expression around Emily.

"Damn animal rights activists," she said. "Pardon my French, but I mean . . . Shoot! How do they expect us to make a living? Not that they care."

"You think it was animal rights activists?" he asked.

"Who else?" She shrugged. "I mean, unless there's something special about that particular animal?"

"Special? No. We just picked her up at an auction to replace a mare that was wore out. I should have known better, but . . ." He shrugged, not caring. "She's got the right organs. Wouldn't do that again, though. She tore up the barn first night we brought her home. Pawing, rearing . . ." He shook his head. "She was nothing but trouble."

"Still, she's *your* trouble, right?"

"I paid good money for her. Had trouble foaling her out last time, too. 'Bout took my head off when we took her colt."

Something flared in Emily's eyes. Casie tensed and jumped into the fire.

"So she's pregnant now?"

"You gotta keep 'em pregnant," he said. "Otherwise their pee ain't worth piss." He laughed and glanced down at them through his lashes, wet lips canted up.

Casie laughed with him.

Emily did not. "What do you do with the babies?" Her voice was low. Maybe she was trying to smile. Definitely she was failing.

He glanced at her. "What's that?"

Casie drilled Emily with her eyes, willing her to be silent. But the girl just shrugged. "We've got some extra space. I'm thinking maybe we could get into the business."

He was shaking his head. "I don't know. I'm starting to think it ain't worth the trouble."

"Yeah, I suppose foaling out mares year-round can be a pain in the rear, huh?"

"Well, naw," he said. "We just run 'em with the stallion for three weeks or so. If they don't settle in that time we send them off to auction."

"You get decent money for them?" Emily said.

Casie ground her teeth.

"Sixty cents a pound is all. Less for the colts. They don't want no ponies or nothing."

"So you sell the bab . . ." Her voice broke. "The colts, too?"

"Sure. I mean, I'm a businessman. I don't have no time to mess with training them. And anyway . . ." He brightened as the thought hit him. "It wouldn't be right to sell them to some poor kid somewhere. I don't want to get anybody hurt."

"Except the horses," Emily said.

"What's that?"

Casie cleared her throat and took a step closer, half blocking Emily from his view. "I heard they're opening the slaughter-houses for horses again," Casie said.

"Can't happen soon enough. Problem is, the meat is almost always shipped off to Europe or Asia." He shook his head.

"Tree huggers," Emily scoffed again, but her eyes looked dangerous.

"Well," Casie said and edged toward him a little, shooing him gently toward his vehicle. "We'll sure keep our eyes open for any suspicious behavior."

Suspicious behavior? she thought, but he didn't seem to notice any weird CSI phraseology.

" 'Preciate it," he said and kept his gaze on Emily for an extended period of time.

Casie felt a shiver whisper over her skin, but if the girl was creeped out, she didn't show it.

"Just so we know . . ." Emily began, "when's that colt due? I mean, if I'm driving around and happen to see a pregnant mare, it might be helpful to know what I'm looking for."

He shrugged, still focused on her. "I dunno. Couple of weeks, I suppose."

"Soon," Emily said. Empathy had crept back into her voice. It didn't take a genius to realize that she and the mare were on the same maternal course. "What does that make her, nine months along?"

"Near eleven," he said. "That's what makes this business work good as it does. They're pregnant a long time." His gaze swept down and rested on her belly for too long a time. "But you don't want to leave them in the stalls past ten, ten and a half months. They drop those colts while they're tied up, they'll about tear the barn down to get at 'em."

"They're still tied up when they foal?" Her face was pale except for two flames of color on her cheeks.

He shrugged and pulled his gaze almost regretfully back to her face. "It happens."

"And they can't lie down?"

"They go down, it messes up the catheters."

"You f—" Emily began, but Casie reached out to grip her arm in silent warning.

"Well . . ." she said, her tone as cheerful as she could possibly make it. "We'll sure do what we can to help, won't we, Em?"

"Count on it," Emily said.

CHAPTER 21

"Who do you suppose that is?" Linette Hartman sat very upright on Maddy as the mare plodded patiently around the arena.

"I wouldn't know," Colt said. He tried to sound bored, but his mind was racing. Who *was* the guy in the muddy pickup truck? Why the hell was he there?

Linette gave him a glance out of the corner of her eye. He had told her during their first lesson to focus on the direction she wanted her mount to go. He didn't have to tell her twice. Still, he had the feeling she could have picked the stranger out of a lineup without half trying.

"You telling me you don't know your neighbors?" she asked.

"He's *not* my neighbor."

"What do you suppose he wants, then?"

"That's none of my business."

She shrugged. "Maybe he's looking for something."

Colt jerked his attention to her face, wondering what she suspected, but her expression was bland. He concentrated on keeping his the same.

"Keep your heels down. You want to come off that horse headfirst?"

"Not particularly," she said, then returned doggedly to their previous discussion. "So you don't recognize the truck? I thought everyone knew everyone around here."

"Well, you were wrong."

"You think he's a suitor?"

"What!" He sputtered the word and she grinned.

Maddy plodded along, slow and steady in a circle around him.

"Suitor . . ." she said. "It's an antiquated but quaint term for boyfriend."

"I know what it means," he said. The words sounded a little irritable to his own ears.

"So, do you?"

"Keep her moving," he said and nodded to the mare.

"I'm trying."

"Squeeze her up with your legs."

She did so. "If he's not a suitor, he must be Freedom's former owner."

"What?" He snapped his attention back toward her.

She shrugged. "He's got kind of a malevolent look about him. I'd bet you my Social Security check there's something in his past. Battery, maybe." She narrowed her eyes in thought. "Or arson."

"Holy hell, Lin, imagine much?"

"You dig deep enough you can find something on anyone." Her voice was low and thoughtful.

"This job you used to have . . . did it involve handcuffs and a nightstick?"

She stared at him a second, then laughed out loud. "Now who's imagining things? Listen, if you don't want me inventing an entire criminal record for that man, you better keep me challenged. Are you really going to let me lope or were you just yanking Casie's chain?"

He studied her with a frown. She was the approximate size of an eight-year-old. Then again, he knew some eight-year-olds who rode like seasoned jockeys.

"You just sat on a horse for the first time a few days ago."

"Yeah, well, I don't have a lot of time to waste. When's it going to happen?"

"When I know you're not going to kill yourself up there."

She smiled. The expression was a little wistful, a little mischievous. "We've all got to die sometime."

"Well, it would be best if it didn't happen when you were on the Lazy," he said and glanced toward the muddy pickup truck. Emily had joined them there. But Sophie and Ty were noticeably absent. Why?

"I don't think you have to worry about her so much," she said.

"What?"

"Casie," she said. "She's tougher than she seems. Although maybe abetting felons isn't the best idea she's ever had."

Abetting felons? He felt his heart gallop in his chest, but tried to keep a stoic expression. "Sit back on your jeans pockets."

"What?"

"You want to lope or not?"

"Well . . ." She looked nervous suddenly, but her tone was jaunty when she next spoke. "I didn't travel a thousand miles to learn how to knit."

But he'd feel better if she was safely ensconced on a couch somewhere. Purl one, knit two. Maybe Casie could join her. They could sip coffee and talk about whatever the hell women talked about. Holy crap! Who was that guy? "All right then," he said, forcing himself to focus on the business at hand. "Her head's going to come up a little when she transitions."

"What?"

"Maddy," he said, trying like hell to ignore the conversation by the truck. "She's going to raise her head when she speeds up. What are you going to do to maintain control?"

"Shorten my reins?"

"Shorten your reins," he said, "but not your legs."

"My legs can't get any shorter."

"Just keep your heels down," he said. "It lengthens your muscles."

She nodded. "What else?"

"What lead do you want her in?"

"We're tracking left. So the left lead."

"How do you cue for that?" She hadn't been wasting her riding time. She questioned everything and remembered just about as much.

"Body weight on my right sitting bone. Left leg off the horse, right heel behind the cinch, tilt her head inside."

Emily was doing most of the talking. He could tell that much from the corner of his eye. Where on earth had she gotten those ridiculous overalls?

"What do you do with your hands?" he asked.

"Keep them low and steady."

"Upper body?"

"A little more forward, maintaining it over the center of gravity."

"Motion," he said. "Over the center of motion."

"Right," she said and licked her lips.

"You nervous?"

"Never been an idiot," she said. Her gaze was now firmly set on Maddy's slowly bobbing head.

"Look up. Between her ears," he said, and losing his battle with himself, glanced at the trio by the truck again.

"I'd like to console you with tales of second chances and happily-ever-afters," she said, "but right now I'm a little bit scared of dying."

"You're not going to die."

"You hope."

"I hope. Don't drop your chin."

"Wouldn't think of it."

"Thumbs up. Shoulders back. Look where you want her to go and throw her a kiss for the lope."

"Now?" She shot him a glance.

"You're not getting any younger," he said, and she took the bait like a cutthroat trout.

Narrowing her eyes, she nodded once, squeezed her legs, and made a kissing sound.

Despite her advancing years, Maddy responded like a trooper. Picking up her left lead, she rocked into the lope.

Linette said something. Colt wasn't sure what it was, but it sounded a little bit like a prayer. Even so, her lips were canted up in a childish grin.

"There you go," he said, raising his voice a little so as to be heard. "You're doing great. Just let your hips roll with the motion. Keep your hands in front of the saddle horn. Snug up your knees and don't look—"

But suddenly everything went wrong. He would never be sure what it was. Maybe she lost a stirrup. Maybe she lost her nerve. Maybe Madeline stopped with no provocation at all. But suddenly her rider was falling, tumbling past the mare's shoulder like an autumn apple.

"Linette!" He lunged forward, then dropped down to squat beside her. "Are you all right?"

She was lying facedown in the dirt, left leg half bent, right sprawled out to the side.

"Linette?" he said, and touched her arm. "You okay?"

She rolled slowly onto her back, eyes glazed, dirt smudged across her nose. "Well, my heels are down," she said.

He skimmed her body. Nothing seemed to be drastically out of place. "A little lower than I had in mind."

"Linny!" Casie said, and suddenly she was rushing across the arena. "What happened?"

His student stared at her with narrow eyes. Either she was analyzing the situation or she was concussed. He rather hoped for the former.

"Who was the guy with the pickup truck?" she asked.

"What?" Casie skimmed her crumpled form before skipping her worried gaze to Colt and then back to Linette.

"The guy in the truck." Her voice was extremely patient. "Who was he?"

"Oh . . . Ah . . . just a neighbor."

Linette stared at her for a second, then snorted. "I've heard better lies from priests," she said and sat up, but Casie leaned in quickly, placing a hand on her shoulder.

"Just take it easy. No rush," she said.

"I don't have . . ."

"A lot of time, I know," Casie said. "But just relax for a second."

Linette did so for approximately that long, then pushed resolutely to her feet. Casie rose with her. "Can you make it to the house?"

"I imagine I could if I wanted to, but Mr. Dickenson promised to teach me to lope."

"I'm sure he'd be willing to do that later."

"Good to know," she said, and shaking her head, creaked painfully past them. "But if I've learned one thing in the last millennium or so, it's to keep punching. Hold Maddy for me, will you?" she asked and hobbled toward the mare.

"Linette . . ." Casie hurried after her. "Listen, you can ride after dinner or something. I really think you should—"

But Colt interrupted. He'd always gotten a kick out of doing so. "She's right, Case," he said. "It's all about the number of times you get back up."

She opened her mouth to argue, but Linette was already grasping the reins in one stubborn hand. She tilted her head once in each direction as if to get the kinks out, then turned to look over her shoulder at him.

"What did I do wrong?" she asked. Her expression was almost comical with that streak of dirt firmly set across her nose.

"You fell off," he said.

Her face softened a little, her expression equal parts humor and exasperation. "Could you be a little more specific?"

"I'd really rather you came into the house for a few minutes," Casie said, but Linette just smiled.

"I would think if there was anyone who understood getting back on the horse, it'd be you," she said and nodded toward where all three teenagers had gathered on the front porch. "Don't worry about me. Your kids need you."

Casie glanced at the trio, brows beetled. "You know they're not really *mine*, don't you?"

The older woman narrowed her eyes. "Your first family maybe didn't turn out exactly like you hoped. Maybe your folks were a little more . . ." She shrugged, seeming to feel her way along. "More tempestuous than you're comfortable with. But nobody's perfect, Casie, and I've got a good feeling about this family."

"They're not *my*—" she began again, but Linette had already moved on.

"How do I get back up there?" she asked, and Colt smiled as Casie turned thoughtfully toward the house.

CHAPTER 22

"Case. Hey, Case."

"Yeah." The single word sounded groggy and misshapen. Since she'd returned to the Lazy six months earlier, sleep had become not only scarce but rather sacred. She lay now in her favorite sleeping position, arms flung out to the side, face squashed against the pillow. She raised her head the slightest degree. "What?"

"Wake up."

"I *am* awake." That might have been an out-and-out lie. She rather hoped it was. "Emily? Is that you?"

"Yeah."

"What time is it?"

"I don't know." Casie could hear her shuffling her feet. "Three, maybe."

"Three in the *morning?*"

"Looks like it."

Casie closed her eyes. "Why do you think people keep waking me up at three in the morning?"

"I don't know. Could just be bad luck. Or maybe it's the fact that some of us are going to have a baby."

"Yeah, that's—What!" She would never remember sitting up, but suddenly she was blinking against the light that dimly backlit Emily's ponderous form. She was standing in the doorway, half in, half out, hand resting on her belly.

"You're going to have a baby?"

"I thought you knew." Emily's face was mostly shadowed, but her dry tone said it all.

"Holy shorts!" Casie breathed. She was out of bed in a second, turning an awkward circle, searching for something she couldn't quite remember the name of. "Where's your thing?"

"What thing?"

"Your . . ." She blinked hazily at the girl. "Are you all right?"

"Kind of tired."

"Get in the truck. Maybe you can sleep on the way. They said you should rest as much as you can until the pain gets too intense."

"Am I supposed to sleep when *every* horse goes into labor or just Freedom?"

Casie stumbled to a halt. "What?"

They stared at each other.

"Oh." Emily narrowed her eyes a little. "You didn't think *I* was in labor, did you?"

There was a pause that stretched out a bit as Casie stared at the girl. "Things are a little blurry." She said the words slowly. It would be wrong to strike a pregnant woman. "But I'm pretty sure I just asked if you were going to have the baby."

"Did you mean right *now?*"

Casie put her hand to her heart. It was still there; in fact, it was pretty active. "I don't know why you hate me, Emily," she said, and plopped bonelessly onto the mattress behind her.

Emily laughed at the drama. "Geez, Case, I'm not due for a couple weeks yet. But Sophie thinks Freedom is ready to pop any minute."

"A couple weeks! Holy Hannah, Em. The baby's not on a time clock. He could come anytime."

"*She.*"

"What?"

"I've decided it's a girl."

"Really? What makes you think—"

"Casie!" Sophie's voice boomed through the house like a cannon volley.

Casie didn't even jump at the sound and wondered if it was a bad sign that these early-morning adventures didn't faze her anymore. "I'm coming," she said, raising her voice a little before lowering it again as she pushed herself to her feet. "What makes you think it's a girl?"

"Girls are nice."

"What are you doing?" Sophie stormed into the doorway, expression mad enough to burn rubber.

"Sometimes," Emily added, noting Sophie's irritable expression.

"How's she doing?" Casie asked, checking a grin as she turned her attention toward the youngest member of their little trio.

"How's she doing? How's she doing!" Judging by the sound of Sophie's voice, the mare was probably doing considerably better than Sophie was. "She's in shock from the move, she's physically exhausted, and she probably has kidney damage from dehydration."

"Sometimes girls are a little bit dramatic, though," Emily noted.

"Just relax a little," Casie said. "Take a breath."

"Take a . . . Just hurry your ass up," Sophie hissed.

"My ass is hurrying," Casie said and turned another groggy circle, searching for who knows what. "It's my mind that's having a little trouble deciding . . ." She shook her head, trying to clear it. "Okay, I'm coming."

The barn was mostly dark. Mostly quiet. Angel thrust her head over the half door, ears pricked forward. Beside her, Freedom circled her stall with restless uncertainty.

Casie scowled, trying to mentally engage. "How long has she been agitated like this?"

"Probably her whole life," Emily said, then, "Oh, were you talking about the horse?"

Sophie glared at her before turning her attention back to Casie.

"I first checked her at three twenty-five. She's lain down and gotten back up at least five times since then."

"Any other signs?"

"She's been dripping milk for about twenty-four hours."

"Join the club," Emily said.

"TMI," Sophie said distractedly and quietly approached the mare's stall.

Emily shrugged.

"What about her water bag?" Casie asked.

"I think it already broke, but I'm not sure."

Casie glanced at her watch. "So we think she's been in labor for at least a half an hour."

"What's the norm?" Emily asked.

"Start to finish . . ." Casie paused, thinking back to her Horse Bowl days when she could recall this kind of information with lightning speed. "Three hours. Maybe four. About the same as a cow. Prey animals need to get the job done quick and move on."

"So flippin' unfair," Emily said. She was rubbing her belly. There was a lot of that lately.

"Yeah, well, you just have to push out about nine pounds," Sophie said. "Freedom has to eject practically a hundred pounds of legs and—"

"Nine pounds!" They were keeping their voices very low. The mare circled again before plopping roughly onto her side with her spine toward them. "If she weighs in over seven, she's staying in there indefinitely."

"I don't think that's physically possible," Sophie said. She was scowling as the mare started straining. "I think this is it. Case—"

"Take it easy, Sophie," Casie said, though her own nerves were cranked pretty tight. "Let's just let nature take its course."

"Nature!" Sophie turned on her. "There's nothing natural about this. Natural was taken away when she was tied up in a stall so narrow she couldn't even—"

"Sophie," Casie said. "Quiet down."

The barn fell silent. Only the mare's soft grunts could be heard. In a minute she had stretched out flat. Sweat darkened her flanks and neck.

"There!" Emily said, trying to peer past the mare's tail. "Is that a hoof?"

The mare groaned long and low.

Sophie jerked toward the stall, but Casie grabbed her arm and reeled her back.

"Just wait."

"She's dying."

"She's not dying," Emily said. Her voice was soft, reverent with hope and trembling excitement. "She's creating life."

They waited in silence. Sophie clutched Casie's left sleeve. Emily was holding her breath.

The lone hoof emerged farther.

"One leg's back. It's malpositioned," Sophie whispered, but just then the other front foot slipped into view. It was followed by a dark nose encased in a bluish-white sac. It slipped farther into the world and drooped toward the well-bedded floor. The mare groaned, heaved, then lay panting.

"We've got to help her," Sophie rasped.

"She's as flighty as a jackrabbit," Casie said. "We don't want to scare her."

Sophie bit her lip. "Better that than losing the baby."

Casie scowled, then nodded in silent agreement.

"Easy, girl," Sophie said and took a step into the stall.

Casie let her go.

"Freedom?" Sophie said. Nothing happened. The mare remained flat out on the straw, neck stretched forward, legs straight and stiff.

The foal, still wrapped in its gauzy sac, still caught half inside its mother's body, was as motionless as the mare.

"Get the afterbirth off its nose," Casie instructed quietly.

Sophie did as ordered. Casie snuck forward, fear squeezing her chest. If they lost this foal, *both* girls would be inconsolable.

"Tug on the legs," Casie instructed. "Nice and gentle."

Sophie shifted her terrified gaze to Casie's, swallowed, then wrapped her fingers firmly around the foal's fetlocks.

Freedom's eyes widened. She lifted her head slightly, then glanced back over her misshapen belly. Her gut contracted. Sophie pulled harder, and the foal, slippery as an eel, slithered onto the straw.

"She did it," Sophie crooned.

The mare, relieved and anxious, gathered her legs beneath her and pushed onto her feet. She turned a rapid circle and nickered low in her throat, but the foal remained unmoving.

"He's not breathing," Sophie said. "I don't think he's breathing!"

"Stick a straw in his nostril," Casie said, rushing up. "If that doesn't work we'll—"

But at that moment the little creature sneezed noisily and shook its wobbly head.

There was a communal sigh of relief, followed by a bevy of activity. Emily applied iodine to the baby's navel as she'd done a hundred times with calves. Casie removed the afterbirth, which had already dropped away from the mare.

"Look at him," Em cooed, fingers pressed to her mouth. He was already preparing to rise, rubbery hooves braced in unlikely positions in an effort to do so. He heaved shakily upward on crooked legs, finding his balance against all odds.

"Isn't he gorgeous?" Sophie sighed.

Watching the ribby, ungainly newborn shake its knobby head, Casie was sure Emily would disagree, but perhaps her maternal hormones had already kicked in full force.

"He is." She breathed the words between her fingers, eyes bright with tears. "He's just perfect."

Casie smiled, reveling in this moment of solidarity. But in that second the mare staggered toward the wall. Emily jumped out of her way. Freedom stumbled, trying to correct herself, but she fell to her knees and then onto her side.

"No!" Sophie gasped.

Casie swore. Emily backed against a wall, wide eyed.

"Call the vet!" Casie rasped. But Sophie was already doing just that. They could hear the answering service on the end of the line. The mare thrashed a little, the motion weak and disjointed.

"Keep her down," Casie ordered. "Sit on her head!"

Sophie shoved her phone in her pocket and did as told. "What's wrong?"

Casie's mind was spinning. "I don't know. Too much blood loss? Calcium deficiency? It could be anything."

"Maybe it's dehydration."

"I don't—"

"Help her," Sophie pleaded, and there was something in the girl's tone, a desperate hopefulness that snapped a half dozen decisions firmly into place in Casie's mind.

"Keep her steady. I'll get the IV," Casie said and rushed out the door. Fingers trembling, she untied the fluids bag from the front of Angel's stall and hurried it next door. "Find me a vein."

"What?" Sophie's eyes were wide with terror.

"The vein, in the neck. You saw them do it to Angel."

"I watched a guy saw a lady in half, too. It doesn't mean I can replicate—"

"Just do it!"

The two of them huddled together over the mare. The animal's eyes were glassy, her body frightfully still as Sophie ran a trembling hand down the length of her neck.

"There!" Casie said. "Push up there."

Sophie jabbed with her thumb, but no vein bubbled above her fingers.

"Push harder!"

A blood vessel bulged away from the mare's chestnut hide.

Taking a trembling breath, Casie jabbed the needle into the swelling and jerked her head toward Emily. "Open it up."

"What?"

"The IV," she snapped. "Turn the screw."

"How far?" Emily's voice was almost inaudible.

"All the way." She had no idea what she was doing. Might as well go for broke.

All eyes turned to the IV bag. No one spoke. Hell, no one breathed. And then the clear liquid began to flow out of the plastic and into the vein.

"Okay," Emily murmured. "Okay."

"Don't move, Soph," Casie warned. If the needle came out of the vein, they were screwed . . . if they weren't regardless. "Get some tape, Em."

"Tape? Like . . ."

Freedom shifted her right foreleg.

"Hurry," Casie said, and Emily catapulted from the stall.

In less than a minute she had returned. "How is she?" Her voice was breathless. She was holding a roll of silver duct tape in her hand. Casie raised her brows.

"It holds the rest of the ranch together, so I figured—" Emily began, but there was no time for explanations.

"Tear off a piece and tape down the needle," Casie ordered.

Emily swallowed and moved closer. In a moment the needle was strapped to the mare's neck. She remained exactly as she was, eyes unblinking, body immobile.

"Okay." Casie said the word softly. "Now a longer strip."

"How long?"

"Couple feet, maybe. We've got to make it as steady as we can."

"But what if—"

"I don't know," Casie said, then inhaled carefully and lowered her voice. "Let's just try it."

Emily unrolled more tape as the newborn bumbled back to its feet. It shambled wildly along, legs going every direction before bumping into the nearest wall and falling onto its rump.

"Is he okay?" Emily's voice was strained, but Casie kept her attention steady on the mare.

"Just make this needle secure, then grab the other IV bag from the tack room."

Emily jerked a nod and hurried away. In a matter of seconds, she was yanking the tubing out of the old bag and jamming it into the new. Fluids flowed out in a steady stream.

But the mare remained as she was, glassy eyed, barely breathing. Behind her, the foal stumbled back onto his feet, took a tottering step forward, and shambled helplessly into another wall.

Freedom remained completely unaware.

"What now?" Sophie's tone was small and broken.

"Try the vet again," Casie said.

She dragged her phone back to her ear. They waited breathlessly as more fluids pumped into the mare's system.

"Answering service," a voice responded.

Sophie flashed a hopeful glance to Casie. "I need to speak to Dr. Sarah!"

"I'm sorry." The voice on the other end of the line was cool and remote. "This is the answering service for Dakota Equine Veterinary Hospital. Dr. Sarah is not available at this time."

"I need her to call me as soon as possible."

"Can I get your name and pertinent information?"

"It's life or death!"

"Please give me—"

But in that second the mare's eyes blinked closed.

"No," Casie breathed.

"Freedom!" Sophie rasped, and dropping her phone onto the straw, stroked the mare's pretty face. "Don't. Please. Not now. Listen. Things will get better. They will. Don't give up." The mare spasmed, head jerking. "Don't—" she sobbed, but suddenly Emily lurched toward the foal. Squatting awkwardly beside him, she wrapped her arms around his barrel and dragged him toward his mother's head.

"Emily . . ." Casie began, tears already blurring her vision. "I don't think—"

"Just help me!" she rasped.

Dropping her hands from the mare, Casie jerked to her feet. The colt was slippery, ears drooping heavily, eyes half closed.

Emily relinquished the foal's torso. They each grabbed a foreleg and dragged him forward.

"I'm sorry," Casie said. "I'm so—"

"Farther," Emily panted. "A little farther."

They heaved the colt in front of the mare's unseeing eyes. She remained exactly as she was, thin and broken, flat against the straw, life depleted.

"Wake up!" Emily ordered.

Nothing happened.

"Get up, mare!" Emily said and squatted beside her to slap her neck. The chestnut body remained entirely flaccid.

Emily swore between her teeth. Scooting over to the foal, she swiped her hands across his ribs before slathering the slime on the mare's nose. "It's your baby!" she snarled. "Don't wimp out now. He needs you."

The world was absolutely quiet, and into that silence, the colt nickered. The sound was as old as the earth, as sweet as life, filled with yearning, and hope, and despair.

And to that sound, Freedom opened her eyes. She blinked once and then her ears shot forward. She answered back. The sound was low and shaky, but in an instant she was scrambling awkwardly to her feet. Casie skittered out of the way, still holding the IV bag. Stumbling forward, Freedom reverently lowered her muzzle to her baby's damp back.

It was a moment Casie would never forget, a space of time when all was well with the world, when things were as they should be. The mare, unsteady but determined. The foal, even more so, a beautiful dance as old as time as they found each other. There were tottering steps and soft nickers, wide limpid eyes filled with instant adoration and audacious hope.

Eventually, the pair was nestled together in the golden straw. Freedom's muzzle was resting on her baby's silky head. He was stretched out on his side, ribs rising and falling, long-lashed eyes closed to the world.

It was then that Beethoven's Fifth Symphony began playing from the depths of the bedding. Freedom cocked her head in that direction but did little more as Sophie dug through the straw for her lost phone.

"Dr. Sarah?" she said, breathless.

"This is Dakota Equine's answering service calling back." The operator's tone was more than a little snooty. "I'm afraid I need more information than 'this is life or death.' "

"Just have her call me," Sophie snapped. "Or there'll be another life on the line."

CHAPTER 23

"So she said, 'Get your ass in gear, or it might just be *your* death.'" Emily stood narrow-eyed near the stove, spatula raised and pointed with deadly accuracy at the milk pitcher. Pancakes bubbled on the skillet behind her.

"I didn't say that," Sophie said and shifted her gaze to Ty. He felt its impact like an arrow to his soul. Her cheeks were pink, her lost girl eyes as bright as shooting stars. If she were any more awe-inspiring, the sight of her would tear his heart clean from his chest.

Emily scowled, canted her head for a moment, then turned to flip a pancake and consider the situation anew. "Maybe it was, 'If she doesn't call me back, you'll *wish* you were dead.' Or—" She paused again, one hip cocked, studying the ceiling as she reconsidered. "Maybe I should be an equine practitioner. I bet they make the big bucks."

"You're afraid of horses," Colt said.

Emily sighed. "It's a conundrum."

Colt chuckled. He sat next to Sophie. The three of them were tucked close around the kitchen table. Casie was filling mugs with coffee. The dark aroma was strong enough to taste, whispering of comfort and peace and a world of emotions Ty couldn't put a name to. The steam wafted lazily into the air, haloing their heads like morning mist. "Way to put the fear of God into someone who has her hands completely tied," Colt said.

Sophie scowled a little as she took her first sip of coffee. "I thought Freedom was dying."

"She *was* dying," Casie said. "She'd given up. Checked out. Then Em dragged her baby up to her." She shook her head, remembering, and the sight of the pride in her eyes caused goose bumps to pebble up on Ty's arms. "It was as if an electric current went off. As if the scent of her newborn went straight to her heart."

"It wasn't because of me," Emily said. "You're the one who pumped two gallons of electrolytes into her." She turned toward Colt, spatula still in hand. "You should have seen her, shouting orders like the sergeant general. 'Get the IV, find me a vein, STAT!' "

"I didn't say 'stat,' " Casie said, tone embarrassed.

Ty watched her settle her hips against the counter and self-consciously sip her coffee just as Sophie tasted her own. Two women. They couldn't be more different, and yet . . .

"Emily butchered the story completely," Sophie said.

"Are they always that . . ." Linette paused in the doorway. "Spindly?" she asked and skimmed her gaze from one face to the next.

They all turned toward her, conversation interrupted.

"Foals," their guest explained. "He's so . . . knobby."

"Spindly!" Emily sputtered the word as if she had birthed the colt herself. "Knobby? What are you talking about? He's spectacular." There was fire in her eye, a threat in her raised hand.

There was a moment of stunned silenced before anyone spoke.

"Let this be a lesson not to cast aspersions on *Em's* baby," Casie murmured against the lip of her coffee mug, but the words were easily heard. Colt chuckled and Emily finally grinned.

"And it might be wise to remember who does the cooking around here," she added.

They did a little salute with their coffee mugs.

"She's right, though," Sophie said. "He's a cutie. At least *I* think so. And he's strong. He was up in . . ." She snapped her fingers. Her hair swung in rhythm to the motion. Her fingernails were perfectly clean. Ty didn't understand how that could be. "Thirty seconds. And with the crap . . ." She paused, glanced at Casie, and adjusted her terminology. "Considering his mother's deprivations, that's amazing."

"Yeah," Emily said. "And he—"

"All right." Linette laughed, holding up a hand as she slipped into an empty chair. "My apologies. I'll know better than to slander any of your equine friends in the future." She glanced up. "So you think they're doing well?"

Casie shrugged, looking worried. "Seem to be right now. The vet's supposed to stop in as soon as she can to check on them."

"How could anyone have treated that mare so heinously?" Linette asked.

"The guy's psychotic," Emily said and shivered a little as if disturbed by the thought of him.

They all turned toward her.

"So you've met him?" Linette asked.

Casie tensed. Sophie's eyes went wide, but Emily just flipped a pancake and calmly corrected her mistake. "I don't have to *see* psycho behavior to recognize its effects," she said. "Maybe I should be a psychologist. Or a psychic. Or, hey, I could be a judge. They're still looking for a replacement for that hang-'em-high gal who resigned recently."

Linette took a sip of coffee, studying her before turning toward Casie.

"I saw you bought the mare a new halter and lead rope."

"*I* did," Sophie said. "I didn't want her to have any memories of her old life."

Linette nodded. "I think green's her color. What did you do with the old ones?"

"The old halter?" Sophie scowled.

"Yes. I just . . ." The older woman shrugged, looking a little embarrassed. "I'd kind of like a memento of the Lazy."

"You want a ratty old halter?"

"It's more the lead I'm interested in," she said. "It was leather, wasn't it?"

"Yeah," Sophie said. "I put it in the trash out back."

"And you don't mind if I take it?"

Sophie shook her head, looking bemused.

"Thanks," Linette said, then smiled her thanks at Emily as the girl slid a trio of pancakes in front of her. "And can I hang around when the vet comes to check out the new arrival?"

"Of course," Casie said. "You'll be around the farm?"

"I have a riding lesson, of course," Linette said. "We're trying bareback today."

"That's—" Casie began, just about to take a sip, then, "What!" Her gaze snapped to Colt.

"Riding bareback," Linette repeated, then widened her eyes as she chewed. "Em, what is in these pancakes?"

"You like them?"

"They're fantastic."

"Bareback?" Casie said.

Colt shrugged, but his expression was sheepish. "What can I say? She's a prodigy."

"Aren't prodigies . . ." Emily shifted her dubious attention to Linette's lined face.

Silence settled in for a full heartbeat.

Ty shifted his gaze from Em to Linette, nerves already cranking tight. "Taller?" he guessed.

The laughter started with Linette, spread to Emily, then caught on like wildfire.

In the end Ty himself could do nothing but laugh. It felt odd—frightening and soothing and helpless all at once—warming his belly, loosening something in his chest he hadn't known was tight.

The sounds were just beginning to dissipate when tires crunched on the gravel outside.

Still chuckling, Casie turned toward the door. "That must be Dr. Sarah now," she said, but Sophie was already on her feet and hurrying around the table.

"I've got it," she said.

"Ask her in for breakfast," Em said.

"Be nice." Casie's voice was very quiet as the girl passed her, but even Ty heard it.

Sophie slashed her glance to his, cheeks pink again. "I hardly ever eat anyone," she said.

Casie raised her brows in mock fear as Sophie disappeared from sight. The door opened. There was a murmur of voices.

Emily shrugged. "Don't worry about it," she said. "Sometimes death threats are extremely effective."

Casie grinned and turned her mind back to Linette. "You'll be careful, right?"

"Careful's for kids," she said. "If I'm not going to take risks now, when will I?"

"After you leave the Lazy perfectly healthy and happy?" Casie suggested.

Linette laughed. "I *am* happy, and sometimes that's all you can hope—"

"Case." Sophie appeared in the doorway. "There's someone here for you."

"What?" She straightened and turned toward the entry.

"It's not Dr. Sarah?" Emily asked.

Sophie shook her head as she retrieved her coffee mug. "Some guy with a briefcase."

"A briefcase," Colt said and chuckled a little as he leaned back in his chair. "He must be lost. Hey, Em . . ." He motioned to his plate. "Someone stole my breakfast."

"Geez," she said, building a new pile of pancakes onto a platter. "We could feed a thrashing crew for less than—" But her words stopped abruptly as Casie stepped back into the room. "What's wrong?"

They turned toward Casie in unison. Her face was pale. There was a manila envelope in her hand.

Colt rose to his feet. All humor had been leached from his face.

Ty felt his gut clench, felt premonition curdle like old milk in his stomach.

"Casie," Colt said, eyes narrowed as he stepped toward her. "What's in the envelope?"

"A subpoena." Her voice was ghostly.

"A subpoena?" Linette glanced from one to the other. "For what?"

"I don't . . ." Casie glanced down. Her hands looked unsteady. "I can't even guess."

"Because you haven't done anything wrong?" Linette asked. "Or because you can't narrow it down to a single event?"

Casie laughed. The sound was shaky. She turned her gaze to Colt, and in that second Ty felt that awful knot of jealousy twist tight in his stomach again. *He* wanted to be there for her. *He* wanted to save her. Make her smile. Make her face light up like a spring morning. Instead, he made her life harder at every turn.

"I don't know . . ." Casie began brokenly, but Colt stopped her.

"It's going to be all right," he said. "Whatever it is, it's going to be all right."

"But . . ." she began and brought her gaze to Ty's. There was no accusation there. No animosity whatsoever. And maybe that's what made the situation unbearable.

Rising woodenly to his feet, he pushed away from the table and escaped.

CHAPTER 24

"How's she doing?" Casie kept her voice low as she approached Ty from behind, but he jumped anyway, his chapped hand jerking where it rested on Angel's neck.

It took him a second to respond. "All right, I guess," he said, but he didn't turn to look at her. It was reminiscent of the early days, when he would come here for refuge. Come here with a bruised face and battered soul. Her heart twisted at the thought, crumbled at the idea that they were back at the beginning.

"We're becoming a regular convalescent camp," she said and stepped a little closer. He didn't respond. She gazed over the stall door at the gray, who nudged Ty with her nose, silently complaining about the lack of attention.

He stroked her distractedly.

"She seems more comfortable," Casie said.

He said nothing.

"Sam's supposed to come today to check on her. I think that will—"

"I'm sorry." He said the words quickly and a little too loud.

"It's okay." Casie forced a smile. "She's not that bad. Maybe she'll even wear a real shirt this time," she said, but he failed to laugh. Instead, he turned his eyes toward her. They were haunted and tired, as old as forever.

"It's because of me, isn't it?"

She shook her head. "I don't know what—"

"The subpoena—" He bit off the word as if it were poison. "It's because of my folks."

She stared at him. "Don't worry about that, Ty. It's going to be fine."

They stared at each other. He shook his head, choked a laugh. "Or is it because I . . ." He motioned toward the pair in the adjacent stall. "Is it because I stole a horse?"

She shook her head, agonized by his expression, by his fault-finding. "Freedom needed saving. It was an act of kindness." She didn't have to force a smile as she turned toward the stall next door. "Look how happy she is."

There was no more pacing, no wild-eyed worry. Instead, the mare stood in the center of her stall, one hip cocked, muzzle resting lovingly on her scrawny baby's bushy tail.

"I shouldn't have done it," he said.

"The way I heard it, it was Sophie's idea."

"It wasn't. It was—"

"You don't need to lie," she said quietly.

He swallowed and shook his head. "I should have talked her out of it."

She laughed, despite everything. "God himself couldn't have talked Sophie out of that, Ty."

"I'm a weakling," he said. The words were almost inaudible.

"What?" She stepped closer, drawn in by the pain in his voice. "What'd you say?"

"Mom's right," he said, and swallowing, turned away. "I ain't got no backbone at—"

"Ty!" Her voice was sharper than she meant it to be. She took a deep breath and steadied her hands. "Your mother's a . . ." She stopped herself, though it took every ounce of fortitude she had. "Your mother's *not* right. Not about that . . . not about a lot of things."

A muscle twitched in his face. He shook his head, but she rushed on before he could speak.

"I'm not condoning theft," she said. "But this horse . . ." She glanced at the mare next door again. She was nibbling gently at her foal's rump, delicate kisses that spoke of adoration, of un-bridled happiness. "Freedom . . ." She smiled. Her eyes stung. She cleared her throat. "It took a lot of nerve to sneak into that barn. A lot of nerve to bring her here."

He shook his head again, expression pinched. "Sophie's the brave one. I just followed along. I didn't mean to cause you no trouble. I didn't think . . ." He paused, winced. "I just didn't think," he whispered. "And now here you are in trouble be-cause of my stupid—"

"It's not something you did," Casie said.

He stopped, scowled.

She cleared her throat, fiddled with a piece of straw caught between the stall door and the frame. "It's something *I* did."

He stared at her in silence for several seconds, eyes narrowed, breath held before he spoke. "You're lyin'," he said. "You're lying to protect me. But I ain't no little kid, Case. I can handle it. Just tell me the truth."

"It's because I didn't guard Sophie closely enough. I shouldn't have allowed her to go out with a guy I knew nothing about. I should have said no, regardless of what her father wanted. I'm sorry you had to be the one to protect her."

He blinked at her and for a second she thought she might have won this battle, but he pursed his lips. "So you *are* in trou-ble cuz of me."

"No!" she said. "The Pritchards don't have a case. They're lawyers—just looking to make trouble because their idiot son is . . ." She shrugged. "An idiot. It's not your fault. Listen to me, Ty. This guilt thing you have going on . . . I'm no therapist, but you've got to quit blaming yourself. It's going to eat you up."

"You afraid I'm gonna go crazy or something?"

She opened her mouth, though honestly, she had no idea what she planned to say.

"You think I'm crazy already?"

Casie exhaled and raised her chin a little. Calm settled in like a fog, making her limbs feel heavy, her mind feel free. Let the bastards sue her, she thought. See where it got them. "I think you're the most honorable person I've ever met," she said.

He shook his head once, but she spoke again before he could argue. "I think that I'm lucky to know you. I think we're *all* lucky to know you. And I think your mother—" She stopped before she found herself climbing into Puke and kicking the stuffing out of the stupid cow again. "She didn't deserve you."

He searched her eyes and she let him. There was nothing to see there but the truth.

He drew a deep breath as if trying to believe, as if struggling for balance. "What you going to do about the subpoena?"

She shrugged, nerves cranking up a little again. "I'm going to show up in court and tell them the truth."

He looked like he was going to throw up. And for some reason that made her laugh. "What's the worst that can happen?"

"They can put you in jail."

The laughter froze on her lips. She suddenly felt sick to her stomach, too, but she took a deep breath and smiled, pretending confidence as best she could. "They're not going to put me in jail," she said.

"You could lose the Lazy."

Well, yes, she thought. *That* could happen.

It was later that night that Casie stood in Freedom's stall. The mare swished her tail, seeming unconcerned by her uninvited guest's after-hours visit. The foal touched his muzzle to Casie's leg tentatively, then jerked away and galloped a wild circuit around the narrow enclosure.

His antics brought tears stinging to Casie's eyes.

She could lose this, she thought. She could lose it all. She gritted her teeth against the injustice of it, but her tears fell nevertheless. Anger flared through her. She banged her fist against the wall.

"It's easier if you use a hammer."

She jerked at the sound of Colt's voice, pivoting away to hide her tears.

"I was just..." She cleared her throat. Closed her eyes. "What are you doing here?"

"I don't know. I was bored."

"It's two o'clock in the morning."

"Yeah, not much going on this time of day."

"Go to bed."

"Is that an invitation?"

She snorted and chanced a glance in his direction. His grin was cocksure, but there was something in his eyes. Understanding, maybe. Or pity. She hated pity.

"Linette's right," he said, changing the subject as he folded his forearms across the top of the stall door. "That is one ugly foal."

She glanced at the colt, then surreptitiously swiped at the tears with the back of her hand. "Is not."

"He looks like a llama."

"He doesn't..." She tilted her head a little, studying the misshapen head, the long curling whiskers on his chin. "Llamas are cute."

He chuckled as he stepped into the stall. For a second she was tempted to brush past him, to hurry out of sight. But she hated being a coward. Or maybe she was just tired. She turned toward him, hoping against hope that he hadn't heard her crying, that he couldn't read her eyes. But his expression was atypically sober, his mouth for once unbent by humor.

"Let me help," he said.

"What are you talking about?" She took a step back and gave him her best look of confusion, her best upbeat tone. "Help with what?"

"Anything." There was angst in his voice suddenly, sounding harsh in the aftermath of her forced cheeriness.

"I don't need any help. Everything's fine. Angel's recuperating. Freedom's doing well. The Lazy—"

"Let me hire an attorney."

She gave him a shocked expression. "For what?"

"You did the right thing," he said, and there was something in his eyes. Something that threatened to warm her belly and soften her heart, but she refused to acknowledge it. Just stood, instead, watching him. "God, I've never been happier than when you beat the crap out of Ty's bitch of a . . ." He stopped himself with an obvious effort. "Just let me help."

The rumbling sincerity of his tone was desperately tempting, but she'd been seduced into letting others run her life before. And look where that had gotten her. She'd all but lost the ranch. All but lost *herself*. She shook her head and reached up to stroke Freedom's face. It was as delicate as a porcelain vase. "It'll be fine. Like you said . . ." She swallowed. "I was justified. Besides, that's not what the subpoena was for."

"What then?"

"David Pritchard's parents are suing me."

"Pritchard! The snotty kid in the Camaro?"

"They allege that he was in danger while on my property. Therefore I'm responsible."

"Are you kidding me? He was drinking. And he's twice as big as Ty."

"I'm still responsible."

"That's bull. That'll never stand up in court."

"Maybe you're not an expert on responsibility," she said.

"What's that supposed to mean?" His tone had gone dark.

She turned to face him. "Are you even paying child support?" she asked and felt a dark release at the change of topic.

He said nothing.

"For your daughter," she said, voice rising as she faced him. "Are you even helping with the day-to-day—"

"I don't have a daughter," he said.

She stared at him, then huffed a laugh. "What is it, Dickenson? Don't tell me you thought the *mother* should be exclusive even if *you*—"

"She had an abortion."

Casie blinked. "What?"

He glanced away. His jaw looked hard, but his eyes were

wounded. "She, ahh . . . she said she was going to if I didn't . . . If we didn't . . ." He swallowed.

"If you didn't marry her?" Her voice was just a whisper.

He cleared his throat but didn't look at her. "I didn't believe her. I mean, I knew she was . . ." He chuckled. The sound was broken. "I knew she was seeing Hedley."

"Brooks? She was dating Brooks?"

"She's a mounted shooter, too. She's good. Nationally ranked. And maybe she didn't want the baby. . . ." He cleared his throat again. "Maybe she thought she'd lose her competitive edge if she was pregnant. Or maybe Hedley . . ." He shook his head. "He and I . . . we always butted heads. I should have known he wouldn't have wanted her to . . ." He drew a deep breath and straightened to face her. "I made mistakes, Case. Terrible mistakes. But the thought of having a baby . . . a little girl . . ." His eyes misted. He glanced away. "I learned everything I could about . . ." He exhaled. "About labor and delivery. I would have supported her in every way I could."

"Except emotionally." She knew all about that. Her own father had been as distant as a mirage. "Except for being a real father to her."

"I screwed up," he said. "I realize that."

"And how do I know what you *would* have done?" she asked.

"I thought you knew me."

"Did you?" she asked. "Really? How would I? It's not like you confide in me. Geez, you were going to be a father, and I would have never even known if Brooks hadn't told me."

"So you want to know about me now? Okay." He jerked a nod. "I broke a couple of ribs last year. I don't like asparagus. I can be a bear in the morning if my coffee—"

"Maybe you *wanted* her to get an abortion."

He stopped cold. "Maybe I did." His voice was very soft. "Maybe in some cowardly part of me I hoped she would." He swallowed and clenched his teeth. "If that's the truth, I'm sorry.

But I can't turn back the clock." His eyes were dark and pained, drawing her in, but she held tight to her reserves.

"Brad lied to me, too," she reminded herself.

"I'm not your damn fiancé!"

"No. As it turned out, he didn't get anyone pregnant!"

The world went silent. He stared at her a long moment, then opened the door behind him and disappeared into the night.

CHAPTER 25

Linette was soaring, flying on horseback. The world below spread out beneath her like a magic carpet, robed in colors so bright they all but hurt her eyes. Between her legs, the palomino stallion glided like a silken ribbon.

She reached forward to caress the animal's neck. His hide was as smooth as sun-warmed satin, as bright as gold. His muscles rippled like waves beneath her palm.

But something sprang at them suddenly. She saw the movement from the corner of her eye, and in that instant the stallion reared. She leaned into his crest, reaching for the mane that sprayed across her waist like corn silk. Her fingers caught nothing but air, and suddenly she was falling.

The earth rushed toward her. The impact hit her like a rock.

She awoke with a start. Pain burned her hip. She put a hand to the ache and sat up slowly, grappling for her bearings. But instead of the white walls and blinking monitors she had become accustomed to, she found she was surrounded by a rustic simplicity that eased her heart rate and steadied her breathing. The burnt-umber walls and rough-cut furniture reminded her where she was. Who she was. Who she used to think she would become.

Lifting her cell from the simple bedside stand, she pressed the appropriate digits and waited hopelessly. The phone rang the usual four times. She closed her eyes, ready to leave another message, but someone answered. A tiny voice.

"Hello?"

Linette sucked in a breath, gripping the phone until her fingers ached. "Lila? Is that you?"

"Who's this?"

Tears sprang into her eyes. Tears from Heartless Hartman. How many people would have sworn it couldn't happen? "Lila." It was hard to say the name out loud. "Is your mommy there?"

There was a moment of silence, then, "I can whistle. Do you want to hear?"

She felt her mouth twitch, felt herself swallow. "Yes. I do. I really do."

The noise she made sounded like a little leak of air leaving a tiny hose.

"Lily bird." The voice in the background was soft, quiet, coming from another corner of the house. Linette held her breath. "What are you doing, honey? Are you . . . Oh no . . ." she said and chuckled.

Linette gripped her cell tighter and prayed for strength as she heard the phone being taken from the child.

"I'm sorry." Maybe there was still a hint of little girl in the woman's voice. Or maybe Linette simply wanted to believe that. "Lila just loves the phone. Who is this, please?"

"Heidi?" Linette's voice almost failed her completely, making the sound scratchy and inhospitable. "This is your mother."

There was a moment of silence. "I don't have a mother," she said. "Haven't for thirty years."

"Heidi, please, I'm sorry. I thought I was doing what was best for you. I didn't want to leave you destitute like *my* father—"

"You were doing what was best for you," she said, and hung up.

Linette sat immobile before sliding the phone shut and exhaling carefully. Across the rustic room, a mirror was framed in deep-grained barn wood. The woman in the looking glass appeared old and worn. Exhausted and beaten. But her gaze fell to the leather lead she had dragged from the trash can behind the house.

Stepping out of bed, she raised her chin and shoved the memory of her abandoned daughter behind her. She had become an expert at that. Lifting a padded envelope from the dresser, she addressed it to Detective Leonard Alderman. There were still a few people who owed her favors. In a moment, she had shoved the leather strap inside.

"So if I get the fiber from Colt's mom, I can learn to spin *and* knit over the winter." Emily put a hand to her abdomen. Fear blossomed as pain knifed across her abdomen. Braxton Hicks contractions, she told herself, and breathed through them. "Come spring I'll be able to make all of Karma's clothes myself." Since deciding the baby was a girl, she had begun with names back at the beginning of the alphabet. So far, Cosima was her favorite.

"Alpaca diapers?" Casie asked. She was leaning back in the kitchen chair, one foot tucked beneath her as she nursed a cup of coffee.

"I said *clothes*," Emily repeated. "Not diapers."

"So you're going to use disposables?" Sophie mused.

Emily turned on Sophie with a start. "Are you flipping? Cloth costs less than a fourth as much as disposable and that's not even considering the environmental impact. If—" It wasn't until she saw the sparkle in Sophie's eyes that she realized she'd been played.

She rolled her eyes. "What about you, Linny? Which do you prefer?"

No one spoke. Emily glanced to her left, but the older woman's gaze was distant as she stared out the window.

"Linny?"

"What?"

"I was just wondering if you used cloth or disposable diapers when Elizabeth was a baby."

"Oh, I . . ." Her face looked pale and drawn. "You know what? I'm kind of tired. I think I'll go lie down for a while."

"Are you okay?"

"Sure. Of course. I'll see you later," she said and left. The screen door slammed behind her.

"What was that about?" Emily asked.

Sophie shrugged.

Casie scowled. "Do you think she's not feeling well?"

"She's got to feel better than I do," Em said and pressed a hand to her ribs.

"What's wrong?" Casie immediately sounded worried.

Emily shrugged, conflicted. She'd wanted a family of her own since the day she was old enough to understand what it meant to be alone. True, she hadn't expected it to be like this exactly, but the thought of having someone to share blood with, to share life with, had always been a need nestled so deep inside her that it could barely be separated from the beat of her heart. But the fear was becoming overwhelming. Fear punctuated by glaring self-doubt and throbbing inadequacies.

"Em?"

"I'm fine," she said, pressing harder on a rogue heel that seemed to be trying to jam its way between her ribs. I just . . ." she began, but just then a knock sounded on the door.

"I got it," Sophie said and hurried into the foyer.

In a moment she was back. They stared at her, waiting for an explanation.

"Oh," she said, realizing their interest. Glancing up momentarily, she sank back into her chair. "It's just Colt."

"Geez, Soph," Colt said, stepping into the kitchen. "You're making me blush." Ignoring Casie, he turned toward Emily. "You got any more of that coffee?"

"Sure," she said and watched her two favorite people in the world pointedly avoid each other. What the hell was their problem now?

"Well . . ." Casie carefully settled her coffee mug on the counter. "I better get that gate built," she said, and brushing past Colt, deftly escaped from the people who loved her most.

Despite its inauspicious beginnings, the day hadn't been a total bust, Casie thought. She was almost finished with the arena gate she was determined to build herself. Potential guests called from Washington State: a mother and her two daughters who were looking for some girl time. Emily whipped up some sort of green-bean concoction that made life worth living, and there was still time after supper to begin halterbreaking the new baby.

In fact, she and Sophie were doing just that, urging the little one out of the stall behind his momma while Emily made ridiculous suggestions, when Philip Jaegar stepped into the barn.

Casie felt her heart jerk nervously as he strode toward them. He was dressed in a pair of high-priced blue jeans and loafers imported from a more romantic part of the world. "Mr. Jaegar! We weren't expecting you." She glanced at his daughter. She looked a little pale. It was a pretty good bet that she hadn't mentioned her sojourn into felony.

"Daddy." The girl blinked, knuckles white against the newborn foal's lead rope. "What are you doing here?"

He laughed. Philip Jaegar was nothing if not charismatic. "Can't I stop by to see my favorite daughter now and then?"

"Sure. I mean . . ." She skimmed her gaze to Casie. Her wild-eyed glance did nothing to settle Casie's stomach. "It's great to see you."

"Really?" He reared back a little, faking shock before his handsome face broke into another smile. "You short on cash or is the world just coming to an end?"

"No. No." She shook her head, glossy hair shining in the overhead lights. "Of course not."

"Who's this?" he asked, nodding to the foal as he took an additional step toward the newborn.

"He's, um . . ." Sophie glanced at Casie again. "He's . . ." She licked her lips.

"He's the Lazy's newest addition," Emily said.

"Yeah?" He stepped closer. Casie tightened her grip on Freedom's lead rope when she fidgeted a little.

"Is that a new mare then?"

"New?" Casie said, and though she tried to avoid shifting her gaze to Emily, she couldn't seem to help herself.

And Em didn't fail her.

"Strangest thing," the girl said, stepping casually into the breach. "We found her in the sheep pasture."

"What?" He reared back on his well-shod feet again. "You mean, she just *appeared?*"

"Like a phantom horse," Emily said, gathering steam. "It was surreal. I was the first one up in the morning because I'd set caramel rolls out to rise the night before and I wanted to see how they were doing. If you let them go too long they'll fall, and with this climate change debacle I was afraid they'd get too warm. Anyway, when I looked out the kitchen window, there she was, running across the pasture. At first I thought I was still dreaming. I mean, I have the strangest dreams. You can't imagine what a miniature person does to your REM when it's cavorting on your bladder. Once I dreamed I was skiing naked in the Amazon jungle. Tarzan was there and . . . Well, never mind. Anyway, when I finally realized I wasn't dreaming, I woke up Casie and Soph."

Jaegar blinked as if just awakening himself. "And she was pregnant?"

Emily shrugged. "Everybody's doing it," she said and stroked her belly.

He laughed, thoroughly distracted. "So you don't even know who they belong to?" he asked, glancing at his daughter.

She stared back at him, not speaking. Maybe Soph's lying ability was as abysmal as Casie's.

"We're not sure," Emily said, yanking up the verbal slack once again. "We think she might have escaped from a kill truck or something."

"A kill truck?"

"Unwanted horses," she said. "They haul them up to Canada for slaughter."

"No," Jaegar said, scowling. "I mean, I know the practice exists. But who would do something like that to such a beautiful animal?" Although he admired the equine pair, Casie noticed that he was careful not to venture any closer. "It wouldn't even make sense. Why breed her if they're just going to slaughter her? At least they would have waited until the colt was born. Right?"

No one spoke. You could cut the tension with a pocketknife. He shifted his gaze from one to the other. Lies seemed to be in short supply.

"Have you called around?" he asked. "It must be one of your neighbors'."

Emily glanced from one to the other as if waiting for them to pull their verbal weight. They didn't. She was carrying the proverbial load alone.

"I put flyers up in town, of course. I mean . . ." She shook her head. "They don't exactly pop. They're just made by hand since we don't have a printer. Living in the dark ages definitely has its disadvantages."

"And no one has called?" he asked, turning back to his daughter finally.

She managed a shrug and a scowl. It looked like the extent of her abilities.

"Tell you what," he said. "I'll put an ad in the lost and found for you if you'll just give me her stats."

"That's . . ." Casie felt her stomach knot up and her knees go weak. "That's not necessary."

He shook his head. "It's no problem. Assurant Realty gives the paper a lot of business. They'll probably cut me a deal. In fact . . ." He snapped his cell from the front pocket of his perfectly pressed jeans. "I'll call them right now. What would you like me to—"

"I stole her!" Sophie breathed the words.

Jaegar's brows rose, his mouth formed a soundless O, before he tilted his head and narrowed his eyes as if thinking very hard.

"What?" he asked.

No one spoke.

He chuckled a little as if waiting for the punch line, then turned expectantly toward Casie.

"I've, um . . ." Her voice was barely audible to her own ears. "I've been trying to contact you."

The barn went silent for two seconds before Emily stepped back into the breach. "I think Sophie is speaking figuratively. I mean—"

"She was being abused," Sophie said. "Confined to a tie stall for months at a time. No exercise. Not enough water. Raped. Neglected . . ."

"You *stole* her!" Jaegar's voice exploded like a nuclear bomb.

"There was nothing else I could do!" Sophie snapped. All hope of being appeasing had disappeared from her voice. "She was pregnant, exploited for her . . . for her *urine* . . . for God's sake. It should be a crime. It *is* a crime if you ask—"

"What the hell is she talking about?" Jaegar turned on Casie like a caged bear.

It took everything Casie had not to back away. "We'll return her to the rightful owner," she said. "We just . . . wanted to make sure she had the foal safely, and now that we—"

"You stole her?"

Sophie shook her head. "Casie didn't—"

"It's my fault," Casie said. "I should have—"

"You're damn right it's your fault!" He swept his hand through the air as if cutting any lingering cords between them. "First she ends up in the hospital because of some juvenile delinquent and now—"

"Ty's not a delinquent."

"Listen, young lady," he said, turning on his daughter with a snarl. "I've tried my best to give you everything you—" he began, but she laughed out loud. The foal jumped, but she held him steady without glancing back.

"To give me what?" she asked. *"Things? Possessions?"*

"I've given you everything," he snapped.

"Yeah?" She laughed. "How about your time? How about honesty? How about a *mother?"*

"A . . ." He shook his head. His cheeks had reddened a little. "Listen, I'm sorry it didn't work out with Amber but—"

"Amber?" She spat the name out like poison. "Are you kidding me?"

"She's a very nice woman."

"Woman! *Woman?* She's barely older than this foal."

"Well, at least she wouldn't . . ." He waved a hand wildly, including the farm and a dozen other things he seemed unable to articulate. "At least she's not a horse thief."

Sophie pursed her lips and narrowed her eyes. "That's because she was too busy getting liposuction to care about anything as significant as another life."

"Are you—" He shook his head in disbelief, then turned abruptly on Casie. "What have you done?"

"I . . ." She had no idea what to say.

"I brought my daughter here thinking you'd be a good influence on her. Thinking, foolishly, I see, that you would make her into a decent human being, not—"

"Is that what you think?" Sophie rasped. "You think I'm not even *decent?*"

He scowled, ran splayed fingers through his perfectly frosted hair. "I didn't mean it like that."

She laughed. "No wonder you don't want me living with you. You think I'm some kind of depraved—"

"I *do* want you living with me. In fact . . ." He raised his brows, squared his jaw. "I insist on it."

She snorted and shook her head, but he persisted.

"Get in the car," he ordered.

Her eyes got wide. "What?"

"Get in the car! Right now."

"No!"

He turned to Casie again, eyes snapping with anger. "You tell her."

"What?"

"Make her come with me."

She took a stumbling step back, shaking her head. "I can't do that."

"Then I'll call child protection and tell them you're abusing minors."

The air had left Casie's lungs with a hiss of disbelief. The barn went quiet, and into that silence, Sophie dropped her bomb.

"And I'll call Mother," she said.

They turned toward her in unison. The anger in his eyes had

banked down to dark embers. The flush had disappeared from his cheeks.

"What?" He barely breathed the word.

She raised her chin a little. "I'm sure she'd like to know about the valuables you had stashed away at the time of the divorce."

He glanced at Casie, face pale. "I don't know what you're talking about."

"I'm talking about the twenty thousand dollars in precious metals you didn't declare during the divorce proceedings."

He shook his head and took a step toward her.

"I've got Mom on speed dial," she said. "I bet she's got her attorney on hers."

"You're mistaken," he said.

"Then it won't hurt to tell her about them," she said and pulled the phone from her pocket.

He stared at her a full five seconds, then turned abruptly on his imported heel and left.

CHAPTER 26

"Did I tell you that alpaca fiber is twenty times warmer than wool?" Emily asked. She was just taking a bacon-and-apple quiche from the oven. Comfort wafted from the steaming dish, curling around her worn oven mitts, easing the tension of the trio of women seated around the table. Still, no one spoke. It had been approximately twenty-four hours since the Philip Jaegar episode. Perhaps, during that time, Sophie had come to accept the fact that Freedom would have to be returned to her former owner. Hell, maybe Linette knew, too, but if she realized the truth surrounding the mare's strange appearance at the Lazy Windmill, she'd kept it to herself. Instead, she was sipping coffee, deeply immersed in her own thoughts.

"It's also one-hundred-percent natural and extremely sustainable even though—"

The sound of tires on gravel stopped her words. Every eye snapped to the window. Sophie jerked to her feet, nearly tipping her fresh-squeezed apple juice as she hurried to look out.

Casie tried to wrangle in her angst, but it gnawed at her like a bad-tempered hound. Her breathlessness was probably caused by panic. After all, there was no telling who was going to show up on her front porch. Maybe the police with a warrant for her arrest, or someone to inform them that the world was about to come to an end. But maybe, just maybe, it was her last conversation with Colt that kept her most sleepless and jittery of all. "Who is it?"

Linette glanced up. "Perhaps Ty caught a ride this morning. He said he was going to hand graze Angel first thing today."

"It's not Ty," Sophie said.

"Is it Colt?" Linette asked.

Casie's chest felt tight, though she was sure she wasn't holding her breath.

Sophie shook her head, craning her neck to peer out the kitchen window. "It looks like a woman." She scowled. Somehow the expression was obvious even from behind. "We're not expecting any new guests, are we?"

Casie shook her head. "Not until next week." She took a step toward the window. "Maybe it's the mail carrier. I heard we were getting a new one."

"She doesn't seem to have any mail."

"Is it Mrs. Dickenson?" Emily asked. "She was going to drop off some fiber . . . you know . . . since it's twenty times warmer than wool."

"Is Colt's mom thirty years old?"

Emily raised one shoulder. "She would have had to give birth when she was about ten if she is, but some of us don't like to procrastinate."

"I don't know who it is," Casie said, but she had a bad feeling.

Emily stepped up beside her. "Oh." She nodded, set her worn oven mitts aside, and headed toward the door. "That's just Mrs. Avery."

Casie turned on her with a scowl. "What?"

"Who?"

"Mrs. Avery." Emily retrieved her backpack from the kitchen floor and stepped into the foyer. "From the adoption center," she said and was gone.

It was almost noon by the time Emily returned home. Casie had been hoping to see her alone, but Murphy's law was still in force, it seemed, since Linette was making herself a sandwich near the sink when the girl chirped a hello and headed for the stairs.

"Emily," Casie breathed. "Where have you been?"

She shrugged and gave a half smile. "Just went for a drive. Listen, the kid's calisthenics have been wearing me out. My spleen feels like a punching bag. I'm going to catch a couple zz's before I start dinner."

"Emily!" Casie said, but the girl had already disappeared into the stairwell.

Casie exchanged a quick glance with Linette.

"Excuse me," she said and hurried up the stairs, but Emily was already shutting the door by the time she arrived on the landing. "Emily," she said, putting a hand on the knob. "Can I come in?" She could just see Emily's left eye through the open door.

"I'm dogged, Case. Sorry. But I'll get started on—"

"We need to talk."

"Oh," Emily said and stepped back. "Okay. What's up?" she asked and slipped the backpack from her shoulders.

"What's—" Casie gestured toward the front yard. This had been the longest day of her life and it wasn't even noon yet. "Where have you been? Who's Mrs. Avery? And what is this about an adoption agency?"

"Listen, I told you I was thinking of giving the kid up for adoption, right?"

Casie huffed a laugh and waited for the punch line, but when none was delivered, she shook her head and struggled for equilibrium. "What are you talking about? You're not serious . . . are you?"

"Well, I'm sure not joking," she said and plopped down onto the bed. "I mean . . ." She shook her head. "Who am I kidding? I'm not mom material. Holy shorts . . ." She laughed and made a silly face. "I'm barely *human* material."

"Em . . ." Casie shook her head and sat down on the bed beside her. "You're not really thinking about giving her up, are you?"

They stared at each other.

"No," Emily said and let her shoulders slump. "I'm not thinking about it."

Casie closed her eyes and felt the breath leave her lungs in a rush of relief. "Thank heavens."

"I've decided for sure," she said, and jumping to her feet, shoved a book into one of the neat rows on her shelves. "I mean, seriously, raising a kid's not for wimps. It's like . . . a job for Superman or something."

"Emily, you can't just—"

"Listen, this is going to work out great. The agency will pay all the hospital bills this way. I mean, do you know what it costs to have a kid these days?"

"If it's just the money, we'll—"

"But it's not *just* the money, Case. It's everything!" she said, sweeping an arm sideways to encompass the world. "I'm just figuring out this gardening thing. I want to learn to knit and spin and weave. You need help around the farm, and you know . . . who am I kidding? I'm not cut out to be a mother. I don't have a career. Hell, I can't even decide on a name. If it stayed with me, it would probably turn out to be a juvenile delinquent or something."

"I think you're wrong."

She paused. Something passed over the girl's face, something painful and desperate and so hopeful it almost made Casie cry, but it disappeared in a flash. "You're so great, Case. And I owe you so much. But how am I ever going to pay you back when I'm strapped with a kid? It's hard enough getting stuff done around here the way it is."

"Emily . . ." She was at a loss for words for a moment and shook her head. "You can't do this."

"I already have," she said and gave one quick shrug. "Listen, it's no big. Women give up babies every day. My mom gave me up and look how well I turned out." She laughed. The sound was short and high-pitched. "I know you're worried, Case, but you don't have to be. I'm fine. The baby doctor said so, and I didn't even have to sleep with him to get a clean bill of health. Although he was kind of cute. Anyway, I'm doing great, I'm just super tired. Do you mind if I just—"

"Is it because of me? Have I made you work too hard? Are you—"

"What? No. Casie, are you kidding? You're wonderful. This has nothing to do with you."

"Then what?"

"Like I said, I just realized that this isn't my gig. I mean, it's been a blast fantasizing about it, but shi . . . shoot," she corrected, and managed a laugh. "I've run out of big vocab words to feed it and—" Her voice broke. She squeezed her eyes shut.

Casie moved closer, heart aching. "Emily, what's going on?"

"I can't do this." The words were barely a whisper. "Geez, Casie, it's a baby! A new life! I can barely be responsible for myself. I can't possibly take care of someone else. I'm a liar, Case. And a thief. Did you know I'm a thief?"

"We've all made mistakes," Casie said. "But what's past—"

"It's not in the past," she whispered. "Not very far past, anyway."

"What are you talking about?"

"I stole your can opener."

Casie raised her brows. "My . . . can opener?"

Emily nodded.

"Honey," she said and ran her hand along the girl's arm. "I used it just this morning."

The girl shook her dreadlocks wildly as if frustrated by Casie's inability to follow her thoughts. "Two weeks ago I was thinking of bugging out, so I took the opener. You know . . . just in case. But then I realized I'd have had to walk all the way to town and . . ." She shrugged, smoothed a palm over her belly. "I put it back."

"You were going to leave? What—" Casie began, then shook her head, trying to get back on track. "It's just a can opener, Em. It costs about two dollars brand new and believe me it's not brand—"

"But that's just the thing. I barely *have* two dollars." Her gaze held Casie's. Her eyes were bright with unshed tears. And in their depths Casie saw a fear so deep it could suck her in. "I barely have a dime. And even if I did . . . even if I was as rich as

Judas . . . or . . . or Jaegars . . ." She shook her head and exhaled a laugh. "Holy shorts, I mean, he has more money than God and even he messed up his kid."

"I don't think money's the determining factor here, Em."

"Then what is?" she snapped and jerked out of Casie's grasp. "Having two parents?" She turned back. "The Jaegars had that. Good jobs? They had that, too. So what makes it work? Maturity? Stability? Extended family? I don't have any of those things. They had them all, and they're still at each other's throats, Casie. Like wolves, like . . . like everyone I've ever known." Her voice caught. "I can't do it," she whispered.

"But you're not them," Casie said. "You don't know what's gone wrong in their relationship. You can only hope to do better in your own."

Emily's eyes searched Casie's for a second. Then she snorted. "Hope?" she said. "I'm supposed to bring a life into the world and *hope* it works out. That's probably what *my* mom did," she said, then exhaled heavily and straightened her back as she turned to look out the window toward the quiet pastures. "Mrs. Avery promised to find a good family."

"You can't—"

"Two parents. With a stay-at-home mom and a dad that'll teach him to hit a baseball. A traditional family." She nodded. Her expression was somber, her eyes as old as forever. "Like *Father Knows Best* or *Leave It to Beaver* or—"

"Emily—"

"Although . . ." She laughed. "I guess that last one has some weird sexual connotations these days."

"Just wait," Casie pleaded, rising carefully from the bed lest she frighten the girl. "Everything's all messed up right now. You don't have to make a decision immediately."

For a moment Emily seemed to waver, but then she laughed. "If I wait much longer, the kid'll be able to choose his own parents."

"You can't—" Casie began, then drew a deep breath and made herself count to three. "Just tell me you'll think things through. Promise me you'll—" she began, but Emily shook her head.

"The papers have already been signed."

Casie felt the blood drain from her face, felt her heart clench in her chest.

"I'm sorry, Case," Emily said and turned away. "But I really am beat. When this is all over I'm sure I'll be able to get a lot more done. But for right now, I'd better rest up. I don't want the kid's new parents to think I deprived him somehow."

"Emily—"

"Please," she said, and there was such desperation in her voice, such mind-numbing hopelessness, that Casie nodded once and turned away. The door felt heavy when she pulled it open.

The stairs groaned as she made her way down them.

Sophie had joined Linette by the sink. They turned toward her in unison.

Casie blinked, dazed. "Did you know anything about this, Soph?"

"About what?"

"This." She gazed sightlessly at the stairs. "The adoption."

Sophie pulled her perfect features into a scowl. "She's not really going through with it."

Casie drew a deep breath, searching for balance. "She says she signed the papers."

Sophie shook her head. "She's lying," she said. "That's what she does."

"I don't think so."

"Why?" Linette asked. Her face was crumpled with worry. "Why now?"

Casie stifled a wince, but couldn't quite manage to keep her gaze from straying back to Sophie.

The girl's eyes went wide even before Casie managed to shift her own away. "It's because of me," she said.

Casie shook her head, ready to deny, retreat, lie, even though she would never have the talent Emily possessed.

"It's because of my dad and me, isn't it?" she demanded.

"No. She's just . . ." Casie struggled with a denial. She was sure there was far more to the situation than witnessing one simple argument. Hell, if she had made life-changing decisions based on her parents' fights, her entire life would have been dictated by arguments. Then again, maybe it had been. "She's just scared. I'm sure she'll change her mind once she gets some sleep," she said, but she was just spouting platitudes. She had no reason to believe such tripe. Emily was as predictable as a tornado.

"Maybe it's for the best," Linette said, but her eyes looked haunted.

They turned toward her like she'd grown a spare head. "What?"

"Parenting isn't easy. Who's to say this isn't the best thing for Emily *and* the baby?"

They said nothing.

"I mean, she's so young." She winced. "Maybe she wants a career. To be an attorney or . . . something." Her voice had gone very soft. Her hands were shaking. "She's very bright. She deserves to have a life."

"Linette . . ." Casie said and took a step forward, but the older woman backed away.

"I think Colt's here for my lesson," she said and escaped out the door.

CHAPTER 27

Maddy stood like an equine angel at the hitching rail behind the barn while Linette tacked her up. The equipment was heavy, and Linny was short; she had to hoist the saddle over her head to settle it onto the mare's broad back. But she liked the challenge, appreciated the strain it put on her biceps, enjoyed the puzzle of cinching it up right. She'd made Colt show her a dozen times a day how to tie the knot in the latigo. Committed to memory how tight to make the cinches.

The bridle came with its own set of problems, but Linette wrestled her way through them, slipping the short-shanked curb between the mare's teeth, buckling up the throatlatch. Through it all, Maddy waited patiently, reins drooping, tail swishing gently from side to side, banishing the few remaining insects that had survived the first frosts.

Autumn had come in earnest in the last week or so. Out east the apple orchards would be bustling with leaf peepers. But the heart of the West had its own rhythm. The cool, dry weather was perfect for harvesting corn and branding weanlings, for digging root vegetables and mending fences.

Linette inhaled sharply, drawing in every second. She could have tacked Maddy up inside, but she had always liked fall. In her mind it was the time for new beginnings. Other people, she knew, thought of spring that way, but not her. Heidi had been born in the fall. In her wallet was a dog-eared photograph of her toddling through the oak leaves outside their little house in suburbia, but the modest little split level had never been right for her. She wasn't the domestic type. Not the kind to sit around and bake cookies. Not even the kind to *eat* cookies. She was a doer. Always had been. She'd been sure her daughter would understand that once she was grown. She'd been sure all her hard work would be worth the sacrifices. Because that's what she'd done. She *had* sacrificed. She had sweated. And she had achieved. That's the kind of person she was. That's why she was here. To learn something new. It didn't matter that she was sixty-four years old. She was still learning. And she would learn this, even if Colt was late and her surgical sites were on fire.

She put a hand to her right hip, took another deep breath, and closed her fingers over the reins near the bit. Maddy followed her willingly into the outdoor arena. Mounting was always a challenge. The stirrup seemed to fall straight from the sky and land practically at her shoulder, but Linette pulled her knee to her chest, shoved her newly purchased Ariat boot into the near leather hoop, and heaved herself into the saddle. That accomplished, she felt better. Hurdles were her thing. She'd cleared a thousand of them in her lifetime, and she'd clear a few more no matter what the doctors said. She wasn't the type to sit around and mope. Neither was she the sort to suffer through another bout of debilitating treatment in the hopes of gaining a few more weeks spent flat on her back.

Maybe things hadn't worked out as she'd hoped with her family, but that chapter wasn't over, either. If they knew her better, they'd know who they were dealing with. They'd know she wasn't the kind to quit once she set her sights on a goal.

Looking ahead, she hugged Maddy with her calves. The big mare moved into a slow walk, beginning her first circle. Linette was tempted to take her down the road, but she was no fool. She knew her limitations. Instead, she would practice here, learn what she could on her own, and show Colt her accomplishments when he arrived.

Those decisions made, she clicked twice, urging Maddy into

a trot. That felt good, right, exhilarating. They did a few circles as Linette screwed up her nerve. The lope was scary as hell, but she threw the mare a kiss, and finally, on the second try, the mare rocked into an easy three-beat gait, gliding along. The rhythm was like magic. The crisp air felt like salvation against her face. With little more than a thought, the mare took the cue to cut through the middle of the ring and change direction. There was a moment of panic as she lurched into a down transition, nearly jolting Linette from the saddle. The extended trot was a bugger to ride, but she'd discovered years ago that easy was not for her. Pushing the mare back into a lope, Linette felt the soaring euphoria of accomplishment once again. She was riding. She was doing it. After dreaming of this since childhood, she was making it happen. Because that's what she did. She set her eyes on an obstacle, she studied the obstacle, she overcame the obstacle. Just like that jump. Shifting her gaze, she eyed the makeshift obstacle Colt had set up along the north rail of the arena. It wasn't tall, just a long branch perched between two hay bales a foot or two off the ground. She'd ridden over it more than a dozen times at a walk and a couple at a trot. Maddy tended to drag the branch down at both gaits, causing Colt no end of entertainment.

Linette narrowed her eyes at the jump. The problem was, it seemed to her, they didn't have enough speed to clear it easily. There wasn't enough lift during the walk and trot to make an effortless arc over the thing.

She licked her lips, urged the pinto back into a lope, and watched the obstacle. It was just a little thing. She could jump it herself. She pushed the mare past it a few times, making sure Maddy knew it was there, building up her own confidence. Then, after passing it for the fourth time, she screwed up her courage, leaned into the center of motion, and urged her mount toward the rail with her inside leg. The mare went easily, picking up her pace a little, and shifting her ears forward.

The challenge rose up in front of them, but Maddy was game. She gathered herself like a champion, thrust off with her powerful hindquarters, and soared. Exhilaration burned through Linette like a flare gun. It was like flying. Like being truly free for the first time in her life. Like being unshackled. But suddenly her mind flickered, just a little misfire of neurons her doctors had warned her about. For an instant, blackness filled her head, and then the earth came flying toward her like a meteor. There was a moment, just a wild second in time, when Linette was sure she could correct herself, could find her balance. But the ground was coming up too fast, hurtling at her, a world of changes in its wake.

"I need you to talk to Em," Casie said. It had taken all of her nerve to force herself out of the house when she saw his truck in the yard. But just because she had finally admitted there would never be anything between the two of them didn't mean he should abandon Emily.

Colt settled a roll of twisted wire into the back of his pickup truck and straightened. Turning his head, he glanced over his shoulder at her. Dark, too-long hair brushed the collar of his flannel shirt. "What's up?" he asked. There was no inflection in his tone and his expression was guarded. But that was fine. For the best, really.

Casie exhaled carefully, steadied her palms against her thighs, and silently assured herself that everything would be okay. Though God knew she was probably lying. "She's planning to give the baby up for adoption."

"What!" He turned fully toward her. His dark brows were low beneath his ubiquitous Stetson.

"She says she already signed the papers."

He swore in near silence and she nodded.

"Yeah," she said.

"I'm sorry." His voice was low and quiet, as steady as the earth, as deep as the river. It sucked her in, but she forced herself to stay back, to stay away.

He glanced off toward the windmill. A muscle jumped in his cheek. "Did you tell her she's making a mistake?"

He shifted his dark gaze to hers, causing her to turn away in self-defense.

"It's not really my place to tell her what to do."

"You think it's mine?" His tone was atypically rough.

"I think . . . I think she needs a friend. You're her friend."

For a moment she thought he would remind her that she'd asked him to stay away from the girl, but maybe he wasn't as petty as she was. He nodded. "Okay. So you want me to . . ." He shook his head, seeming at a loss. When was Richard Colton Dickenson ever at a loss? "What do you want me to say exactly?"

"Tell her not to—" She stopped abruptly, reminding herself that she couldn't live someone else's life. Hell, she could barely manage her own. "I don't know what to tell her."

He nodded slowly and glanced toward the cattle pasture. Worry was etched on his face, but there was more than that. There was pain, too. An inordinate amount of honest agony. Making her wonder what would have happened if his daughter had been born. She pictured a child with his dark good looks. His mischievous smile. The idea made her stomach clench.

"Well . . ." She made her voice brisk, straightened her spine. "I'd better get back to work."

"Where is she?" he asked.

"She's still napping," Casie said. "I waited until you were done with Linette's lesson to talk to you. She should be up soon."

He scowled. "Lin doesn't have a lesson until later."

"She said . . ." Casie began, then remembered the agony on the other woman's face during their talk about giving up babies. "I guess she was just making excuses to get out of the house."

"Tormenting your guests again, are you?" he asked, and for a second the old Colt shone through. It was like seeing light at the end of the tunnel, but she didn't need that light. She could make it on her own. Hell, she *was* making it on her own.

"Well . . ." He shoved his hands into his jeans pockets and glanced away. "I guess I'll go find Lin. She probably wants to learn to wrestle steers or something."

Casie nodded. Colt shuffled his feet. They both cleared their throats.

"Well . . . thanks," she said and turned, pulling herself toward the house as he headed in the opposite direction.

"Case . . ." She turned at the sound of her name, breathless, hoping for something she dared not try to define.

"Yes?" Her tone was too breathless, too hopeful, but he was still facing away from her, body suddenly tense.

"Why's Maddy in the arena?"

"What?" Something jangled in her soul . . . premonition or worry or a horrific mixture of the two.

"Why's . . ." He took two more strides and stopped short. "Call an ambulance," he ordered.

"What? Why—"

"Now!" he snapped and disappeared around the corner of the barn.

Casie pivoted away and raced toward the house, breath coming like a windstorm. "Soph!" she yelled as she burst into the kitchen. "Sophie!"

The girl's footfalls tapped down the stairs. She appeared before Casie had lifted the receiver from its cradle. "Take a blanket out to the arena," she ordered, and dialed 911.

"What?"

"For Linette," she said, but just then someone spoke through the receiver.

"This is Casie Carmichael!" Holding the phone in a death grip, she rasped the words into the ancient receiver. "There's been an accident at the Lazy Windmill!" she added and rattled off the address.

Sophie swung around and galloped up the stairs. She was back in a matter of seconds, racing past Casie and out the door.

The woman on the other end of the line asked something, drawing Casie back to the conversation. "I don't know how long it's been. Twenty minutes? Maybe more. A helmet? I don't know. Just . . . please . . . send an ambulance quick," she said and hung up.

By the time she reached the arena, Colt and Sophie were both squatting in the dirt. Linette lay perfectly still between them. Casie's limbs felt wooden as she ducked between the planks and straightened. The world seemed hazy, rotating in slow motion.

"What happened?" she asked.

Colt rose to his feet and moved toward her with long strides.

Casie stopped in her tracks, momentarily forgetting to breathe. "What—" she began again, but he spoke before she could complete the question.

"It's probably not as bad as it looks."

"What are you talking about?" she rasped and jerked past him.

He didn't try to stop her.

Linette looked inordinately peaceful. They'd covered her with a red-striped blanket. Her eyes were open. She smiled a little, but the expression was somehow off, tilted a little.

"Linette," Casie crooned, and squatting beside her, reached for her hand. "What happened?"

The elderly woman shifted her eyes sideways and said nothing.

"Linette?" Casie said and wiped a smudge from the other woman's creased cheek. "Where does it hurt?"

"She injured her leg." Colt spoke softly from behind her.

Casie turned slightly, snapping her gaze frantically to his. "What?"

"Her leg . . ." He paused and glanced at Linette's face, but when there was no reaction, he continued on. "It's not good."

"Oh." It was strange that her first inclination was to move away. Even though her eyes traced along the outline of Linette's body to her leg, she didn't really want to see. She didn't want to be there. She simply wanted to distance herself from this woman on the ground. This new disaster. But she remained where she was, maybe held there by fear. "Is it . . . Is she going to be okay?"

He didn't answer. Beside her, Linette shifted as if trying to sit up.

"No!" They all spoke at once, urging her back onto the ground.

"Just . . ." Casie swallowed. "Just lie still. Everything's going to be all right." She wrapped both hands around Linette's cool fingers, encasing them in her palms.

"What—" Linette's face scrunched slightly beneath the helmet that remained askew on her silvery hair. She looked disoriented, only slightly concerned. "What happened?"

Casie swallowed her fear as best she could. "You fell off Maddy."

The scowl intensified. "Maddy?"

Casie stopped a wince, smoothed her expression. "Colt's horse."

"I was on a horse?"

"You don't remember?"

Linette moved her head from side to side the slightest degree. "Well . . ." Her voice was a little hollow, a little empty. "At least I was *on* a horse."

Casie smiled woodenly. "How are you feeling?"

Linette blinked and half shrugged but didn't answer. Her eyes drifted closed.

"Keep her awake," Colt ordered quietly.

"Linette!" The name sounded panicked to Casie's own ears.

She opened her eyes slowly. "How'd it go?"

Casie glanced toward Colt. He shook his head, obviously as uncertain as she. She hurried her gaze back to Linette. "What?"

"The transplant. How'd . . ." She scowled, lifted her left hand vaguely. "What happened?"

Casie swallowed, fear turning to terror at the repeated question. "You fell off a horse."

"I was riding a horse?"

Dear God.

Her eyes went dreamy. "I've always wanted a horse." Her face seemed strangely slack, her skin gray.

"Linette!"

She shifted her gaze groggily back to Casie. "But Mommy says we can't afford one. Not until Daddy comes home."

"An ambulance is on its way," Casie said. "Just hold on. Okay?"

"He's coming back. I know he is," she said and let her eyes fall closed.

"Colt!" Casie rasped.

He was beside her in an instant, shoulder brushing against hers, body warm and solid. "Linny, honey, come on." He squeezed her arm. "Wake up."

She did so, remained expressionless for a moment, then focused with seeming difficulty on his face. Her lips twitched up at one corner. "You're a good-looking devil," she said, then shifted her gaze to Casie. "The handsome ones are always trouble, aren't they? What are the charges?"

Casie scowled at her nonsensical words. "I'm sorry," she said. "So sorry. But it's going to be okay. Hold on."

Linette shifted her gaze, face becoming vacant again. "Daddy's handsome, too."

Casie felt sick to her stomach.

"And he'll come back."

"I'm sure he will," Colt said and stroked the hair away from her face "No one could leave a pretty girl like you."

"I'm not pretty." She scowled as if confused by his compliment. "But I'm smart. And Daddy says if I work really hard I can be whatever I want to be."

"Where's that ambulance?" Casie wasn't even sure who asked the question. It might have been her.

"And I'm tough. Daddy told me I had to be. Not like Mother." She shook her head. The movement was disjointed. "She cries all the time. She thinks I can't hear her, but I can." She shifted her gaze upward. "When I grow up I'm never going to cry."

"Where's that stupid—"

"There it is!" Sophie cried, and jerking to her feet, waved her arms before striding to the far side of the arena to catch up Maddy's dangling reins. In a moment she had disappeared with the mare and the ambulance was inside the corral. No lights flashed. No siren sounded. The vehicle sat there like a bulky bug waiting to swallow them up. It regurgitated two men in button-down shirts and blue jeans.

"My name's Michael. I'm an EMT for Fall River County," said the taller of the two. "Can you tell me what happened?"

Colt spoke first, voice low as he moved away from them. "We think she fell off a horse."

"You weren't here?"

"No."

The EMT moved toward them. Casie set Linette's hand carefully atop the blanket and scooted back, out of the way. Michael pulled a tiny flashlight from his shirt pocket and shone it in each eye. "How long ago did this happen?"

Colt shifted his gaze to Casie's. She shook her head, uncertain of everything as she rose to her feet. Her legs felt shaky. "We're not sure." Colt spoke again. "We called you as soon as we found her."

"Was she unconscious?"

"No."

Michael nodded. "Hi there," he said, addressing Linette for the first time. "Can you tell me your name?"

She blinked. "Linny Sue," she said.

"Do you know this gentleman beside me, Linny Sue?" he asked and felt along her arms as he spoke.

"I—" She paused, glanced toward Casie, and scowled. Her eyes filled with tears. "Heidi . . . I'm sorry, honey. I'm so sorry."

The EMT glanced at Casie. "What's she talking about?"

Casie gripped her hands together, gaze never leaving Linette. "My name's not Heidi."

"Then—"

"Check her legs," Colt said.

Their gazes met. Linette was weeping softly as Michael lifted the blanket and glanced down. Casie couldn't see past his body, but she knew the moment he identified the problem.

His body jerked involuntarily, then he settled the blanket

back over Linette and rose quickly to his feet. "Let's get her on the board," he said.

The other EMT spoke for the first time. "But if there's spinal damage—"

"On the board," he snapped. "Now!"

CHAPTER 28

"Emily! Em!" Casie shouted, and started up the stairs, but suddenly the girl was there, eyes wide, expression worried.

"What's wrong?"

"It's Linette." She felt breathless and terrified, but she forced her voice to be steady, her body to move slowly. "I think she's broken her leg. Colt's riding in the ambulance with her. I'm driving separate."

Emily shook her head, taking a second to orient herself. "I'll go with you."

"You don't have to," Casie argued, but Emily stared at her for a second, then yanked her backpack from the floor.

"I think you're wrong. Do you want me to drive?"

"You don't have a license."

"But I'm not in danger of passing out." Emily moved toward the door, movements ponderous. "Are you okay?"

"Of course. I'm fine," Casie said, but her head felt light.

The drive to the hospital took forever.

"Why are they going so slow?" Casie asked. Ahead of them, the ambulance bumped along at what seemed like a ridiculously leisurely pace. She loosened her grip on the steering wheel, trying to ease the ache in her fingers.

Emily leaned back against her seat and exhaled as if enjoying a day at the beach. "They can't legally exceed the speed limit, but they sometimes modify that rule if they have extraordinary circumstances."

"Well, I think this qualifies." Casie glanced sideways, remembering her passenger's current state. "What about *you*? Are you okay?"

"Better than Linette. Do you know what happened?"

"Not really." She shook her head and held herself carefully together. "I thought she was taking a lesson from Colt. But I guess I was wrong. We found her on the ground in the arena. Maddy was saddled."

"How badly is she hurt?"

"I'm not sure," she said and didn't mention how the EMT's face had paled when he'd seen Linette's leg.

It felt like déjà vu as she parked illegally beside the hospital and jumped out of the truck. In a matter of moments the paramedics were lowering the legs of the stretcher.

Casie wanted to rush to Linette's side almost as much as she wanted to stay away, but her desires were a moot point. The patient was already surrounded. Hospital personnel buzzed around her like anxious bees.

"You okay?" Colt asked.

Casie turned jerkily toward him, noticing him for the first time since their arrival. "Yeah, sure." She glanced around, disoriented and jumpy. "Where's Emily?"

He shook his head, but didn't shift his gaze from hers. "Maybe you should sit down for a while," he suggested and took her elbow in one hand. His palm felt large and strong against her arm, but she pulled from his grip and turned a full circle, oddly panicked.

"I'm fine. Where's Emily?"

"Listen," he said, and slipping a hand carefully behind her back, guided her inside. "I'll find her. You'll have to fill out the paperwork."

"Miss . . ." He turned to a fortyish woman who was rushing by. Overweight and harried, she came to an abrupt halt, already scowling. Colt smiled. "Where can my friend here sit down to fill out the necessary forms?"

Her scowl deepened. "You'll have to go to the front desk."

"There's been an accident," he said, gaze steady. "You're probably used to that sort of thing, but we're pretty skittish. I'd really appreciate it if you could help us out."

Casie scowled down the nearest corridor. It was empty but for a pair of young men in scrubs.

The nurse glanced at her. "Around the corner to the right there's a visiting room," she said. Her voice had softened grudgingly. "Grab a seat there."

"You're why nurses should run the world," Colt said.

She chuckled quietly. "I'll send someone with the necessary forms," she said and shook her head, but when she strode away, her steps were a little jauntier.

Casie scowled after her, anxious and out of sorts. "Don't feel you have to charm anyone on my account."

"Not everything's about you, Head Case," he said and steered her around a corner. "Sit down."

"I'm—"

"Listen, you can pass out later if you want to, but right now it'd be kind of nice if you'd remain conscious for Linette."

"I'm not going to pass out."

"Excellent. Then sit down," he said and motioned toward a couch anchored between two chairs. It looked hard and nondescript.

She sat down. Maybe because she'd never heard him sound so angry. Maybe because she was exhausted. And maybe, just maybe, because she was in danger of passing out.

"Thank you," he said, and giving her one last glance, turned and walked away.

She was found by a barrage of hospital employees in just a matter of minutes. It seemed that everyone in the world asked her the same questions. She answered them as best she could until the tide of staff finally ran out and she was left alone.

Minutes passed slowly. Worry gnawed at her in concert with fatigue.

". . . just a friend."

She jolted awake and glanced around, trying to get her bearings as she pushed herself to a sitting position. An older man in a white lab coat smiled at her. He occupied a chair identical to the one upon which Colt sat not fifteen inches from her couch.

"You must be Casie Carmichael," he said.

"Yes." Her voice was nothing more than a croak. She cleared her throat, wiped her knuckles across her lips, and wondered if she'd been drooling. Colt was staring at her. He was as wickedly handsome as ever, but his grin was noticeably absent. Fear crept up her spine.

"I'm Dr. Deacon."

She nodded, still groggy, as she turned back toward the older man. "How's Linette?"

He sobered a little, but the crow's-feet remained around his eyes as if he was accustomed to smiling. "She sustained some pretty serious injuries to her right tibia, as I'm sure you know."

She didn't take time to tell him she knew nothing. "How serious?"

He tilted his head a little. "Compound fractures such as this one can be somewhat difficult. But Dr. Lucas is an excellent surgeon."

"Compound . . ." She felt herself blanch. "That's when the bone . . ." She swallowed but kept her focus directly on the good doctor. "That's when the bone . . ." She couldn't finish the sentence.

"It's when the bone pierces the skin. Yes, I'm afraid that's the scenario we're dealing with. But Dr. Lucas is very experienced with that sort of thing, and . . ." He smiled again. "I'm not exactly a first-year resident."

She nodded. That's when he reached for her hand, looked into her eyes. "Try not to worry," he said. His eyes were a silvery blue. "She's in surgery right now. Be assured we're doing everything we can for her."

She nodded again. He squeezed her hand and stood up.

She blinked and watched him walk away. It was no easy task to gather her wits, but she made a game effort as she faced Colt. "You shouldn't have let me fall asleep."

He stared at her, expression bland. "I'll remember the cattle prod next time."

She scowled and glanced at the doctor's retreating back.

"Emily's fine," he said. "If you're interested."

She scowled at him. "Of course I'm interested. Where is she?"

He shrugged. "Probably flirting with an MD. What is it about you Lazy Windmill girls?"

"What are you talking about?"

He opened his mouth, but a woman in a skirt and heels had arrived with another battery of questions.

By the time yet another person finished interrogating her, Colt had left. He returned just as Casie was finishing up and bent to shove a white paper bag into her hand.

She glared at it. "What's this?"

"Food."

"I don't need—"

"I know. You're too tough to eat."

"I never said—"

"Just eat the damned thing," he said, voice peeved.

"Listen," she began. If anyone had the right to be irritable she was pretty sure she had dibs, but just then a dark-haired nurse stepped into the room. She was young and attractive, her smile effervescent.

Colt glanced up at her.

"She's at four," she said, leaning around the corner.

"Thanks, Shelly."

"You bet," she said and left.

Casie sat there like a block of salt, paper sack on her lap. "Got a hot date in room number four?" she asked.

"Just eat your sandwich," he said.

"How come you're not hustling out of here? Are you waiting for someone to get discharged so you have a free room?"

"I spent good money on that meal."

"Your hot date's not in labor or something is . . ." she began, but in that second the truth struck her like a blow. "Who's at four?" she asked.

"When was the last time you ate?" he asked, but she jolted to her feet. The paper bag tumbled to the floor.

"Is Emily in labor?"

He gritted his teeth at her. "Damn it, will you eat—"

"You son of a bitch!" Rage trembled through her, though she didn't really know why. "Em's in labor, and you didn't even tell me?"

"What good do you think you're going to do her if you're passed out on the floor?"

"Where is she?"

"I'm not going to tell you until—" he began, but she caught his shirtfront in both fists and pulled herself up to him.

"Where is she?" she growled.

His brows rose a little. "You are turning into one scary chick, Head Case."

"Tell me—" she began, but he spoke before she finished the threat.

"Room two seventy-four," he said. "But she told me not to bother you."

"Not to . . ." she began, then snorted and jerked down the hall.

The hospital was like a rabbit warren, but she finally found her way. It took her a while to get permission to visit Emily, who was lying in bed, looking out the window.

"Emily," she said, slowing her pace as she entered the room. "Why didn't you tell me?"

"Hey, Case," she said. Her eyes were dilated, her tone a little groggy. "What's going on?"

"What's going on?" She forced a laugh. "Well, apparently, you're having a baby."

"Oh, yeah. It'll be over pretty soon, I guess, though. Then I can get back to getting things done. I'm thinking maybe I can sell my rhubapple jam on the Internet. You know, get a bigger market for it."

Casie settled herself on the edge of the girl's mattress. "I don't think now's the time to think about jam."

"How's it going?" A woman in turquoise scrubs stepped into the room.

"Fine," Emily said. Her eyes were dull. "When do you think I'll be done?"

"Everything's going according to schedule," she said, and glancing at the monitors, wrote something on her clipboard.

"Well, the sooner the better," Emily said. "I got miles to go, if you know what I mean."

The nurse gave Casie a dubious glance, then ducked back out of the room.

"Em," Casie said and reached for the hand that was not plugged into the overhead bag of fluids. "Are you okay?"

She shrugged. "Well, I'm higher than a kite. I mean, I figure, why not go the pain-free route? But the docs say I'm fine. I should be home the day after tomorrow. Don't feel like you have to wait around."

"Of course I'm waiting around," Casie said. "But you're not still thinking of giving up—"

"Did I tell you? They found a family for it," Emily said. "Isn't that great? An endodontist and his wife. She's a gardener. Has a greenhouse where she grows orchids and stuff. Can you imagine growing orchids? I can barely get the carrots to grow. And she does charity work. Volunteers at the food shelves. She wears those shoes with the funny name. Berkenshoes or . . . What are they called?"

"Emily . . ."

"Birkenstocks," she said. "Ugly things, but they probably cost more than my hospital stay. The kid'll be spoiled rotten. Like one of those mean girls in school that I always hated."

"Emily, I think you need to—"

"Hi," someone said.

They glanced up in unison.

"My name's Linda. I'll be taking over for Sue. I'm told you're just about ready."

"I *am* ready," Emily said. Her face was flushed. "Let's roll."

"Well, let me take a look," Linda said, and snapping on a pair of gloves, pushed up the blanket that covered the lower half of Emily's body. "Great," she said, replacing the sheet. "You're almost there. I'm going to call the doctor and then we'll get down to business."

"Sounds like a plan, man," Emily said and turned back toward Casie. "You should get something to eat. You look kind of pale."

"Are you okay?" Casie asked again.

"Never been better."

"I really think you need to give this more thought, Em. You're under a lot of stress right now, and this is a huge decision. Maybe—"

"So, Emily . . . it's that time," said a man who entered the room briskly. "Hi." He glanced up from his clipboard. "You must be Casie. I've heard a lot about you. Emily and the baby are going to be living with you at the ranch, isn't that—"

"There's been a change in plans, doc," Emily said. "I'm giving the kid up for adoption."

"What?" He scowled and glanced at Emily. "Are you sure about this?"

"Absolutely. I mean . . . I'm just a kid myself, right?" She paused and smiled, though there was sweat on her brow. "I gotta live my life before I can be tied down with that kind of responsibility."

"Well, maybe now's not the time to decide something of that importance," the doctor said.

"I'm giving it up," Emily said. "And it's going to have a perfect life. Two parents. No money troubles. A private school."

"Those things don't make—" Casie began, but Emily interrupted her.

"The decision's been made." She gritted her teeth. "Now let's get this show on the road."

Even with an epidural it was a difficult birth, but finally the baby crowned. Casie cut the cord as a doctor drew the infant into the world. Wrinkled and purple and as loud as a cyclone, she arrived with a gargled wail.

"It's a girl," the doctor said.

A nurse sucked the fluid from her nose and mouth, then wrapped her in a blanket and handed the little bundle to Casie.

She caught her breath and stared into the disgruntled little face. It was wizened and ruddy, with slits for eyes and tiny fists clenched angrily beside its goopy head. "Oh, Emily . . ." Her words were barely audible even to herself. "She's amazing. Just look—"

"Take her away," Emily said.

Casie glanced up. Emily was facing the wall, expression stony, eyes dead.

The room went silent. Even the infant was quiet.

"Emily—"

"Get rid of her," she said and squeezed her eyes closed.

CHAPTER 29

The next few hours seemed interminable. But at last the baby was in the hospital nursery, asleep in her glass bassinet like a tiny soldier lined up with her fellow cadets behind the plate-glass windows. Colt stood a few feet and a couple lifetimes away, expression somber as he watched the tiny bundle.

"She's so . . ." Casie shook her head.

"Helpless?" he said.

She glanced toward him. Their gazes met. Apologies trembled on her lips, but Dr. Deacon appeared before they could escape her mouth.

"Ms. Hartman is out of surgery," he said.

"How is she?" Colt asked.

"Better than we had any right to hope," he said. "She was lucky you found her right away. She'll be in a wheelchair for a while. Chemotherapy weakens the system for some time even after the treatments stop, but she seems like a fighter."

"Chemo!" Casie said.

The doctor raised his silvery brows. "You didn't know?"

"No, I . . . No," she said.

His expression was grave. "I'd better let her tell you about it. You can see her now if you like."

They walked together to her hospital room, but they seemed worlds apart.

Linette looked small and narrow beneath the nubby white blanket.

"Hey," Casie said, easing into the room. "How are you feeling?"

Linette shifted her gaze sideways. "I've been better. I just can't remember when."

Casie forced a smile. "You're going to be all right."

"Am I?" she asked. She sounded worn and defeated.

Casie refrained from glancing across the mattress toward Colt. She didn't need him, didn't need anyone, but sometimes that was hard to remember.

"The doctor said you're lucky. Everything went well."

"Lucky," she said. "I guess that's a relative term." She glanced out the window again. There was a dynamite view of the pediatrics wing. "Did he say anything else?"

"Why didn't you tell us about the cancer?" Casie asked.

"What ever happened to patient-doctor confidentiality?" Linette groused. "He'll be lucky if he doesn't get charged with a lawsuit."

"If we had known—"

"What?" Linette asked, facing her again. "You could have wrapped me in cotton batting and put me up on a shelf?"

"We could have been more careful. We could have—"

"You did everything right," Linette said. "You're legally and morally exempt from blame. Listen . . ." She cleared her throat. "I hope I didn't say something too asinine earlier?"

Colt shook his head. "You were a little disoriented. That's all."

"Disoriented as in I forgot the current secretary of state or like I forgot my own name?"

He smiled at her. "Once I came off a bull headfirst in Reno. Made everyone call me Garth for a week and a half."

"And here I had you pegged for a George Strait fan," she said and took a deep breath. "How's Madeline?"

"She's fine."

"You sure?"

He squeezed her hand. "Would I lie to you?"

"Probably," she said, and he smiled, showing that irresistible light at the end of the tunnel.

She sighed, seeming to relax a little as she glanced from one to the other. "And what about you two? You okay?"

"You're the one we're worried about," Casie said.

"Maybe you should worry about yourselves for a while," Linette suggested.

"Well, we don't have any broken bones," Colt said.

Linette scowled a little. "That's not exactly what I meant. You know . . ." She drew a deep breath and winced a little. Maybe the painkillers were already wearing off. "It might not seem like it to you, but life's short. I think you two should—"

"Emily had her baby," Casie burst in.

Linette lowered her brows, but allowed herself to be distracted. "When?"

"A few hours ago. While you were in surgery."

She nodded slowly, working out the lost hours in silence. "She probably just didn't want to make a separate trip to the hospital," she said finally. "Carbon footprint, and all."

They smiled. She looked exhausted.

"So everything went okay?"

"Yes. It's a girl."

"How long was she in labor?"

"Five hours. Maybe six."

"Not bad. When I had Heidi . . ." She stopped herself, glanced toward the window. It had started to rain, pellet-like drops against the window. "So she's keeping her, right?"

Casie scowled, confused about the older woman's family, but Linette was speaking again.

"You've talked sense into her, haven't you?"

"It's not my decision," Casie said and felt her toes curl at her readiness to cop out at a moment's notice.

Linette stared at her for several seconds, then shifted her gaze to Colt. "How about you?" she asked.

He remained silent for a moment. His eyes spoke of regrets so deep they burned his soul, but he said nothing of the daughter he had lost before ever seeing. "I guess she's already signed the legal documents."

"Documents can be amended," she said, eyes sharp.

Colt shook his head. "I'm in no position to try to change her mind."

Linette drew a deep breath, and for a moment Casie thought she would disagree, but the phone rang beside her bed. Her hand looked bruised and fragile as she reached for it.

"Yes." Her voice was hard. She waited in silence. "She's right here. Tell her yourself," she said and handed the phone to Casie.

She took it with a scowl. "Hello?"

"Ms. Carmichael?"

"Yes?"

"This is Stephanie Pritchard from Pritchard and Pritchard." The attorney's voice was low and flat.

Casie winced at the sound of it. Too many crises were coming too fast. She felt it like a blow to her psyche. "Yes?"

"Mr. Pritchard and I have given this case a good deal of deliberation."

"Listen . . ." She felt panicked and beaten. "I'm not saying Ty was justified in his actions, but—"

"We've decided to drop the charges."

"He was just trying to . . ." Casie paused. "What?" The word was barely audible.

"Just don't expect our son to be coming around in the future."

"Oh . . ." She nodded numbly. "Okay," she said.

In a second, the phone went dead. She stared at it for a prolonged instant, then handed it back to Linette.

"What was that?" Colt asked.

"I just . . ." Casie shook her head, trying to make sense of things. "I don't know."

"Who was it?"

"It was Mrs. Pritchard."

"The attorney? David's mother?" His back was suddenly straight, his expression confrontational. "What the hell is she doing calling here?"

Casie shifted her gaze to Linette. "I don't have any idea. Why did she call you?"

She shrugged. The effort looked exhausting. "They must have gotten my phone number by mistake."

"But how—"

"I'm tired," Linette said, and turning toward the wall, closed her eyes to the world.

"So she's okay, right?" Sophie asked. Her face was drawn. Casie hadn't seen her smile since her father's visit. They were on their way up to Emily's hospital room. Two days had passed since the baby's birth.

"I think she's fine. Physically, at least."

"Physically?" She could feel Sophie's scowl.

Casie shrugged. It wasn't as if *she* had any experience with this sort of thing. "I'm sure it's not easy giving up a baby," she said, and wondered if she'd ever know what it felt like to produce another human being. Wondered if she'd ever have the nerve.

"It's not easy giving anybody up," Sophie said.

Casie glanced at her, but they had already reached their destination. The door to Emily's room was open. Dressed in a baggy sweatshirt and oversized cargo pants, she was sitting with her back propped against the pillows, bare feet flat on the bed. Her eyes looked flat and dull as she stared out the window.

"How you doing?" Casie asked.

The girl turned quickly toward them.

"Hey, you're finally here," she said and shifted to the edge of the mattress. "Let's blow this joint."

"You okay?" Sophie asked.

"Couldn't be better." She was brusque and businesslike, as if she were leaving a long shift at the Chill and Grill. "How 'bout you?"

"I'm fine." Sophie seemed atypically uncertain of her footing.

"How about Ty? How's he doing? He seemed a little down when I talked to him on the phone."

"I don't know," Sophie said. "How would I know?"

Emily gave her an odd look, then shifted her gaze to Casie while shoving a box of confiscated tissues into her backpack. "I figure these are already paid for, right? I might as well take them home with me. Colt didn't come along, huh?"

"No. He—" Casie said and shuffled her feet, struggling not to say any more than necessary. "Do you have everything you need?"

"I think so."

"Well, you're wrong," someone said.

They turned toward the voice. Linette sat in a wheelchair in the doorway.

"Hey," Emily said. "How are you?"

"You forgot this," said the older woman, and wheeling into the room, nodded to someone behind her.

A nurse entered the room. She smiled at the pink bundle she carried in her arms, then glanced wistfully at Emily. "She's just beautiful," she said and handed the baby to her mother. "Congratulations."

"No!" Emily rasped. She stepped back a pace, but the nurse followed, settling the infant into her unwelcoming arms. "The adoption agency is taking care of everything."

"Guess they backed out," Linette said. "Said the contract is null and void."

"What?" Emily tore her eyes from the serious little face that gazed up from its tight swaddling.

Linette shrugged. "Something about needing the birth father's signature."

"That's not true." Emily looked pale and young and so panicked it made Casie's heart ache. "They said that wasn't necessary."

"All I know is what they told me."

Emily's lips twisted. Her eyes were bright. Tears spilled from the corners. A muscle jerked beside her lips. "I can't be a mom. I'm not—"

"What's wrong with you?" Sophie blurted. "You already *are* a mom. Like Mother Earth or something. Holy crap! Half the people on this planet would give their souls to have a mother like you."

"What, are you, nuts?" Emily hissed. "I can't do this. I can't!"

"Yes, you can," Sophie said. Her voice was soft suddenly. The room was as quiet as a prayer. "You're going to be great at this."

Emily shook her head.

"You are," Sophie said. "You know I wouldn't say something nice if it wasn't true."

"I can't—" she whispered again, but in that flicker of time the child made a noise, a small inarticulate sound that drew her gaze like a fire in the darkness. Their eyes met, brown to blue in an exchange of emotions as raw as a wound. Not a soul spoke. Not a breath was whispered. "Baby Bliss," Emily murmured. The world stood still, waiting, and then she cried. Settling back onto the mattress, she hugged the infant to her chest, tipped her dreadlocks over her tiny face, and sobbed.

CHAPTER 30

Life settled slowly back to normal, or at least back to its previous state of abnormal. Sophie treated the scratch on Maddy's knee, cared for Freedom, and gave riding lessons to seemingly every girl in the state of South Dakota. Ty dutifully tended Angel and pretended not to care about Sophie.

As for Emily, she returned to the orchard with Bliss nestled inside a basket beneath the dormant apple trees. And cooking . . . with Bliss on the kitchen table. And goat milking, with Bliss swinging gently from a bough of the ancient cottonwood. But mostly she sat and stared into her baby's eyes and smiled until she cried.

Evening was settling in with comfortable quiet. The western horizon was a scalloped palette of violet and periwinkle that backlit Sophie and Tangles as they cleared a series of low jumps. Emily was picking apples with Baby Bliss snuggled fast and warm in a sling against her chest.

Watching them from across the yard made something deep inside Casie ache.

"There's nothing quite like it, is there?" Linette asked. Casie swallowed the lump in her throat and turned toward the woman who hobbled carefully into the barn on underarm crutches. The doctors had recommended that she remain in a wheelchair, but it was hard to slow her down. She would be flying out in the morning, but had finally relented when Casie insisted that she call her family. They would be arriving within the hour. She drew a deep breath. "So what's on the docket for Cassandra Carmichael?" she asked.

Casie exhaled, careful not to unload too much onto Linette's exhausted shoulders. "Oh, I don't know. Keep chugging along like we're doing, I suppose. Try to put the Lazy back in the black. Make a place for Emily and Baby Bliss and—" Her words stopped as she caught sight of Ty striding down her driveway.

His frayed cap was pulled low over his face, hiding his eyes, but there was an easy rhythm to his steps, making him look almost carefree. What she wouldn't give to make that true, Casie thought, and felt love tangle messily within her heart as he headed toward the apple orchard.

"He's a good kid," Linette said.

"Yeah," Casie agreed and cleared her throat. "Yeah, he's all right."

"Everything's going to be okay," she said.

Ty tilted his battered cap down and said something inaudible. Emily laughed and hit him on the shoulder. He bounced back a step and gazed down at the baby. Lifting little Bliss out of her snug carrier, Emily gazed at the infant for several prolonged moments, then settled her carefully into the boy's arms.

The poignancy of the moment brought tears stinging to Casie's eyes.

"Casie . . ."

"I'm sorry." She zipped her attention back to her paying guest . . . her paying guest who could, conceivably, sue her for any number of missteps. "What did you say?"

"I said everything's going to be okay."

Casie cleared her throat. "As someone quite intelligent once told me, 'Okay might be a relative term,' " she said.

Linette chuckled, but the sound faded as her attention was diverted to the driveway. "Who's that?"

Casie turned. Her body stiffened. She shifted her eyes toward the arena where Sophie rode, then hurried toward the approaching pickup truck just as Pete Whitesel stepped out of his vehicle. His gaze was honed in on the girl just dismounting from the dun gelding.

Casie's chest felt tight, her legs stiff, but she kept walking.

"Mr. Whitesel," she said. Her voice sounded weak to her own ears "Still haven't found your mare?"

He kept his gaze on Sophie's approaching form for several more seconds before shifting it down to Casie. His lips curled into what might be misconstrued as a smile. "Looks like I have."

"Really? Where was she?"

"Don't know, but I'm betting *she* does," he said, and jerked his chin toward the arena.

"What do you mean?"

"What'd you do with her?" he asked, addressing Sophie who had just arrived from behind.

"You can't have her." The girl's voice was as steady as a rock, but when Casie turned toward her, her face was pale.

"She's my property, honey buns," he said. "It's me or the cops."

No one spoke.

He snorted as he jerked toward the barn, but Casie blocked his path again. "You heard her," she said. Her heart was beating overtime, her hands sweaty, but she held her ground. "You can't have her back," she said. "You've lost your rights to her."

"I don't know what's going on with your merry little band of sluts. But nobody steals from me," he growled and stepped to the side again. Casie moved with him.

"It's your word against mine. You can't prove—" she began, but in that instant he grabbed her by the shirtfront and hauled her up against him.

"And it's my *fist* against your—"

"Whitesel!" Linette's voice cracked like a whip through the evening air.

He snapped his attention to her.

Linette hopped toward them, balancing carefully on her crutches. "Or should I call you Warren?"

Whitesel's eyes darted to her, then off to the right where Emily and Ty approached from the orchard. Ty's expression was grim. Emily hugged Bliss close to her chest. "I don't know what you're talking about," he said.

"Don't you?" Linette asked. "Well, maybe the sheriff will. The way I heard it, Pat Warren is a pretty famous name in some parts."

The world went absolutely silent, and then Whitesel shoved Casie away. She stumbled backward but Ty caught her, helped her find her balance.

"Fine. That's just fine," Whitesel snarled. "Keep the worthless nag. I hope she tears this whole place apart," he said, and backing away, climbed into his truck and roared away.

Casie blinked after him. Sophie exhaled noisily. The world settled gratefully into silence.

"What just happened?" Emily asked.

Casie shook her head. "I don't have any idea. Linette . . ." She turned toward the older woman. "How did you—Who's Pat Warren?"

Linette shrugged. "Em said there was something wrong with him, and she seems to be a pretty good judge of human nature, so I just checked into his past a little. It wasn't pretty."

"Hey, Ty, could you help me back to the house?"

"Checked into his past? What do you mean? How could you check his past if he had another name?"

Linette shrugged. "Turns out fingerprints show up pretty well on leather."

"What—"

"Listen, I'd love to chat, but it looks like my ride's here," Linette said, glancing toward the dark vehicle just turning into their drive.

"Oh . . ." The world felt shaky beneath Casie's feet. "I suppose your daughter's worried sick about you."

"Probably. Say, I'm not one for long good-byes so don't feel like you have to wait around. I'm sure you have things to do," Linette said, but no one moved as the black SUV came to a halt. Jack barked once as dust settled slowly on the gravel road behind it. A woman in a sensible gray suit stepped out of the car.

Her hair was pulled back in a severe bun. She wore low pumps and dark-rimmed glasses.

Casie shook herself free of her trance and tried for conviviality as she stepped forward. "You must be Elizabeth."

"Yes," she said simply.

"I can't tell you how much we've enjoyed having your mother with us."

The woman scowled. "She's not—"

"Well . . ." Linette said, voice brusque. "I don't have much time. We'd better get going."

"Yes, ma'am."

Casie shifted her gaze from one woman to the other, confused by the dynamics, but Linette spoke again before she could work things out. The kids stood huddled together some twenty feet behind her, trying to take it all in.

"You're doing good work here, Casie," Linette said. Her voice was soft, her expression sincere.

Casie scowled, trying to keep up. "I don't—"

"But you've won now."

"What?"

"They're doing well." From the cottonwood, a mourning dove spoke to the approaching darkness.

Casie shook her head.

"The kids," Linette explained. "They're going to be okay . . . because of you."

"No, it's—"

"Do you need anything else before we leave?" Elizabeth asked.

"No, I'm fine," Linette said, not turning toward the woman near the SUV.

Elizabeth nodded briskly and opened the passenger door.

"It's because of you," Linette repeated. "You can do it all. Work a ranch, save a life, keep your family together."

"They're not really my family."

"Not all family's blood kin, Casie," she said. "Sometimes it's your pastor, or your next-door neighbor, or your administrative assistant." She smiled fondly at Elizabeth. "And sometimes kin lets you down. Or you let them down." She glanced out over the endless hills. There was an eternity of sadness in her eyes, but she drew her attention back to Casie in a matter of moments. "You've proven you can make it on your own," she said, and handing her crutches to Elizabeth, climbed gingerly into the SUV under her own power. "But you'd better make damn sure that's really what you want before it's too late."

"What?"

Linette smiled a little, then sighed and looked out the windshield. "Let's go," She said.

"Yes, your honor," Elizabeth agreed and, stowing the crutches in the backseat, slammed the passenger door shut.

"Your—" Casie began, but the SUV was rolling quietly away.

"Holy Hannah," she said.

"Judge Heartless?" Emily breathed.

They silently watched the vehicle turn onto the gravel road. Quiet settled back in. The evening air felt heavy with the promise of upcoming storms. Bliss began to cry. Emily soothed her. A horse snorted. A lamb bleated. But Casie's mind was still in turmoil. Had the Pritchards dropped the lawsuit because of Linette? And what about Whitesel? The memory of a discarded leather lead line galloped through her mind, but the thought was interrupted by the sound of a diesel engine. Casie brought her attention back to earth as Colt's pickup truck pulled into the yard. He stepped out of the vehicle, all rugged strength and dark regrets. He glanced at her, nodded, then strode off toward the barn.

The kids, she noticed, had miraculously disappeared, leaving her alone with Linny's words reverberating in her brain.

Something curled up tight in her stomach. Uncertainty tangled with hope, and hope was the winner.

"Dickenson," she called.

He turned toward her, eyes shadowed by the brim of his Stetson.

She paused, her nerve skittering into a dark corner. "Nothing," she said, and glanced away, but the black SUV was still in sight, dredging up quiet words of wisdom.

"I need help." She said the words more to herself than to him.

Colt tilted his head a little, face barely visible against the dark clouds behind him. "What?"

She cleared her throat, desperately marshaling courage she doubted she possessed. "I'm having trouble . . ." She glanced to her left, thinking hard. "Hanging that new gate."

He paused a second. The world waited in silence. "The one you built yourself?" he asked.

"Yeah."

"For the fence you put up?"

"Yes." She scowled at him, trying not to fidget.

"Well . . ." His lips tilted into a slanted grin filled with promise and anticipation and endless possibilities. "Let's get at it," he said, and the sun slipped from behind a bank of lavender clouds.

HOME FIRES

Lois Greiman

ABOUT THIS GUIDE

The suggested questions are included
to enhance your group's
reading of this book.

DISCUSSION QUESTIONS

1. Although Emily Kane has significant problems of her own, she's extremely upset that Colt and Casie can't seem to work out their differences. Why do you think this concerns her so much?

2. Do you think the loss of Colt's unborn daughter will make him more or less likely to form a lasting relationship with a woman in the future?

3. Although Tyler Roberts and Sophie Jaegar come from very different backgrounds, they both have dysfunctional families. Is that fact apt to make it easier or more difficult for them to relate to each other?

4. Linette Susan Hartman reveals very little about herself during her stay at the Lazy Windmill. Why do you think she's so secretive?

5. Ranchers deal with death on a daily basis. Do you think that makes them more sensitive or less sensitive to the frailties of human life?

6. Although Casie is obviously attracted to Colt, she's certain she should be with someone who is more like her former fiancé, someone solid, pragmatic, and unemotional. Do you think she's right, or would someone more lighthearted better balance her own practical nature?

7. For a short period Emily believes she should give up her baby for adoption. In reality, do you think that would be the best decision for a young woman in her circumstances?

8. Ty sees some similarities between his abusive mother and Sophie Jaegar, yet he can't help but be attracted to Sophie. Knowing something about the girl's volatile nature, do you think he should avoid her, or will she become the kind of woman who could make his life better?

9. With which character in *Home Fires* do you most closely relate?